NATIONAL ACCLAIM FOR THE
BESTSELLING NOVELS OF

BARBARA DELINSKY,

"ONE OF WOMEN'S FICTION'S
TRUE MASTERS"*

THE SUMMER I DARED

"Delinsky excels at combining a compelling mystery with an insightful portrayal of captivating people facing challenges both ordinary and dramatic."

—*Booklist*

FLIRTING WITH PETE

"Dramatic and satisfying."

—*Houston Chronicle*

"Sophisticated and fast-moving. . . . It will satisfy her fans and . . . win her some new readers."

—*Publishers Weekly*

"Scintillating. . . . [An] emotive novel of discovery and denial, love and liberation."

—*Booklist*

"Another 'I didn't want to put it down' novel from Delinsky. . . ."

—*Library Journal*

AN ACCIDENTAL WOMAN

"[A] powerful domestic drama . . . from one of women's fiction's true masters."

—*BookPage**

"Delinsky has strong characters in Blake, whose disability never impedes her work, and Hughes, who looks past his lover's disability to the woman within."

—*Baltimore Sun*

"The twisty plot and icy late-winter backdrop . . . will keep you chilling on a hot afternoon."

—*People*

"A good story in an idyllic and lovingly rendered setting."
—*The Calgary Sun*

THE WOMAN NEXT DOOR

"An achievement. . . . Delinsky's adept and compelling exploration of the inner workings of the modern upper-class American family makes for one of her best books to date."

—*Booklist*

"Delinsky peers into the dark corners of ideal marriages, loving families, and ideal neighborhoods and makes you realize that 'the woman next door' could be you."
—*Roanoke Times* (VA)

"The Woman Next Door . . . has something in it that will stir everyone who reads it. . . . Likely to go down as one of [Delinsky's] best."

—*The Anniston Star* (TX)

THE VINEYARD

"High drama, beautiful scenery, and resilient yet sensitive characters make this a must for all Delinsky fans."
—*Booklist*

"Another enjoyable novel."

—*Library Journal*

LAKE NEWS

"[An] engaging tale."

—*People*

"An engrossing story of strength in the face of cataclysmic life changes."

—*Library Journal*

"Delightful. . . . Readers will be sorry to reach the end of *Lake News* and yearn for more about its cast and characters."

—*The Pilot* (Southern Pines, NC)

"[Her characters] . . . become more like old friends than works of fiction."

—*Flint Journal* (MI)

COAST ROAD

"Heartwarming."

—*Star Tribune* (Minneapolis)

"A remarkable journey."

—*The Cincinnati Enquirer*

THREE WISHES

"Touching and delightful. . . . A story of genuine love, sacrifice, redemption, and the cohesiveness of life in a small town."

—*Chattanooga Times* (TN)

"Delinsky's prose is spare, controlled, and poignant."

—*Publishers Weekly*

BARBARA
DELINSKY

The
Summer I Dared

POCKET BOOKS
New York London Toronto Sydney

POCKET BOOKS
A Division of Simon & Schuster, Inc.
1230 Avenue of the Americas
New York, NY 10020

This book is a work of fiction. Names, characters, places and incidents are products of the author's imagination or are used fictitiously. Any resemblance to actual events or locales or persons, living or dead, is entirely coincidental.

This Pocket Books paperback edition June 2011

POCKET and colophon are registered trademarks of Simon & Schuster, Inc.

For information about special discounts for bulk purchases, please contact Simon & Schuster Special Sales at 1-866-506-1949 or business@simonandschuster.com

The Simon & Schuster Speakers Bureau can bring authors to your live event. For more information or to book an event contact the Simon & Schuster Speakers Bureau at 1-866-248-3049 or visit our website at www.simonspeakers.com

Cover art by Christine Triebert/Aperture; hand lettering by Iskra Design.

Manufactured in the United States of America

ISBN: 978-1-4516-4842-3
ISBN: 978-0-7432-5867-8 (ebook)

10 9 8 7 6 5 4 3 2 1

Acknowledgments

The *summer* I dared? Try the entire *year* I dared. In writing this book, I dared write of two topics about which I knew absolutely nothing. Those topics were Angora rabbits and lobstering. I say "were," past tense, because I did learn. I'm still not sure I've done them right, though literary license gives me some leeway. But I would have been at sea without a paddle if I hadn't had the help of Debbie Smith, who breeds Angora rabbits at her Iron Horse Farm in Sherborn, Massachusetts, and Betty Ann and Don Lockhart, Vermonters who aided me in researching maple syrup production for *An Accidental Woman* and who turned out to know lots about lobstering as well. My thanks to Jason Marceau, of Irwin Marine in Laconia, New Hampshire, for crucial info on boats in a storm. On the matter of lobstering, others were key as well. They know who they are; I thank them for their time and generosity.

As always, I thank my editors, Michael Korda and

Chuck Adams, along with Susan Moldow and the Scribner team. I thank my agent, Amy Berkower, who only gets better and better. I also thank my assistant, Lucy Davis, who makes my life immeasurably easier.

To my family, I send thanks and love—to my husband, Steve, for his patience during the odd and sundry moods that hit me when I'm writing a book; to my sons, Eric, Andrew, and Jeremy, for indulging me with quick answers to the questions I sometimes shoot their way; to my daughters-in-law, Jodi and Sherrie, for feedback on subject, content, and emotion.

The more I learned about lobstering, the more I came to respect the men and women who eke out a living through endless days of hard work at the mercy of the elements, and who juggle the issues of conservation and commerce as best they can. I salute you all.

Finally, I dedicate this book to Gabrielle and Jesse, with a love beyond words.

The Summer I Dared

Prologue

The *Amelia Celeste* was born a lobster boat. An elegant lady, she ran a proud thirty-eight feet of mahogany and oak, from the graceful upward sweep of her bow, down her foredeck to the wheelhouse, and, on a straight and simple plane, back to her stern. True to the axiom that Maine lobstermen treat their boats with the same care as their wives, the *Amelia Celeste* had been doted on by Matthew Crane in much the way he had pampered the flesh-and-blood Amelia Celeste, to whom he had been married for forty years and on whose grave every Friday he continued to lay a dozen long-stem roses, even twelve long years after her death.

Matthew had the means. His grandfather had made a fortune logging, not only the vast forests of northern Maine but the islands in its gulf that bore trees rather than granite. He had built the family home on one of those evergreen islands, aptly named Big Sawyer. Two generations later, Crane descendants were equally represented among the fishermen and the artists who comprised the core of the island's year-round residents.

Matthew was a fisherman, and for all his family money, remained a simple man at heart. His true delight, from the age of sixteen on, had been heading out at dawn to haul lobster traps from the fertile waters of Penobscot Bay. A purist, he continued to use wooden traps even when the rest of the local fleet had switched to ones made of wire mesh. Likewise, he would have died before trading in his wood-hulled boat for a newer fiberglass one, which would have been lighter and faster. Matthew didn't need speed. He lived by the belief that life was about the "doing," not the "done." As for gaining a few miles to the gallon with a lighter boat, he felt that in a business where no two days were alike, where the seas could change in a matter of minutes and abruptly unbalance two men hauling loaded traps up over the starboard rail, the stability of the Amelia Celeste was worth gold. And then there was the noise. Wood was a natural insulater. Cruising in the *Amelia Celeste* was quiet as no fiberglass craft could be, and quiet meant you could hear the gulls, the cormorants, the wind, and the waves. Those things brought him calm.

Reliability, stability, and calm—good reasons why, when Matthew turned sixty-five and his arthritis worsened enough to make his hands useless in the trade, he fitted the vessel with a new engine and tanks, rebuilt the pilothouse with permanent sides to keep out the wind, polished the mahogany to an even higher sheen, installed a defogger on the center window and seating for passengers in the stern, and relaunched the *Amelia Celeste* as a ferry.

During the first few years of this incarnation, Matthew skippered her himself. He made three daily runs to the mainland—once early each morning, once around noon, and once at the end of the day. He didn't carry cars; the ferry run by the State of Maine did that. Nor did he publish a schedule, because if an islander had a special need, Matthew would adjust his schedule to meet it. He charged a nominal fee, and was lax about collecting it. This wasn't a job; it was a hobby. He simply wanted to be on the boat he loved, in the bay he loved, and if he made life easier for the local folk, particularly when the winter months imposed a craze-inducing isolation, so much the better.

On that Tuesday evening in early June, however, when the idyll went tragically awry, Matthew—to his deep regret—was not at the helm of the *Amelia Celeste*. She was being piloted by Greg Hornsby, a far younger cousin of his who had spent all of his own forty years on the water and was as skilled a fisherman as Matthew. No, there was no shortage of experience or skill. Nor was there a shortage of electronics. As a lobster boat, the *Amelia Celeste* had been equipped with multiband radios, fish finders, and radar. As a passenger-toting vessel, she had the latest in GPS navigational systems along with the rest, but none of it would help that day.

Riding low in the water as lobster boats did, the *Amelia Celeste* left Big Sawyer at six in the evening carrying the photographer, art director, models, and gear from a photo shoot done earlier on the town docks. The sun had come out for the shoot, along with a crowd of locals wanting to watch, but the water remained cold, as Atlantic waters did in June, and by late afternoon, the approach of a warm front brought in fog.

This was no problem. Fog was a frequent visitor to the region. The lobsterman who let fog keep him ashore was the lobsterman who couldn't pay his bills.

Between the instruments at hand and Greg Hornsby's familiarity with the route, the *Amelia Celeste* deftly skirted lobster buoys clustered in the shallows leading to inlets at nearby Little Sawyer, West Rock, and Hull Island. After taking on a single passenger at each pier, she settled into the channel at an easy twenty-two knots, aimed at the mainland some six miles away.

Fifteen minutes later, the *Amelia Celeste* docked at Rockland and her passengers disembarked with their gear. Eight others were waiting to board, dressed not in the black of that city crew, but in the flannel shirts and hooded sweatshirts, jeans, and work boots that any sane islander knew to wear until summer truly arrived. These eight all lived on Big Sawyer, which meant that Greg would have a nonstop trip home, and that pleased him immensely. Tuesday was ribs night at the Grill, and Greg loved ribs. On ribs night, the wife and kids were on their own. His buddies were saving a booth; he'd be joining them there as soon as he put the *Amelia Celeste* to bed.

He took two bags and a large box from Jeannie

Walsh and stowed them under a bench while she stepped over the gunwale. Her husband, Evan, handed over several more bags and their one-year-old daughter before climbing aboard himself. Jeannie and Evan were sculptors; their bags held clay, glazes, and tools, and the box a new wheel, all purchased in Portland that day.

Grady Bartz and Dar Hutter, both in their late twenties, boarded with the ease of men bred on the water. Grady worked as dockman for Foss Fish and Lobster, the island's buyer and dealer, and was returning from a day off, looking only slightly cleaner than usual. Dar clerked at the tackle and gear store; once in the boat, he reached back to haul in a crate filled with stock, set it by the wheelhouse wall, and moved down to the stern for a seat.

It was a wise move, because Todd Slokum was the next to board. Thin and pale, Todd was the antithesis of a seafaring man. Even after three years on the island, he still turned green on the ferry to and from. Local gossip had never quite gotten a handle on why he had come to Big Sawyer in the first place. The best anyone could say was that Zoe Ballard was a saint to employ him.

Now he stumbled over the gunwale, hit the deck on rubbery legs, and tripped toward the nearest bench as he darted awkward glances at the others already there.

Hutchinson Prine was only a tad more steady. A lifelong lobsterman, his aversion to talk hid a wealth of knowledge. Nearing seventy, he still fished every day, though as sternman now, with his son at the helm. Hutch wasn't well. He had been in Portland seeing doctors. The scowl on his face said he didn't like what they had told him.

"How's it goin'?" Greg asked and got no answer. He reached for Hutch's elbow, but the older man batted his hand away and boarded the *Amelia Celeste* on his own. His son Noah followed him aboard. Though Noah was taller, and even smarter and better-looking than his father, he was just as silent. His face, at that moment, was equally stony. But he did reach to untie the lines.

The *Amelia Celeste* was seconds shy of pulling away from the dock when a pleading cry came from the shore. "Wait! Please, wait!" A slender woman ran down the dock, struggling under the bulk of heavy bags that bounced against her body. "Don't leave!" she cried beseechingly. "I'm coming! Please wait!"

She wasn't a local. Her jeans were very dark, her blouse very white, her blazer stylishly quilted. The sandals she wore wedged her higher than any islander in her right mind would be wedged, and as if that weren't odd enough for the setting, fingernails and toenails were painted pale pink. Her hair was a dozen shades of blonde, fine and straight, blowing gently as she ran. She was simply made up, strikingly attractive, and married, to judge from the ring on her left hand. The large leather pouch that hung from her shoulder was of an ilk far softer than that worked by local artisans; same with a bulging backpack.

Big Sawyer often saw women like her, but not in early June, and rarely were they alone.

"I have to get out to Big Sawyer," she begged, breathing hard, addressing Noah first, before realizing her error and turning to Greg. "I had my car reserved on the five o'clock ferry, but obviously I missed that. They said I could park back there at the end of the pier for a day or two. Can you take me to the island?"

"That depends on whether you have a place to stay," Greg said, because he knew it was what everyone on board was wondering. "We don't have resorts. Don't even have a B and B."

"Zoe Ballard's my aunt. She's expecting me."

The words were magical. Noah took her bags and tossed them into the pilothouse. She passed him the backpack, then climbed aboard on her own, but when Evan Walsh rose to give her a seat, she shook her head, and, holding the rail that Matthew had installed when he had turned the *Amelia Celeste* into a ferry, worked her way along the narrow path to the bow.

Noah released the stern line and pushed against the piling of the pier. He said something short to his father, but if there was an answer, Greg didn't catch it. As he edged up the throttle, Noah stalked past the wheelhouse. Stationing himself on the far side of the bow from Zoe Ballard's niece, he folded his arms and stared into the fog.

Quiet and graceful for a boat that was broad in the stern, the *Amelia Celeste* slipped through the harbor at headway speed. Although two hours remained yet of daylight, the thick fog had drained the world of color. Only the occasional shadow of a boat at its mooring altered the pale gray, as did the clink of a hook the silence, but these were quickly absorbed by the mist. Once past the granite breakwater, the waves picked up and the radar came on, little green dots marking the spot where a boat, rock, or channel marker would be. Painted buoys bobbed under the fog, signaling traps on the ocean floor. The *Amelia Celeste* gave these as wide a berth as possible, throttling up to speed only when she was safely in the channel.

The chop was fair to middlin', not overly taxing to the boat, even riding low as she was. In turn, she elicited little noise beyond the soft thrum of her engine, the steady rush of water as the point of the bow cut through the waves, and an occasional exchange of words in the stern. Nothing echoed. The fog had a muting effect, swallowing resonance with an open throat.

Far to starboard, a hum simmered in the thick soup before growing into the growl of a motor. In no time, it had grown louder and more commanding, belying the soundproofing of the fog, just as its owner meant it to do. That owner was Artie Jones, and he called his boat *The Beast*. Infamous in an area dominated by the boats of working fishermen, it was a long, sleek racer of the alpha-male type, whose aerodynamic purple body shot over the surface of the water driven by twin engines putting out a whopping 1,100 horses. It was capable of going seventy-five without effort, and from the rising thunder of those twin Mercs, it was approaching that now.

Noah shot Greg a *What the hell?* look.

Bewildered, Greg shrugged. The fog yielded no

sign of another boat in the area, but his radar screen painted a different picture. It showed *The Beast* tracing a large arc, having sped from starboard to a point astern of them now, crossing through the last of the wake left by the *Amelia Celeste* and heading off to the north. The rumble of the racer's engines faded into the fog.

One hand on a bronze spoke of the wheel and one on the throttle, Greg kept the *Amelia Celeste* aimed at the island. Dreaming of ribs, he forgot about Artie Jones until the sound of *The Beast* rose again. No mistaking the deep chain-saw growl that came from the monster engines in the tail. The racer was headed back their way. Radar confirmed it.

He picked up the handset of the VHF, which was preset to the channel the local boaters used. "What the hell are you doing, Artie?" he called, more in annoyance than anything else, because he didn't care how macho it was, no man in his right mind would be playing chicken this way in the fog.

Artie didn't answer. The roar of those twin engines increased.

Greg sounded his horn, though he knew it didn't have a chance of being heard above the noise. His eyes went back and forth from the radar screen, which pinpointed the racer, to the GPS screen, which pinpointed the *Amelia Celeste*. It occurred to him that if he didn't do something, the two boats would collide. For the life of him, though, he didn't know what to do. Artie wasn't behaving rationally. The radar screen showed him cutting through prime fishing grounds, plowing past buoys at a speed that was sure to be destroying the pot warp tied to hundreds of traps. If he was aiming at the *Amelia Celeste,* playing some kind of perverted game, he had the speed to follow wherever she turned.

"Artie, what the *hell*—throttle down and get out of the way!" he shouted, uncaring that he might alarm his passengers, because what with the way they were all staring wide-eyed into the fog in the direction of the oncoming howl, they were already highly alarmed.

He sounded the horn again and again, to no avail.

What to do, with the island barely a mile away, the responsibility of nine people in his hands, and Artie Jones a loose cannon in his muscle boat, capable of calling on all those horses, shooting off like a bullet with his bow in the air, propelled who knew where in the fog at a speed faster than the *Amelia Celeste* could ever hope to move?

Studying the radar screen for a final few seconds, Greg tried to guess where *The Beast* would go based on where it had been and what it could do. Then he made a judgment call. Unable to outrun the powerful boat, he yanked back on his own throttle to let *The Beast* pass.

It would have worked, had *The Beast* continued along its established arc. What Greg couldn't possibly have known, though, much less plugged into the equation, was that Artie had been hugging the wheel of his beloved machine at the moment his heart stopped and was slumped, frozen against it, unconscious at the end—but that at the same moment the

Amelia Celeste made her defensive move, his lifeless body began to slide sideways, pulling the wheel along with it.

Matthew Crane knew what had happened the instant he heard the explosion. He had been in his usual spot on the deck of the Harbor Grill, nursing a whiskey while he waited for the *Amelia Celeste* to emerge from the fog and glide to the pier. His ear was trained to catch the drone of her engine, distant as it was at the mile point, and he hadn't been able to miss *The Beast.* He had plotted its course in his mind's eye, had foreseen bisecting paths and felt the same sense of dread he had known when his flesh-and-blood Amelia Celeste had been admitted to the hospital that final time. The horrific boom had barely died when he was hurrying down the steps and across the beach. Scrambling onto the dock, he ran waving and shouting toward the handful of men who had just returned from hauling traps, and who were themselves staring into the fog in alarm.

Those men set off within minutes, reaching the scene quickly enough to fish the first two survivors from the water before they were overcome by smoke from the fire or cold from the sea. The third survivor was picked up by another boat. None of the three suffered more than minor bruises, a true miracle given the fate of the rest.

Chapter 1

Julia Bechtel was airborne only as long as it might have taken had a large someone picked her up and heaved her high into the ocean. She went underwater in a stunned state, but she never lost her orientation. Even before her downward plunge slowed, she was clawing against the sea to propel herself back up. When her head broke the surface, she gasped for air. The waves rose around her, but she fought them. Focusing on that singular need to breathe, she used her arms and legs to create a rhythm matching that of the sea in an effort to keep herself afloat.

Her breath came in shallow gasps, along with a creeping awareness of what had happened. She heard in echo the sound of screams, an impact, and an explosion, all drawn from immediate memory. Pushing wet hair from her eyes, she looked around, trying to get her bearings. The waves were littered with pieces of wood, ejected from the boat just as she had been, but where the rest of the *Amelia Celeste* should have been there were now flames furiously devouring wood and God knew what else, and the line between black smoke and white fog was lost.

Instinct told her to move away from the fire, so she fought the tug of the waves and pulled herself backward. Her sandals were gone, as was her pocketbook, and when she felt the weight of the wet quilted blazer dragging her down, she slid her arms from that, too. She was trembling, though she didn't know whether from cold or from shock. Fear hadn't yet set in.

"Hey!" came a shout from the smoky haze, then a head appeared. It was the man who had been with her in the bow. He was swimming toward her. "Are you hurt?" he called loudly enough to be heard above the roar of the flames.

She didn't think she was. Everything seemed to be working. "No," she called back.

"Hold on to this," he said as he pulled forward what he'd been towing. It was a long seat cushion, clearly buoyant. "I'm going back in."

Grasping the cushion, Julia was about to ask if that was possible, when another staggering explosion came. She barely had time to take a breath when the man pulled her under to escape the falling debris. By the time they resurfaced, gasping and sputtering, treading water in the churn of the waves, the hail was done.

Going back in was a moot point, then. The flames were louder, the smoke more dense.

In obvious anguish, the man stared at the devastation. Seemingly as an afterthought, he tore his eyes from the smoke, looked around for the cushion, swam for it, towed it back. "Hold on," he said, and when Julia complied, he dragged the cushion through the waves, farther away from the wreck. All the while he stared into the smoke and the flames.

Suddenly, he did an about-face in the water and turned those anguished eyes in the opposite direction. *"Hey!"* he screamed in desperation toward what Julia assumed was the shore. *"Get out here! Hey! There are people who need help!"*

Julia knew he wasn't referring to himself or to her. They appeared to be unscathed, but there were all those others on the far side of the flames, who might have been hit by debris, knocked unconscious by the explosion, or burned by the fire.

Incredibly, the man began to swim toward the smoke.

"Don't go!" Julia cried. She had visions of his disappearing and never being heard from again—or perhaps she just didn't want to be left alone. The fog was thick, the fire close, and she had no idea how far they were from shore. For the first time then, with a marginal grasp of what had happened, she did feel fear. The ocean was a big place and she an infinitesimally tiny dot in its midst. Two dots were better than one.

He kept swimming. After a minute, though, he stopped. He bobbed in place, staring at the flames, before recalculating and swimming to the left of the fire, but the waves fought him there, pushing him back when he might have moved on. So he let himself be carried back to where she was and, once there, grabbed hold of the cushion.

"Did you see anyone else?" she asked. She was breathing hard, but nowhere near as hard as he was.

He shook his head, then twisted it back toward shore again. It was another minute before Julia heard what he had, and another minute after that before a boat emerged from the fog. A working lobster boat, it was smaller than the *Amelia Celeste* and nowhere near as polished, but Julia had never seen anything as welcome in her life.

In no time, she had been helped over the side and into the boat, wrapped in a blanket and settled in the small cabin under the bow. Once there, though, she began to shake in earnest, because not only were those sounds reverberating in her mind—screams, impact, explosion—but she could see it again: the sudden emergence of a huge purple point coming out of the fog, just high enough to start right over the side of the ferry, before crashing down in its midst.

Unable to sit still, Julia went back up to the deck, where she stood, dripping wet and trembling under the blanket, now with a hand at her mouth and her eyes on the fog. The smell of smoke was overwhelming; she raised the blanket over her nose to diffuse it.

The man who had been with her in the water was also aboard, but there was no blanket for him, no coddling. He and two others were leaning over the side, peering through the fog and smoke as the boat dodged its way along between pieces of wood, fiberglass, and miscellaneous other matter that Julia couldn't identify. Some were burning, some were not.

The ghost of another search boat flickered briefly in the fog before heading in the opposite direction. When a third search boat appeared, it drew alongside, and the man who had been with her in the water climbed into it.

Julia didn't ask questions, and he didn't look back. He was clearly a local, known by the men in both boats, no doubt known by the rest who had been in the *Amelia Celeste*. He was worried.

Feeling a deep sense of dread, she watched the third boat pull away. She followed the sound of it, struggling to see through the fog, until her own boat turned away.

"We're gonna get you in," the captain explained as the boat picked up speed.

"You don't have to," she said quickly. "I'm okay. Shouldn't we stay here and help with the search?" She felt a need to do that.

But the captain simply said, "I'll drop you ashore and come back," and sped on.

Chilled as the wind whipped through her wet hair, Julia took shelter in the wheelhouse, eyes on the front windshield, waiting for sign of land. Within minutes, a darkness materialized, a body of land rising from the water, with a serrated skyline rising high above it. Another minute, and the mist thinned to reveal a small fishing village built into a hillside.

The boat pulled up at the dock. Of the islanders already gathered there, one woman ran forward.

Zoe Ballard was Julia's mother's youngest sister, a late-in-life child, barely twelve years older than Julia. That closeness in age alone would have been enough to justify the bond Julia felt. More, though, Zoe was interesting and adventurous, irreverent, independent. She was everything Julia was not but admired nonetheless.

And now here she was, wearing a woven patchwork jacket and frayed jeans, her chestnut hair windblown, her features delicate like Julia's, eyes filled with tears. But her arms were strong, helping Julia as she stumbled off the boat, then hugging her tightly for what seemed like forever. Julia didn't complain. She couldn't stop shaking. Zoe's strength helped. She felt safe with her, safe on dry land, safe and alive—and suddenly terrified that others were not. She looked back at the boat in time to see it head out again.

That quickly, the crowd closed in, and the questions began.

"What happened?"

"How many were on the *Amelia Celeste*?"

"Have they pulled others from the water?"

Not knowing where to look, Julia focused on Zoe. "A boat hit us. There were six, seven, maybe eight others on the ferry."

"Did you catch any names?" Zoe asked and Julia understood why. Ferries like the *Amelia Celeste* were casual things. Tickets weren't booked ahead; there would be no list of passengers. Any information Julia could give would be a help to the islanders gathered there.

But she could only shake her head. The rest of her

body continued to tremble. "I was in the bow. They were in the stern."

She tried to picture the group she had seen when she boarded the boat, but the image was vague. Running down that dock, she had been distracted and tense after a harrowing seven-hour drive up from Manhattan. It should have been an easy drive—*would* have been, had she left when she had originally planned. But her husband had given her a raft of last-minute errands, treating her as usual like a maid, something she had come to sorely resent. Driving out of the city, she had wallowed in that resentment, mentally arguing with Monte as she didn't dare do in person, venting a frustration that had been building for years. Add to that the growing realization that she was late enough to miss the ferry she was booked on, that she didn't know if there was another ferry that day, and that she had no idea where she would spend the night if she didn't get to the island, and her level of tension had risen. She had driven above the speed limit much of the way, a problem in and of itself. She didn't drive often, least of all on the highway. What she had hoped would be a pleasant drive had turned into a white-knuckle experience.

The only good thing had been her luck in finding the *Amelia Celeste* ready to leave.

Lucked out? Well, perhaps. She was alive and well. But others?

"Her arm's bleeding," said a man who emerged from the crowd. He didn't appear to be out of his thirties, though he carried an air of mature confidence. "Can I check her out?"

Julia was startled to see the blood on the underside of her forearm.

"He's a doctor," Zoe explained quietly. Stepping out of her clogs, she knelt to put them on Julia's feet.

Julia put a hand on her shoulder for balance. "Won't a Band-Aid do?" she asked, because she didn't want to leave the dock.

"His clinic's right around the corner," Zoe said as she straightened. Sliding an arm around Julia's waist, she guided her away.

"Now you have no shoes."

"I have socks," Zoe said, keeping her moving until a large man wearing a khaki uniform stepped in their path.

"I have to talk with her," he said.

"Not now," Zoe replied, clearly unintimidated.

"Something happened out there. I'm opening an investigation."

"Not *now*, John," Zoe repeated. "She hasn't stopped trembling. She's likely in shock. Jake is taking a look, then I'm taking her home."

Julia whispered, "I want to stay here."

Zoe ignored her.

The police chief stepped aside.

With Zoe holding her on the left and the doctor close on her right, Julia was ushered down the dock. When they turned onto Main Street, she saw little of it. Island store, tackle and gear shop, offices for newspaper, postal service, and police—all passed in a blur.

She was barely over the threshold of the small clinic, though, when she balked. Something was starting to feel familiar—the same thing she was running from, the sense that she didn't have a mind of her own.

"I am *not* going home right now," she told Zoe. She kept her voice low, just as her aunt had done with the police chief, but there was no doubting her determination.

"You need to dry off and warm up," Zoe said, albeit with greater deference.

"I need to be down on the dock," Julia insisted, and something about the sureness in her voice must have registered, because Zoe gave in.

"Okay, then. Give me my clogs. While Jake checks you out, I'll drive back to the house for dry clothes."

Only then did it strike Julia that she had none of her own. No clothes. No shoes, no socks. No makeup. No books, no camera equipment. All of the things that she had so carefully gathered—been putting aside for months, if the truth were told—for her two weeks on the island were gone. Same with her pocketbook, which meant she had no driver's license, no credit card, no money. She had no cell phone, no picture of Molly that she kept in her wallet, no dog-eared photos that dated back to her own teenaged years and had been the object of so many dreams. Nor, it dawned on her, did she have any of those other personal papers that she had so painstakingly gathered.

She was grappling with the realization of all that when Zoe slipped out the door. By the time she returned, twenty minutes had passed, and Julia had been judged in fine health aside from the jagged tear on her arm, which the doctor stitched.

"A week for the stitches," she heard him tell Zoe, while she pulled on the dry clothing Zoe had brought. "The shaking will stop. I offered her a sedative, but she refused it. She's apt to feel bruised all over by morning. Call me if there's pain."

Julia zipped the jeans, pulled a T-shirt and sweater on carefully over her bandaged arm, then wool socks and sneakers, and a fleece jacket, appreciating the warmth with each layer. She used Zoe's blow-dryer for a minute, brushed out her hair, and pulled on a baseball cap that said *Foss Fish and Lobster*. Then she joined the others in the front room.

"I'm ready," she said quietly, and was grateful when—rather than tell her how pale she was, that she needed food, a hot bath, and sleep more than she needed to return to the dock—Zoe simply nodded.

The three retraced their steps. The mist over the harbor had thinned some, and the visibility was improved, but what had been gained was being quickly consumed by dusk. Enough light remained to show Julia a maze of side docks meandering off the main. Empty slips, along with a dearth of lobster boats at harbor moorings, suggested that the entire local fleet had joined the search. As Julia approached, another pulled away from its dinghy and motored toward open water with its running lights on, spotlights blazing from the wheelhouse roof.

The dock itself was lit by tall torches and crowded with people. The town had come out en masse, a throng of worried faces, watchful eyes, and joined hands.

Holding Julia by the arm, Zoe waded right in. "What's the word?"

"Not good," said a woman with a cell phone in her hand. "Rescue boats have come from the mainland. Emergency vehicles are waiting on that end." She stopped short, but the look in her eyes went farther.

"What are they expecting?" Julia asked, needing confirmation.

"Burns," the woman said, but again stopped short.

Julia closed her eyes for only a second, but it was enough to be right back out there with the others in the ferry, enough to see that purple boat burst out of the fog, enough to hear the screams and feel the impact, enough to be thrown by the explosion. *Body parts.* That was what the woman hadn't said, and suddenly Julia glimpsed the scope of the horror.

Trembling head to toe, she wrapped her arms around herself and turned to the water, though there was little to see and even less to hear: the roar of flames, the rumble of rescue vessels, the sirens were gone. Except for the occasional low talk over a cell phone or radio transmitter, she heard precious little other than the waves that slapped pilings under the pier, rocked boats at their moorings, and broke resoundingly against granite boulders that lined the outer shore.

Behind Julia, the conversation went on in hushed tones, muted by a fear that was heavy and stark.

Glancing over the crowd, she could have picked those closest to the missing. They were at the center of each small group. By contrast, a gray-haired man stood alone at the very end of the dock. His hands were anchored in the pockets of a worn brown jacket that hung over loose corduroy pants.

"Matthew Crane," Zoe said, following her gaze. "The *Amelia Celeste* is his. He's probably wishing he'd been at the helm himself, instead of Greg. Greg has a young family."

Julia was trying to absorb that information when the woman with the cell phone said on a note of accusation, "It was Artie Jones's racer. They're picking up purple debris."

Again Zoe explained to Julia, "Artie's up from Portsmouth. He has a house down on the shaft. You remember."

Julia did. Big Sawyer was shaped like an ax. It was broadest and most densely populated at its head, which included the harbor, near the flat of the blade, the fishing village, which climbed the wooded hill, and, at the back of the head, viewing open ocean, the artists' homes. The shaft, extending off to the southeast, was long and narrow. Seasonal residents lived there, putting a certain distance between the lavishness of their homes and boats and the down-to-earth functionality of the locals. The arrangement suited both groups just fine.

"Artie made it big in the Internet boom," Zoe went on, "and if he suffered when the whole thing went bust, you'd never know it. His house is huge.

No expense was spared." She caught a breath. "If it was *The Beast,* Artie was the one at the helm. No one else drives that boat. He's out there, too."

"Is his family here?" Julia asked softly.

"No," answered the woman. "They don't move up until the kids finish school. Artie comes alone to open the house and put *The Beast* in the water." She looked past them. A boat had come in and was approaching the dock, drawing the crowd. "There's the *Willa B.* Looks like she has someone." She set off.

That someone, Zoe told Julia as soon as she made the identity, was Kim Colella. She was standing on her own steam and appeared to be unhurt. Wrapped in a large towel with her hair soaked and her head bowed, she looked to Julia to be little more than a child, but when, in a voice tinged with horror, she said just that, Zoe was quick to correct her.

"Kimmie's twenty-one and tends bar at the Grill. Life hasn't been easy for her. She was raised by her mother and grandmother. They're two tough ladies."

Julia felt a tug of protectiveness, not only because her own daughter was close to Kimmie's age, but because Kimmie Colella didn't look tough at all. Her chin stayed low as she was helped from the boat to the dock, and when a barrage of questions hit her, she recoiled. Huddled into herself, she let the doctor guide her away.

The boat that had delivered her was already heading back out. "How long can they search?" Julia asked, because it was fully dark now.

"Awhile. They have floodlights."

Julia had been frightened enough out there in daylight; she couldn't begin to imagine the terror of being in the water at night. Moving closer to Zoe, she tucked her hands in the pockets of the fleece jacket. "Maybe other survivors have been taken to the mainland?"

Zoe's eyes were understanding, but she didn't offer easy comfort. "We'd know," she said gently, even apologetically. "Someone would've called. Are you sure I can't take you home?"

"I'm sure."

"Does your arm hurt?"

"No." But she didn't think she would notice if it did. The emerging horror dwarfed aches and pains.

"Want something to eat from the Grill?"

"I don't think I can eat."

"Coffee, then?"

Julia gave in on that, though she didn't drink much. She had adrenaline enough in her body without caffeine, but the warmth of the cup in her hands did feel good. As time passed, though, that warmth faded, along with the hope that others would be brought in alive. And still she resisted when Zoe would have taken her home. She wouldn't be able to sleep, not with the weight of grief on her chest—and not with the rest of the townsfolk still on the docks. As long as they stayed and waited, she had to as well. She had been on that boat. She might not know the names of these islanders, but she was one of them on this night.

By eleven, the fog had dispersed, and the mood of

the crowd lifted with the hope that survivors would be more easily spotted. By midnight, though, when no good news was radioed back from the boats, that hope waned. By one in the morning, those on the dock stood in silent huddles.

Shortly thereafter, word came back that the Coast Guard had called off the search for the night and would return with divers in the morning—but still the local fleet kept at it. By two, however, even they began to return. One boat after another slipped into the harbor, their engines rumbling in exhaustion. The faces of the men who climbed back on the dock were pale and drawn in the flickering light of the torches; they had little to say and simply shook their heads.

Julia searched until she saw the man who had helped her right after the accident, the man from the *Amelia Celeste*. Zoe identified him as Noah Prine. Though he hoisted himself to the dock now with the others, the depth of the pain on his face set him apart. He didn't look around, didn't acknowledge any of those who had been waiting there all night, and they, in turn, gave him wide berth as he strode along the planking and off into the night.

"He was with his father," Zoe explained softly. "Hutch is still missing."

Julia was horrified. She could only begin to imagine what Noah was feeling, fearing that his father was dead but not knowing for sure. Her own father was still alive, as were her mother and her brothers. And her daughter.

"I need a phone, Zoe," she said, feeling a dire

need, right then, right there, to hear Molly's voice. The girl was a culinary student, normally studying in Rhode Island, but now doing a summer apprenticeship in Paris. It would be morning there. If Molly had worked the night before, she might still be sleeping, and under normal circumstances, Julia would have waited. But what had happened—and what she felt—were far from normal.

Zoe produced a cell phone, and Julia quickly punched in the number of Molly's global phone. As it rang, she moved away from the others on the dock. It seemed forever before a groggy voice that Julia knew well said, "Mom?"

Julia felt such a swell of emotion that she began to cry. "Oh, baby," she gasped in a choked voice that, quite naturally, terrified her daughter.

Sounding instantly awake, Molly asked, "What's wrong?"

"Nothing. I'm fine," Julia sobbed softly, "but it's a miracle."

The story spilled out in a handful of sentences, to which Molly injected "Omigod" with rising frequency and fear. When Julia finally paused, her daughter said with a mix of disbelief and awe, *"Omigod!* Are you *sure* you're okay?"

"I am, but there are others who aren't. I'm sorry to wake you"—she was crying again, though less wrenchingly now—"but with something like this, you need to talk to people like your own daughter. Email doesn't do it. You need to hear a *voice.*"

"I'm *glad* you called. *Omigod.* Mom, that's just *so*

awful! Here I am, pissed off that the chef at the restaurant won't give me the time of day, and there you are dealing with life and death. When'll they know about the others?"

"The morning, maybe."

"That's so bad. And you—you've been looking forward to this for months. It was supposed to be your vacation. Are you going right home?"

The question startled Julia. "No," she said. Odd, but there wasn't a doubt in her mind. She couldn't list her reasons, because her thoughts were too disordered. But leaving wasn't an option. "I'll be at Zoe's. You have her number."

"Are you sure you want to be there after all this?"

"I'm sure."

"Do you want me to come?"

"No. You have a job. You need the experience."

"Is Dad coming?"

Julia was startled for a second time. In all that had gone on, she hadn't once thought about Monte, which was odd, too. Or perhaps it wasn't. Monte had no place here on the island. She had visited Big Sawyer three other times since her marriage, and he had opted out each time. Nor had he shown any interest in coming this time. She was sure that he had made other plans for these two weeks, well beyond those he had shared with her; she was as sure of *that* as she was that she couldn't leave the island and race back home.

Unable to explain all this to Molly, she hedged. "Honestly, I don't know. We'll probably talk about it in the morning."

"Let me know?" Molly asked and rushed on. "Email me later. And call again whenever you want. I love you, Mom."

"Me, too, baby, me, too."

Alone, Noah Prine tromped down Main Street, turned left onto Spruce, and began the short climb up the hillside to the house he shared with his dad. It was a fisherman's cottage in a neighborhood of other fishermen's cottages, clapboards weathered gray by the salt air, blue shutters in need of paint—always in need of paint, because the wind was abusive to *everything,* and boats and buoys came first. It wasn't a big place, a fraction as large as the monstrosity Artie Jones owned down on the shaft, but it was honestly come by, the product of years of hard work, and it was paid for in full.

He bet Artie's place wasn't. He bet there were hefty mortgages on both the house and *The Beast.* He bet that the guy didn't have an ounce of insurance either, because guys like that didn't think past the moment. What *that* meant was that if eight people turned out to be dead, all the lawsuits in the world wouldn't produce enough money to adequately compensate two orphaned Walsh kids, Greg Hornsby's wife and kids, Dar Hutter's fiancée, Grady Bartz's parents, and whomever Todd Slokum might have left in the world.

Money certainly couldn't bring back his dad—not that Noah was convinced he was gone. Hutch had spent his whole life on the water and had done his share of time in the drink. He had survived storms that might have killed another man—and besides, it wasn't like it was the middle of winter, with water almost at the freezing point. This was June. Hutch could do it. A night in the sea might even slow the growth of cancer in his blood.

The problem, of course, even beyond that of the initial crash and whatever those mammoth propellers had chewed, was the explosion. Who knew what damage it had done? Noah would be out there still searching if he had floodlights on the *Leila Sue*. Radar alone wouldn't have helped, not in the chop. He would go out again at first light. In the meantime, he didn't know what to do with himself.

He turned in and went up the short path. His mother's lilacs were in bloom. He could smell them as he went past, though he couldn't make them out in the dark. There wasn't even a light on out front, because he and his father had planned to be back well before nightfall. Noah had intended to cook the bass that had come up in a lobster trap the day before. Hutch loved bass, and, sensing that their day at the hospital would be a disaster, Noah had wanted to please him.

Noah hadn't had a clue what the real disaster would be. He had always seen the island as safe and low-key and familiar. Yes, death came. They had been through it with his mom three years before, but not with this kind of violence, not with this kind of . . . stupidity, this kind of preventability.

Bursting with anger, he opened the door, and a forty-pound creature raced past him and out into the small yard. "Lucas," he said with a mixture of dismay and guilt, anger draining instantly away. He had forgotten about the dog, shut in all day. Like the bass he had intended to cook for Hutch, he had planned to be back for Lucas, too. Leaving the front door ajar so that the dog could return, he went inside.

The emptiness was overwhelming. He put his hands on his hips and hung his head. After a moment, he raised it and pushed a hand through his hair. What to do? he asked himself. Was Hutch dead or alive? He just didn't know. No one knew anything for sure. How could they know without proof? He felt the need to talk to someone, but whom could he call? Most everyone who meant anything to Hutch was here on the island.

Ian ought to be told. Noah went to the phone. He lifted the receiver, punched out the number, but hung up before the call could go through. Ian was his son, seventeen years old and difficult. Noah had trouble communicating with him in the best of times. He didn't know what to say now.

Still in the dark, he went down the hall to the bathroom, stripped off clothes that had dried stiff with salt, and turned on the shower. One hand high on the wall and the other limp by his side, he let the water course over his head, though he barely felt its heat or its pulse on his skin. He scrubbed every inch of himself to erase the smell of fish, a habit that was unnecessary today, since he hadn't been fishing. He was going through the usual motions—come home, shower, put on dry clothes, fix something to eat.

He got on the dry clothes, still without lights, but wasn't up for eating, and knew enough not to even try to sleep. Lying in the dark, with his mind having nowhere to go but back on the water, he found himself staring down at the sneaker of a one-year-old child. No, he couldn't do that. But he had two hours to live through, before he went back out in the boat, back to the search. Not knowing what else to do, he did the one thing he did best.

Grabbing an anorak from the coat tree, he went out the door. Lucas was beside him—a surprising comfort—before he reached the end of the walk and raced on ahead, while Noah strode back down the hill to the small shack by the water's edge where he kept his traps. He had already set several hundred, mostly in the warmer water of the shallows, because this was June, and the shallows were where lobsters would hide before molting. Come July, once the molt was done, they would move to the shelter of deeper water to let their new shells harden. The traps he set now would head in that direction.

Most were ready to go, stacked in eights from floor to ceiling. Over the winter, he had repaired those in need of attention, but there were a few last casualties, victims of marauding seals, hidden rocks, or plain old wear and tear. His wire mesh traps were more hardy than the old wooden ones, but they weren't invincible.

He set to repairing them now, working by the light of an old oil lamp, because there was no electricity in the shed. He didn't mind the smell of the oil, or that of fish or ocean air. Or that of fresh paint, drying on buoys that hung in bunches from the rafters. Or that of old gloves that had handled their share of fish bait. These scents were part of his history, part of who he was.

He worked on the wire with his pliers, twisting one piece around another to close a gap, reattach the netting inside, or repair a door. He replaced hog rings and attached trap tags. When he finished with one trap, he went on to the next, then the next. By the time he was done, he had a tall stack of traps ready to go, as well as a sore back. But the two hours were nearly up. He could see it in the whisper of light that came through the window, could feel it in bones that screamed to him, *Get on out there now, man, right now!*

He blew out the oil lamp, left the shed, and, with Lucas still full of energy, running every which way ahead, he set off for the harbor. Lights were on up the hillside; Noah could pick the homes where they had probably been on all night. Those people would be down on the dock soon, resuming the vigil while they waited for word. Until then, the gulls had free access, swooping through the predawn light to perch on pilings, deck rails, and wheelhouse roofs, sitting statue-still, then setting off with a cry.

He reached the Grill. Inside its door, his thermos was filled with hot coffee and waiting in its usual spot alongside those of the other lobstermen. This time, though, the owner of the Grill was waiting, too.

Rick Greene was a man with a large body, a large

mind, and a large heart. He had single-handedly turned the Harbor Grill into a destination eatery; come summer, day-trippers planned expeditions to the island around lunches of mussel salad, lobster chowder, or curried cod, all fresher than they would find anywhere else.

Now he pressed a bag into Noah's hand. "You gotta have food."

Noah stared at the bag. He wasn't surprised by the gesture, but he was by his own need for it. For a man who prided himself on being self-sufficient and independent, he was touched. The heaviness he felt inside was eased, if only briefly, by the sense of another person sharing the weight.

"Did you sleep any?" Rick asked.

"Nah," Noah said and raised bleak eyes to search the harbor. "Anyone else here yet?"

"The *Trapper John* left ten minutes ago, and they aren't heading out to haul traps."

Noah was relieved. The more boats joined the search, the better the odds.

"Maybe you shouldn't go out alone," Rick said.

Noah smiled sadly. "Lucas'll have to do, since I don't seem to have my sternman." That would've been Hutch.

Pain crossed Rick's face. "What can I do?"

Noah looked out at the sea. The waves were tipped with the same shade of lilac as his mom's beloved shrubs, a new day rising, though with a sense of dread. "Not a helluva lot," he said, feeling the kind of despair he hadn't yet allowed himself to feel, but exhaustion did that—poked holes where holes wouldn't normally be. "I'll go out looking again. Could be we missed something. Could be we misjudged the area. Could be there's a whole crew of them hanging on to a piece of the hull."

"Let me know," Rick said kindly. "You need anything, radio it in."

Noah tucked the bag under his arm, hooked his fingers around the thermos lid, and set off down the dock. The planks underfoot were damp as usual, but the harbor chop wasn't bad. The *Leila Sue* rocked gently in her slip, flanked by lobster boats of different sizes and states of repair. Each had a buoy pegged to the wheelhouse roof. Noah's was bright blue with two orange stripes. These were his colors, registered with the state, marked on his lobstering license, and repeated on every one of the hundreds of buoys he attached to his traps. Blue-orange-orange—originally his father's colors, for the past ten years his own.

Lowering himself to the deck of the *Leila Sue* seconds before Lucas leaped aboard, he stowed the food in the wheelhouse, then got the engine going. He didn't look at the yellow oilskins that hung from hooks, one for Hutch and one for him. His jeans and sweatshirt would do today. And his Patriots hat. He reached for that and pulled it on. He and Hutch shared their love for the team, and, killer though that had been at times, the wait was worth it. That first Super Bowl season had been something. And the Snow Bowl against the Raiders two weeks before the big game? That had been something! It had been a good day. Driving down to the game that day, he and Hutch hadn't argued a bit, a rare and memorable thing.

Noah untied his lines fore and aft, then gave the *Leila Sue* enough gas to back her out of the slip and turn her. Throttling up, he headed out, but he saw little of the harbor boats, the buoy field, or, passing the lighthouse, the rocks that the gulls made white, now shaded the palest pink with the dawn light. Nor did he see the lime-grape-lime buoys that were out farther, in waters traditionally fished by Big Sawyer lobstermen, because he couldn't begin to think of the gear war that loomed. The *Leila Sue* might have been in forward, but his thoughts remained in reverse.

No, he and Hutch hadn't argued going to Foxborough that day in the snow, but they sure had bickered yesterday. Hutch had criticized Noah's driving, his choice of a tuna sandwich in the cafeteria, his inability to answer the questions that—Noah countered—Hutch should have asked the doctor himself. They had bickered about how to negotiate traffic leaving the hospital, about waiting in the toll line rather than producing exact change, about radio stations, about refilling the gas tank of the borrowed truck. By the time they had returned the truck and were boarding the *Amelia Celeste,* Noah had had it. When Hutch grumbled that *he* didn't want to sit after he had been doing nothing but sitting all day long and that *he* would stand in the bow during the ride to the island, Noah had balked.

"Sit," he'd ordered his father in no uncertain

terms. "I need air." He had held up a hand in warning and reinforced it with a warning look. *Stay there!* it said. *Don't argue! Gimme a friggin' break!* He'd remained where he was long enough to make sure Hutch understood, then marched up to the bow. And so he lived through the crash.

Guided now by the GPS, he pointed the *Leila Sue* toward the spot that had been the focus of the search the night before. Other boats would be searching, as would the Coast Guard. With a little help . . . a little luck . . . a miracle . . .

Lucas settled in against his leg, nearly sitting on his foot, looking up, and Noah allowed himself a moment's distraction. He had rescued the dog from euthanization three years before, and hadn't once regretted it. Lucas was a retriever, and a handsome guy at that. His coat was red, with white markings on his nose, his bib, and the tips of his feet. He had a feathered tail that wagged constantly. And freckles. And gentle eyes. And undying love. How could he not save a dog like that, even if it had meant arguments with his father ever since?

No place for that dog on this boat, Hutch had argued. *Dog like that has to run. Why'd you think no one else wanted him? Dog like that'll exhaust you. You watch. You'll see.*

What Noah had seen was that Lucas could run himself ragged around the island, but was good as gold on the boat. Not that Hutch ever admitted that.

Noah stroked the dog's head and scratched his ears, but his father's voice filled his mind. Straightening, he held the boat steady at twenty knots and kept his eyes peeled. As soon as his radar picked up the bleeps of other boats near the site, though, he turned off. He couldn't go there. Just couldn't. The best he could do was circle the perimeter and wait for word on the radio. He didn't remind himself that the search had gone on for seven hours the night before, that the nature of the debris picked up then did not bode well, or that even before turning in for the night, the Coast Guard had begun talking about recovery rather than rescue. He didn't remind himself of any of those things because they only made him feel heartsick and empty—empty and helpless—helpless and angry—angry and confused. And there he stayed at the end of the list, with anger and confusion foremost in his thoughts.

He was a lobsterman. Lobstermen knew that they couldn't control the wind or the waves any more than they could control where lobsters chose to crawl on the ocean floor or what bait they decided to take. But there were certain givens, and Noah loved those. He loved the freshness of the morning air, loved heading out with a boat full of bait and a belly full of breakfast. He loved pulling up a trap that held a breeder loaded with eggs, loved notching her tail and setting her gently back in the sea. He loved knowing that she would drop many thousands of lobster larvae and that in six or seven years he would pull up some of those very same lobsters, now big enough for keeping. He loved knowing that he had some control, however small, over the preservation of the species.

He had no control over people like Artie Jones,

though. He had no *understanding* of people like Artie Jones, and his anger grew as he approached the site of the crash. Artie Jones was a hotshot. Infinitely worse than rogue lobstermen planting lime-grape-lime buoys where they shouldn't be, Artie bombed around in *The Beast,* polluting the air with its roar, adding its wake to the rock of the sea. That said, he wasn't suicidal. He might be an irresponsible, arrogant cad, but he wasn't a maniac.

So why in the *hell* had he done what he'd done?

The one person who might have given them a clue wasn't saying a word about what had happened—not to the fishermen who had pulled her from the sea, nor to the other searchers, the police chief, the doctor, or, with the rising sun now, the families gathering again on the dock, waiting for word. She wasn't talking to friends or to her boss, and certainly not to her mother or grandmother. She wasn't talking, period. For all intents and purposes, the accident had stolen her voice and rendered her mute.

Chapter 2

Zoe Ballard lived in a farmhouse that had been built by an original Crane with the stones he had taken from his field when he cleared it for his sheep to graze. In recent years, she had updated the electrical and plumbing systems, but where insulation was concerned, the stone was wonderfully effective: the house needed nothing more than a woodstove in winter and open windows in summer. Zoe had lived through three hurricanes in the house, and though she had lost tiles from the roof, the wind had barely penetrated the walls.

Julia had always found the farmhouse comfortably warm both in temperature and atmosphere. The furniture was large and cushiony, the colors leaning toward earth tones, with accents of yellow and red. Woven throws were everywhere, along with an assortment of spinning wheels and baskets filled with new-spun yarn, because that was what Zoe did—raise Angora rabbits, pluck their fur, spin it, and dye it. She supported herself by selling prime pluck to weavers, spun yarn to knitters, and rabbits themselves to off-island buyers.

Julia was in one of two guest rooms in the house. It had a big double bed topped with a huge comforter of goose down, and before slipping under it in the wee hours of the morning, she had taken a long, hot bath. Though her bandaged arm stayed out of the water, the rest of her was submerged, so, technically, she was warm. But a chill remained; all it took was a burst of memory to start her shivering again.

She slept poorly, waking every little while to one of those bursts. It helped when she left a lamp on; then she didn't have quite the disorientation she suffered waking in utter dark. Once dawn came, she felt better. Even then, though, she didn't sleep for more than half an hour at a stretch. Well beyond the sting of her arm, her whole body had started to ache. The reminder of what had happened was therefore instant each time she awoke. Trying to ignore it, she looked at her watch, turned over, pulled the comforter up to her ears, and lay wide-eyed until exhaustion finally claimed her again.

Shortly after seven, the phone rang. Though it was distant and quickly answered, she awoke with the first ring and lay staring at the pine beams above, wondering who was calling, what they were saying, whether Zoe would be coming to get her. She didn't move, didn't want to be reminded of the stiffness that had come from her time in the sea or of the tension that still gripped her.

She waited long enough to assume that the caller wasn't Monte, before dozing off again. She awoke again soon after, though, when another call came. Another followed that. And still Zoe didn't come for her. Slipping out of bed, she wrapped herself in the chenille robe that was draped on a spinning wheel in the corner and, moving gingerly, went down the hall to the kitchen.

The sight of Zoe was a comfort. Totally unadorned, she wore a sweater and jeans and, at fifty-two, was more fit than many women half her age. Standing barefoot in a kitchen filled with light wood, aged ceramic, and an assortment of art created by her friends, she was the real thing.

She was at an open window, looking out over the meadow. Fog moved gently through the trees, dissipating even as Julia watched.

"No, I will *not* wake her up," Zoe was saying into the phone. "She doesn't need that." Glancing behind her, she saw Julia but didn't miss a beat. "No, Alex. She's been through a trauma. Any idiot would know that. Does she need to spell it out for the press? Hey, I hafta go. See you later?" She ended the call and raised her brows. "Do you mind?"

"No. *No.* I don't want to talk with the press." Julia could barely deal on her own with what had happened, much less discuss it with someone else—and for public consumption? She didn't think so. "How did they know to call here?"

"Alex Brier is local. He saw you on the dock last night and knew you were mine, but others will be coming around. I asked him to ward them off. How'd you sleep?"

Julia answered her with a telling look.

Reaching out, Zoe tucked a strand of blonde hair behind her ear in much the way Julia's mother had done when Julia had been very, very young. It was a gesture of affection of the kind that Janet had neither the time nor inclination to show now.

"Did the phone wake you?"

"The phone, my mind, daylight." Julia wrapped her arms around Zoe and hugged her before dropping into one of the chairs that circled the table. "Sorry. My legs feel strange." She spread her hands over the table, which, like the chairs, was made of oak. She had paid a fortune back home in New York for a set with a distressed finish similar to the kind these had—the only difference being that the marks here were from love and use.

"Achy?" Zoe asked, reaching for the teakettle. "How's the arm?"

"Sore."

"Do you want something for it?"

"No. Who were the other calls?"

Zoe busied herself filling the kettle with water. "A couple of friends here, just askin' about you."

She was a tad too casual for Julia's mood. "There's word on the search, isn't there?"

"Not much."

"Zoe."

Zoe lit the gas under the teakettle. When she turned, her expression was grave. "They've found bodies."

Julia put her fingertips to her forehead and pressed hard. Dropping her hand, she looked at Zoe again. "Any survivors yet?"

"No. But they haven't given up hope."

"Oh, Zoe," Julia chided quietly, because they both knew that if searchers had reached the point of recovering bodies, they would have already spotted survivors. The day was clear. Sunlight spilled across the kitchen floor, warming the wood under Julia's bare feet. "That's what's drawing the media, isn't it?"

Zoe looked tormented. "Yes. We think there may be nine people gone."

"Nine? I hadn't thought so many."

"Eight from the *Amelia Celeste,* plus Artie Jones. We're still pretty much going on who was supposed to show up here and hasn't." Her eyes saddened. "One of them is the fellow who helps me in the barn. His name is Todd Slokum. He's twenty-three, five-ten or so, dark-haired, a little awkward. Do you remember seeing someone like that?"

Julia searched her memory, trying to separate out individuals from the cluster in the stern of the *Amelia Celeste,* but the group was as amorphous in the light of day as it had been the night before. "I don't remember. I'm sorry. There was a cabin between me and the people in the stern. Do you know for sure that Todd was on the ferry?"

"No. I know that he was on the mainland yesterday. He's usually here by seven. It's almost eight now."

"Have you called him?"

"He doesn't have a phone. The guy's kind of a

lost soul. He's been with me for three years now, because he just doesn't know what else to do or where to go, and he's one of the best workers I've had. Once I show him what to do, he's compulsive about doing it right. He loves the rabbits. That's why he always comes to work so early. He loves it when he first walks in and they start butting against their cages to get his attention. They're his friends. He doesn't seem able to make others."

Julia held out a hand, which Zoe came and took. "I'm *so* sorry."

"So is it worse," Zoe asked, eyes haunted, "when someone who is all alone dies, or when someone dies and leaves family and friends? I don't know."

One of the things Julia had always loved about Zoe was her honesty. Given what Julia had been through herself the night before, another person might have tried to shield her from grim talk. But Zoe was right out there; what you saw was what you got. Unfortunately, that kind of forthrightness—and independence—hadn't sat well with her family, which was why, from early adulthood, Zoe had been branded a rebel and distanced from the rest. The ill will remained. Julia's mother, Janet, hadn't even spoken more than a sentence or two to Julia since she had said she was visiting Zoe. The occasional drop-in with Molly along was one thing; two weeks alone with Zoe was something else entirely.

Feeling a swell of love, Julia rose and wrapped her arms around her aunt. The answering hug said Zoe needed it as much as she did this time.

Finally, Zoe set her back, searched her face, and smiled. "What do you do with the years, Julia? The world ages, and you look every bit as beautiful at forty as you did at twenty."

"Look who's talking," Julia replied. "I live and breathe makeup, moisturizer, and sunscreen, and here you are, going with the bare basics and still looking younger than me." It was an argument they'd had before. "I love your hair." In the light of day now, she could see that its natural chestnut color was shot with bits of blonde.

Zoe seemed pleased, if self-conscious. "I did it for you. I didn't want to look like your island hick of an aunt. I knew you'd arrive looking gorgeous." She paused, then added, "Gorgeous, but tired." And the gravity returned. "Physically, is there anything hurting you other than the legs and the arm?"

Julia actually felt like she had been hit by a truck. But she wasn't about to complain. "I'm alive. How can I gripe about aches and pains?" With that reminder, her stomach turned over. "Does anyone know why the purple boat plowed into us?"

"Not yet. They just recovered Artie's body. The medical examiner will do an autopsy."

"Do you think he was drunk?"

"Don't know."

"How many others have they found?"

"Three. The captain of the *Amelia Celeste,* my friend Evan Walsh, and Grady Bartz, who is a dockman for the local lobster buyer."

Julia put her head to Zoe's shoulder, but brought it back up quickly. "Noah Prine's father?"

"Not yet."

"Noah and I were the only ones in the bow. Everyone in the stern died, except for that girl."

"Kimmie."

"Yes."

The phone rang. Julia looked at it with dread. Zoe picked it up, seeming as unsettled as Julia by the prospect of who might be on the other end of the line.

"Yes?" Seconds later, she let out a breath and rolled her eyes. "I know you have an investigation to do, John, but can't it wait?" She paused. "Later, then. Give her a chance to rest. Then she'll be more help." Zoe politely ended the call and turned in apology to Julia. "You will have to talk with him at some point. First, though, you need to call Monte."

Julia's hopes rose. "He called?"

Eyes knowing, Zoe shook her head.

"Ah." Hope died. "Well, of course, I guess he wouldn't," Julia rationalized in an attempt to ease her disappointment. "He doesn't know about the accident, and we left it that I'd call him. So you're right. That's what I should do."

"What he should do," Zoe suggested softly, "is call *you* because he's concerned that you haven't called *him*."

Julia forced a smile. "Well, he hasn't. So I'd better do it." She held out her hand. When Zoe passed her the phone, she carried it out to the porch, punching in her home number as she went. The screen door shut behind her with a trio of echoing claps. Settling into a rocker, she put the phone to her ear.

He picked up after the third ring, sounding groggy. "Yeah."

Julia was immediately concerned. "Monte. Hi. Were you sleeping?" He should have been ready to head off to work.

"It was a late night," he said in a way that suggested he was stretching. The stretch ended. "Since you weren't here, I figured I'd stay at the office. A group of us went out to dinner, then I worked afterward. I don't know—maybe I'm getting something—the flu or a cold. I'm bushed. I think I'll stay in bed awhile longer."

"You should," Julia said, because Monte suggesting that he sleep in, rather than race to the office to monitor the stock market in Japan, was totally out of character. "Are you running a fever?"

"No. I'm just tired. What's up?"

Julia's eyes found the meadow. Fog drifted around the upper leaves of the oaks; splotches of yellow hinted at buttercups in the grass; nearby sheep grazed quietly with only the occasional *baaaa.* Soothed, she was able to tell Monte about the accident without crying.

By the time she was done, he seemed fully awake. "You sound okay."

"I'm alive. Others aren't, and we don't even know the extent of it yet."

"You lost everything? Clothes, books . . . *everything?* Maybe they'll be able to recover some of it. I'll call about the credit cards this morning, and they'll send replacements. They may need to invalidate our account number and give us new cards, though, because if divers don't find your bag, and two or three months from now some fisherman finds it, he could charge up a bundle."

"I'm not worried—"

"How much did you cash?"

"A thousand."

"*That* much? Why that much?"

"That was what you told me to cash. You were going to do it for me, remember? Then you didn't have time." He hadn't had time to drop his tuxedo at the dry cleaner, pick up razor blades, or buy a book for a hospitalized client, either—all of which he had asked her to do yesterday morning at breakfast, after she had begged him for days to let her do things in advance, so that she could be on the road by nine. If she had done that, she wouldn't have missed the car ferry.

"And your camera equipment," he trotted on like a horse with blinders, "there was a *fortune's* worth of equipment in that bag—all the gifts I've given you in the last three years. You were signed up for a course with that photographer Himmel."

"Hammel," she corrected quietly. She looked up when Zoe joined her with mugs of tea for them both.

"That's why you went up there in the first place," Monte went on, "to take his course, but even if it's recovered, the Nikon is ruined." His voice grew resigned. "We should have insured that equipment. You make a judgment call about these things. You weigh their value against the cost of insurance. Oh, boy, did I call it wrong."

"Monte," Julia cried in dismay, "they think nine people are *dead!*"

"Well, thank God, you're *not!* And thank God you missed the car ferry. If we'd lost the car, too, it'd be bad."

Quietly, factually, Julia said, "If I'd made the car ferry, I wouldn't have been in the accident at all."

"The car is insured. Isn't it always the case? It's actually too bad. If the car had gone down, we could have gotten a new one."

Julia stared at Zoe, who sat on the porch rail leaning back against a post. Yelling and screaming wasn't Julia's style, but she was hard-pressed not to react that way now, her frustration with Monte was so great. Molly had felt the tragedy of the accident. Monte didn't get it at all.

Julia felt distant and disconnected from him. Unfortunately, it wasn't a new feeling.

He had been talking on through her musings. Now she realized he had stopped. "I'm sorry, what did you say?" she asked.

"I was wondering," he sounded cautious, "if you were coming home."

Had he said something sweet—that he missed her already and really wanted her home, even that he thought she would be better off in New York after what had happened—she might have been swayed. But there was nothing. So she said, "I want to wait here until the searching is done. There are families of people who died. I feel a kind of responsibility."

"For what? You didn't cause the accident. You had nothing to do with it."

"Not responsibility, then. Connection."

"Okay. That makes sense," he said, sounding more upbeat. "As easy as it would be for you to run home, it's probably better that you don't. Kind of like getting back on the horse after it throws you. Getting back on the bike after you fall. So . . . do you think you'll stay for the whole two weeks, like you planned?"

"At least," Julia said. She sensed he wanted that.

"I'll be fine," he assured her. "The important thing is that you recover from the trauma. Zoe can help with that. I'll overnight you more money and a credit card. And a new cell phone. I mean, hell, we're paying for the service whether you use it or not. Do you want me to send clothes?"

She looked at her wedding band. It was an arc of sapphires and diamonds on a platinum band, and had a matching engagement ring, which she had left in New York. That part of the set was far too large for Big Sawyer, far more showy than Julia wanted to be here. But that was Monte—grand and showy. She shuddered to think which of her clothes he might pick from her closet.

"No," she said. "I can always buy a few."

"The car keys!" he exclaimed. "Where are *they?*"

"In my pocketbook."

"On the ocean floor. Ah, Christ. Okay, I'll send a set up with the cash. What else?"

Julia couldn't think of anything. Her life in New York was far removed from this island, this porch, this rocker.

"Call your parents, Julia," Monte instructed. "You

don't want them to read something about this in the news before they've heard your voice. Will you tell Molly?"

"Uh-huh." There was no point in saying that she already had. Monte simply wanted to know that it was taken care of so that he didn't have to do it himself.

"Good. Y'know," he mused, "I'll bet some of that camera equipment is covered by our homeowner's policy. I'll make some calls."

"Fine."

"So what you need to do is to sit in the sun and get some rest. It's a shame about the photo stuff, but you can still salvage your vacation."

"Uh-huh."

"Okay, then. Be good."

"Yes."

"Bye."

She ended the call with a press of her thumb and dropped the phone into her lap. With the severance came a feeling of emptiness that was overwhelming. She didn't understand how she and Monte could be at such opposite ends of the spectrum after living together for twenty years. Couples were supposed to grow more alike as time passed, not more different. But he had no idea what she was feeling, after surviving an accident like that. Worse, he didn't seem to care. He was worried about the cash. She was worried about lives lost.

"What was that about?" Zoe asked softly.

Julia raised her eyes, then shut them and laid her head against the back of the rocker. "I'm not sure."

"I was surprised you agreed to come for two weeks. I didn't think Monte would let you."

She pulled up her legs, tucked them under her robe, and rested the mug on a knee. "He was fine with it. The course was supposed to run for two weeks. He's heartsick about the lost camera equipment."

"Are you?"

Julia shot her a dry look. "It was his thing more than mine. I asked for a simple digital camera. He interpreted that as meaning I was interested in photography, with a capital P. I figured his heart was in the right place, so I thanked him when he bought me the Nikon, and then he bought me a tripod, and a zoom lens, and a macrolens, and before long I couldn't tell him none of it was what I wanted."

"He's a self-centered man," Zoe said.

Julia didn't respond. Setting her tea aside, she rose quickly and went to the railing. "Where was the accident? Which direction?"

Zoe pointed off to Julia's left.

Julia searched for an ocean view through the trees, but between leaves and the fog, she couldn't see a thing. "Do you think they've found more?"

"They will. The water where it happened wasn't very deep—only six or seven fathoms. That's fortyish feet."

Julia tried to picture the ocean floor at forty feet. What she came up with was dark and littered with grisly debris. "How did *I* escape it?" she asked in bewilderment. It wasn't guilt she felt, so much as incredulity. Her being in the bow of the boat had been pure chance. Had she reached the pier ten minutes earlier and taken a seat in the stern, or had the water been a tad rougher or the oncoming boat a hair faster, the outcome of the accident might have been entirely different. "One of the fellows in the stern offered me a seat. He was the one with the wife and . . ." it hit her then, " . . . and baby." She was stricken. "They had a *baby* with them."

"Kristie," Zoe admitted solemnly. "She just turned one. They have two others, ages three and five."

Julia's heart ached. "What about Artie Jones?"

"He had four."

"Did any of the others have children?"

"Greg Hornsby, the captain. He had two."

She was trying to process the idea of eight children whose lives would be forever changed, when the phone in her hand rang. Startled, she managed to pass it to Zoe.

"Hello? . . . Who is this? . . . What makes you think she's here?" Zoe looked at Julia with dawning anger. "I'm sorry, she's not talking to the press. If you have questions, give the police chief a call. His number is . . ." Her voice trailed off. She held the phone away from her ear, stared at it, lowered it to her side. "He hung up. There's class for you. And from *The New York Times*."

Julia caught her breath. She was about to ask how *The New York Times* had known to call here, when something in Zoe's expression registered.

"*Monte?*" Julia asked and, feeling a blow to her belly, let out a quick puff of air. "He didn't waste any time, just turned around and picked up the phone! How *could* he? He *knows* how private I am."

Zoe didn't say anything, but the anger remained in her eyes.

"He wanted the publicity," Julia decided. Monte was always angling for exposure.

"They'd have mentioned him in the piece."

"That is *sick!*" Julia was shaking again.

Zoe was suddenly on her feet. She reached inside the kitchen door and pulled out a pair of garden clogs. "Put these on." As soon as Julia had done so, she led her down the back stairs and around the side of the house toward the barn. The path was wide and well worn, though bordered by grass in need of a cut. The air was cool and moist, welcome against the heat of anger.

Julia didn't ask questions. Nor did she balk when they reached the door to the barn. She wasn't normally a barn person. She had been raised to believe that barn animals were dirty creatures who could pass on disease. In past visits here, she had been content to view them from afar and even that was more out of politeness to Zoe than true interest.

Zoe opened the door and pushed it wide to stay, but there was plenty of light without it. The openings where horses had once hung their heads out for fresh air were now covered by screens. Same with skylights in the roof. Both had shutters on pulleys, ready for closing in inclement weather.

"I shut the doors at night," Zoe explained, "because, believe it or not, there are foxes in the woods. They'd make a tasty meal of my crew here."

Her "crew" had started making little sounds, but it wasn't until they got closer that Julia could see what they were doing. A large area in the barn, stalls included, had been taken over by cages. They were stacked two high in some places, three in others. Each looked to have a single rabbit inside, a good many of which were now pushing their noses against different parts of their cages—some against the wire, some against a crockery food bowl, some against the tubes of their water bottles.

Julia was startled. She had seen the rabbits before, but only from the door. A glimpse of fur, and she had conjured an image of the classroom rabbit Molly had brought home to care for one first-grade weekend.

Close up now, Julia wouldn't have known these creatures were even rabbits if she hadn't known that Zoe raised them. The traditional bunny ears, eyes, and twitching nose were lost in a cloud of fur. Most of those clouds were white, but others were beige, gray, or black. Some had a lilac tinge. Others were mottled.

"Good morning, little sweeties," Zoe crooned and explained to Julia, "English Angoras are the smallest of the Angoras. They may look big, but it's all fur. My largest rarely hits eight pounds." She went to one of the cages, opened it, and reached inside. Slipping one hand under the rabbit's belly and another over its ears, she lifted it out and cradled it against her middle. "They like the sense of confinement that comes when you put a hand on their ears this way. This is Gretchen," she said, crooning again. "Gretchen, say hello to Julia."

Gretchen said nothing, of course. Julia couldn't even tell if Gretchen was looking at her, her eyes were so hidden in fur.

Zoe carried the rabbit to a grooming table. Its top was eighteen inches square and lined with carpeting. A raised compartment closed in one end. The other three sides were bounded by a three-inch-high lip of wood.

"Sit," Zoe instructed Julia, hitching her chin toward a chair by the table.

Julia was no sooner in the chair when the rabbit was on her lap.

"I need to dole out food and put out clean water bottles," Zoe said. "I want you to hold Gretchen while I do. Put one hand here," she said, replacing her hand with Julia's on the rabbit's ears, "and the other here by her chest, so that she won't jump off."

"Does she nip?" Julia asked, feeling a little uneasy.

"Nope. She's my therapy bunny. One of my friends here lives with her grandmother, who is ninety-two and suffers from severe dementia. She can be ranting and raving seconds before I put Gretchen in her lap. Then she calms. Instantly."

"Maybe it's sheer terror," Julia said, only half in jest.

"Is that what you're feeling?"

Actually, it wasn't. Edging past the uneasy part, Julia was intrigued by the creature's warmth and the softness of its fur. She saw nothing remotely related to dirt. There were no bugs, no matted parts, no smell, only a luxurious puff of fur. She found herself gently stroking the rabbit's ears, which she could make out clearly now. The motion started small. When the animal didn't seem to mind, it broadened.

"Is this okay?" she asked Zoe.

"Perfect. She loves it. You're a natural."

Julia didn't know about that, but she was encouraged when the rabbit actually seemed to relax in her lap. She let her fingers sift deeper, until she was finger-combing the feather-light fur. After a minute, she tipped her head sideways and smoothed enough fringe away so that she could see the rabbit's eye.

"Hello," she whispered.

The creature looked at her, then away. The simple gesture reminded her of Kimmie Colella, but the memory didn't start her trembling again. She did feel calmer, holding the small rabbit. So she kept at it, stroking the ears—first one, then the other—combing its fur with her fingers, and exploring its shape, all in smooth, gentle motions. She found herself breathing more easily, relaxing more completely, even shifting the rabbit sideways so that she could see its nose.

It did have a bunny nose. It wasn't quite pink, but it twitched.

"How many of these do you have?" she asked Zoe.

"Currently? Twenty-three adults, twenty-five babies."

"Babies?" Julia did look up then. "I don't see any babies."

"See the wood boxes in some of the cages? Those are nest boxes. The kits are inside."

"How do they fit?"

Zoe laughed. "They are lit-tle, Julia. Here, I'll show you." She opened one of the cages and reached in. "Come here, cutie pie," she cooed. Closing the cage again, she carried the baby to Julia. Though she used both hands, the baby would have fit comfortably in one.

Julia caught her breath in delight. The kit was pure white, with tiny ears, eyes, and nose. "How old is it?"

"Three weeks. It's just beginning to fuzz up."

"But it looks more like a rabbit than these biggies."

Zoe chuckled. "More like a rabbit than cotton candy? It does. Give it another little while and it'll sprout fringe on its ears and face." One small leg kicked its way through Zoe's hands. She shifted to hold the kit more securely. "This little guy is the dominant one in the litter. He's the biggest of the bunch."

"How do you know it's a boy?"

"I've sexed it."

"Ah." Julia wasn't ready to ask how *that* was done. Both hind legs poked out this time. "He's an active little guy."

"I'd be worried if he wasn't. The strength of their hind legs is really the only defense Angoras have. If one kicks you, you feel it. You'd be amazed at how fast they can move."

"Twenty-five babies?"

"Four litters, with five, seven, seven, and six kits, respectively," Zoe said, ticking them off with a glance at each cage. "My rabbits do well at birthing, because the environment here is ideal. The temperature's just right—never too hot, which would spell death for an Angora carrying this kind of fur. Angora wool is seven times warmer than lambs' wool. Anything over seventy-five, and they start panting. Forty-five to fifty-five degrees is perfect for them. Once in a great while, in the dead of winter, we have to hook up supplementary heaters, but the walls of the barn deflect the wind, and the air coming off the ocean is always more moderate than it is on land. The screens here provide the kind of cross ventilation the rabbits need. Give them shade and a breeze, and they're great."

"How did you learn all this?" Julia asked, because she had seen nothing of this magnitude in earlier visits. Yes, those visits had been brief, stolen time when Molly had been her excuse to come. And, yes, Zoe had emailed her bits and snatches of information in between. But Julia hadn't imagined such a serious operation.

Zoe carried the kit back to its cage. "I did a lot of reading. I visited with breeders. I had a friend in Rhode Island, Caroline Ellis, who raised Angoras and was a *huge* help when I first started out. Now a group of us is in constant touch on the Web, but in the final analysis," she closed the door and returned, "it's been trial and error. I began small, while I worked out the bugs. The thing is, no two rabbitries are exactly alike. For starters, the weather here is unique. Rabbits are like a green plant, in a sense. A plant may thrive in a nursery, then wither and die when you get it home because the light isn't right, or the food you give it isn't right, or your cat eats it up." She glanced toward the barn door and said with gusto, "That's why I don't bother with houseplants, right, Ned?"

Ned was a cat. He was large and black, and would have faded into the shadow of the door had Zoe not singled him out.

"Mind you," Zoe went on, "Ned might eat up these kits, too, if I put them on the floor. He'd think they were rats."

"Will he harm the adults?" Julia asked. The cat was certainly larger than Gretchen.

"No. He's trained to consider them friends and is actually protective. He might not be able to catch a fox or a raccoon, but he'll make enough noise to bring me running." She looked at the nearest cages. "I have to do some cleaning."

"Let me help," Julia offered. The creature in her lap was so sweet. "Show me what to do."

Zoe gave her a curious smile. "Is this the woman who was three weeks in replying when I first emailed her that I was buying rabbits?"

Julia protested, "We were away for two of those weeks and returned to no heat in the condo, so we had to stay in a hotel. Did I ever tell you not to buy them?"

"No, but you never offered to help with them, either."

"I never narrowly escaped death before."

"What does A have to do with B?"

"Todd Slokum, for one thing," Julia said. "If he were here, you wouldn't be doing these chores yourself."

Zoe's shoulders sagged. "I skipped it yesterday, because I figured he'd be in today. I have to run down to his place. He may just be sick."

"I'll work here while you go."

"Later, maybe. Have you called your parents?"

Julia shook her head.

"I would. We have no way of knowing what Monte told the *Times*. I wouldn't want them getting a call from a reporter. They'd be hurt."

"*They'd* be hurt?" Julia cried. "Know how much support they've given me lately?"

"The problem is Janet. Not your dad."

"Well, it hurts just the same."

"I know," Zoe said. "I've been there."

Julia went back to stroking Gretchen. When she spoke again, her voice was calmer. "I know you have."

"Which is why," Zoe said quietly, "I can't make that call for you. I'd do most anything else. But not that."

Julia had been born knowing that Zoe was considered the black sheep of the family. Back then, though, Zoe and Janet had still talked. Julia didn't know what had caused the final rift, only that it had happened when she was fifteen. For a while, she had blamed herself for annoying Janet by loving Zoe too much. Her father had assured her that wasn't the case, but he had never given her anything in its place, and she quickly learned that the subject was too raw to pursue.

Quietly now, she said, "I don't understand my mother."

Zoe sighed. "With a little luck, she'll have left for work, and George will be the one to pick up the phone."

Julia didn't need luck. Without fail, Janet was on her way to work by eight. She claimed that the hour she had before the rest of her staff arrived was the most productive of the day, and who was Julia to argue? Janet was an important person. She headed one of the largest charitable organizations in greater Baltimore and was responsible for raising millions of dollars each year for the underprivileged. Life didn't get any more important than that, Julia was taught, and from the time she was twelve, with brothers nine and seven, she had covered for her mother during those oh-so-important absences.

Watch the boys for me, will you, sweetheart? Make sure Mark wears his jacket.

Or, *Oh my, I forgot! Jerry needs cookies for school. There's a roll of those Pillsbury things in the freezer. Slice them up and bake them like a good girl, Julia?*

And it wasn't only helping her brothers at the start of the day. Julia was often the mommy at the other end, as well.

I've left a container of frozen stew on the counter. If you put it in a pot when you get home from school and put the gas on low under it, we can eat as soon as I get home.

Or, *If Mark comes home with grass stains on his uniform, will you just throw it in the wash? I'll put it in the dryer myself, but the head start will help. He needs it clean for tomorrow.*

How could Julia possibly object? How could she be the one to make things hard for Janet, when Janet was doing such meaningful work? And Janet couldn't have been more appreciative. If it wasn't, *You are the best daughter, Julia, I am a very lucky woman*, it was, *The boys listen to you, Julia, you have a knack for this*, or, *My friend Marie is struggling with her career because she doesn't have a daughter like you at home.*

Julia thrived on the praise. She became the best homemaker there was, the best cook there was, the best helpmate there was. Only in hindsight, when she looked back on both her childhood and her marriage, did she wonder if she hadn't been used more than necessary.

"Hello?" came the wary voice of Julia's father now.

George was a whole other issue, so different in temperament from Janet that Julia had often wondered what had brought them together in the first place. An accountant by profession, George was introspective and shy. The most conventional of men in his navy suits and pressed sportswear, he was as supportive of Janet's whims as he was supportive of Julia.

Hearing his voice now, she felt a surge of warmth. "It's me, Dad. Thank goodness I caught you before you left. I have to tell you—"

"This isn't a good time," he cut in. "Your mother has a headache. She's late leaving for work."

Julia was instantly concerned. Janet was in good health, but she was, after all, sixty-four. "A headache?"

"Just tension," he said and added in a whisper, "but it wouldn't help seeing Zoe's name on the caller ID."

Julia felt chastised. "I had no choice. This is the only phone I have. I had an awful experience last night."

"Be right there, Janet," he called, then said impersonally, with innocent curiosity, as if he were talking to a friend, "Can I phone you later?"

Julia wasn't a friend. She was his daughter, and she needed comfort. "There was an accident."

"What kind of accident?"

"A boating one. I was on a ferry—"

"Are you hurt?"

"Miraculously, no. But—"

"Thank God. Listen, sweetie," he said under his breath, "I will call you back. Right now, I need to get your mother some tea. She has an important meeting at ten. I'm going to try to get her there. She won't be happy if she misses it. Later, Julia." Without another word, he hung up the phone.

Julia wasn't as quick. Stunned, she held the receiver in midair, realizing only then how much she had wanted to talk, and not only with George, but with Janet. Her parents had given her life. She had nearly lost it last night. She couldn't think of any more appropriate people to give her comfort.

Disconnected. That was what she felt as she slowly returned the receiver to its cradle. Disconnected. And it went beyond the call to her parents, even beyond the call to Monte. She was feeling disconnected from *everything* back in those places she had called home. It was as if the accident had created a barrier between past and present, as if a wall had sprung up out of the water and was now separating the two.

She would have thought that if anyone could moor her again, it was her parents. Apparently, she had thought wrong.

Chapter 3

Noah felt thwarted. He needed to blame someone for the accident, and Artie Jones fit the bill. Big
boat, big noise, big wake—big house, big dock, big
wallet—Artie was everything year-rounders dreaded
and lobstermen despised. It didn't matter that he
hadn't hurt anyone before. He would have made a
perfect scapegoat for a disaster that shouldn't have
happened.

Early word on the autopsy, though, ruled that out.
Artie hadn't been playing chicken. Nor had he deliberately aimed his boat at the *Amelia Celeste*. He'd had
heart failure before the crash ever occurred—which
meant Noah had no one to blame but fate.

That realization came midday Thursday. Shortly
thereafter, the Coast Guard recovered his father's re-
mains.

With Hutch's death confirmed and no fall guy,
Noah was numb. He sat in the stern of the *Leila Sue*,

staring out at sea, so overcome with frustration and regret that they canceled each other out.

His cell phone lay beside him. He couldn't go ashore to make the call, because something held him there on the water. He didn't know whether it was Hutch's soul, not yet fully risen, or the bond he had always felt with the sea. If there was comfort to be had anywhere, it was here.

Determinedly, he picked up the phone and dialed his ex-wife's number. Sandi had moved twice since the divorce, following teaching jobs that had carried her steadily into administration. She still taught history, now at a private high school in Washington, D.C., but she was also the dean of studies there. He phoned her office, guessing that her administrative responsibilities went on even though the school year was done.

"Sandi," he said when she picked up.

"Yes," she replied blankly.

"It's me."

There was a brief pause, then a cautious, "Noah? It doesn't sound like you. Is something wrong?"

"Hutch is dead."

In the ensuing silence, he saw her close her eyes and bow her head. Sandi had never been particularly fond of either of Noah's parents, but she was a compassionate woman. She was also acutely aware that regardless of her feelings for Noah's family, they were Ian's forebears. She had been sympathetic when Noah's mother had died. She would be no different now.

"I'm sorry," she said quietly. "How?"

"Badly. There was an accident." He gave her the bare outline.

She was appalled. "I hope he died instantly."

So did Noah. The alternative was too horrible to consider.

"How are you?" she asked. "Are you hurt?"

"No."

"Not at all?"

"Not at all."

"How?" she asked with some of the same bewilderment he felt.

"Beats me."

"Were you the only survivor?"

"No."

There was a pause, then, "One other? Two?"

"Two."

"Are they hurt?"

"Not much."

"What does that mean?"

"One has a small cut."

"And the other?"

"She can't speak."

"Is it a physical problem? Burned windpipe? Crushed vocal chords?"

"No."

"Trauma, then."

"Apparently."

"But you're fine?"

"Yes."

A long moment's silence. Then she sighed. "I'd

say you're traumatized, too, if I didn't know that even in the best of times, you suffer from an inability to speak. Why is it that every conversation with you is like pulling teeth? Okay. Don't answer that. We've been through this before. I don't know why I always expect more. I guess it's because there was more when we met. So if *this* is your natural state, where did *that* come from? Or if *that* was your natural state, where did *this* come from? Is it just with me that you can't say more than three words at a stretch?"

Jaw tight, Noah waited until several seconds passed. When she remained quiet, he said, "Here's more'n three words, Sandi. Hutch died night before last. I'm not going into my inability to speak right now. I just want to tell Ian the news. Hutch was his grandfather. His grandfather's gone."

Sandi was quickly contrite. "I'm sorry."

"For his death or the outburst?"

"Both. I'm always amazed at how close to the surface everything is, even ten years after the split."

Noah didn't pretend that she still held feelings for him. Nor did he want it. They had failed as a couple. The divorce was mutually agreed upon.

The problem was that Sandi didn't like to fail. She had been analyzing their marriage since the day it fell apart, and, naturally, she blamed him. He worked unconscionable hours, she claimed, and was distant when he was home. He excluded her from his thoughts and was insensitive to her needs. He was impatient with her colleagues and couldn't stand her friends.

So maybe she was right. Maybe the whole lot of it

was his fault. Just then, though, he couldn't have cared less.

"Where's Ian now?" he asked. At three in the afternoon, the boy would normally be playing baseball, but this was June. The varsity season, like the school year, was done until fall.

"Stewing. He mouthed off to the coach yesterday, so he's warming the bench today."

"What bench?"

"It's a local league," Sandi explained. "I needed him to be involved in something until summer school begins. He isn't an easy kid."

"Seventeen's tough."

"*I'll* say."

"I was thinking of him, not you."

"I *was* thinking of me," she charged, "because you're not around to deflect any of what's going on. *I* didn't have trouble being seventeen. I was busy with school, I had friends and dance class and soccer. I was excited about being a senior and excited about looking at colleges. Ian is none of those things."

"And you see no other kids like him?" Noah asked knowingly.

"Of course, I do. That's my job. But those are other kids. Ian's mine. I take him personally."

Noah couldn't argue with that. He had always felt Sandi was a good mother. "So when'll he be home?"

"Maybe four. Maybe five. He's been somewhat unreliable lately."

"Have him call me when he gets there?"

"When's the funeral?"

"Tuesday." Noah would have rather it be sooner, but the medical examiner wanted Hutch for a while, and by the time Noah talked with the minister, three other funerals had already been lined up.

"Should I fly him up?" Sandi asked.

"Only if he wants to come."

"Noah." She sighed. "That's a cop-out. Do you *want* him there?"

"Yes."

"I'll tell him that. It may not hold much weight. Lately, defiance is his middle name."

Noah was suddenly weary. "Just tell him. If he doesn't want to come, he won't come. I can bury Hutch just fine without him."

There was a pause, then a guarded, "I could bring him, myself. Do you want me there?"

"Why? You couldn't stand Hutch."

"It wasn't that. It was just that over time I was seeing in him all of the things I had to struggle with in you. But that takes us back to the talking thing. I didn't know Hutch. How could I? He didn't have much to say to me. He didn't seem to have much to say to your mother either, but she was used to it, being a Mainer and all, and there's a whole *other* issue. There were times when I was up there and I'd see a bunch of local guys on the dock, talking and laughing. I'd approach, and they'd go stone silent. So was it just that they hated outsiders? That's what I always felt like when I was there. An outsider."

Again, Noah waited until the silence lasted long enough to suggest she was done. Then, quietly, he said, "This isn't the time, Sandi. Just have Ian call me, okay?"

Julia didn't get a call from her father. She did get a call from her friend Charlotte, who had heard about the accident from her husband, who had heard about it through Monte. Charlotte wanted to know for herself that Julia was all right, and once she was satisfied, she begged Julia to let her send clothes from the store. Charlotte sold the finest of Italian imports. Julia's lost bags had held several of her outfits. But those clothes seemed all wrong now.

Unable to explain this to Charlotte, she must have come across as being disturbed, because, less than an hour later, Julia got a call from their mutual friend Jane. Jane taught psychology at City College and was, actually, just the person Julia wanted to speak to. She described the accident and told her about Kim Colella. By the time she hung up the phone, she had learned the rudiments about post-traumatic stress disorder and muteness.

It wasn't until even later, though, when she was accessing her email on Zoe's computer, exchanging comforting notes with her lawyer friend Donna, when she received one from George.

SORRY I HAVEN'T CALLED, BUT IT'S BEEN A BAD COUPLE OF DAYS, he wrote in the all-caps style he insisted on using, though shouting was not his way. He was a quiet man of necessity;

being married to as forceful a woman as Janet, he couldn't get a word in edgewise. Julia had often suspected that since Janet didn't use a computer, he spoke loudly on the web simply because he could.

I GOT YOUR MOTHER SET YESTERDAY AND THEN HAD A MAJOR PROBLEM HERE AT WORK. I'M JUST NOW COMING UP FOR AIR. SUFFICE IT TO SAY THAT WE'RE BOTH GRATE-FUL YOU CAME AWAY FROM THE ACCIDENT UNSCATHED. GIVEN THE SITUATION, JANET FEELS YOU OUGHT TO RETURN TO NEW YORK. LET US KNOW.

Stung, Julia didn't reply.

Actually, "stung" barely covered it. She was angry.

Heart pounding, she closed out her email, turned off the computer, and, putting the anger to use, set off for town. There, she bought the makings of half a dozen casseroles and as many batches of cookies. The first of the funerals wasn't until Monday, but she wanted to take something to the families involved—and she was a good cook. She couldn't do gourmet the way her daughter could, but she knew basics. She had thrown innumerable parties for Monte's colleagues, and even apart from what a caterer brought, she always prepared something herself. She often gave home-baked bread or cookies as gifts when they went to friends' homes for dinner. As for bereaved families, someone was always dying in Monte's circle of clients, which went to show what happened when you represented clients who had taken long lifetimes to amass a fortune worth investing. Bottom line?

Julia was a pro at making homemade little some-
things to satisfy one or another of Monte's professional needs.

That said, she would have gladly cleaned rabbit
cages if Zoe had shown her what to do. She found
the rabbits surprisingly clean, and the scent in the
barn unexpectedly pleasant, what with those little
bursts of chrysanthemum extract and rosemary oil to
keep the flies at bay.

But Zoe was still out with the search, looking for
Todd Slokum.

So Julia baked. The familiarity of the activity was
a comfort at a time when she was feeling unhinged.
Monte hadn't helped. Her parents hadn't helped. If
her life were a boat that had been torn from its mooring, she was all on her own as far as tying up again
went. Embracing the old and familiar was one way to
do it, albeit a stopgap measure. She didn't know what
the long-range answer was.

Four o'clock came and went, and still Noah
waited for Ian to call. He didn't budge from the boat.
There was nowhere better to go. Lucas was aboard
one minute and loping down the dock the next,
seeming unfazed by the gravity of the moment. But
Lucas was a dog. He had no way of knowing Hutch
was gone for good.

Noah knew it and grieved. But grief wasn't all.
Making plans for the funeral had been an eye-
opening experience in a pathetic kind of way. Had
he known what Hutch wanted? No. They had never

talked about funerals. They had never talked about Noah's divorce. Or about his mother's death. They had never talked about Ian. Or about why Noah had returned to Big Sawyer to haul traps after the divorce, rather than continue on in New York. He was good at what he'd done there, and had made a lot of money in a very short time. They had never talked about that, either.

What did they talk about? They talked about the weather. They talked about the boat and the traps and the buoys. They talked about the day's catch, the price it would bring, the new minimum-size regulation the state was rumored to be considering. They talked about the *Trapper John*'s engine overhaul and *My Andrea*'s new GPS. They talked about the lime-grape-lime buoys that were popping up in waters traditionally fished by Big Sawyer lobstermen. And they talked about the weather, again.

These were the things lobstermen discussed. Noah could discuss them as well as he had discussed the pros and cons of an IPO with colleagues in New York. They were real. They interested him.

Small talk did not.

Julia visited the Hornsby house. Nestled not far from the harbor, it was filled with friends. She dropped off a chicken casserole, offered her condolences, and left. She did the same at the homes of Grady Bartz and Dar Hutter.

The situation was different at the Walsh house. It stood on Dobbs Hill, where so many of the artists lived, and artists liked open space. At the high crests, jagged spruce tips grazed the sky, but the face of the hill was an expanse of rolling meadow. There were no crowds at the Walsh house, no neighbors milling about. A lone Volvo station wagon sat in front of the barn, which in turn sat not far from a weathered farmhouse.

Julia climbed the steps, crossed the porch, and knocked on the frame of the screen door. The woman who quickly appeared was in her early thirties, which Julia knew only because Zoe had filled her in. This was Jeannie Walsh's sister, Ellen Hamilton. She was single and taught high school math in Ohio. With the accident, she had become an instant parent. Despite sandy hair and a face full of freckles, she looked ten years past her age.

When Julia introduced herself, Ellen put a finger to her lips and slipped outside, silently closing the screen behind her. She gestured Julia to a wood swing halfway down the porch. Once seated, she whispered, "They're both asleep on the sofa. They're exhausted."

"You must be yourself," Julia said softly. "I've brought dinner. Is there anything else I can do?"

Ellen smiled sadly. "No. Thanks, though." Her smiled faded. Age and anguish returned. "Evan's family is handling the funerals. Most of their friends have gone back with the bodies. We agreed the girls were too young to go. They're coming to live with me in Akron. It's really just a matter of packing up this place, and I'm the only one who can do that." She looked bewildered. "How do you decide what to take? I live in a small place, so I can't take it all. I'm trying to imagine what might have meaning for the girls when they're grown." Her voice had begun to waver, her eyes to water. Seeming unable to say more, she looked at the far horizon.

A soft sound came from the door, the breeze of a small child slipping out. She had dark hair in a tumbled mass, a ketchup-stained jersey and shorts, and dusty bare feet. Eyes barely open, she put her thumb in her mouth, slipped between the nearest pair of legs—which happened to be Julia's—and laid a head on her thigh.

Without a thought, Julia scooped her up. The child was instantly asleep on her shoulder.

"I'm sorry," Ellen whispered.

Julia wasn't. She loved the feel of the little body against her. "It's fine. I'm good at this."

"She's three. She has no idea what's going on. Neither of them do. Boy, I'm not up for this."

"You'll manage."

"But what harm will I do in the process? The thing is, there's no one else. I'm Jeannie's only surviving relative. Evan's parents are older, and his two brothers already have nine children between them. I wouldn't be comfortable with that for the girls." She made a sound of disbelief. "Talk about life-changing moments. Little did I know when my phone rang yesterday morning . . ."

Five o'clock came and went without a call from Ian.

Noah pulled a beer from the stash that he kept in the cabin cooler now that summer was coming.

Nothing else quenched thirst better on those days when the sun beat down with so much heat that the wind just couldn't cut it. Nothing better chased down a lunch of two peanut butter and jelly sandwiches on a hot day than a beer. It didn't matter that he didn't have even one sandwich now or that it wasn't particularly hot. The beer was good.

A second beer followed the first, and by the time six o'clock came and went with no Ian, Noah had mellowed enough so that he wasn't wholly annoyed. There would be less pressure this way, he reasoned. He'd have an easier time doing the funeral without having to worry about what to say to his son.

It wasn't as if Ian and Hutch had been friends. The boy hadn't been up to the island more than a handful of times. It had always been easier for Noah to visit him on his own turf.

Besides, contrary to what his ex-wife thought, Noah wouldn't be alone at the funeral. He had lots of people here. Hadn't they been coming by the *Leila Sue* all afternoon to pay their respects? They didn't say much. They didn't have to. Noah knew that they truly meant what few words they did say.

Sandi could never understand that. She could never understand the concept of communicative silence. She could never understand that when you were with the right people, you didn't need words in order to know what they felt.

It was nearing seven when a woman appeared in the reflection his windshield gave of the shore. He spotted her the instant she reached the dock. There was no mistaking the crazy multicolored angora sweater that Zoe wore all the time. Nor was there any mistaking that this woman wasn't Zoe. She stood apart just as much as she had back on the mainland, running down the dock to catch the *Amelia Celeste*. It might have been her fine blonde hair that was distinctive, or the delicacy of her build, or even the way she held herself, which was straight, as people did when looking good was part of who they were. She wore sneakers this time, likely Zoe's also. And she wasn't weighed down by luggage now, only by a light canvas bag that hung from a shoulder.

Several yards onto the dock, she grew tentative and stopped. She seemed lost. The wind was blowing her hair over her eyes. She held it back while she scanned the boats.

He imagined she was looking for him, then decided it was only wishful thinking. He was male, and she was female. He wasn't so numbed by Hutch's death—or by beer—that he couldn't appreciate that. But there was more. The two of them shared something that had to do with life and death. In that sense alone, he wanted her to be looking for him. He didn't quite know why, but there it was.

His wish was granted. Her reflection said she had spotted him. He decided it was a consolation prize after forty-eight hours of hell, but he wasn't complaining. Without turning, he followed her approach in the glass. His heart was finally beating a notch above numbness. He felt relief, even comfort.

He waited until she was turning onto the *Leila Sue*'s arm of the dock before looking around to show he had seen her. He stood up, but didn't move more than that. She seemed a little nervous. That made two of them. It was an odd situation, her being a total stranger who had shared something intimate with him. Intimate. Yes, that it was. Though he'd been born and raised here and had known most year-rounders nearly as long as that, he hadn't shared an experience this intimate with any of them.

She came up to the side of the boat and stopped. "I'm, uh, Julia. I just heard about your father. I wanted to say how sorry I am."

He nodded.

"And how grateful," she went on, seeming more sure here. "You saved my life. I'm not sure what I'd have done if you hadn't given me that cushion to hold."

"You'd have been okay," he said, because he was no hero, not after he'd ordered his father to the stern of the *Amelia Celeste,* as if the man were a dog. "Rescue wasn't long in coming."

"But would they have spotted the speck that was me without the cushion?" she asked with a speed that suggested she had been agonizing over the question. "Would I have swallowed too much water and been taken under by a wave? Would I have been too close to the ferry when that last explosion came?" Her eyes went out to sea. They were haunted when they found his again. "Until this minute, I hadn't even thought about that second explosion. I keep stumbling over these little memories that I didn't know I had. All these questions. And then there's the big one."

The big one. He didn't need to wonder what *that* was. "Why us?" he said. "Why were we spared? Why not them?"

She nodded, seeming relieved that he knew what she meant. "I've asked myself that a hundred times. I mean, there's the whole thing about mortality. I've been lucky. This is the closest I've ever come to death, and that's enough to get me thinking. But then there's the randomness of what happened. If we'd been in the stern . . . or if the racer had hit the bow . . . I don't know how to explain that."

Noah didn't either. "My father wanted to stand in the bow," he blurted out. It had nothing to do with his aversion to being a hero, and everything to do with his own inner torment. "I made him sit in the stern."

She didn't blink. "Evan Walsh offered me his seat. I turned him down." She took an unsteady breath. "It could so easily have gone the other way."

He nodded with feeling.

Neither of them spoke for a full minute, and he was fine with it. She was easy on the eyes. More than that—she was *beautiful*. But it was more than that, too. With her standing here, something raw in him was soothed.

"Well." She pressed her lips together, nodded, seemed ready to wrap things up. "I just wanted to express my condolences." Her eyes abruptly widened. "And to give you this." She slid the bag from her shoulder and passed it down to him over the gunnel.

He peered inside at a foil package.

"It's dinner. I cooked. It's one of the few things I'm good at. Today it was therapeutic. Not that I can eat much myself. My stomach keeps turning over."

Noah knew the feeling. The only thing he'd eaten since the accident had come on the fly from Rick Greene. He had eaten it without tasting a bite.

But whatever Julia had cooked smelled good. "Thanks," he said. "This is really nice of you."

"It's the least I can do," she said with a smile that came and went so quickly he might have missed it if he hadn't been watching closely. He was thinking that there was something shy about her when, looking haunted again, she said, "Zoe called just before I left. The divers found the body of the young man who worked for her."

"Todd." Noah had already heard. "Does she know if he has family?"

"She thinks so. She found mail in his apartment. She's working with your police chief to track down the senders. Todd was the last one missing."

"Yes. Now they're looking for anything that might help them reconstruct the accident."

"Why do they have to do that?"

"It's their job. There may be insurance issues. They have to investigate. Who knows? They may find your bags in the process."

"I don't care about my bags," she avowed soundly—then blinked and blushed. "Oh. You mean life insurance issues. I guess they would want to learn as much as they can because of that. Have you talked with Kim Colella?"

Noah kept forgetting about Kimmie. Or maybe he was just preoccupied with Hutch. "I haven't. I think she's with her family. How long are you here for?"

"Two weeks. I was supposed to take one of Tony Hammel's courses, but my equipment . . ." She moved her hand in a telling arc.

"He could loan you some."

She wrinkled her nose, gave a tiny smile. "I've lost my taste for it."

"And not for Big Sawyer? I'll bet you head back early."

"No." She said soberly. "Don't ask me to explain. It's complex, and I'm not up for complex things right now. I'm feeling . . ." She searched for a minute or two, finally looked at him in bewilderment. "What am I feeling?"

She was so beseeching—and *sweet* at it—that he might have smiled if the situation hadn't been so dire. What was she feeling? He considered the options.

She might have been afraid of going on a boat again, hence unable to leave just yet. But he didn't think it was that.

She might have been tied to the island out of guilt. Hadn't she mentioned Evan? Evan might have survived if she had switched places with him. But Noah had mentioned Hutch in the same regard, and it wasn't guilt he felt as much as regret. Hutch could have stood in the bow with him. Then neither of them would have died. Julia struck him as being a sensible person. She wouldn't be feeling guilt, per se.

She might have been feeling an obligation to the

people here, but he ruled that out the minute it came to mind. Part of being sensible was being smart, and smart people understood the nature of islanders. Islanders were independent and strong. They chose to live off the water and knew the risk that went with leaving port in a small boat each day, and any who might have forgotten had seen the movie of *The Perfect Storm* a hundred times. The video remained the hottest commodity at the rental counter in Brady's Tackle and Gear.

What am I feeling? her eyes continued to ask.

"Singled out," he said. He didn't know where the words came from, hadn't thought them before. But that was what he was feeling. He was feeling different from the old friends who had come by today. Yes. Singled out.

Her eyes lit up. She nodded. In the next breath, though, the spark faded. "Singled out for what? Survival?"

"No," he said. That wasn't it.

"Recompense? I've had a good life. I'm not owed anything."

"Me neither."

"Singled out by whom? God?"

He felt an instant annoyance. He didn't want to *think* about the God issue, not with the games He had played on the water two nights ago.

"I'm sorry," she said quietly. "You have enough on your mind. I shouldn't be bothering you with this. It's just . . ." She gave a tiny shake of her head and another of those touch-and-go smiles. Then, raising a hand in a wave, she turned and started back down the dock.

He didn't stop her. It wasn't his place. He had nothing to add to the conversation, though he wished he did. He was as confused as she was.

But he felt better now, he realized. Being confused wasn't so bad when someone else felt the same. It was the old misery-loves-company thing, and it took the edge off his angst—at least until the angst took on a new focus. That happened the following Tuesday, at the tail end of his father's funeral.

Chapter 4

The island graveyard sat on a hill overlooking the sea. Given the nature of those who lay there, this was fitting. Equally fitting, the headstones were cut of island granite and locally carved. A small chapel stood off to the side, built of stone for practical reasons. Exposed to the elements on the hill, a chapel of wood might have crumbled under a regular battering by wind, sea salt, and rain. On this spot, everything had to be solid. "Eternity" was the operative word.

Of the victims of the accident, the Walshes, Todd Slokum, and Artie Jones were being buried back near family homes on the mainland. The rest were buried on Big Sawyer. They were islanders related to islanders, which meant that their funerals were attended by just about everyone who lived there. Dar Hutter's was Monday morning, Greg Hornsby's that afternoon, and Grady Bartz's the next morning, all in fog, reminiscent of how they had died. For the most part, Julia stood with Zoe, and at those times was as much a part of the community as any stranger could be. It was when the eulogies were done and Zoe turned to talk with friends that Julia felt separate.

At those times, rather than stand idly at Zoe's side, she drifted off to the edge of the cemetery and gazed out over the sea. It calmed her. It was as though she was familiar with the ocean in a way that she wasn't with these people, as though she and the ocean were connected. Likewise Noah. She didn't talk to him, but she knew he was there. That knowledge grounded her.

Hutch's funeral was the last. It was held Tuesday afternoon at four, a time that allowed members of the local lobster fleet to return from their day's work and attend.

For Julia, the scenario here was the same as the others; ostensibly, she was neither more nor less a part of the gathering. But this funeral was different for her. She had never met Hutchinson Prine—could no more pick him out from the memory of the people gathered in the stern of the *Amelia Celeste* than she could pick out any of the others—but she did feel a connection to his son. This time, it didn't bother her to be on the fringe of the crowd. She was even comfortable enough to stay on when Zoe slipped away to meet the afternoon ferry. Todd Slokum's brother was coming to take Todd's things back home, and Zoe felt responsible.

Comfortable with the silence of being alone, Julia

stood at the end of the line of funeral-goers waiting to pay their respects to Noah. The sun had broken through the fog for the first time in two days. Its rays heated the trees on the slope of the hill, sending the fragrance of pine and spruce up into the graveyard.

As she moved slowly forward over the grass bordering the granite headstones, she thought about the quiet words that had been said about Hutch. A loyal man, one friend said. An independent man, another said. An able man, said a third.

She found herself wondering what would have been said about her, had she been the one who died. Loyal wife, surely. Loving mother. Able homemaker. Obedient woman.

Obedient woman. She didn't know whether being called "obedient" was a compliment, but it was true. Obedient she was. She had been an obedient daughter to her parents and an obedient sister to her brothers. She had been an obedient student—always obedient in school—and an obedient bride. Oh, yes, she was that. Ten years her senior, Monte wanted babies, and Julia accommodated him. Miscarriages followed their initial success, though, and by the time it became clear that there would be no other children, he was successful enough in the world of high finance that he needed Julia as his hostess. Which she was. Obediently.

It could be said, she realized as she neared the front of the line, that taking this two-week trip to Big Sawyer without Monte was the most independent thing she had done in her life. Not that he appeared to mind. As promised, he had sent a package containing everything she would need to prolong her stay—money, credit cards, a set of car keys, and a new cell phone.

Loyal. Loving. Able. Obedient. Running through the list, she stopped short at the end.

Loyal. Loving. Able. Obedient. And . . . what else? She felt there ought to be something. But she couldn't come up with a word.

When the person in front of her moved off, she approached Noah. He wore a sweater and slacks, the islanders' equivalent of a jacket and tie. His were of fine quality, accommodating his significant height, well fitted over a trim, tapering body and the longest of legs. His dark hair was flecked with gray and the skin around his eyes was creased, but the impression was less of age than of exposure. Likewise, his face held color from the spring sun, though she sensed that the last few days had washed out much of it. His eyes were the dark blue of the sea, and they looked weary.

Still, she felt the same comfort she did each time she saw him. It was especially nice that he managed a smile. It was small, perhaps more a spasm than a smile. But for a few seconds it softened his face.

"My condolences," she said. "Again."

"Thanks. And thanks for the dinner. I ate it all."

"The heating instructions were okay?"

"I don't know. I didn't bother to heat it up."

She had to smile. "Was that laziness or hunger?"

"Hunger."

"I'm glad it helped." She looked over as a trio of workers began lowering the coffin into the ground. When she glanced up at Noah, he was watching them, too. His eyes held a whisper of horror. She saw him swallow.

"This is the hardest part," he said quietly.

"Perhaps you'd rather be alone."

He shot her a quick glance. "No. Stay." As they watched, the coffin descended. It landed softly. The workers gently pulled the straps free and out of the hole. "Bet you didn't think you'd spend your vacation going to funerals," he murmured.

"I couldn't have imagined any of this. It's ironic, really. I've never been a good flyer. When I'm on an airplane, I'm holding the plane up by the arms of my seat, waiting for an accident to happen. But a boat ride? Safe as anything. Shows how much I know."

"It usually is safe. For the ferry, at least. Working fishermen always face a weather risk. A big blow can come up in no time. Even the best of fishermen gets caught by surprise. If you have to go, it's an honorable way. My father would have preferred that to this."

Julia could understand it. The men in her life had always been cerebral, whereas men like Noah and his father relied on brawn. To die in a physical duel with nature was one thing; to die at the hands of a runaway boat was far less noble.

Had Monte been skippering the *Amelia Celeste,* he would have taken pride not in outrunning but in outwitting Artie Jones. Of course, Monte wouldn't have been skippering the *Amelia Celeste*. He wouldn't have been caught dead doing that kind of work. The son of a man who worked the docks in Boston, he had turned his back on physical labor and those who did it.

Noah suddenly looked over her head. She glanced back to see the police chief, John Roman, climbing the hill to the cemetery. A Crane cousin, he had the same kind eyes as Matthew, though he was far taller and rounder. That ample body was moving quickly enough now to suggest purpose.

Julia didn't think he was coming for her. She had talked with him over the weekend, and hadn't been able to tell him anything he didn't already know. He seemed satisfied at the time.

Now his eyes held Noah's. When he was near enough, he removed his cap and said a slightly winded, "Sorry, Noah. I wanted to be here. But there was a development ashore. I'm just now coming back." He regarded Julia. "Did you hear?"

"Hear?"

"They brought up some of your things."

She wanted to show excitement. Someone had put in extra effort to recover those things. But she felt as distant from her belongings as she continued to feel from her life. The best she could manage was a curious, "They did?"

"There's a bag of clothes that's kinda torn apart, but your pocketbook's intact." He turned to Noah again. "I'm coming from the medical examiner's office. They finished the autopsy on Artie. There's a twist."

"It wasn't his heart?" Noah asked.

"Sure was. The heart was gone before he hit the water, but it wasn't just an ordinary old heart attack. Artie didn't have a history of heart problems. His wife insisted on that. So the examiner went back and looked closely at some of the wounds to see if they could have caused the heart to give out. He just assumed those wounds were from fragments of debris that came from the explosion." John Roman shook his head. "Gunshot wound."

"*Gunshot?*" Noah asked.

Julia, too, felt the force of the word.

"Gunshot," the police chief confirmed.

Noah frowned. "Around here we have spats and grudges. Some of 'em aren't even so little. But if you're saying that a man's heart stopped because of a gunshot wound, that's murder. We've never had anything like that here before."

John gave a mirthless laugh. "Don't have to tell me that. This is a one-man department. Gear war's the worst it gets."

Julia was startled enough by the prospect of murder. She was wondering what "gear war" was—and whether she had *totally* misjudged the island—when Noah asked, "Are they sure?"

"It was a shoulder wound. The bullet shattered the bone and passed on out the other side, but there's no doubt it was there."

"A bullet, and not a piece of debris," Noah specified.

"A bullet."

"Could it have been an old wound?"

"Not with that kind of shattering. That kind of shattering would have needed repair. No, it was fresh."

"Not, like, done the night before?"

"Nah. He wouldn't have gone that long without treatment."

"Would he have been shot on land and then gone off in *The Beast*?"

"Not likely."

"Which means," Noah concluded, "he was on the boat when he was shot. Was someone with him on *The Beast*?"

"I was gonna ask you that," John said, broadening his gaze to include Julia. "Think again. Did you see anything in the fog? Anything during the first pass Artie made around the *Amelia Celeste*? Anything in the seconds before the collision? Anything at all on *The Beast* to suggest someone else was aboard?"

Julia tried to relive those moments and see something she hadn't seen before, but the only image that came to mind was the one that continued to wake her in the middle of the night. "Just that purple bow shooting out of the fog."

"That fog was thick," Noah reminded John. "Greg was using his instruments, visibility was that poor. The first time around, we only heard him. The second time around—well, you know how those racers are built. They're all nose. The cockpit was easily fifteen feet back from the bow. Visibility was less than that."

"How about noise? Like a gunshot?" John asked.

"Above those engines?" Julia shook her head.

"The boat circled around us and went up to the north," Noah said. "We didn't hear it at all then. And we were making noise of our own—the motor, the chop against the hull. We wouldn't have heard a gunshot. What about Artie's wife? Did you ask if someone was with him?"

. "She says he was alone. Divers are going down again to look for a weapon. And for another body, in case someone else was aboard."

Noah ran a hand around the back of his neck. "If it wasn't for the fog, he might have been shot from another boat or even from shore."

"Maybe it was an accident," Julia said. "Maybe he had the gun aboard and hit it or stepped on it. Maybe he was innocently putting it away when it discharged." When neither man replied, she asked, "Did he have any enemies?"

"The wife says no," John said and eyed Noah again. "What do you think?"

Looking back at Hutch's grave, now half-filled with dirt, Noah chewed on his cheek before speaking. "I don't know who or what he was back where he lived. Enemies up here? I think he annoyed lots of us with that boat, but that's all it was, an annoyance. Nothing to kill someone over."

"What about Kimmie?" John asked. "Would someone have killed over her?"

Julia was trying to make the connection, when John answered himself. "Nah. I don't see it. It'd be too much of a coincidence to think that someone shoots Artie for her sake and then she nearly dies on the *Amelia Celeste*."

"Is she talking?" Noah asked.

"Not yet. I'm going there now." He put the cap back on his head. "I was hoping to catch the last of Hutch's service. He was a good man." Giving a clap to Noah's shoulder, he went to the grave for a minute, before turning and striding down the hill.

"Kimmie?" Julia asked as soon as he was out of earshot.

Noah drew in a tired breath. "There were rumors she and Artie were an item."

"How true were they?"

"You'd have to ask Kimmie. For what it's worth, there are always rumors about Colella women."

"With married men?" Artie Jones had a wife and four children.

"Yes."

"So. What do you think? Is there a murderer involved here?"

Noah averted his eyes. "I've been looking for someone to blame, and that'd do it. But it'd only be a diversion. Wouldn't change the outcome any." Chewing on his cheek again, he set off for his father's grave. The men were finishing up. He watched them shovel the last of the dirt onto the mound. When they were done, he shook each hand. He continued to stand there after they left.

Julia watched quietly, until she began to feel awkward. When she turned to leave, he said, "Hold up. I'm coming."

"There's no need. This is your time with him."
She was barely past the cemetery gate, though, when
he was walking beside her. Seconds later, a beautiful
red-and-white dog bounded up the hill from the road
and danced excitedly around his legs.

"Is he yours?" she asked.

"Yes. His name's Lucas. He's probably thrilled the
old man's gone. They were never the best of friends."

"He's a striking dog," Julia said, admiring a feathered tail, white bib, silky ears, and freckled nose.
"What kind is he?"

"A Nova Scotia duck tolling retriever."

"That's a big name for a medium-size dog," she
said with a curious smile. "What's a 'tolling retriever'?"

Noah stopped walking and bent to scrub the dog's
ears. The dog raised adoring eyes to his. "Tollers are a
breed of dog used as decoys for ducks. They jump
around onshore to distract the duck while the hunter
takes aim. Since we don't hunt ducks here, it means
that this one's forever running back and forth, up and
down the dock, in and out of the boat. It means he
likes the water, which can be a problem when he goes
after a gull and finds himself in rough chop."

The instant he straightened, the dog shot off
down the hill after the departing cemetery truck. The
only two vehicles left were Zoe's little Plymouth and,
down the road a bit, Noah's dark blue pickup.

They started walking again.

Julia watched the dog. He followed the cemetery
crew for a minute, was distracted and chased a bird,

was distracted again and made for the woods. "Does he ever stop?"

"Now and then. He probably slept through the service in the bed of the truck."

They walked toward the bottom of the hill. Noah seemed deep in thought, but the silence was a comfortable one. The sun had come out, warming the ocean breeze to a perfect temperature. Birdsong came from the trees, close enough not to be drowned out by the surf. Julia took a deep breath and relaxed.

They were nearly at the car when Noah spoke. "I keep thinking about what his friends said. You know, about the kind of man he was. I wonder what they'd say about me, if I was the one who had died."

Julia wasn't surprised that his thoughts mirrored hers. It went with the territory of missing death by a hair. "What would they say?"

"Nothing interesting. I'm an average kind of guy."

"Is there anything wrong with that?"

"Actually, there is," he said with feeling. "I could be more." He stopped speaking. Julia waited for him to go on, but he was frowning, lost in thought, eyes focused on the road below. Suddenly, he looked at her. "What about you? What would they say?"

"Loyal. Loving. Able. Obedient." The words were fresh in her mind.

"Obedient?"

"I'm a very docile person. Or was," she added with a half smile. "I'm not identifying with that woman at this moment."

"How not?"

"Being here on Big Sawyer, for one thing. I was breaking new ground when I decided to visit Zoe for two weeks. I've never left my husband for this long. He's . . . dependent."

"Physically?"

"No." She was about to say emotionally, but Monte wasn't really that. "Custodially," she finally said. Not caring to elaborate, she rushed on. "My mother thinks I should hurry back to New York, because of the accident and all. But I want my time away." She smiled in self-deprecation. "That's out of character. I'm not a very independent sort. But you all are. Maybe there's something in the air here. I'm feeling a little like a stranger to myself."

It was an opening. She might have liked to talk more about that, because Noah was the only other person who had experienced what she had. Well, Kimmie Colella had experienced the same thing. But Kimmie wasn't talking.

Noah didn't pursue the issue. Her disappointment was short-lived, though, because he smiled. It was a gentle smile for a man who seemed rock-hard and somber.

"Maybe it's Zoe's clothes," he suggested.

Julia wore Zoe's slacks and sweater. She plucked at the latter. It was charcoal angora, shot with ribbons of blue at random spots. "The sweater gave me away, huh?"

"Her things are distinct," Noah said with respect. "Maybe you'll feel more like yourself once you have your own clothes."

But Julia didn't think so. More to the point, she didn't know if she wanted to feel like her old self. Looking back at the woman she'd been, she knew she wasn't a very interesting person. Interesting people weren't content to play second fiddle all the time. They didn't fade into the woodwork or defer to their husbands. They didn't always play it safe.

Looking back at that woman, Julia found her wanting.

She was saved from confessing this to Noah, though, when Zoe's truck rumbled up the road. After bucking erratically, it came to a stop.

"Sounds like gear trouble," Noah said, which reminded Julia of gear wars, which she wanted to ask him about but instantly forgot, because Zoe wasn't the one climbing out of the truck. It was a petite young woman who, with one marked exception, looked very much like Molly.

"It's not gear trouble," Julia said in a rising voice. "I believe that's my daughter, who doesn't have a *clue* about driving a stick shift." She set off across the grass, walking at first as she stared in disbelief, then running when she realized that, despite the boyish haircut, it really *was* Molly.

By contrast, Molly was frozen in place, one foot on the running board and one on the ground. She was looking in Julia's direction, her expression registering something akin to horror.

By the time Julia reached the truck, her excitement had turned to concern. Molly had Julia's blonde hair and slim build, but she was less fair-skinned, and she had Monte's dark eyes rather than Julia's hazel ones. That skin was washed of color now, and the eyes were red-rimmed.

Julia took Molly's face in her hands and spent only the briefest seconds looking at that startling short hair before focusing on her eyes. "What's wrong?"

"Who's that man?" Molly asked.

"Noah Prine. He survived the accident with me. This funeral was for his father. What's *wrong,* sweetie?"

There was a tiny pause. Then a tense, "Nothing."

"Yesterday morning you were in *Paris!*" They had talked then. "And what is this?" she asked, moving hands lightly over Molly's head.

"It's the rage there. I thought it looked great."

"It does. I'm just startled. You've always had long hair. I wasn't prepared."

Molly shot Noah another glance before refocusing on Julia. "That makes two of us. It's weird seeing you with a man who isn't Dad." Her eyes filled with tears. "Men are so bad." Seeming to simply crumble, she wrapped her arms around Julia's neck and, weeping softly, held on more tightly than she had done in years.

Julia's mind went in a dozen different directions at once. "What happened?"

"Nothing."

Julia held her back. "If it was nothing, you'd still be abroad. How did you . . . when . . . ?"

"Last night," Molly said, brushing at tears with the palm of her hand. "I kept thinking that my job stunk, that my boss sucked, that my roommates were totally selfish and unfriendly, and here you were nearly killed, and how could I stay there when someone should be with you? Only they routed me through Chicago," she wailed, crying again, "and the plane back to New York was two hours late, and by the time I took a cab home it was after one, and Dad didn't know I was coming, and we had a big fight."

"About the hair?" Julia asked uneasily. Out of the corner of her eye, she caught sight of Noah heading for his truck. He raised a hand; talk *later,* it said.

"About *men,*" Molly cried. "The things they do. They were just so disgusting at the restaurant, Mom. I could have been someone walking in off the street, and they would have been nicer. It's like they were doing me a big favor letting me watch them work— which they were—but they were also supposed to let me work, too. I mean, there I was, their *slave* for the summer, doing an internship for *no pay,* and they were rude. Like *I* was the one who offered to sponsor an internship. I haven't spent the last two years at culinary school just so I could smile and nod and say, '*Vous êtes brilliant, monsieur*'!"

Julia was oddly relieved. "Why didn't you tell me things were so bad?"

"Because I kept thinking they would get better. Dad kept insisting this was going to be a worthwhile summer, quote unquote, and I kept reminding myself of it, but then I kept thinking that I'd had a choice. I wanted New York, but Dad thought Paris would look better on my résumé. Well, I don't care about my résumé. What's a résumé worth if you're miserable? And I was, Mom. That was *not* where I wanted to be."

Julia smoothed that short blonde hair. "I'm so sorry, sweetie. I wish you'd told me."

"What good would it have done? I accepted the internship, and I probably would have stayed, because *God forbid,*" she drawled sarcastically, "Dad should think I'm a quitter. Then you were in the accident, and it changed everything. I had to see for myself that you were okay."

"So you flew to New York by way of Chicago. But how did you get up here?"

"I flew to Portland and took a bus the rest of the way."

Julia wasn't surprised. Molly had always been resourceful, particularly when she wanted to do something that one or both of her parents did not want her doing. Julia took pride in Molly's independence. Now, she also felt relief. It was nice knowing that Molly could take care of herself, in case something had indeed happened to Julia. "Did Dad give you money?"

"I didn't *ask* Dad for money. I used my bank card. Dad doesn't know I'm here. I just showered, packed a bag, and left."

Julia's unease returned. She wondered if there was more Molly wasn't saying. "Did he see you leave?"

"Yes, but we didn't talk."

"Didn't he ask where you were going?"

"Yes, but I didn't answer."

"He's probably worried sick," Julia said.

"I doubt it."

"Why do you say that?"

Molly leaned against the truck. With her short hair, three earrings per lobe, and the angry look on her face, she seemed uncharacteristically rebellious. "Because he has a busy life, and that life revolves around him. It always did. Remember the time he was supposed to be looking at colleges with us? Or the time he was supposed to be vacationing in Washington, D.C., with us? Or the time he was supposed to be chaperoning my senior prom? Or the time—"

Julia put her fingers to Molly's mouth to stop the flow. "We've been through this before. But he loves you. I'll call him as soon as we get back to Zoe's." She looked again at that hair; it was going to take some getting used to. "I'm sorry about the job. It sounded like such a good opportunity—and you were getting academic credits for it. What'll you do now?"

"Go back to New York with you and look for something else," she said. "I know it's late. But I can talk my way into things."

"You certainly can." The apple didn't fall far from the tree. Molly might have Julia's sensitivity, but she had Monte's drive—and his tongue. "Only I may stay here a little longer," she added. The idea of extending her stay had been a germ, floating around without concrete form until now.

Molly frowned. "I thought the deal was for two weeks. One's gone."

"Deal?" Julia echoed with a puzzled smile.

"Plan."

"It was. Then the accident happened. I haven't done much of what I thought I'd do."

"Like photography? But if your equipment is lost, how can you do it at all?"

"I don't know. I'm trying to figure things out. It's been an emotional week," she said with a glance up the hill.

"Not much fun? Nor for Aunt Zoe. She looked pretty stressed when I saw her. I mean, I couldn't believe she was there at the dock when the ferry pulled in. I saw our car back on the mainland, only I didn't have the keys, and then I stepped off the boat at this end, and there she was. I thought, like, she just . . . had a vision of my coming. Then she explained that she was meeting someone else." Her voice lowered, taking on greater weight. "Mom, the guy who died wasn't much older than me."

"I know."

"And his brother wasn't much older than him. Zoe borrowed another truck and made me take hers. She told me you were here." She glanced up at the cemetery, much as Julia had just done. "Can we leave now? This place freaks me out. Besides, you need to call Grandpa. I talked with him while I was at the bus station. He said he was waiting for you to call."

Yes. There had been that order at the end of his email. There hadn't been another email since, though there had been emails from Charlotte, Donna, and Jane. There had been calls from Julia's brother Jerry and from the wife of her brother Mark, but nothing from either Janet or George in the days that had passed between then and now. If Julia's parents felt any of the concern that had brought Molly home from France, Julia saw no evidence of it. Not in them, and not in Monte. Forget concern. If Monte even missed her, Julia saw no evidence of it at all.

Chapter 5

Back at Zoe's, the first call Julia made was to Monte. He picked up with a terse, "Yes," but she was grateful he picked up at all. He didn't always do that—not for clients, not for family.

"Hey," she said, as chipper as could be. "It's me." She smiled at Molly, who stood nearby, chewing on a fingernail.

"I've been trying you all day," he replied, sounding put out. "What's with the new cell phone?"

"I left it at Zoe's. I've been at funerals all day."

"It'd help if you checked for messages once in a while. Molly's back."

"I know," Julia said. "She's up here now."

"*There*? How in the hell did she get *there*?"

"She flew to Portland and took a bus to the ferry."

"He'll love that," Molly muttered.

"A *bus*?" Monte exclaimed. "Do you know the kinds of scuzzbags who take buses up there?"

"Are they any different from the scuzzbags who take buses down there?"

Molly snickered. Julia held up a warning hand.

"Ah," said Monte. "We're in a mood today, are we? Well, let me tell you, Molly was almost incoherent when she walked in here last night. I don't know whether it was exhaustion or whether she was on something she got in France, but she wasn't making any sense. What did she say to you?"

Julia didn't for a minute think that Molly had been "on something." She knew her daughter. They were far closer than many a mother and daughter, for which Julia was particularly grateful now. If Molly had behaved badly, it was either from exhaustion—or from Monte. "She says you two had a fight. She says you're upset that she came home early."

There was a heartbeat's silence, then an arch, "Well, aren't *you*? It was a good internship."

"She didn't think so."

"She's twenty years old. What does she know?"

Julia bridled on Molly's behalf. Turning away from the girl, she told Monte with a vehemence she didn't often use, "If she was male, and we were at war, she'd be old enough to use lethal weapons. Let's give her a little credit. We weren't in Paris. We didn't see what was going on. She felt that the internship wasn't going to give her the experience she was there to get. She also felt that it would mean a lot to *me* for her to come here and make sure I was okay. And it has."

"You're okay," Monte said lightly. "You're always

okay. So you did get the package I sent? It might have been nice if you'd called and told me it arrived."

Julia bit her tongue. Monte knew it had arrived. He had FedExed it from work, just like he did all the other important papers in his life. To hear him talk, which he usually did, he would trust FedEx with his life.

"Thank you," she said obediently.

"You got the credit card, and the cash?"

"Yes. It was all in the package. Thank you."

"And the car keys? Have you brought the car over?"

"Not yet."

"Why not? I thought the whole idea was to have it there so you wouldn't have to drive Zoe's truck."

That was true. She didn't know how to handle a manual transmission any more than Molly did, and she wasn't as daring as Molly. "I've been driving an old car that a friend gave Zoe, but I haven't gone far. Lately it's been to funerals. They just held the fourth one in two days."

Remember the accident? she wanted to ask. *How can you carry on about cell phones and car keys when nine people are dead?*

Monte was oblivious. "If you weren't going to be needing our car, I could have used it here."

To go where? she wondered. Monte had insisted—and more than once—that he wasn't leaving the city during the two weeks she planned to be gone, and that cabs would do him fine. But pointing that out would only invite argument, and she rarely won. Monte was a master at verbal jousting.

She, on the other hand, was a master at suppression. Though part of her simmered, her voice was calm. "I'll go get the car," she assured him. "Especially now that Molly's here, I have reason to do it."

"She's staying with you, then? She should. There's no sense in her coming back here. She won't find another job now. She might as well stay there for another week."

Julia wasn't going into the possibility of staying longer, herself. "Yes."

"I wouldn't be able to keep an eye on her here. There's too much going on. She can help you spend the money I sent. Did I tell you that our insurance will cover the camera equipment? See if you can replace it somewhere up there. That fellow will know where to go. Himmel."

"Hammel."

"You'll do it?"

"I'll see."

"Why the doubt? You loved that equipment. Learn how to use it, and you'll have an artistic outlet. That's what it's for."

Julia could just as easily have found an artistic outlet using a simple point-and-shoot camera.

Monte went on. "By the way, call your father, will you? He called here yesterday wanting to know what's wrong with you that you haven't returned his call."

"He never called," Julia said, mildly annoyed.

"Maybe he did, only you weren't answering your cell. Do me a favor, Julia. Keep it with you, please? I don't care whether cell phones are politically correct or not up there, but it'd be nice for the people in your life to be able to reach you. Okay?"

"Okay."

She ended the call, simmering now at the condescension in his voice, and accessed her voicemail, but other than three increasingly irritated messages left earlier by Monte, there was nothing from her father. She had no doubt that he had tried the line, but he hadn't bothered to leave a message. That only added to the hurt she felt.

She was of half a mind to turn off the cell and wait until later to call. But the annoyance that remained from her conversation with Monte gave her the backbone to call now—not to mention the fact that with Molly still standing close, watching and listening, she would have to explain herself if she put it off.

Still, old habits died hard. Her stomach was jumping as the phone rang. It got even worse when her mother's voice came on. "Hello?"

"Mom, hi." There was silence on the other end. Quickly, hopefully, she said, "Talk to me, Mom. Please talk to me."

But George came right on. "Julia? We've been trying to reach you. Why haven't you called?"

Julia was deflated. "Things have been a little busy."

"Busy? Up there?"

He might have spoken neutrally, but the words hit her wrong. Every bit of the annoyance she had felt talking with Monte was back, and then some. Yes, she was a whiz at self-control, but she couldn't let the jibe pass.

Curbing anger, she said, "There was an accident, Dad. Nine people died. There are eight children, two wives, one fiancée, and dozens of parents and siblings and friends who have lost people they love. When I haven't been at funerals, I've been making meals for families of the ones we've buried, and when I haven't been doing that, I've been helping Zoe out, because her assistant died on the ferry. Yes, it's been busy up here."

Despite her efforts to stay calm, her voice had risen. Uncharacteristic? Definitely. Even Molly looked startled.

Her father must have been startled as well, because he immediately backed off. "I understand, Julia. It's just that we've been waiting for your call. We're your parents. We worry."

"Mom, too?"

"Yes."

"Is that why she handed the phone off to you?"

"Julia."

"If you were worried, why didn't you call me yourself?"

George didn't reply, and Julia felt instantly contrite. She wasn't accustomed to talking back to anyone, much less her father.

"I'm sorry, Dad, but we've had a difficult time here. This wasn't just another car crash on the Beltway. Big Sawyer's a small place. Everyone knows everyone else. When nine people die, it is felt."

"I can imagine," he said quietly, sincerely. "How many more funerals are there?"

"None here. The rest are on the mainland."

His voice brightened. "You're coming home, then?"

"Not yet."

There was a pause, then a surprised, "Why not? It's been a week." Julia heard murmuring in the background—surely her mother's voice—though she couldn't make out the words.

Determined not to wither, she said, "I had initially planned on two weeks. Besides, I can be a help here. There are still things to do."

"What does Monte say?"

"He's all for it. He's about as much into the ferry accident as you and Mom are." The words were so laden with sarcasm that Julia surprised even herself. But she didn't take them back. Nor did she make any effort to fill the ensuing silence.

Finally, kindly but tactfully, with Janet clearly standing nearby, George said, "I'm not sure I understand what you're saying."

Julia didn't hesitate to explain. She didn't care that Molly was standing right there. Molly was an adult. She should know what her mother was feeling.

"I'm saying that the accident was about as traumatic an experience as I've ever had in my life. I don't know why you and Mom are having so much trouble understanding that. I could easily have been one of the ones who died."

Molly cried, "Don't *say* that!"

"Don't say that," her grandfather said with the greater gravity of his age. "You didn't die. That's all that counts."

"No. You see, it isn't," Julia went on, struggling now to express herself. "I didn't die. But I could have. So why didn't I? There has to be a reason."

"No reason. Just sheer luck."

"There's a reason," she said with conviction. "I just haven't figured out what it is. And anyway, even aside from that, I'm looking at things differently now."

"Differently how?"

"Differently . . . like, who I am and what I am doing with my life and what people will say when I die."

"Mom!" Molly squealed.

Julia angled the phone away from her mouth. "Someday, Molly. I'm not planning on doing it any time soon. That's the whole point."

"What's the whole point?" George asked when she returned to the phone.

"I'm forty," she said, holding Molly's gaze. "God willing, I'll have another forty years. I need to make the most of them."

"Are you doubting the first forty?" George said over more background murmuring and aimed an impatient *"Shhh"* away from the phone.

"No," Julia said, but caught herself. If the point was to be honest—saying what she felt, rather than saying what the listener wanted to hear—she had to change that. "Make that yes. Some parts. I wouldn't change a thing about others."

George said something muffled to Janet. His tone sounded less indulgent than before.

"If Mom has something to say," Julia invited, "why doesn't she pick up the phone?"

"Why *doesn't* she?" Molly asked. "Why won't she talk with you?"

"You know why," George muttered on his end of the line.

"Actually, I don't," Julia said. "We all know that she and Zoe had a falling-out, but I'm not sure what it was about. To carry the grudge all this time is absurd. Zoe's her only sister, and she lives up here totally alone."

"By choice," George reminded her.

"Has Mom invited her to live in Baltimore? Has Mom ever expressed an interest in having her closer? Has Mom ever picked up the phone and called her?"

"Julia," he cautioned.

But Julia was on a roll. "Zoe has friends but no family, and there Mom is, head of a charitable foundation. Her specialty is supposed to be communicating with people, but she won't talk with Zoe and now, because I'm here visiting Zoe, she won't talk with me. Charity begins at home, doesn't it? If forgiveness is part of charity, why can't Mom forgive Zoe? What did she do that was so terrible?"

"Ask Zoe."

Zoe chose that moment to walk in the door.

Holding her gaze, Julia said, "Zoe won't say." When Zoe arched her brows, Julia mouthed, *Dad*.

Molly went to Zoe and slipped an arm around her waist.

George sighed, sounding tired. "Julia, this has nothing to do with you and your life."

"It does," Julia insisted. "It has to do with honesty. That's one of the things I'm feeling different about."

"You've had a shock. It's understandable. Give yourself a little time. Things will return to normal." There was more background murmuring. This time, though, George raised his voice enough so that Julia could hear. "Be *still*, Janet, and let me talk. Yes. Yes. Here, do you want to tell her that?"

Of course, Janet didn't. But Julia was intrigued by the thought that her father might be standing up for her.

Moments later, though, in a purely perfunctory way, George repeated what Julia was sure Janet had said. "You have to move on now."

She straightened her spine and smiled. "I am."

"Come home. We'll talk more once you're back in New York."

"Fine."

"When *will* that be?"

"I'm not sure."

"Don't you think it'd be better if you got back into your usual routine? You don't sound like yourself at all."

Julia didn't doubt it. She didn't usually challenge her parents. She didn't usually challenge her husband. She was, after all, obedient. "That might be good."

"I'm worried, Julia," George said.

She softened immediately. Her father wasn't the problem. In many regards, he was a victim himself. What Julia said to him was aimed at Janet. "I'm not asking you to worry. I'd just like you to try to understand what I've been through and what I might be feeling."

"Yes. I'll try," he said, but in an inattentive way that indicated he was done with talk.

Julia ached. No, George wasn't the root of the problem. Nor, though, should he act like a robot. He was a man, with the ability to think and feel. And he was her father. No matter how cowed he was by his wife, he could have emailed Julia again or called her from work, and Janet would never have known.

"Zoe's just come in," she said. "I have to go now, Dad. Ask Mom to call. Please." She disconnected the phone, held the cell to her middle, and raised stricken eyes to Zoe and Molly.

"What's *wrong* with Gram?" Molly asked. "Why won't she talk with you?"

Julia squeezed her eyes shut and shook her head. Opening her eyes again, she drew in a long breath and let it out slowly. Her stomach remained clenched. On top of that, she felt suddenly, acutely restless.

"I need a breather," she said and made for the kitchen door.

"Where are you going?" Molly asked worriedly.

"The barn. There's work to do there."

She was halfway out the door before Molly managed a startled, "Excuse me?"

Gretchen was waiting for her. At least, that was what she chose to believe, because the instant she entered the barn and approached the cages, of all the rabbits who began their little scrabbles and butts and tugs, only Gretchen moved to the very point in the cage where the door could easily open. Reaching in with confidence, Julia put one hand over the rabbit's ears and another under her belly and gently lifted her out. Cradling her, she went to the chair.

The rabbit settled comfortably on her lap, which was another sign of recognition, Julia decided. Gently, she stroked the fringed ears, forward to back, forward to back.

Like everything about Zoe, the barn was a mix of old and new. The walls were made of wood that had, in its heyday, sheltered cows. There were no cows now, though the sound of them echoed in the *ooooo* of the breeze through open skylights. Those skylights were new. Zoe had installed them when she bought the rabbits, because rabbits like light. Any danger that might have been posed by the sun heating things up was offset by the oaks outside, whose leaves sheltered the roof. Diffused light and fresh air came in; heat stayed out.

The air was comfortable now, cool but not cold. The breeze carried the smell of new hay, waiting in bales. The sun was lower in the sky and the light was easing. The result was a pleasant shade. Ned was nearby, his presence betrayed only by stunning amber eyes. Statue-still, he stood watch now over Julia as well as the rabbits. Above the gentle sounds of movement in the cages came the sound of the sea. It was distant but distinct, the ebb and flow of water on rocks.

Gradually, Julia's pulse slowed and her breathing leveled. The restlessness that had hit her so abruptly in the kitchen eased. The knot in her stomach began to loosen.

"Hello, pretty little one," she crooned to Gretchen. "How are you today?"

The rabbit didn't respond, didn't even look up, but Julia knew not to expect that. If she leaned over and smoothed back the brow fur—as she did now—Gretchen might shift her eyes and make contact—which she did now. Under Zoe's tutelage, Julia had learned to accept these small gestures for the shows of affection that they were.

She had also learned how to refill water bottles and measure out pellets, how to empty the trays under the cages and fill the hay trays with fresh hay. Zoe had taught her these things once they had learned that Todd wouldn't be coming back, and Julia was glad to fill in. She had changed diapers when Molly was a child. Emptying cage trays was much the same thing—easier, actually, since there was neither wiping of bottoms nor odor involved. Hay, pellets, and water were a cinch.

She didn't do any of that yet, though. Nor did she give other rabbits a turn at being held, though Zoe insisted upon giving each a little one-on-one every day. Zoe prided herself on maintaining people-friendly Angoras, and Julia understood the importance of this. Many of Zoe's rabbits would eventually find homes with owners who weren't as interested in plucking fur as they were in playing with pets. People-friendly Angoras—it made total sense. Angoras would never run and fetch like a dog, or jump up on the bed at night like a cat. But they did know the difference between human warmth and a cage.

Julia wondered if they knew enough to miss Todd. It had been a week since he had last held them. According to Zoe, he had given each rabbit far more than a little one-on-one. Zoe claimed he had spoiled them rotten.

But Julia didn't know about that either. All she knew was that holding Gretchen was a powerful sedative. She continued to stroke the billowy fur and murmur little words of affection, until her own body was thoroughly relaxed. Only then did she gently return Gretchen to her cage and see to the chores—and they were therapeutic, as well. Even so late in the day, even so late in a *dismal* day filled with funerals and angst, she felt energized.

It wasn't mindless work at all. There were things to monitor, things having to do with the health of the rabbits, like the contents of those waste trays and the amount of hay that had been eaten. In addition to having people-friendly rabbits, Zoe prided herself on having healthy ones, and though healthy ones took a little extra work, she was willing to do it.

So was Julia. She topped off the hay racks to make sure each was brimming, then deposited the refuse from the cage trays in a wheelbarrow and wheeled it out to Zoe's chosen spot in the back field. Returning, she sat for a few minutes holding in turn several of the rabbits she hadn't held that morning—first Maria, then Jasper, then Pretty Boy, Petunia, and Swizzle. She even removed the nest box from Bettina's cage and took turns holding each of the seven kits—and all the while, she refused to think about Monte, refused to think about her parents, refused to think about that other, distant life. She focused on the babies' tiny eyes, their scrawny little legs, their silky new fur. The miracle of birth gave her a lift.

She was totally engrossed when something made her glance back at the barn door. Molly stood there, with Zoe at her shoulder.

Startled anew by the sight of her short-haired daughter, back so suddenly from France, Julia's spirits rose even higher. "I didn't hear you come in."

"Obviously," said Molly. "We've been here awhile." She sounded amazed. "Look at you. Holding rabbits. Is this the same woman who wouldn't let me have a cat?"

Still smiling, Julia focused on the kit in her hands. Like each of its siblings, it was pure white. Julia's favorite rabbits were actually the ones with color—the blacks, the tans, the lilacs and torties. But she understood Zoe's excitement over this litter. White pluck could be dyed, which gave it added value from an economic point of view.

"You kept me busy," Julia teased. "A cat would have been one responsibility too many." She hitched her chin toward the shadows not far from Molly and Zoe. "There's a cat here."

Molly looked around and caught her breath. "Oh, pretty cat," she cooed and approached, crouching as she went. "Come here, kitty," she coaxed, hand outstretched.

Ned put his tail in the air, walked off several yards, sat, and stared, daring her to try again.

Molly straightened. "Oh, dear."

"He's on duty," Zoe advised. "Catch him when he's dozing in a puddle of sun, and he's a sucker for an ear scratch."

Molly went to Julia, who had replaced one baby and was holding another. She held it out to Molly, who took it readily, but, perhaps needing to save face after being dissed by the cat, remarked, "Your nail polish is chipping."

"Now, there's a message," Julia decided.

"Here's another," said Zoe to mother and daughter. "This is ribs night at the Grill. I'm not sure we're ribs women, but Rick has a mean salad menu. Lobster salad, shrimp salad, scallop salad, Caesar—field greens, Bibb—you name it, all fresh. It's been a hell of a day. We deserve a treat. What do you say we clean up and go?"

Chapter 6

The Harbor Grill was as unpretentious as the rest of Big Sawyer. Made of cedar shingles that had gone gray in the salt air, it stood two stories high. The main entrance, marked by double doors shaded by an awning, was on the upper story, at the top of a broad staircase that took two turns, with an ample landing at each. The name of the place was on the flap of the awning, though it was hardly needed. There was only one eatery on the island, and of the other buildings perched on the rim of the harbor, none exuded as inviting a scent. If it wasn't buttered buns being grilled for lobster rolls, it was fried clam bellies, fish chowder, seared sirloin, or—this night—barbecued ribs.

The lower level housed the kitchen and had only what windows were necessary for light and ventilation, but the upper level, devoted to diners, was something else. Large banks of glass offered a three-sided harbor view that was broken only by a pair of screen doors in the middle. Those doors led to an open deck that stood over the water on thick pilings.

In winter, action often centered around the bar. Thanks to a satellite dish on the roof, the television there aired a steady stream of sports events. With the advent of warmer weather, though, the deck was the place to be. A built-in bench ran around its three open sides; like the floor, they were of solid wood and weathered gray. Tables filled the rest of the space, dressed with hunter-green cloths, multicolored plates, and small vases of fresh flowers. A retractable awning, rolled back more than halfway now, offered shade from the daytime sun. At night, a warm glow came from torchlights similar to those that lined the dock.

The torchlights weren't yet burning when Julia, Molly, and Zoe arrived. Though the sun had lowered, it was still more than an hour shy of setting. Julia couldn't help but remember that she had arrived on the island at nearly the same hour one week before. There was no fog this night; the air was mild and the harbor calm, but the memory was sharp.

It was stoked by the gray-haired man who sat alone in a corner of the surrounding bench. He had one leg crossed over the other, and an elbow braced on the wood rail. The other hand, knobby at the knuckles, held his drink. He was staring out past the harbor boats, toward the open sea.

Zoe led them to a table, but they had no sooner taken seats when Julia rose again. "Be right back," she whispered, then made her way to the man in the corner.

He was nursing his whiskey, seeming preoccupied, and for a minute she considered retreating. But she needed to talk with him. Silently, she slipped onto the bench. She left plenty of room between them, but there was no doubt why she was there.

His eyes flew to hers, ice cubes tinkling in his glass with the shake of his hand. Those eyes were gray, like his brows, his hair, and the bench on which he sat. Though his shirt and pants were tan, they might have been gray as well, he seemed such a faded sort.

"I'm Julia Bechtel," she said gently. "I was on the ferry the other night."

He nodded.

"I just wanted to say . . ." What *did* she want to say? She had no idea. "I just wanted to say . . . well, I've seen you at the funerals. It's a tragedy, the loss of life. But you also lost the *Amelia Celeste*. I'm told she was like a person to you."

"My wife," Matthew confirmed in a voice that was rusty with age.

"And she's gone. I just wanted to say I'm sorry."

He nodded again.

She smiled and started to rise, then hesitated. There had to be more to say to a lonely man. She tried to come up with something, but the small talk she was so skilled at back home didn't fit. He wouldn't want to discuss the Italian Old Masters exhibit at the Met, the new sushi bar in Soho, or the latest on the mayor of New York City.

So she smiled again, nodded, let out a breath. She

looked out at the diners. Two more tables had just been taken. Only one was left.

"Quite a crowd," she observed.

"Always is," he said.

"Is it ribs night that brings them in?"

"No. They just come."

She looked out over the group. Of the tables taken, nearly all had four people; a few even had five, with an extra chair drawn up. By comparison, her own table looked empty with just Zoe and Molly. "I'm eating with my aunt and my daughter, but there's a spare seat. Would you like to join us?"

Matthew managed a small smile. It was one more line, albeit slanted, in a weathered face. "Thanks, but I'll just sit here awhile."

A voice rose at the other side of the deck. It had a tipsy joviality to it, and was followed by raucous laughter.

Matthew muttered something.

"I'm sorry?" Julia said, leaning in.

"The fruit guys," he repeated. "Loud sons of Bs. *Insensitive* sons of Bs."

Julia agreed. As charming as the deck was, it didn't erase the week that had been. She felt it; surely others had to feel it as well. Loud laughter was out of place. "Why do you call them the fruit guys?"

"Their buoys are painted like fruit. Green and purple. Lime and grape. It's a problem."

"The colors?"

"The buoys. They're all over Big Sawyer waters. But they're not allowed."

"Can't the Coast Guard stop them?"

"It's not federal law, not even state law. It's Big Sawyer law." He was looking at her now, apparently seeing her confusion, because he started to talk with an ease she hadn't expected, given the brevity of his speech to that point. There was color beyond gray now. His voice was low, but it held feeling. "Every island has its own territory where its fishermen work. It's an unwritten rule. Outsiders don't sink traps here."

Julia was intrigued. "How do you know where one territory ends and another begins?"

"You just know," Matthew said patiently. "Oh, the lines smudge some come winter, when you have to go out past the usual turf to catch anything good in your trap. Lobsters may have pea brains, but they're not stupid. They don't want to be near the surface cold in January and February. So they crawl along the bottom of the ocean into deeper waters. 'Course, if you want to trap them, you have to follow them there. That means taking longer to reach your buoys and going through worse weather. There's not a lot of men willing to do it."

"Because of the danger?"

"That, and the sun."

She smiled, puzzled. "The sun?"

"Florida. Arizona. Tortola. There's a group from up Hull Island goes south for four months every winter to escape the cold. 'Course, there's some who fish *only* then."

"Only in winter?"

"January to June."

"Not at all during summer?"

"Nah." He took a drink.

Julia said, "I would have thought summer was the height of the season."

The ice settled back to the bottom of his glass, the glass to his thigh. "It is. There's many more lobsters hauled in August and September than in January, February, or March. 'Course, that means the price is higher in the winter months. You catch less, but you make more."

"Do you go down south?"

"Nah. I run the ferry." He stopped abruptly and looked away.

Julia ached for him. "Have the police come up with anything more?" she asked.

He shook his head.

"Will you buy another boat?"

He shrugged.

She smiled sympathetically. "I guess it's too early to say."

He nodded, then looked up when a young waitress delivered his meal. She wore a dark green camp shirt, khaki shorts, rolled-down crew socks, and sneakers. She had her hair in a ponytail and a sweet smile on her face. "Here you go, Cap'n Crane. Breaded cod, a twice-baked potato, and green beans almondine." She set it on the bench with an ease that said this was nothing unusual. He drained the last of his whiskey and handed her the glass, taking in exchange the napkin-wrapped utensils she offered. The napkin was cloth, the same dark green as the servers' shirts. She was barely gone when, with care—almost gingerliness—he began to unwrap the neat roll.

Julia sensed she was watching a ritual. It was time to leave. "Are you sure you won't join us?" she asked.

He nodded, concentrating on the emergence of a fork.

She rose. "The extra seat is there, if you change your mind. Thank you for talking with me. What you said about lobstering is all very interesting."

He raised a hand just enough to signal a wave, but was quickly focused on his meal.

Julia headed back to her table. As she crossed the deck, people were watching. *Singled out,* Noah had said. She wasn't used to that. It was with relief that she settled into her seat.

"He has to keep certain staples, like burgers and steaks, even meat loaf," Zoe was telling Molly, "because some of the men here won't eat anything else."

"Not lobster?" Molly asked in amusement.

"Oh, all the time, but they eat it at home with culls from the catch of the day. Here, they want something different." She filled Julia in. "I'm talking about Rick Greene. Molly's surprised at how eclectic the menu is, and I was saying Rick is a savvy guy. When he bought this place, it wasn't much more than a fisherman's shack. No one from outside came. Then people began building big houses down on the shaft, and luxury boats arrived, and he knew he had to do something different or he would squander the business. So he spruced up the place, enlarged the kitchen, and printed a menu."

"Up till then," Molly informed Julia, seeming enchanted by the thought, "the menu was written by hand on a board each day, and it constantly changed. He would cook up whatever the local catch brought in."

"He still does," Zoe said, passing a menu to Julia. "That's what the specials are about."

"We got you iced tea, Mom. Did you want wine?"

Julia smiled. "Tea is perfect. I'm sorry for that diversion. I wanted to talk with him. I feel bad that he's all alone over there. I invited him to join us, but he wouldn't."

"Not surprising," Zoe said gently. "He likes being alone. He isn't a big talker."

"But he did talk. When I asked about lobstering, he said a lot."

"Bingo. Ask him anything, any time, about lobstering, and he'll tell you all you want to know. Dinner is something else. Most nights of the week, he's right there in that corner. He drinks his whiskey, eats his breaded cod, and—you watch—he'll have tapioca pudding for dessert. He likes it warm."

"Doesn't he have family? Children? Siblings?"

"He has all of the above. Big Sawyer is packed with Cranes. He's probably related to half the people on this deck."

"Then why is he sitting alone?"

"Because he chooses to. And he isn't one of a kind that way. There are probably half a dozen tables inside with one, maybe two people. There are lots of loners around here. That's one of the things I've always loved about Big Sawyer—or any of these islands, for that matter. No one looks at you funny if you sit alone. There's no stigma to it. People like space—it's as simple as that. They're used to having it. Lobstering is a solitary profession."

"They don't actually fish alone, do they?" Molly asked.

"Usually in pairs, but it's still pretty solitary, when it's day after day, week after week."

Julia was perplexed. "I'd have thought that *precisely* for that reason they'd appreciate being with people when they're back on land." She glanced around the deck, but didn't see Noah Prine. She wondered if he was inside.

"Oh, the lobstermen congregate," Zoe went on. "They talk about the weather and bait and the size of their catch, but it isn't the kind of chitchat you and I know. People who can survive lobstering—or fishing in general—or living on an island, for that matter, are people who like being alone. Which isn't to say," she added, looking up, grin wider, "that there aren't people here who are social." She opened an arm to greet a trio who approached, two men and a woman, all midthirties, give or take, wearing sweaters and jeans. "Gouache, giclée, and silk screen," she said, pointing at each respectively to indicate his or her artistic medium, and the threesome couldn't have been nicer. They asked Julia about the accident and how she was feeling; they expressed concern for Kimmie Colella; and they talked about the possibility that Artie Jones was murdered. Apparently, it didn't matter whether one knew the man personally or not. If it turned out that he was murdered, islanders would go after the perpetrator with as much fervor as if he had truly been one of their own.

As discussions went, it was heavy. By the time the artists moved off, Julia was feeling a whiff of the restlessness that had hit her earlier. Sensing her mother's mood, Molly changed the subject.

"How big is the kitchen here?" she asked Zoe.

"Rick plus three do the cooking, six wait tables, another three out back doing clean-up."

"Where does he get his meat?"

"It's delivered fresh from Portland every day."

"Is the fish local?"

"Not all of it. Our fleet can't get tuna, or halibut, or shrimp. That's up from Portland, too."

Their drinks arrived, iced tea for three. The waitress delivering them was the same perky young woman who had delivered Matthew Crane's meal. By Julia's estimate, she was no older than Molly. "Ready to order, ladies?" the girl asked.

Julia studied the menu. It was extensive—and, yes, included the kinds of staples Zoe had mentioned, though done with a twist. Steak was served on couscous, with a trio of sauces and sides of corn pudding and wood-grilled asparagus. Meat loaf contained peppers and basil, and was served with garlic mashed potatoes and salsa. Fried chicken had a cornbread crust and was served on a bed of mesclun greens, with a hash of honeyeyed carrots and beets. The fish choices were extensive, including novel incarnations of cod, bass, tuna, shrimp, scallops, mussels, clams, and lobster. And, of course, there were ribs—all you could eat for a fixed price. And more salads than Julia had expected. Many of them were on the specials menu along with the ribs, a separate page inserted into the larger menu, this one beautifully designed, with the day's date at the top.

She looked up to find all eyes on her. Zoe and Molly had already ordered. They were waiting for her to decide. "Oh. I'm sorry." She smiled at the waitress and ordered the tuna salad, which wasn't made with any ordinary, canned tuna. This tuna was billed as being fresh, lightly grilled, served warm and thinly sliced over mesclun greens, with Parmesan bread sticks and a Chianti vinaigrette.

"How would you like that cooked?" the waitress asked.

"Rare, please," Julia said and passed her the menu. As soon as the girl was gone, she said to Zoe, "Great menu. Is this all Rick's doing?"

"It's a joint effort. Anyone who travels brings back ideas."

"And the printing?"

Zoe smiled proudly. "We computer-literate artists take turns. Rick pays with free meals. Our dinner tonight is on the house."

Loud laughter erupted from the fruit guys' table, erasing Zoe's smile. She turned and stared—as did half of the people on the deck. The men continued to snicker and snort, seeming oblivious to the attention they'd drawn.

Zoe faced front again, angry now. "We get summer people who are loud. Artie Jones was one, but he and eight other people are dead. We've just buried four of them right here, yet those guys are laughing away. They're trouble."

The same sentiment prevailed down the street in the cavernous back room at Brady's Tackle & Gear. Cartons lined the walls, stacked haphazardly, three thick at places, five high at others. A pair of desks stood under fluorescents in the open space, along with an assortment of chairs. Some were made of wood, some metal; all were old. Conversely—by island standards, at least—the men occupying them were young. Seven strong, they formed the core of the local lobstermen's association—the trap group, as it was known—and were generally accepted to embody the future of Big Sawyer. They were cleaner than usual now, most having showered for Hutch's funeral. Those who had worn slacks then were back to T-shirts and jeans. Some held beer cans, others coffee in Styrofoam cups. Some straddled their chairs, others rocked on back legs.

Hayes Miller ran the *Willa B.* out of a slip at the pier. A full-bearded barrel of a man, he was a third-generation lobsterman and knew all the rules. "They're trouble," he charged. "No good's ever come of a West Rock boat down here. West Rockers are supposed to drag for scallops. They got no business hauling traps."

"Leastways not in *our* waters," remarked Leslie Crane. He was a distant Crane cousin, a man of medium height and wiry strength. He hauled traps from *My Andrea,* named for his wife, who was currently expecting their fifth child. All those mouths to feed made Leslie more possessive of his catch. Traps set near his, where they had no right to be, took money from his pocket, bread from his table.

Joe Brady was the unofficial moderator of the group and as close to a harbormaster as Big Sawyer had. Dark-haired, with a trim beard and a less weathered look, he didn't run a lobstering operation himself, just the tackle and gear store. But he came from a family of lobstermen and knew as much about the trade as the others. The little distance he had from day-to-day fishing gave him perspective. When tempers rose, his was the voice of reason. "So what do we know about them?" he asked now.

"Names are Haber and Welk," said John Mather. A quiet, bespectacled man, he owned the *Trapper John*. "They bought the boat up in Nova Scotia and outfitted it with everything you can imagine. They're up from Florida themselves."

"Word is, they bought eight hundred traps."

"That's legal," said Elton Hicks. At fifty-five, he was the senior member of the group and its most traditional.

"Bet they've gone over."

"More'n eight hundred?"

"Well, why not? Who's gonna know?"

"Hayes is right," said Mike Kling. He and his father hauled from the *Mickey 'n Mike*. Mickey was something of a legend with regard to the size of his catch, not to mention the speed of his boat. He was the perennial favorite in the lobster boat races each Fourth of July. His son promised to inherit all that, which was why he was part of the group. At twenty-nine, he was its youngest and only shaved-headed member. He was also its most imaginative. "Remember those guys up on Salinica Island year before last? They dropped three hundred traps over the limit, all with forged tags They'd have gotten away with it, if the Coast Guard hadn't got a tip. So maybe one of us has to make a phone call. If you ask me, those guys are prime suspects."

"Prime suspects in what?" Noah asked. He had been listening to the discussion with his elbows on his knees and his jaw set tight. "Are we talking lobstering or murder?"

The room was still.

Joe was somber. "Both. Think about where the fruit guys have the greatest concentration of traps."

"Up Little Sawyer," Mike answered. The front legs of his chair hit the ground. He shot Noah an excited look. "Isn't that where *The Beast* went after its first buzz of the *Amelia Celeste*? So what if Artie ran those twin props right through the fruit guys' lines, and what if Haber and Welk were pissed enough to pull out their rifle and take a shot?"

"If he's hit, why's he keep driving *The Beast*?" Joe asked reasonably.

"Maybe he's hit too bad to move. Maybe the loss of blood made his heart give out sooner rather than later. Maybe he's dead there and then."

"What about the kill switch?" Leslie asked. "If he fell, that would've stopped the boat."

Hayes gave a grim laugh. "Artie? Guy like that's too macho to hook himself up to any kill switch."

"So if I'm right," Mike went on, "Haber and Welk committed murder. Get 'em on that charge, and we can say bye-bye to their buoys."

"But can anyone prove they were the ones shot Artie?" Joe asked. "Last I heard, the medical examiner couldn't tell for sure what kind of gun was used."

"It's simple," Mike maintained. "Search the fruit guys' boat, find a weapon, show it was fired last Tuesday."

"Hah," Elton exclaimed. "And what if they say they were shooting at seals? It's done all the time. Hell, I do it myself. Damn seals get in our traps and eat our catch. We all shoot at seals."

"You could prove they were on the water at the right time," Mike insisted.

"But you couldn't prove exactly *where* they were on the water unless you had a witness," Joe said.

"You could find a witness. Someone must've seen them during the day. We all know roughly where the rest of us were. Wouldn't that be neat, killing two birds with one stone?"

The group fell silent. It was a minute before Joe said, "You're quiet, Noah. What're you thinking?"

Noah was thinking about Hutch and Ian—Hutch, because he wasn't cold in his grave, and Ian, because his absence was huge. It hadn't helped seeing the excitement on Julia Bechtel's face when her daughter had pulled up in that truck. Noah had felt an even greater emptiness then, an even greater sense of failure.

He could have made more of his life. He had said it to Julia and had repeated it a dozen times to himself since then—and it had nothing to do with lobstering. Nor did it have anything to do with a college education or making money in New York. He meant personally. Sandi. His son. His father. Hell, he hadn't even talked much to his mother, sweet as she was.

"Noah?" Joe coaxed.

"There's one problem with the theory," Noah said. "Fog." And suddenly that infuriated him. If it hadn't been for fog, Hutch would be alive and Noah would have gone on living the same life he had lived for the past ten years.

For a time, no one spoke.

Finally, Joe said to the others, "He's right. We were in a thick of it when the accident happened. The fruit guys couldn't have seen who was cutting their lines."

"They didn't have to see," Mike insisted. "They could hear. Everyone knows Artie's boat. It's the only one like it up here this early in the season. What if they took a blind shot and lucked out?"

"It's a stretch, Mike."

"That kind of fog, it wasn't a shot from shore," John put in with quiet certainty.

"So," Joe reasoned, "if the shot didn't come from another boat or from land, it had to have come from aboard *The Beast*."

Hayes looked flummoxed. "You think he shot *himself*?"

Mike's eyes widened. "Suicide. That'd be something." He made a face. "What kind of moron thinks to kill himself with a shoulder shot?"

Leslie had been quiet for a time. He remained thoughtful now. "I'd say maybe someone shot him before he left his dock, only Artie'd have to be a *double* moron to have left the dock with a gunshot wound."

"Unless he feared for his life, so he had to leave."

"Or he wanted to die on the water. Remember Caleb Dracut?"

"Caleb was terminally ill. Artie Jones was not."

"How do we know?"

"The Chief woulda said. He talked with Artie's wife."

"Maybe she needs a suspect. Insurance doesn't pay for suicide."

"Now there's *another* thought," Mike picked up. "What if she hired someone to kill him?"

Hayes snorted. "Listen to you. Why would a hit man aim for the shoulder, any more than Artie would himself?"

Joe sighed. "I'm beat, I want to get home, and Noah just buried Hutch and is doing us a favor being here, so we need to make a decision. What're we going to do about the fruit guys setting their traps over ours? My brother Gil is ready to shoot *them*."

"I'll shoot them," Noah remarked so coolly that every face turned his way.

"Very funny," Joe said.

"I'm serious," Noah said. For a week, he'd done nothing of merit. He was ready to act. "A few holes at the waterline? They'd bail like hell, but they wouldn't sink, and even if they did sink, they wouldn't drown. They have flotation. Let them spend a few hours in North Atlantic water." He thought of Hutch, who had probably died so suddenly he hadn't felt a thing, cold or otherwise, and again, he felt a dire need to act. It didn't much matter whether Haber and Welk had shot Artie. Those intrusive buoys were reason enough for a little mayhem. *More* than reason enough.

"You're angry," Joe said.

Noah turned on him. "Damn right, I'm angry."

"Shooting isn't the way to go."

"It'd sure make me feel better." That said, his anger was marginally diffused.

"No shooting," said Elton. "Not yet. First, we send a message."

"Want me to cut a few lines?" Mike asked, searching the group for an okay. "There's a message."

"Knots are better," John reasoned, pushing up his glasses. "Knotted lines can't get through the winch. They wouldn't be able to pull any traps."

"That'll only slow them down," Mike argued. "If we cut their lines, they lose their traps. That'll cost them."

"What if they cut our lines right back?"

"We'll cut more of theirs. We'll haul their traps and empty them out."

"Hell, I don't want to spend my day hauling *their* traps," Leslie argued. "And I can't get into a full-fledged gear war. It costs too much. Look. The goal's to get them out of our space. We don't care where the hell they go, as long as it's somewhere else. I agree with John. Knot the lines. If they knot ours back, we'll know where they stand."

Joe looked around. "Everyone agree?"

No one disagreed. The plan was considered adopted.

Feeling suddenly, acutely restless, Noah rose from his chair. He shook hands with Joe and Leslie, nodded briefly at the others, and went out the door at full stride. Had he looked off to the west, he would have seen a horizon layered with orange and gray, where the last of the day's sun spilled around distant clouds. But his eyes were low as he went up the alley between the health clinic and Brady's, and once he rounded the corner and started down Main Street, Lucas was by his side.

The view of the horizon was gone. Dusk had fallen here. The island store was still open, screen door slapping against its frame with each coming and going. This time of day, though, most of the activity was at the Grill. He could hear the muted drone of talk from the deck and the clink of dishes and flatwear from the dishwashers at the back window.

He and his dog weren't alone. There were others on the road leading down to the dock, but he didn't look at them. He didn't want any more condolences, wasn't in the mood. He was still thinking of Hutch, still thinking of Ian, but he was thinking of Artie now, too. It would be convenient if Artie's wife had hired a hit man—convenient if that someone had just propped Artie at the wheel of *The Beast* and aimed the boat out to sea, thinking it would keep going until it was swallowed up, as if the ocean were a black hole. Then there'd be someone for Noah to go after. It would be very convenient.

But plausible? He didn't think so. He had his own theory, and it was making him uncomfortable.

He could be wrong. He had been distracted that night, upset about Hutch and bone tired. He hadn't looked hard at the others in the stern. So how could he know for sure? Taking his venom out on the fruit guys was one thing; they were guilty as sin when it came to trespass. Tossing out accusations that might hurt the innocent was something else.

The one person he could talk to without doing instant damage was Julia Bechtel. She might have seen something without realizing it—or *not* seen something. He'd have to think about talking with her.

Meanwhile, he couldn't sit and do nothing. So he made for the *Leila Sue,* released her lines, and backed out of the slip. With Lucas near his leg, he steered out of the harbor. Once past its limits, he throttled up. Night fell. He turned on his instruments, but barely gave them a glance. Guided by his familiarity with the waters and a keen sense of purpose, he cruised to the spot with the largest aggregation of lime-purple-lime buoys and began knotting lines. He didn't knot every one, deliberately skipped bunches in a row. There was satisfaction in thinking that Haber and Welk would find a few knots followed by a clear stretch and think they were done, then be annoyed all over again when they ran into more a mile on.

He enjoyed himself so much that he stayed out longer and covered more ground than he planned—knotting lines for Hutch now, even more than for himself. Hutch believed in the law of the seas. He believed that local fishermen had a moral authority when it came to protecting their turf. Noah couldn't think of a more fitting tribute to Hutch, on this day of his burial, than this.

Chapter 7

Julia didn't want to be on the water. She hadn't been in a boat since the accident, and would have been perfectly happy never to step foot on one again. Of course, she knew she would have to, since Big Sawyer was an island. There was no other way to leave, and she couldn't stay forever.

Plus there was Monte, who was harping on her getting the car.

And now there was Molly, too. Molly wanted to shop with Julia for clothes to replace those lost on the *Amelia Celeste*. She wanted a frivolously fun mother-daughter day on the mainland—had the whole thing planned by the time Tuesday evening was done—so what could Julia say?

What she *wanted* to say was that this was *her* vacation and she would do *what* she wanted, *when* she wanted.

But part of her liked the idea of frivolous fun. She

had woken up during the night with more of those restless moments. They were starting to feel like a stomachache that wouldn't go away. Being busy was the best medicine.

So, Julia reasoned, shopping with Molly would serve on two fronts: it would keep her mind busy, and it would force her to face her fear of the ferry. What message would she be teaching Molly if she refused to get back on the bicycle after a fall?

Not that the accident was a fall, exactly. It was more like a hundred falls rolled into one, the kind of thing that, in the split second of its occurrence, was indelibly etched on the psyche. She didn't fall asleep without thinking of it, didn't wake up without remembering, and then there were the jolts in the middle of the night, and the restlessness that set in when the jitters eased. The stitches on her arm were gone, and the scar would fade, but she suspected that the emotional blow would be slower to heal. Her world had been shaken, her sense of mortality tweaked. She didn't think she would be taking things for granted again, not the least of them being the safety of a boat ride.

Molly didn't see it that way, of course. Nor did Zoe, apparently, because neither of them batted an eyelash when mention of ferrying to the mainland came up—and part of Julia understood. The ferry was a way of life here. It ran multiple times each day and had done so safely for years, the lone exception being the accident the week before. She tried to tell herself it would be statistically next to impossible for something to happen to a second ferry she was on. Today's ferry was bigger, meaning it should be safer. She told herself that. Still, her stomach was in knots when she woke up Wednesday morning and saw the fog.

She washed her face. The fog outside remained. She put on her wedding band, but it brought no comfort. She followed the sound of voices into the kitchen, where she found Molly and Zoe, and, trying to sound nonchalant, asked, "Should we put it off?"

"Oh, no, Mom, this is a perfect day to go. You need clothes."

"The thing is, though, I don't. Do you mind my wearing your things?" she asked Zoe, who was stirring pancake batter at the stove.

"Be my guest."

But Molly was determined. "You'll need your own if you're staying longer. Think we can make the nine o'clock ferry?"

"Nine o'clock's *way* too soon," Julia said. "It'll have to be later. I have work to do first." This was true. She had to help with the rabbits.

"The ten-thirty ferry, then?"

Ten-thirty it was, though only after Julia had therapy in the barn. The shutters were raised and the skylights open, allowing cool morning air to circulate among the cages and stalls, and diffuse light to penetrate even the darkest corners. She wore the sweat suit and sneakers that Zoe had loaned her for barn work; they were welcomingly warm in the moist air.

Fog blanketed the barn. Other than the *whoosh* of

the mister every few minutes, the rustle of the rabbits, and the occasional songbird in the meadow beyond, there was no noise. Julia didn't speak, nor did Zoe. The stillness of the morning held a precious peace.

Julia didn't feel restless here. There was something about the rabbits—something elemental and pure—that didn't allow it.

Savoring the moment, she changed the water bottles hooked on each of the cages and measured the proper amount of pellets to add to each bowl. She held Gretchen first—didn't want her pal to feel slighted—then held other rabbits whom she hadn't yet come to know. She was learning the differences between them. Some were easygoing and could be held most any which way, while others would sit on her lap only if their rumps were against her stomach and they looked out. Yet others needed to bury their faces in the crook of her elbow.

Zoe worked close by, whispering sweet nothings to the rabbits. When she spoke to Julia, it was in a soft, instructional voice. "Now here's Madeleine," she said, standing at a cage that held a puffy lilac Angora. "She'll be dropping her kits within the week. See how she's staying far back in the cage? She doesn't want to be touched. I'll put a nest box in later. She'll need to get it ready."

Julia continued to stroke the rabbit she held. It was a chocolate named Hershey. "How does she do that?"

"I give her fresh hay with the box, then she moves it around and shapes it to her liking. Inevitably, that's a shallow bowl of sorts. Then she starts adding fur."

"Her own?"

"Uh-huh. She plucks her middle to get fiber for the nest. Kits are born hairless and blind. Hay would never keep them warm enough. It's the fur that insulates them and keeps them from dying of the cold."

Julia returned Hershey to his cage and opened the cage beside it. Inside was Maria and a nest box containing her seven babies. The babies were nearly two weeks old. With the kits burrowed deep in their bed of fur, and that bed moving gently with squirming and breath, the initial impression was of a single pulsing organism.

"They're always so warm when I reach in for them," she said. "I can't imagine their getting cold enough to die."

Joining her, Zoe opened the cage and lifted out the nest box. "I've never lost an entire litter. The few I've lost have been accidents following feeding. The mother nurses them twice a day. She climbs right onto the nest box with her belly to the kits, and they latch on and drink. It doesn't take more than five minutes, which is all the patience she has. Then she climbs off the box and goes about her business." She set the nest box on the grooming stand, worked a hand into the fur, and lifted out a small gray kit. "Every so often, Mom leaves the box with one of the kits still clinging to a teat, and she doesn't realize it's there. Eventually it lets go. If it's small enough, it slips between the bars of the cage and falls to the tray underneath. It isn't the fall that kills it. It's the cold. There have been times when I've spotted a kit in the tray in time to save it. Other times, I'll come in in the morning and it's gone." She held the gray baby in the cup of her palms, moving her thumbs gently around its tiny closed eyes. "Watch this."

Julia watched. In less than a minute, the kit's eyes opened, first one, then the other. Her own eyes widened. "You did that?"

"The other kits in this litter have done it themselves, but this little one needed some help. They should be seeing by the tenth day. We're at the thirteenth now. If I'd left it much longer, this little one would be blind." She replaced the kit in the nest box and glanced at another group of cages. "I'll do some plucking today. Chipmunk over there is ready. Same with Gardener and Mae."

"I want to watch," Julia said. She loved the peacefulness here. "Maybe I can put Molly off a day."

"Oh, no. You go with Molly. I'll be plucking next week."

"Can I learn to do it?" Even aside from the serenity of the barn, Julia was starting to feel a personal investment in the rabbits. Like human babies, they were totally dependent on someone to provide them with food, water, and shelter.

Zoe nodded.

"And to spin?"

"Sure."

"What about staying beyond my allotted two weeks?"

"Hey," Zoe chided with a smile, "you were the one who set the time limit. If I had my way, you'd be here all summer."

"What if Molly stays, too?" Julia asked. Her gut told her that Molly would be here as long as she was. "That'll make for a fuller house than you're used to."

"I'd love it," Zoe said and lowered her voice. "But what about you? I had the feeling when you decided to come here that you wanted time away." She stopped short of saying that Molly's arrival put a chink in that.

But Julia heard. She had thought it herself more than once during those middle-of-the-night moments when she had been jolted from sleep by the sight of a long purple bow bursting from the fog, and had lain awake, restless and unsure. *Who am I?* With Molly's coming, she was an active mother again, doing things for her daughter that she might never have chosen to do on her own—like take the ferry to the mainland so soon.

"I love being with Molly," she reasoned. "In the last few years, she's become a friend. Not every mother is as lucky as I am. Besides, Monte didn't rush up here after the accident. Nor did my parents."

"What's going on with you and Monte?"

Julia pressed her lips together, shook her head. She didn't want to talk about that.

Zoe didn't push it. "And your parents? What *is* wrong with them? Okay, if they didn't want to come here, they could have sent something—clothes, flowers, even just a card."

Julia smiled sadly. "To me? But why would they do that? I'm strong. I'm able. I'm the one who takes care of everyone else. They don't have to worry about me."

"They nearly *lost* you," Zoe argued.

"Apparently my mother is okay with loss. Look what she's done to you."

"We're estranged."

"Estrangement implies a mutual distancing, but you still send her cards and gifts. The door's open on your end."

"Okay. She disowned me."

"Why?" Julia asked, but it was a rhetorical question, asked so often in the past and never answered that she was startled when an answer came now.

"Way back," Zoe said, "we loved the same man."

Julia gasped. "Loved the same man? But Janet is so much older than you."

"Men can be with someone far younger, and no one looks twice."

"Who was it?" Julia asked, scrambling to do the figuring. The math didn't work. "You were twelve when I was born. My parents were married then. You would have been too young before that. Even twelve is pushing it."

"It wasn't before. It was after."

"*After*. My mother fell in love with someone *else*?" The thought was barely out when her eyes widened. Her voice fell to an astonished whisper. "You and *Dad*?"

Leaving Julia with the nest box, Zoe went to another cage and lifted out a rabbit. She settled it in the crook of her arm and began to stroke its fur.

"Zoe?" Julia prodded, needing an answer.

"You all used to come up here to see me. Janet

was good that way. Back then, she did want to keep the connection going, despite what I was."

"What were you?"

"The family oddball—raising sheep then, weaving, speaking my mind about things people often don't care to discuss."

"What things?"

"Politics and religion. Always the two no-nos." Alive with feeling, Zoe's eyes met hers. "God forbid you offend someone by saying you disagree with them." A passion entered her voice. "I grew up believing that the beauty of a democracy was *precisely* that it's all right for people to think different things. Well, it's not all right. Some people get offended when you don't agree with them. That's my family." She paused, took a breath, and stroked the rabbit, visibly calming. When she went on, her voice was quieter. "I was twenty-seven when it happened. Janet had a problem at work and had to leave early, but George stayed on, and you and the boys kept busy. If the three of you weren't at the beach, you were hanging out at the island store or holed up in the movie theater." She smiled and looked up at Julia. "Remember the theater?"

Julia did. It was musty and small, packed with kids sitting on rows of bolted wood chairs, eating hot buttered popcorn and Milk Duds—surely a memory to explore, but *not now*. Her mind was shooting off in that other, shocking direction. She could no more imagine Zoe being drawn to her father than she could imagine his being drawn to Zoe. They were city versus country, math versus art, Brooks Brothers versus L.L. Bean—as alike as night and day.

"Back then, we had first-run movies," Zoe was saying, lingering briefly with the memory, stroking the rabbit again. "Even the little theaters could get them in those days. Then, suddenly, we couldn't get them, and videos arrived, and the theater closed." Her smile waned. "George stayed on after Janet left. I'd always thought him *the* nicest man in the world, and then, there he was, in his prime, trying to adjust to the fact of having a wife with a burgeoning career at a time when women were only starting to *consider* having careers outside the home. He was vulnerable. Maybe I played on that."

Of all the things Julia had imagined over the years that might have come between her mother and Zoe, this wasn't one she had ever considered. She was struggling to absorb it. "Did anything *happen*?" she whispered, not daring to ask it any louder, it was such a bizarre thought.

Zoe let out a breath. Looking out the window into the fog, she nodded.

Julia was stunned. Zoe and her father. She was *stunned*. "And Mom found out."

Eyes distant, Zoe chewed on her lower lip. When she spoke, her tone was dry. "Not from me, that's for sure. I knew it would be the final nail in the coffin."

"*Dad* told her?"

Zoe looked at her now. "Apparently he couldn't live with the guilt. He's a very sweet man."

"Then you don't hate him?"

"Because he chose Janet over me? How could I hate him? Janet is a remarkable woman. She was remarkable even back then. And look at the life he had with her. He had the three of you, had the house, had a social life that he might have attributed to Janet, but that was part of him, too. What would he have had with me? I live on an *island,* for God's sake."

"Oh, Zoe. I'm so sorry."

"No, Julia. I'm the one who's sorry. I should have known better than to let anything happen."

"Don't absolve *him* of all responsibility," Julia warned. She had her own current gripes with her father, and was therefore feeling a tad less than sympathetic toward the man—that, on top of her feelings for Monte, which were so closely, disturbingly related.

"Oh, I don't. But it takes two to tango. If I'd said no, nothing would have happened, and if nothing had happened, you all would have continued coming up here to visit, I'd have family, and Janet would be talking with you now."

Julia felt a burst of anger. "Well, how *stupid* is it of her to be holding a grudge all this time? She got the man. She won. You lost. Doesn't she see that?"

"I'm sure she does," Zoe said reasonably. "That's probably why she let you kids keep on coming to visit. But only you kids. Do you remember that?"

Julia nodded. "We took a train to Portland, and you met us there. I was in charge of making sure my brothers behaved. My parents didn't come, but it seemed a perfectly natural thing, with us old enough to travel alone. I assumed they used the time to be together."

"They probably did."

"With an ulterior motive," Julia charged.

"Can you blame your mother?" Zoe asked. "Think about it. She's behaving just like women with straying husbands behave all the time. The affair can end, and be well and truly done. The husband can be attentive and adoring for years, but let him be unexpectedly late coming home from work, and the wife's thoughts shoot off in one direction, and one direction only. Trust can be rebuilt. But it's like a heart. Once there's been an attack, there's always a vulnerability."

Julia knew that truth all too well. She had been feeling vulnerable with Monte for a very long time.

"Mom?" Molly asked from the door of the barn.

And right there was the major reason Julia stayed with him. Feeling not the slightest inkling of regret, she looked at her daughter. Molly had grown up in a household with two parents who loved her, just as Julia had.

Now, the girl tapped the Rolex on her wrist, her high school graduation gift from those two parents who loved her. "The ferry?"

Fog was hovering still when the ten-thirty ferry motored out of the harbor and picked up speed. It was only then that Julia realized how sheltered the harbor was from the waves in comparison with the open sea. The ferry was heavy and wide. It had an enclosed area with seats, plus benches out front on the bow and, above the wheelhouse, a small upper deck. Carrying two cars in its stern from earlier stops, it plowed through the water with remarkable steadiness.

That steadiness notwithstanding, Julia would have rather been anywhere else. Where to sit? Outside would mean feeling the fog and the full brunt of memory. Inside would mean feeling confined, trapped in a space from which she might not be able to escape in the event of a crash. She had survived the other night precisely because she had been at the front of the boat and been thrown out of harm's way.

Choosing the lesser of the evils, she opted for outside and in the bow. There were plenty of free seats on the benches for Molly and her, and enough other people around to make this ride different from the last one she'd taken. She wore another Zoe outfit, this time denim capris, a tank top, and sandals. More notably, she carried a handsome leather shoulder bag made on the island by one of Zoe's friends. Zoe had given it to her as a gift.

So she was feeling well dressed and put-together.

But she couldn't relax. If there had been no fog, she would have been able to see for herself that the channel was clear of other boats. Granted, she didn't hear one, the way she had heard *The Beast*. But then, this ferry was larger and louder, so she might not hear another boat at all. She trusted that whoever was at the helm had radar. Of course, the *Amelia Celeste* had had it, too, and it hadn't helped.

Eyes alert, Julia scrutinized the fog. She had no idea what she would do if she actually saw another boat headed their way, had no idea how she personally would be able to avert a collision. But she didn't take her eyes from the cottony denseness, moved them slowly to the right, then ahead, then to the left. She saw shadows, but they went nowhere. She saw the occasional flash of color, likely a channel marker, and all the while her thoughts were tugging her back to the boat ride the week before. Her heart was hammering by the time they reached the area where she calculated the accident had been.

She heard a noise, but it was only the ferry clearing its throat. She saw—or imagined she saw—a Coast Guard boat with divers. It was a ghostlike presence, perhaps conjured up by her imagination, since she knew that divers would still be at work trying to recover whatever was still recoverable on the ocean floor, before it was all swept away and scattered by the tide or by scavenging creatures of the deep.

"Mom?" Molly asked, her voice distant. "Are you okay?"

Julia brought herself back, forced herself to breathe, and took Molly's hand. "I'll be fine."

And she was. Another five minutes, and the fog began to thin. Another five, and Rockland emerged crystal clear beyond what little was left of the mist. Lit by the sun, the harbor glittered, a gift to Julia if ever there was one. The ferry docked stern first, dropped her gates, and extended her ramp to let off the two cars. Passengers followed.

Joyful to be alive, Julia was in high spirits. Molly was every bit as lighthearted, though Julia didn't know whether her daughter's mood was from life, Julia's presence, or the prospect of shopping. Molly loved to shop, so shop they did. They explored every store in Rockland, then fetched the car from the pier and drove north to Camden for more.

Molly was in her glory, picking one article of clothing after another from shelves and racks, and all for Julia, who couldn't help but be amused. For the very first time, the tables were turned. Just as Julia had taken Molly on innumerable shopping trips for school clothes, camp clothes, college clothes, so now outfitting Julia was Molly's mission.

"You need these, Mom," she said, holding up a pair of embroidered jeans, "or—wait, wait—what do you think of *these*?"

"I think they're perfect for you at your age," Julia replied with a smile, much as Molly had often done in reverse, "but a little too cute for me. I want plain, ordinary jeans. Does this store have plain, ordinary jeans?"

It certainly did, and Julia indulged. She bought plain, ordinary jeans. She bought plain, ordinary T-shirts. At another shop, she bought shorts and slacks, shirts, and a quilted blazer not unlike the one she had lost. At yet another, she bought a fleece robe, and two doors down splurged on a nightgown and nice underthings, because she *liked* nice underthings, and because she was so impressed to find a store carrying them that she wanted to support it, *and* because Molly insisted.

"You deserve it, Mom," she said, holding out her hand for the credit card so that she could give it to the salesclerk, playing the mommy in this, too. "After what you've been through? Dad owes you."

Julia focused on the after-what-she'd-been-through part. She kept that in mind at the next store, when she bought not only sneakers and sandals with a gently wedged heel, but Birkenstocks, which she had never owned in her life. The ones she chose were of mocha nubuck, with three straps crossing her foot. She stood before the mirror, turning every which way, playing Molly here, too, wanting to be convinced.

"People on the island wear them all the time," she reasoned aloud. "Zoe has half a dozen pairs."

"Get them," Molly said. "I think you should get *two* pairs. See those other ones, the ones with the single wide strap across the top of the foot? Get them in red." Catching her breath, she pointed at yet another pair. "No, get *those* in red, the ones with the flowers. With rolled-up jeans, they'd be totally cool. Actually, I want a pair, too—but you first. I think you should get three—the mocha ones, the ones with red flowers, and the ones with the wide strap in white."

"I don't need three, Molly."

"Forget need, think *want,*" Molly said, just as Julia had said little more than four weeks before, when Molly learned she had made dean's list for the spring semester, and they had splurged with a spa weekend. There had been absolutely no practical merit to some of the treatments they'd had, any one of which was more expensive than the Birks, but each treatment was pleasurable. So now, Molly said, "These are fun. After the accident, you deserve fun. Dad owes you. And I *love* the red ones. You have to get those."

The drugstore was a whole other adventure. Julia bought nail polish remover, cold cream, and moisturizer. She bought shampoo, conditioner, and a hairbrush. She bought foundation, blusher, and eye shadow. The brands weren't the ones she knew in New York, and, as far as the makeup went, she chose those with the least amount of coverage. Heavy makeup didn't fit with Big Sawyer. She guessed that much of the time she wouldn't wear any makeup at all. But old habits died hard. She had felt naked at the funerals, then again going out to dinner last night at the Grill. It didn't matter that most other women on the island wore no makeup at all. She wasn't most other women. She was Julia.

So she added several bars of creamy soap to use in place of the no-nonsense soap Zoe kept at the house. She added a bottle of coral nail polish. She added covered elastic bands for her hair, and several tortoiseshell clasps. She added a pair of sunglasses, then, when Molly said that the rectangular ones were fine but that the oval ones were *totally* adorable, added those, too.

By the time she reached the cash register, her basket was overflowing, and she was embarrassed. "Look at this stuff," she said in dismay. "I don't know how long I'll be here. Do I really need all this?"

"Every bit," Molly said, adding three last-minute bottles. "Bath gel, body lotion, and cologne. The scent is Lily of the Valley. It fits you." Grinning at the girl waiting to ring up the sale, she said, "We're all set," and began unloading the basket. To Julia, she whispered, "You're replacing what you had in your bags. Didn't you say insurance was covering this? So if Dad's getting the money anyway, why shouldn't you spend it? *He'll* spend it, if you don't. I'd rather you get the benefit than someone else."

Julia's heart tripped, old suspicions turning over inside. "What does that mean?"

Molly scowled. Seeming frustrated, she finally said, "He'll spend it on ties. I mean, he has *the* largest collection of ties. My high school friends used to joke about those ties. Like, the girls wanted to wear them as belts with jeans. Each one probably costs more than any belt I've ever owned."

Turning away to afford them privacy, she scolded gently, "Your father works hard. He doesn't smoke, doesn't drink, doesn't gamble. If ties are his only indulgence, who are we to begrudge him that?"

"All I'm saying," Molly argued, but quietly as well, "is that you have a right to buy things, too."

"Have I ever denied myself?"

"Yes. You're careful. I watch. You splurge more on me than you ever do on yourself." She slid an arm around Julia's waist, gave her a hug, and grinned. "That's why this is such fun. We're splurging on you for a change."

Julia smiled at the clerk and handed over her credit card.

"Besides," Molly added, "whatever of this stuff you don't use, Aunt Zoe will."

"Lily of the Valley toilet spray?" Julia asked doubtfully. "It'll attract bugs."

"It'll attract *men*. I've never understood why she isn't with someone. She's adorable. Men should be crawling all over her."

Julia felt a twinge. Apparently one man had done just that years before. George, the romantic hero—the philanderer—the unfaithful husband. Trying to reconcile that with the vision she had always held, Julia was shaken. She had assumed her parents' marriage to be inviolate. Learning that it wasn't would take some getting used to.

She was spared replying to Molly by the presentation of the sales slip for signing, followed by the transfer of two large bags filled with her purchases. After depositing them in the car, they hit a little bookstore, where Julia replaced the books and magazines that had been lost to the sea. Famished by then, they went to a quaint restaurant overlooking the harbor. An assortment of trees, some flowering pink, some white, all with a lush canopy of green leaves, shaded the wrought-iron tables and chairs. They ordered lobster rolls, which were served on croissants with barbecue chips on the side. After consuming everything before them, they ordered a single serving of strawberry shortcake. It was a huge thing, delivered with two long spoons.

"Totally decadent," Molly remarked.

"It's strawberry season," Julia countered. "The waiter said these were grown nearby. How can we say no to local fruit?"

"Said Adam to Eve. But this is *real* shortcake. Real shortcake, real strawberries, real whipped cream." She put a large spoonful in her mouth and talked around it. "So what's left?"

"Left?"

"Clotheswise," she said more clearly, speaking after a swallow. "You need sweaters. It was cool here last night."

"Not sweaters. Zoe would never forgive me if I wore anything but something she knitted herself. I could use a sweatshirt, though."

"A hoodie," Molly decided. "Something touristy."

"Excuse me? You *hate* touristy things. Tacky, is what you usually say."

"Okay, but I'm not talking *tacky* tacky. I'm talking classy tacky."

Classy tacky proved to be hooded sweatshirts with CAMDEN written in large block letters across the chest. Molly got a navy one with red lettering to match Julia's gray one with navy lettering.

"And these," the girl said, adding to the pile a yellow rain jacket and another sweatshirt, this one solid green. She grinned, said, "When in doubt, think of Dad's ties," and went off to the register to pay.

Julia acquiesced, in part because the prices were so reasonable and in part because the shopping was such fun. She opted for practicality at a luggage store, purchasing a large canvas bag to hold her new things, but she balked at the camera store, when Molly dragged her inside, straight to display cases holding the same equipment Julia had lost to the sea.

"I don't think so, Molly."

"Didn't Dad tell you to replace what you lost?"

"I'm not sure I want to."

"Why not? He owes it to you."

Julia felt a twinge. "Why do you keep saying that, Molly? Your father doesn't *owe* me anything."

"Yes, he does. You make his life possible. He thinks about work, while you think about everything else. You've given your life to him."

"And it's not been a bad life," Julia pointed out. "I have a beautiful daughter and a beautiful home. I eat at the best restaurants and shop at the best stores. I've been to Europe, to Australia, to the Near East. I've been *multiple* times to the Caribbean, during that time of year when New York is dirty and cold. And I've had all of this without financial worry. Most women would give anything to live the way I do. Most women would give anything to have a husband who treats her like your father treats me."

Molly made a dismissive sound.

"*Molly,*" Julia whispered, uneasy now, "what *is* this about?"

Molly held up a slender hand. "I'm just annoyed with Dad. Okay?" She looked away. "Maybe I'm just down on men."

Julia wanted to think it was that, rather than something Monte had done—and it did follow, she supposed, after Molly's fiasco in Paris. "They aren't all bad," she mused. "I wouldn't be here today if it weren't for one last week. He didn't have to go tugging a seat cushion through the ocean to help me, but he did."

"Ah," Molly said and seemed to revive. "The alpha male." She dismissed Noah in the next breath. "I still think you should get a camera. You used your point-and-shoot to death. Aren't there things you want to photograph on the island?"

There were, though whether Julia could capture the tranquillity of the barn at dawn or the hush of the meadow at dusk, she didn't know, and those were the things she would want to remember once she was back in New York.

But the temptation was great. Having done her homework when she had first asked for a digital camera, she moved down the display case. "I'd like to see this, please," she said to the salesman.

Molly laced her fingers in delight. "Oh, *good*. But wait, wait. Show her this one."

Julia put a hand on her daughter's arm. "That's not the one I want."

"But it's a better model."

"It has features I don't want, and it's much more expensive. I don't care who's paying for it. I don't want a camera that will overwhelm me with buttons and dials for advanced features that I'll never use in a million years."

"You may," Molly said meekly.

Julia smiled. "Well, then, if and when that happens, I'll just hit your father up for the newer model. Right now, this is the camera I want." When Molly opened her mouth to argue, she held up a hand. "Are we buying this for you or for me?"

"You," Molly conceded. "But at least get a tripod. And a case. And whatever other little extras you'll need."

"I will," Julia assured her. She knew about all those little extras, had kept lists of what she wanted when she had done that original research. She didn't have the list with her now, but what items she forgot, the salesman eagerly supplied.

An hour later, they walked out of the store with everything she would need to take, print, and email pictures. The camera itself hung from her shoulder, its battery charged and its first pictures already recorded, thanks to the salesman's able instructions and a charming deck behind the store. Those first pictures were of Molly in every degree of close-up, every angle of light, every type of flash—and Julia was delighted. She loved snapping away, knowing she could later decide what was worth printing and what to delete. She loved seeing the picture in the monitor, and being able to zoom in on any part of it she wanted. She loved *holding* this camera, which was so much smaller and more comfortable in her hand than the one she had lost. She felt an immediate intimacy with it.

"This is exactly what I wanted," she announced as they returned to the car.

Molly beamed. "I'm proud of you, Mom."

Julia smiled back. "I'm proud of me, too."

Julia clung to that thought when she drove onto the ferry an hour later. Her first instinct was to stay in the car for the short ride to the island. The car was familiar. It was safe. She could sit inside and pretend she was on dry land.

But Molly wanted to go to the upper deck, where the air was sunny and warm. And with no fog in sight, a part of Julia wanted this to be the crossing she had been robbed of, herself, the week before.

So she left the car and went up on top, and she felt perfectly safe. Yes, she kept an eye on the water and monitored the boats that were nearby. Yes, she was mildly uneasy when the ferry's motor made the same intermittent noise it had that morning. But this time there was lots to see. Weekend boaters were taking advantage of the weather; all, though, respected the ferry's space and kept their distance. Rockland's pier, its landings and cottages faded gradually, while before them, the islands took shape and grew. To the north were the granite bluffs of West Rock and Hull, to the east, the meadows of Little Sawyer. Beyond that were the forested crests of Big Sawyer, gaining prominence the closer they came. If the island hadn't stood out from the others for its lushness, it would have by dint of sheer size.

Julia was biased, of course. Big Sawyer was the only island of which she had childhood memories. As the ferry docked, she felt a sense of homecoming. Moments later, though, driving the car onto Big Sawyer soil, she felt something else. She was trying to identify the emotion when Molly said, "Stop here," and directed her to a parking space. "I have to run into the Grill for a minute."

Julia didn't blame her. The bathrooms in the restaurant were far preferable to the ones on the ferry. Nor did she mind waiting. Lord knew, she was practiced at it. Hadn't she spent a good part of Molly's first eighteen years waiting, if not at school, then at a dentist's office, a dance lesson, or some such activity? Usually, she had a book with her. Or a pad of paper to make a grocery list. Even stationery to write thank-you notes to friends who had hosted them for a weekend in the country.

She had none of those things now. So she rolled down the driver's window and settled back in her seat to enjoy the first quiet moments she'd had in hours, and the emotion came to her then. Actually, more than one. She felt blessed. She felt strong. She felt . . . liberated. Yes. Liberated. She had tussled with fate and survived. That opened doors.

And as quickly as that, it was back—the restlessness, the little niggling in the pit of her stomach, the sense of something pending. She might have blamed it on the confines of the island, if she hadn't known better. This was big-picture-of-life stuff.

Opening the door, she swung her legs out. Seconds later, she put one back in and reached for her phone. Whom to call, though?

She had talked with Monte just last night. There was no reason to call him again. He wouldn't know what to make of her restlessness, would only feel threatened and grow defensive, and she would end up feeling worse.

Both legs out of the car again, she put her elbows

on her knees and thought about calling her parents. But her mother wouldn't speak, and her father would be cryptic with her mother nearby, and, anyway, what would she say to *him,* knowing now what she did?

She straightened. She put her hands on her knees. She glanced at the Grill, her watch, the pier.

Then, snatching up her new camera, she climbed out of the car.

Chapter 8

A trio of men talked beside a pickup. One had his arms folded over his chest; another had a booted foot on the running board; the third stood free, his stance wide. All were local. All glanced at Julia as she passed. They didn't stare. Just glanced. They didn't acknowledge her, though they knew who she was. She could see it in their eyes as she walked on.

A young woman sat on the top of a piling at the start of the pier, talking with what looked, from the intimate slant of their bodies, to be her boyfriend. They, too, glanced at Julia as she turned onto the dock. They didn't stare. Just glanced. They didn't smile, didn't speak, though they knew who she was. She could see it in their eyes as she walked on.

A pair of lobstermen anchored each end of a large locker as they carried it ashore from a boat. The locker was heavy; they struggled with it as they walked. One of them did nod at Julia as they passed, but the other just looked. Neither of them spoke.

She felt totally conspicuous. She was wearing the same tank top and denim capris she'd had on that morning, but she might as well have been wearing neon pink, had a green streak in her hair or two noses for the visibility she felt—which was truly ironic. She had spent a lifetime being the least visible person in the world. First her mother was the attention-getter, with Jerry and Mark duking it out for second place, then when Julia married, Monte became the main attraction. She was perfectly content to be in the background. It suited her quietness.

Nothing in her experience had trained her for being watched. She didn't want it. It made her very uncomfortable.

So, maybe it was in her mind.

Of *course* it was in her mind. Being glanced at was not the same as being watched. But that didn't change how she felt—which was precisely why she wanted to see Noah Prine. He wasn't family, wasn't even a friend. But he understood.

She had spotted the *Leila Sue* pulling into its slip when the ferry had first entered the harbor. Turning down that arm of the dock now, she singled it out. Noah was hosing down the boat, cleaning up after a day's work. What she could see of his T-shirt was gray under spatters of blue and orange paint, but from midchest down he was covered by yellow oilskins. Wide bands cinched them at the shin. At the ankle, big rubber boots took over, and from what Julia could see, it was a good thing. Both oilskins and boots were dripping wet.

His hair was mussed and fell damply on his brow, over the curve of his ears, down the nape of his neck. He had regained color during a day of sun on open seas and was lightly bronzed. His eyes followed the spray from the hose. His bare arms gleamed, muscles flexing as he moved things aside with a gloved hand.

He didn't see Julia, who stopped just shy of the boat. She was aching to take a picture or two. That felt like an intrusion, so she took the opportunity of his preoccupation to study the boat. It was long, with the same up-curved bow and low stern as other boats nearby, the same flat rail running all around, the same rubber-skidded platform on the back. The wheelhouse was enclosed on three sides, front windows angled open. On one side were steps that led to the cabin, with hooks along the way holding hats, jackets, and other gear. On the other side, a console housed the throttle, three separate screens, and numerous gauges. The steering wheel protruded from its front.

There was no seat at the wheel. Noah would be in and out, back and forth all the time. In keeping with that, immediately to the right, where the wheelhouse ended, were long hooks, winches, and pulleys. In the center of the boat, bolted to the floor, was a worktable; Noah was washing that down now. A pair of large crates and a trio of tanks were overturned in the stern. The water from the wash ran away through small holes at the sides of the deck.

She didn't see any lobsters, though from the way

Noah was scrubbing the boat and the soapy smell of whatever he was using to clean, she assumed they had been there not long before.

When he turned to hose down the crates in the stern, he happened to look up, and for a split second, his face was intent, blue eyes as dark as the North Atlantic. Then, incredibly, he smiled. It wasn't a large smile, but it was spontaneous.

"Hi," he said and continued with his work, but in a more relaxed way.

More relaxed now herself, she smiled and stepped forward. She stopped at the side of the boat and watched him work. He was quite handsome—every bit in control of his work—yes, alpha male here, which made watching him a delight. After a minute, he hosed down his overalls and boots. Turning off the water, he coiled the hose and tossed it aside.

"Where'd the lobsters go?" she asked.

He hitched his head toward the far side of the harbor. "The boxy building out there. Foss Fish and Lobster. Foss is the local trader. I catch, he sells."

"Was the catch good today?"

"Not bad." He tossed his gloves back toward the wheelhouse. "Pretty good, actually. I've missed a lot lately, so most of my traps were full."

"Not all?" she teased.

"Nope."

"Why not?"

Still smiling that small smile, though crookedly now, he said with a one-shouldered shrug, "Bad place? Bad bait? Vandalism? You choose."

"Vandalism?"

"Seals. Or men."

"Oh, don't say that."

He pushed an arm up to mop his brow, leaving his hair all the more mussed. "Men? I don't want to say it, but a couple of my traps were bone empty. Two in a string. Like someone pulled the line and helped himself."

"Can't a seal take lobsters from both?"

"Oh, it can. Definitely. Seals can steal from as many as they want."

"But you don't think this was seals." She could see it in his face.

"Seals make a mess of the trap. Men are pretty neat. These were neat."

"I thought there was honor among fishermen."

"There is," he said, unhooking the straps of his overalls. He bent to dispense with the boot bands, then in deft movements kicked off the boots and slipped out of the overalls. His bare feet were well formed. His jeans were faded and fit him well. "Once in a while, you get bad guys. We're working on it." In a movement eased by long arms, he hung the overalls from a hook just inside the wheelhouse, and caught up a towel.

"What does 'working on it' mean?" she asked.

He stepped into clogs as each foot was dried. "Trying to get a message to the offending party."

"Then you do know who it is?"

"Oh, yeah."

She did, too, she realized. "The fruit guys?" When

he gave her a quizzical look, she said, "Matthew Crane told me." She had another thought. "Is this a gear war?"

"Not yet, but it could become one if they ignore the message."

"What would happen then?"

"Not good stuff. It can get ugly. Part of me's itching for it. I'd like to have a good go-round with someone." He angled his chin toward her camera. "Been playing tourist on the mainland?"

"Uh-huh. Clothes shopping, mostly."

"How'd it feel?" he asked. Those dark blue eyes were suddenly sober. He wasn't talking about the mainland or the shopping. This was why she had come to see him.

"The ride out was hard," she admitted. "Coming back was better. Did you feel anything like that?"

"No. But it'd be pretty bad if I did. I've spent most of my life on the water. I'm avoiding the place where the boats went down, though. That's tough. How're you sleeping?"

"Badly. Dreams wake me."

"Itching wakes me."

"Itching?"

He moved closer to the gunnel. His eyes were troubled, his voice low. "I wake up restless. Like I need to move or I'm going to die. Like there's something I'm supposed to do."

"Oh, boy," she said, because it sounded familiar.

"Like something's unfinished," he added, though he sounded unsure of the word.

"Incomplete?" she put in.

He sputtered out a breath in agreement.

"That is *so* what I feel," she said in relief.

His voice was cautious, his blue eyes baffled. "Have you figured out what you're supposed to do?"

"Not yet."

"How do you get past the restlessness?"

"I cook. Or I tend the rabbits. That's calming. Does your work calm you?"

"Yes. There's more to do, working alone. It keeps my mind busy."

"Is it safe to work alone? What if something were to happen?"

"I have the radio. Friends are never far off."

Julia wondered if he would hire another sternman once things settled down. The question seemed callous, though, with Hutch only buried a day. So she asked, "Where's your dog?"

"Lucas?" He scanned the dock, looking down the row of boats. "He's around."

"Doesn't he go out with you?"

"Sure does, only he runs off when it's time to clean up. There he is." He was looking at a boat two slips down. Lucas sat on its stern platform, looking straight at Noah. "He's not much help with cleaning up, or with catching lobster, for that matter."

"Can I help?" she asked.

His eyes returned to hers. "Nah. It's grunge work."

"I could do it," she offered.

"If you had trouble on the ferry, this'd be worse. The ferry was big. The *Leila Sue* is even smaller than the *Amelia Celeste*."

"I'd be okay," Julia insisted, feeling strong still. She had survived the ferry today. The sea wasn't taking her now. Besides, Noah had saved her life once. He wouldn't let her drown.

"Ever handled a live lobster?" he asked.

"Yes."

"With banded claws?"

"Uh-huh."

"Know why those bands go on?"

She certainly did. She had asked the question at her local fish market, where lobsters filled a huge tank. "To keep them from cannibalizing each other."

"And from taking a finger from the person picking him out of the tank. Those bands go on here in the boat. It isn't easy."

"Neither is diapering a squirming two-year-old who has diarrhea."

He was momentarily startled.

She grinned.

He grinned back and put a hand on his hip. "Think about rotting seaweed and gull droppings. And fish in the trap that are half-eaten by the lobsters."

Julia was defiant. "Kids throw up. It's all over everything. Someone has to clean it up."

"What about herring body parts?" Noah countered. "That's my bait. Each trap that comes up has a bait bag that has to be refilled. Doesn't smell like any perfume you ever bought."

Julia wasn't being beaten. "Did you ever open a fuse box and find a mouse nest filled with mouse stuff? Or open a cabinet and disturb a cockroach feast?"

"You haven't."

"I have. I live in Manhattan. Pests go with the territory."

Apparently ceding the gross-out contest and opting for a new approach, he gave her a quick once-over. "You're . . . slight. Lobstering takes strength."

Julia stood straighter. "Doesn't the winch do the hauling?"

"Sure does, but that's only a small part of it." He opened and closed his hand. "It takes strength to use the bander."

"Same with using a manual can opener when the electricity goes out. Or lugging twenty-four-bottle packs of spring water in from the car. Or turning a king-size mattress."

"You don't do that yourself," he said skeptically.

"Well, with someone else, but the point is, I'm not a weakling. And I really would like to see how you catch lobsters. Think of it as my island education. Besides, it'll occupy my mind."

"Until you figure out what it is you're supposed to be doing?"

She smiled sadly. "Yes. Until then. Have you seen Kim Colella?"

"No. You?"

She shook her head. "I'm not sure I'd recognize her if I passed her on the street. I've only seen her dripping wet when they brought her in after the accident."

"You didn't see her in the boat?"

"No. Do you think she's feeling the same things we are?"

He shrugged. "I don't know. She still isn't talking."

"Maybe she'd talk with me, my being a woman and all. Is she getting professional help?"

"Counseling? I doubt it. The Colellas wouldn't go for something like that." Noah looked at her arm. "How's it healing?"

Julia turned her wrist to show the red zigzag mark. "I forget about it most of the time."

Noah's gaze shifted. She followed it in time to see Molly start down his arm of the dock. The girl's cheeks were flushed, her eyes excited.

"I did it," she said with a smug smile as she reached Julia.

"Did what?" Julia asked.

"Convinced Rick Greene to hire me. It took a little talking—he likes his lean operation—but he knew my restaurant in Paris, and I told him a couple of things he could do with lobster, things I learned there, and then I said I'd work for free. I mean, it was a total no-brainer." She grinned. "So I'm here for as long as you are, chaperoning."

"Chaperoning," Julia repeated quizzically.

"Making sure you're all right," Molly stated and turned to Noah with something that, to Julia, looked suspiciously like a challenge. "I'm Molly." She stretched forward, extending her hand. "And you're Noah."

Noah started to put out his hand, pulled it back and wiped it on his jeans, started to extend it again, then paused. "This hand's been working all day. You don't want to shake it."

"But I do," Molly insisted and waited until the

handshake was done. "Thank you for saving my mother's life."

"I didn't do that."

"She believes you did, and that's all that counts." Dismissing him, she turned to Julia. "I have to go back and shower. I'm starting tonight." She took Julia's arm.

Julia stood her ground. She pulled the keys from her pocket. "You go on up. When you get back here, I'll take the car myself."

"You're staying?" Molly asked, less pleased now. "Here? On the dock?"

"I want to play with my camera," Julia said.

Molly darted Noah an uneasy glance. "What about Zoe? She's expecting you for dinner."

"It's too early for dinner. I'll be there in an hour. Please tell her."

Whispering now, Molly said, "That's not very polite. She's your hostess."

Bemused, Julia whispered back, "Who was the one who insisted we leave Zoe for the entire day today? Who insisted I buy this camera? Who'll be deserting Zoe tonight and every other night to work at the Grill?"

"But she was counting on you," Molly argued. "You were the one who planned to vacation here with her."

"That's right," Julia said, still quietly but with conviction, "and it's my vacation. I want to spend another hour here. End of discussion."

Molly looked startled. Julia was vaguely startled, herself. She wasn't usually so forceful. But it felt good. She really did want to stay here—not for long, just for a bit—maybe even just to make a statement, rather than to be swept docilely along.

Recovering her tongue, Molly said, "Fine," in an annoyed tone, and walked off.

Julia watched her for a minute, then gave Noah an apologetic smile. "I really do want to play. Could I photograph you?"

"No. Want to do the boat, be my guest. Me, I need a shower and food." He went back to the wheel-house, ducked inside the cabin and came up with a logbook, his thermos, a sweatshirt, and a cooler. Whistling for the dog, he used the rail as a step. His other foot had barely touched the pier when Lucas bounded past. Lifting a hand to Julia, he followed the dog.

By the time Noah let himself into the house, he was feeling disgruntled. Given his druthers, he'd have stayed awhile on the boat. That was where he felt most calm. Here in the house, there were ghosts. It didn't help that the place was dark, but he didn't see the point in raising the shades, when he was gone so much of the time. Besides, if he let light in, he'd see the emptiness. It was a trade-off, emptiness for ghosts.

He strode through the house to the laundry room, where he stripped down and put every item of clothing he'd worn into the washer. Naked, he went into the bathroom, turned on the shower, and stepped into the stall. The water was cold at first, but he didn't mind. Physical discomfort was a welcome diversion, so he focused on it until the water heated, then he took the soap and scrubbed himself, first with his hands, then with a brush. When he was done, he stood for a while, head bowed, under the spray, and he enjoyed it, until the itching returned.

Turning the water off, he reached for a towel and did a cursory job of drying off. *Unfinished . . . unfinished . . . unfinished.* With cach swipe of the towel, he heard the word again. He would have had to be an idiot not to know what it meant. The accident had left a gaping wound in his life, and it wasn't only Hutch's place there that left its emptiness.

Wrapping the towel around his waist, he went to the kitchen, picked up the phone, and punched out Sandi's number. It had barely started to ring when he felt the old anger rising up, accusations hurled his way, endless analysis of every word he breathed, making him feel less than little—and she was probably right. He could tell himself that a million times to Sunday, and it wouldn't change things, at least not with Sandi. The sound of her voice brought it back.

"Hello?" she said.

"It's me," he said, struggling to sound kind. "Ian never called."

There was a pause, then a resigned, "I know. He and I had a big fight about it. I think it really bothered him that Hutch died, and he didn't know how to deal with it. I tried to talk with him, but he refused. I told him to call you, but the thought of doing that was even worse. He's going through a hostile stretch. Right now, that hostility is directed toward you."

"What have I done?"

"Nothing," Sandi said with pleasant factuality. "Absolutely nothing for the last ten years. You're there, Ian's here. Yes, you call every week, but if he's not home, you talk with me and that's it. Talk? Well, I talk. I tell you what's going on in his life, and you ask just enough to keep it going. I know you love him, but you're so damned silent about it, how's he supposed to know? As far as he's concerned, you loved him until he turned seven, then you moved out and everything changed."

Noah pinched the bridge of his nose with a forefinger and thumb. "I've seen him."

"In New York, twice a year. Not down here, and this is where he lives. When I said he should go up for the funeral, he argued about all the important things in *his* life that *you've* missed. He didn't understand why he should go up there to be with you."

"Not me. His grandfather."

"I told him that. And I told him you wanted him there, but let's face it, Noah. You didn't call. You didn't talk with him directly. You didn't ask him yourself. You could have tried the number. You could have left a message. You could have pestered a little. Sometimes that's the only way you get things done with kids this age. But no. You just let it ride. You sat and waited for him to call. Well, that's not how it happens. Maybe when he's a bona fide adult, you can sit back and wait for him to take the initiative, but at seventeen? Forget it. And it's not just Ian. I see this all the time, well-meaning parents who want to be good guys and reason everything out with their kids, but for certain kinds of kids and certain kinds of things, issuing orders is all that works."

Noah waited until she was done. Then quietly he said, "I'm issuing an order, then. He's to come up here next week."

There was a pause, then a disbelieving, "Where have you *been*, Noah? He starts *summer* school next week. I told you that way back!"

"You said there were two sessions. He can spend three weeks here with me, then go back for the second session."

"We were going to look at colleges then."

"Do it afterward."

"Can't. I have faculty orientation programs to run then. Besides, Ian doesn't *want* to look at colleges."

"Well, there's your answer," Noah said. "If I change his mind, either I'll take him looking, or you can do it in the fall."

Sandi was silent, before asking a suspicious, "Why do you want to do this? Ian's going to want to know. Is it because Hutch is gone and Ian's all you have left? Or because you really want to spend time in his company? Or because you need help with the boat and he's free labor?"

Noah hadn't thought out the details. He said the only thing he knew. "He's my son. I want him here. Where is he now?"

"At Adam's for the night. He'll be back in the morning."

"When?"

"Elevenish. He won't be pleased, Noah. Three weeks away from his friends? Who'll he hang with?"

"Me."

Again, she was silent. Then came a guarded, "Are you sure you want to do this? Maybe you ought to think it over. Once you mention it to him, you can't change your mind. You'll have to be firm."

"Do I sound firm?" Noah asked in his firmest voice. Sandi would call it cold, but that was because she had never spent enough time among Maine men to know the difference between cold and firm.

Then again, maybe she had wised up. Either that, or the prospect of being free of Ian and his teenage moodiness for three weeks was simply too appealing to resist. She relented with a quiet, "Yes. You sound firm. Do you want me to have him call you?"

"No," Noah said. He wasn't making the same mistake twice. "I'll call him."

Determined, he called Thursday morning at eleven, with the *Leila Sue* idling in the ocean swells and fresh traps on the rail waiting to be emptied. He called again at ten-minute intervals after that until finally, at noon, the boy was home and answered the phone. Strangely, what Noah got then wasn't so much hostility as indifference. Ian didn't show surprise. He didn't argue. He didn't ask any of the pointed questions his mother had asked. If he was pleased that Noah wanted him there, he didn't let on. His tone was neutral to the point of being remote.

Belligerence might have been easier to handle. Noah had lined up his arguments and was prepared for a fight. Remoteness was something else. It said nothing about what Ian was thinking or feeling. It did say, however, that Noah had his work cut out for him.

At the same time that Noah was talking to Ian, Julia was driving to the southern tip of the head. Here, bordering the town beach, were streets of bungalows, all in a row. Some were owned by summer people, either used by them or put out for rent. Most had been opened for the season and had lawn chairs on the porch, grills on the lawn, even cars in the carport. A few remained boarded up.

Other houses were owned by locals. Kimmie Colella lived in one of these. Julia found her street and cruised slowly down it until she reached number forty-three. It had the same beachy feel as the others, with the same weathered shingles, the same battered shutters, the same rangy lawn. This one had a pink door, but it wasn't a pastel pink. This pink was strong. Number forty-three was a house of women who made no bones about who they were.

The driveway was a bed of pebbles. A small red pickup and a vintage Mustang were parked there. Parking on the street, Julia followed a sandy path that time and feet had worn through the grass. There was no doorbell, so she knocked.

At first glance, the woman who answered didn't seem much older than Julia, which made it hard for Julia to decide whether she was the mother or the grandmother. She had pale, strawberry blonde hair twisted up on the top of her head and a pair of sun-glasses propped on top of that. She wore a blouse and jeans, and was barefoot. On closer look, her skin gave her away. The sun had toughened it to a leathery sheen. Same with the fingers curled high up around the edge of the door. They were slim, attractive fingers, but there was nothing soft to them. Nor was there softness in the brown eyes skewering Julia.

Julia forced a smile. "I'm Julia Bechtel—Zoe Ballard's niece?"

The woman emitted a gravelly "Uh-huh" that raised Julia's estimate of her age even more.

"I was in the boat—"

"What can I do for you?"

"I wondered how Kim is doing."

"She's doing fine."

"She isn't fine," came another voice, and another woman appeared. The family resemblance was there—pale reddish hair, brown eyes, slim, attractive fingers, several of which were half-hidden in the front pockets of body-hugging jeans. But the face was less leathery, the voice less coarse, the eyes less hard. "I'm Kim's mother, Nancy, and this is my mother, June. Kimmie still won't talk."

"She's stubborn," June said crossly.

"She needs help."

"She needs time."

"She's had time," Nancy insisted. "She's gone more'n a week without saying a single word."

"How do you know? Maybe she's talking to other people."

"Well, she's not talking to the doctor, and she's not talking to the Chief, and she's not talking to any of her friends."

"She came close to dying. So maybe she's talking to *God*. Who else is up there on the bluff?"

Nancy looked at Julia. "She's not talking to anyone. She just sits up there staring out at the water."

"How do *you* know?" June asked.

"Because I went there," Nancy argued. "Three times yesterday I went there. I brought food. I brought beer. When in your knowledge has that girl refused beer?" She returned to Julia. "She may be twenty-one, of age and all, but she has me worried sick."

Julia could see it in her eyes. "Do you think she's suicidal?"

June snapped, "She is *not!*"

Nancy didn't look quite so sure. She raised her shoulders as much in a gesture of fear as of uncertainty. "She's always been okay. But she's never done anything like this before."

"What did she do?" June argued. "*She* wasn't driving that boat."

"Oh, hush," Nancy said without so much as a sidelong glance.

"You're the one who should hush," June said, dropping her hand from the door and drawing herself up. "This person's a stranger. Kimmie is no business of hers." She held up a hand. "But you want to talk to her, go ahead. Kimmie's your daughter. I'm just the one who raised her while you were out running around."

Nancy glared at her mother then.

"Do what you want," June muttered and disappeared into the house.

Julia felt awkward. "I'm sorry. I didn't meant to make trouble."

Nancy waved the apology aside. "The trouble was already there. She's right. She did raise Kimmie. I was only seventeen when she was born." She raised a brow. "Just like June was seventeen when she had me, only she had no one to help her, so she's forever telling me how easy I had it. I did run around when Kimmie was little. That doesn't mean I don't love my daughter."

"Has she been here at the house at all?"

"Only to sleep. Dawn to dusk," she hitched her chin northward, "she's up there on the bluff."

"Would she talk to me, do you think? She doesn't know me at all. Maybe that would help."

Nancy raised her shoulders again. "It can't hurt to try. You were there on the boat. You survived the accident, like she did. Maybe that'd mean something."

Julia was hoping it would. If she and Noah were feeling similar things, she guessed Kim might be feeling them, too—at least, some of them. Of course, there was the issue of muteness. Neither she nor Noah had experienced that.

Thinking about it as she returned to her car, she had to smile. Noah was miserly with words from time to time, but being laconic was a far cry from being mute. He talked just fine once he got going.

That thought gave her added incentive to see Kimmie. Leaving the beach behind, she headed north. The bluff was a straight shot from there, up on the highest point at the back of the head. While the rest of the island was green with meadow and spruce, here was a mass of granite-gray cliffs, rearing high above the tumble of rock to the sea. A lighthouse stood watch; its light was automated, and the keeper's house long since decayed, but there was an authenticity to it. Julia had visited the spot before. She had felt that authenticity, along with a certain wildness.

The bluff road was well marked, the pavement here broken, but her SUV handled it well. As she climbed, trees that had flanked the road thinned, then receded. Ahead were boulders, sky, and a rustic stone tower with a rotating eye at the top. The pounding of the surf, magnified by all that baldness, was strong enough to penetrate the walls of the car.

Pulling up beside the ruins of the keeper's house, she parked behind a small blue Honda. The instant she opened her door, the roar of the waves came full force, and one step out, she was hit by a stiff breeze. Leaning into it, she climbed over a short stretch of granite to the lighthouse, but it wasn't until she was past it that she saw anyone there, and then she wondered if she had the wrong person. The one sitting out on the rocks facing the sea was a small, childlike bundle with her knees drawn up, arms cinching them to her chest. But it wasn't the pose that was odd.

It was the hair. It was bright red—not at all odd in and of itself, given the hair color of Nancy and June.

What was odd was that Julia always noticed hair first. She noticed it when she was at the gym, when she was out to lunch, when she was at the theater.

Monte said she simply wanted to know that other people worked as hard to maintain their natural color as she did. But the truth was she had always been attuned to hair, even way back when her color *was* her natural color, which was why she felt such an odd twist inside now.

She didn't remember seeing anyone in the stern of the *Amelia Celeste* with red hair. She didn't think she would have missed it, regardless of how harried and rushed she had been. If there had been a flash of hair that red in the stern of the ferry, she would have remembered. And if Kim had not been in the stern, there was only one other place she could have been.

Chapter 9

Hello!" Julia called loudly enough to be heard over the pounding of the surf.

Kimmie Colella looked around quickly. Her face was pale, her eyes blank. She showed no sign of recognition—and with good cause. If she had not been on the *Amelia Celeste,* she would not have seen Julia before, surely not in the crowd on the dock in the dark that night.

Julia could be wrong. She couldn't swear under oath that Kim hadn't been on the ferry. Her own memory might be faulty. Yes, she noticed hair, but she had been preoccupied with getting herself and her bags aboard. If Kim had been sitting behind someone, or if she'd been wearing a hat, Julia might have missed the hair.

That had to be it, Julia decided. A hat.

She stopped ten feet from the girl. Girl? Just as on the night of the accident, she couldn't think of Kimmie as a woman, though she knew her to be twenty-one. Then, she had been a sopping figure swathed in a blanket, her hair color muted by water and night. She was no longer wet now—wore jeans, a sweatshirt, and sneakers—but she looked smaller and more forlorn. That vivid red hair was as straight as Julia's, though longer. In the hands of the wind, it became a shifting veil.

"I'm Julia Bechtel," Julia began gently. "I was on the *Amelia Celeste.*"

Kim's eyes held hers for another minute. They fell to her clothes, studying, and went to her car. Then they returned to the sea.

Julia came closer. "I've been wondering how you are." She squatted on a nearby rock. "There were three of us who survived—you, me, and Noah Prine. He and I talk every so often. We have this thing in common. It's not often that people survive accidents that take so many other lives."

Long strands of silky red hair blew over Kim's cheek. She tucked it back behind her ear.

Taking that as a sign she was listening, Julia began to chat. "The accident was the last thing I anticipated when I left New York Tuesday morning. An auto accident? Maybe. I always think about those when I'm on the highway. How not to? Drive long enough, and you pass some sort of mishap. I did on the drive up that Tuesday. It was a minor accident, I think—no ambulances, only police."

She was talking, just talking, wanting to be pleasant and approachable. And maybe it was working, she decided. Kim wasn't telling her to leave, and there were ways to do that without speaking. She could have thrown Julia dirty looks, turned her back, moved to a distant rock, even stood and left the bluff.

"I'm here to visit Zoe Ballard," Julia went on. "She's my aunt, but more like a friend, since we're only twelve years apart. I've visited before. I've come up from time to time with my daughter. She's twenty and wants to be a chef. The field is a big one now. There's a whole art to food presentation. And then those celebrity chefs."

You have a daughter? Kim might have said. *Just about my age?*

Instead, she put an elbow on her knee and braced her head with a hand.

"I was initially planning to stay for only two weeks, but I've extended that," Julia said. "My parents think I'm crazy. They think that what with the accident and all, I should go right back home."

Your parents think you're crazy, too? It was another opening, but ignored.

"Have you been on a boat since the accident?" Julia asked. When Kim didn't react, she said, "I was dreading that. But my car was back on the mainland, and I needed clothes to replace the ones that went down with the boat. I also had to go because my daughter would have thought I was a total wuss if I didn't." No smile from Kim. "There was fog, like there was at the time of the accident. I kept waiting for the nose of a purple boat to break through. I wake up in the middle of the night with that image."

She wanted to ask if Kim woke up with the same image. Only, if Kim hadn't been on the *Amelia Celeste,* but rather on *The Beast,* the question would have been threatening, and that was the last thing Julia wanted to be. Kim might not be speaking, but she was listening. That was something.

Julia continued. "Taking the ferry back to Big Sawyer was better. The sun was out, so I could see things. I was also feeling like the ocean might have swallowed me up on Tuesday night and it didn't, so maybe there was a kind of truce between it and me. I almost feel an affinity with it." She paused. With genuine curiosity, even beseechfulness, she asked, "Do you feel anything like that?"

A wave spent its force against the rocks below, sending spray nearly up to the bluff. Julia waited for another. It came after several smaller ones, but she appreciated those, too. The power of the sea was raw, its effect hypnotic.

"I've always read that the ocean is as basic to our existence as amniotic fluid," she mused. "So maybe any connection we feel with the sea is a primal thing?"

She looked at Kim, but the girl was somewhere far away. Her eyes were glazed. They suddenly widened. She jerked. Her eyes flew to Julia's.

Oh, yes, she relived the crash. It was there, clear as day.

Gently, Julia said, "They say that fades with time."

Kim blinked. She put her chin on her knees and looked out at the sea.

"Is it different for you, living on the water? You were

born here, weren't you?" Kim didn't answer. "The accident was something else. All or nothing. You either died, or you were unscathed. I think about that a lot. I think about why I was spared, and what I want to do with my life now. Like I have a chance to be someone different, and I have to decide who that is." She paused. Very quietly, she said, "Do you feel *any* of that?"

Kim met her eyes then, and there was something so bleak in them that Julia nearly reached for her. In that split second, she imagined the girl hurling herself over the edge of the cliff to her death on the rocks far below.

Urgent now, she said, "You and I share something, Kim. We've had an experience that not many people ever have. It's been good for me having Noah to talk with, but Noah's male. I'd like to talk with another woman. I'm an outsider—a *New Yorker,* of all things," she drawled in self-derision, attempting to lighten the mood, "and I'm not sure any of my friends back there will be able to relate to what I'm feeling. My husband doesn't. My parents don't. Even Zoe can only understand to a point. The chief of police just wants the facts, and the pastor at the church will pray for me. But I need other things. Talking with you would be therapeutic for me. Maybe you'd get something out of it, too."

Kim's eyes grew accusatory, and Julia read them well.

"No one sent me here," she assured her. "No one even knows I'm here, other than your mother and grandmother. I stopped at the house, hoping to find you there."

Though the accusation eased, distrust remained.

"One of the reasons I like talking to Noah," Julia went on, "is that he doesn't know me or my friends, so if I say something awful or just plain stupid, it doesn't go any further than him. I assume he feels the same about me, like I'm not about to turn around and tell any of his fishing buddies if he confesses to feeling weak or vulnerable or even *guilty*."

The word hung in the wind, suspended between one explosive burst of water on rock and the next. If Kim had been with Artie Jones on *The Beast,* it gave credence to rumors that there was something between them, which, totally aside from who had survived and who had died, would be cause enough for Kim to feel guilt.

Julia smiled sadly. "I guess what I'm saying is that maybe I can help. You're not talking to anyone, but I'm a stranger and an off-islander. If you ever want to talk with someone about the accident, I'm as safe a bet as any." She pushed herself to her feet. Kim's eyes followed her as she stood. "I'm staying at Zoe's. You know where she lives, don't you?" She took silence as an affirmation.

In that last moment, she fought an urge to physically drag Kim farther back from the edge of the cliff. But she didn't delude herself. If Kim wanted to die, she would do it whether Julia tried to hold her or not. Leaving her alone was another matter. Part of Julia felt she was abdicating her responsibility as a sensible adult by returning to the car.

So she gave it a final shot. "Are you hungry? Want to go somewhere for lunch?"

Kim returned to the sea.

"How about Zoe's barn?" Julia tried. "Working with her rabbits is peaceful. Want to help me there?" Kim said nothing. "I'd even go out on a boat with you. We'd have total privacy. You could say whatever you wanted and no one but me would hear. Of course, I don't have a boat or even know how to drive one. You'd have to be in charge of that."

Kim didn't crack even the smallest of smiles.

Not knowing what to do other than momentarily cede defeat, Julia turned quietly and left.

Julia turned quietly and left.

Driving back down from the bluff, she grew annoyed with herself. *Julia turned quietly and left.* It was the refrain of her life. Julia didn't make noise. She didn't say things people didn't want to hear. She didn't rock the boat.

Wondering if she was simply an inveterate coward, she actually slowed the car and considered going back. Prudently, she did not. Kimmie Colella needed the help of a professional, and Julia was far from that. The last thing she wanted to do was make things worse for the girl.

That said, Julia knew she would go back for another visit. She shared something with Kim. The affinity grew murky when it came to the girl carrying on with Artie Jones, and grew even murkier with regard to who was or was not in the stern of the *Amelia Celeste.*

Still, there was a bond. Of a dozen people, only three survived. Kim was the youngest of the three, and the most vulnerable, and Julia was a born care-taker. It was only natural that she would want to help the girl.

Not knowing how best to do that, she returned to Zoe's and began to bake. She made Congo Bars this time, following a recipe she could make in her sleep, she had used it so often over the years. A favorite, in-herited from the mother of a childhood friend, it called for brown-sugar batter layered with chocolate and butterscotch bits, coconut flakes, marshmallows, and pecans. Her own mother had always balked at the name—*Why in the world are they called Congo Bars?* she asked whenever Julia baked them, and Julia made up any number of answers, though none really mattered. Janet didn't want to know the meaning of the name, so much as simply to place the bars in a too-bizarre-for-my-own-effort category. She was too busy to bake. But she did eat her share of the bars.

This day, Julia made them for the Walsh children. As soon as they had cooled enough to be cut into child-size bites and layered in foil, she drove them over. The children were in the front yard of the weathered farmhouse, playing in a plastic pool filled with sand. Their aunt sat on the grass nearby in a rumpled T-shirt and shorts, her tawny hair un-combed, her freckles stark in a pale face. She looked exhausted.

Julia knelt beside her. "I brought goodies for the kids. Are they allergic to anything?"

Ellen regarded her bleakly. "There's another thing I don't know. Jeannie never mentioned it. She was always here when I visited, so there was no need for me to know. She didn't plan on this."

"Is their pediatrician here on the island?"

"The only name I ever heard was Jake. If there are medical records to be picked up, I assume he has them. I'll stop by his office before we leave."

Julia imagined it was one more thing on an ever-growing list; all that, on top of the shock of losing her sister, brother-in-law, and niece. "How's the packing going?"

"Slow." Ellen's voice fell to a whisper. "I'm trying to do most of it when the girls are asleep and leave just enough out and around so the place doesn't look so bare. They know they're going back to Akron with me, but they think Jeannie, Evan, and the baby are meeting us there. I try to explain that they're in heaven, but I'm not getting through."

"They're so young. Heaven is only a word. They can't grasp the meaning. It'll take time."

Vanessa, the dark-haired three-year-old, climbed out of the sandbox and, smacking her hands free of sand, made a beeline for Julia. She pointed a small finger at the foil pack and, in a barely baby voice, asked, "What's there?"

"Little munchies."

"I'm hungry."

Julia unfolded the foil. Vanessa watched closely, leaning in with two little hands braced on her knees. "Oooo," she said when the first of the bars came into sight. She looked up at Julia with pretty blue eyes. "Can I have one?"

"You can." Julia separated one small bar from the rest. Vanessa took it from her, bit off a corner, chewed for a minute with a thoughtful look on her little face, then gave Julia a gooey grin. Pushing the rest of the piece into her mouth, she settled in against Julia's thigh.

By this time, her sister, Annie, had joined them. "What's Nessa eating?"

"It's a Congo Bar," said Julia and handed the five-year-old a piece. Then she held the foil pack out to their aunt.

With a tired smile, Ellen shook her head. "Not much appetite here."

"Want to take off for a little while? I can stay."

Ellen perked up at that. "Would you? There are errands I'd be better doing alone."

"Go," Julia said.

For the next two hours, Julia was focused enough on the girls not to worry about Kim, Monte, or Janet, and busy enough not to be restless. She took them for a walk through the meadow, read to them, helped them build sand castles, let them run under the sprinkler to clean up. They were precious children, curious, well behaved, and smart. The younger was more physical than her sister, wanting to hold Julia's hand, sit on her lap, stand against her leg. The older asked questions.

What's this flower? Where's the yellow from? Do you know my mommy? Where do you live? Why's it called a buttercup? Can I pick one for Kristie?

Each in her way, they were needy. They might not understand what had happened, but they knew something was up. *My daddy made my face in clay, want to see?*

Julia's heart broke for them. When Ellen had returned, and it was time to go, leaving the little one, in particular, was hard. Vanessa clung. "I'll be back," Julia assured her, holding her tightly for a minute, before whispering in her ear, "with chocolate chip cookies."

"I love those," Vanessa whispered back, but solemnly.

Driving away, Julia thought about love and loss. She hadn't gone far when the thought of her mother loomed before her. The Walsh girls had lost their parents. Julia couldn't help but think how lucky she was to have hers, and how tragic it was that she and Janet couldn't talk.

Pulling to the side of the road under the shade of a gnarled old oak, she put down the windows to let air in while she gave them a call. Her father answered.

"Hi, Dad," she said tentatively.

"Julia. How's it going?"

"Pretty well, but I really need to talk to Mom. Is she there?"

"She's out on the patio."

"Would you take the cordless to her?"

There was a pause, then a quiet, "She's relaxing, Julia. Maybe we ought to let her be."

Julia feared that if she let the moment pass, she might lose her resolve. "Please give her the phone, Dad."

"Are you all right?"

"Dad."

"I'm on your side, Julia. I'm pushing her every chance I get, but she's a stubborn woman."

"Right now, so am I," Julia decided, and there must have been enough conviction in her voice to give him pause.

After a murmured "Okay," he put her on hold—which, of course, meant that Julia couldn't hear whatever coaxing he had to do to get Janet to take the phone. Enough time passed that Julia began bracing herself for another flat-out refusal.

Then Janet came on with a curt, "Yes, Julia."

Julia's heart beat faster. "Can we talk?"

"That depends. Is this an apology?"

Julia swallowed. "If you want it to be. If I've offended you, I'm sorry."

Janet was silent.

"I'm sorry, Mom. I don't know what you want me to say. You're upset that I'm here. But it's not like I'm forcing *you* to come. This is me, not you. *My* need to get away, not yours. I don't understand why you're so angry."

"Zoe betrayed me. End of story."

"Not end of story, because the two of you are still alive. It'll only be end of story when one of you dies, and that's what I've seen up here, Mom. I was just with two little girls who've lost their parents. *That's* the end of a story."

Janet said nothing.

"Mom?"

"Are you trying to reconcile Zoe and me?"

"No. It's me needing to talk with you, me needing to know that you're there and you care."

"We'll talk when you're back."

"I want to tell you about the accident. About what I'm feeling."

"It'll hold until you're home."

"But I won't be home right away."

"So your father said. That's not wise, Julia."

"I need this time."

"Have you told Monte that? What did he say?"

"He's fine with it."

"He's your husband. You ought to be with him. Men behave badly when they feel they've been abandoned."

Exasperated, Julia cried, "Oh, he *already* behaves badly! Mom, I need to talk about who I am and where I'm going, and what you really think of me, because I haven't done anything like what you've done, and sometimes I think I'm less of a person for it, and now, here I am with half a life ahead of me, and I'm feeling like there are things I need to do, only I can't pin them down—and, yes, I want to talk about Monte, because I don't, for the life of me, know what to do with my marriage, and you've had experience with this." She hadn't planned to say the last, would have taken the words back if she could. "Mom?" she said fearfully. There was no answer. "Are you there, Mom?"

Janet had hung up. What Julia didn't know was whether it had happened before those words, or after.

Chapter 10

Heart heavy, Julia sat in the car with her hands limp in her lap. Her hair was caught up by a gentle breeze as it came in one window and went out the other. She felt the breath of it on her skin, but it went no deeper.

She could have used the soothing inside. Everything there was raw, everything in turmoil, flowers that had grown year after year suddenly tugged from the soil, roots and all.

There were no sounds of the ocean on this road; they were blunted by waves of spruce, pine, and birch. She might have been on any country road in any little town in the heart of America—except that she wasn't, and, suddenly, the pull to Big Sawyer that she had felt over the years was stronger than ever. It went beyond familiarity. Being here was *right*.

Far down the road, a dark blue truck rounded the curve. It was a late model, bumpers gleaming even as its tires kicked back a cloud of dust. It slowed as it neared. Driver's window to driver's window, it stopped.

"Hey," said Noah Prine, straight-faced as ever. "You've led me a merry chase."

Julia felt a tiny lift, a little nudge against the ache in her heart. "Following me, were you?"

His eyes were the darkest of blue and direct. "You look a little down. I'm doing chores. Want to come?"

It was the invitation she needed. Leaving the car without a second thought, she rounded the front of the truck. By the time she reached the other side, he had the door open. She climbed in, closed the door, and looked around. The seats were leather, the steering wheel wood, the stereo system advanced.

She ran a hand over the leather. "Very nice," she said in admiration and sent him a bright smile. "I'm all set."

He wagged a finger at the seat belt, which she quickly fastened—but the fact that she had forgotten it got her thinking. "So here's a question. Would it be possible for us to survive the crash the other night, only to die in a car crash today?"

"Possible? Sure." He shot her a glance. "Are you feeling immortal?"

"No. But some people who've been through what we have do feel that way. They tempt fate. They take every risk possible."

"They don't have kids," he said with some weight.

Julia studied his profile—serious forehead softened by spikes of dark hair, straight nose, firm chin— and it struck her that he wasn't talking only about her. "I didn't know you did."

After shifting gears for the cruise down Dobbs Hill, he put his right hand on the top of the wheel. His left elbow was on the windowsill, fingers just grazing the wheel. The pose was relaxed. Not so his voice. "I have a son. He's seventeen. He'll be coming up next week."

"Where does he live?"

"Washington, D.C. My ex-wife is an educator."

Julia pictured the island school. It was housed in a small, square building of wood and served Big Sawyer children until they reached high school, when they were ferried to the mainland each day. "Was she originally from here?"

"No. We met at college."

"Were you an education major, also?"

"Economics. We spent the nine years of our marriage in New York."

Julia broke into a surprised smile—then yelped a split second later when something brown and wet appeared between the seats. It was a nose, and might have been followed by a freckled white muzzle and a pair of soft brown eyes had Lucas not been startled himself by her yelp and shrunk back. She pressed a hand to her chest and began to laugh.

"I did *not* know he was there." She turned as much as the seat belt would allow to see the dog, wedged now in a corner of the extended cab. She held out a hand. It was a minute before he sniffed it, another before he decided she was harmless, at which point he curled up and went back to sleep. Julia turned back to Noah. "What did you do in New York?"

"I was an investment banker," he said with the twitch of a diffident smile.

"You *were*?" She never would have imagined it. Noah was light-years removed in appearance and behavior from the investment bankers she had met through Monte. "That's very different from lobstering."

The road curved. He drove it one-handed, with ease. "Not as different as you'd think. There's the same lone wolf mentality, the same competitiveness. I was working with MBAs who saw me as a lesser breed because I wasn't one myself."

Julia knew how that worked. Monte was acutely aware of credentials. When he introduced people, it was so-and-so MBA, or so-and-so Ph.D. or so-and-so CEO or CFO or COO or EVP. He sought out colleagues with advanced degrees as a validation of his own. She—who had no college degree at all—had come to find the habit annoying.

"That actually helped me out," Noah went on. "If they keep you at arm's length, you can be more independent. I wasn't driven by their opinion. I often rowed against the tide, but my instincts were good. I did well." He slid her a glance. "We're goin' for bait. You mind?"

"Of course not. Where do you get it?"

"There's a bait house far side of the harbor. A supplier keeps it stocked. It'll likely be herring. Pieces of," he tacked on.

"Will I need to hold it raw in my lap?" she asked and, when the corner of his mouth quirked in reply, moved on. "Were you always interested in business?"

He raised his fingers from the wheel only enough to acknowledge the driver of a passing truck. "Only as it related to lobstering. I'd probably have stayed here those four years, if it hadn't been for my parents. They wanted me to go to college. They wanted me to be one step ahead of the lobstermen who didn't go and couldn't see the larger picture."

"Larger picture?"

"Supply and demand. The food chain."

"Human or animal?"

"Both. I studied marine biology, ecosystems, business. The business courses interested me most. I worked back here the first summer, then worked in the city the next. The money was good. I was able to send back double enough for my father to pay a sternman in place of me."

"What about after graduation? Hadn't you planned to return?"

They reached the end of the road. Shifting gear again, Noah turned right. "Yup. Then came Sandi, who had her choice of teaching jobs in New York, and I got an offer myself that was too good to pass up. I told my folks it was a temporary thing. I figured I'd earn a bundle, invest it, and come back here with no money worries at all." Absently, he acknowledged a pickup, then said in a drier voice, "That's pretty much what I did."

"What happened to your marriage?"

His voice remained dry. "Know what kind of hours investment bankers keep?"

"I know they're bad."

"I was working nine in the morning to three the next, plus at least one weekend day. When I was home, I didn't have much taste for anything but sleep."

Julia could see it. Monte didn't work quite those hours, but her friend Charlotte's husband did. Charlotte had bought her boutique precisely to fill the void left by his absence.

"I'm sorry," she said, feeling oddly responsible, as a New Yorker, for the kind of life that ate people alive.

"Don't be. My marriage was never that strong. We fell in love with the idea of it, more than with each other. Sandi's doing fine now. She has a portfolio that gives her lots of extra income. She can spend time with people she's more compatible with than me and my friends. My only regret is Ian. I'm never quite sure what to say to him."

"How long will he be here?"

"Three weeks."

"Does he come every summer?"

"No. This is the first."

"Could he not come for the funeral?"

"Didn't *want* to."

"Oh, dear."

"My fault," Noah said. "I should have called him directly and said I wanted him here. I guess I was anticipating a fight. I wasn't up for it then."

"Are you now?" Julia asked.

"No."

"But he's coming. Whose idea was it?"

"Mine."

She admired his courage. Seventeen-year-olds wal-

lowed in the fear of the future and anticipation of responsibility and stress. They often fought with their parents for no other reason than to feel better about leaving
home. Seventeen had been difficult even with Molly,
and she was a breeze to raise. Julia figured that if Noah
had trouble communicating with his son under the best
of conditions, they would be at the crisis stage now.

Not knowing how to help, she looked out her
side window. Having left the uplands behind, they
were on a flat road that skirted the far side of the harbor. The vegetation was more sparse here, the tended
feel at the heart of the harbor replaced by Atlantic
wear and tear. In the absence of shade trees, the road
was bleached by the sun and worn by the salty air that
blew now through the cab of the truck.

Small businesses stood in twos and threes as they
had for decades—an auto body shop and a gas station,
a convenience store, a store selling island furniture.
Their signs varied from the faded canvas banner to
ones carved in wood, but the late afternoon sun
didn't discriminate. Its glow fell on each, rendering
this workingman's turf in a softer hue.

Farther on, rising beyond a marshy stand of beach
grass and the occasional abandoned hull, was the boat
repair shop. Noah pointed at the large hangar out
front. "Used to be only two rows high, now it's four.
Come winter, there are boats all the way up, waiting
their turn for repair. Not much there now."

The road curved as they passed, giving Julia a
view of the water side with its rough pilings and
piers. "There are plenty out there," she remarked.

"Damage happens in season. Some of those may be in just for tune-ups."

"Like a car?"

"Pretty much. You need an oil change every hundred and fifty hours. That's every other week in summer. Most of us do it ourselves. Some don't."

He turned off the main road. The truck bumped along for a mile before coming to a stop in front of a stone shed. "Be right back," he said and was out of the cab with Lucas on his heels. As the dog dashed into the tall grasses, Noah opened the tailgate, pulled out a fiberglass locker, and hauled it inside. By the time he returned, it looked significantly heavier.

He whistled for Lucas, who came on the run and leapt into the truck without missing a beat. Noah followed, closed the door, backed around, and returned to the road.

"Tell me about Kim," Julia said quietly. She didn't want to make an out-and-out accusation. Nor, though, could she forget what she had seen, or more precisely, *not* seen. The police were investigating the accident. Kim Colella could be a major piece of the puzzle.

"Did you see her?" he asked with what she thought was caution.

"This morning, up on the bluff. I wasn't prepared for her hair."

"All that red."

"I don't remember seeing it on the *Amelia Celeste*. Was she wearing a hat?"

Noah didn't answer.

"If she wasn't," Julia said, "I'd have seen her. I always notice hair. I was thinking maybe she was inside the wheelhouse, but if she was there, she'd have died in the crash." She paused. "Don't you think?"

"Maybe not. Stranger things have happened. Did you ask her where she was?"

"I didn't dare."

"Did she say anything?"

"Not a word."

He slid her a glance. "Is that what had you so sad back there?"

Julia didn't have to struggle to think back. Heavy-heartedness was a pot on the back burner, simmering right alongside the issue of bright red hair. "That. And the Walsh girls. Actually, though, mostly my mother."

He slid her a second glance. "Is she sick?"

"Oh, no. She's well—well and strong-willed as ever. I had been talking with her right before you drove up. Talking. That's putting it nicely."

"You argued."

Julia felt a whisper of the sea on her face. As they neared the center of town, she could see the harbor filled with boats moored for the night. They rocked gently in water that was surprisingly calm. She took comfort in that.

Pushing her fingers into her hair, she piled it in a twist at the top of her head and held the twist with both hands. "Yes, we argued."

"Is it chronic?"

"Arguing? No. I rarely give her cause. I'm usually the good daughter." She released her hair. It slid down. "Not for the last month, though. She doesn't want me here. She thinks I should be back in New York with my husband."

"What does your husband say?"

"He says I should stay. But I'm staying for me. I came here for me, and I'm staying for me, and I want my mother's support." She looked at him. "Why does her opinion matter so much to me? I'm forty years old. Why do I care?"

Pulling up at the pier, he faced her. "Because you're a caring person. It's written all over you."

"But I can't always do what my mother wants. Where do you draw the line between the obligation you have to your family and the one you have to yourself?"

He thought for a minute, brow furrowed, dark eyes deep. Then he said a simple, "After the accident, you draw it here."

That quickly, she was reassured. "Thank you," she said quietly.

He smiled. "Any time." He hitched his head toward the bed of the truck. "There are three traps back there. I'll take the bait first and come back for two of the traps. Can you get the third?"

She certainly could. The traps were four-footers, not so much heavy as bulky in size, but she managed to carry one without any trouble. When everything had been stashed on the *Leila Sue*, they returned to the truck.

"Time for more?" he asked.

"Sure," Julia said without so much as a glance at

her watch. She guessed it was close to six, but Molly was working, Zoe was helping a friend assemble a floor loom, and Julia had no reason to run home. "What's next?"

"Out back under the tarp? There's wood to deliver and a leak to fix."

"Where?"

"Hawks Hill."

She fastened her seat belt and they were off, heading out of town in the opposite direction this time. Hawks Hill was the southernmost of the island's hills. There were no meadows here; it was an ascent through pure forest. That meant the roads were heavily shaded this late in the day. *Dark,* Julia thought, and felt a chill. "So what about Kim?" she asked.

Noah drove on.

"I keep imagining," she said, self-mockingly enough to keep the accusation light, "that maybe she wasn't on the *Amelia Celeste* at all." She looked at Noah and saw no reaction. "If she was having an affair with Artie, wouldn't it be more likely that she was with him on *The Beast*?"

Noah took a breath. "That would mean she was likely the one who shot him."

"Oh no, there could be—" *Another explanation,* she would have said if he hadn't squelched the thought with a meaningful look. The road might have been dark and his face shadowed, but the weight of that look wasn't lost. "So you think she did?"

His eyes returned to the road. "I don't want to."

"But you're leaning that way."

"It's hard not to," he said in a voice that held a touch of desperation, "but if they were involved, it couldn't have gone anywhere good. That means she'd have motive."

"Anger?"

"That, or disillusionment. If they were involved, he may have promised to divorce his wife. Married men do that all the time."

Julia couldn't argue. "Has she ever been in trouble before?"

"No."

"Would she have access to a gun?"

"Probably."

Letting that reality sink in, Julia watched the road. Paved, it reflected the forest green of the woods on each side, with the spill of lavender where bits of late-day light filtered through. Every few minutes, a gap in the trees marked a narrow drive on the left or the right. Some were marked by mailboxes, others by name signs. The occasional tree limb dipped low enough to brush the top of the truck, but Noah drove with confidence, as familiar with this road as he was the ones below.

"Who lives up here?" Julia asked, spotting another mailbox.

"Transplants."

"Artists?"

"No. Most of them prefer Dobbs Hill. It has meadows and is more open and varied—flowers, wood, and stone. Here we have trees. Bringing up services is harder. It's like most things, though. The harder the work, the greater the reward."

Julia didn't have long to wait to see what he meant. They hadn't climbed much farther when he turned right onto a dirt road. There was neither a mailbox nor a sign with a name, and the road dipped and rose, but it was groomed with sand and was surprisingly smooth. What was at its end couldn't rightly be called a clearing, because many trees remained, but where several might have stood once, there now stood a house.

It was an A-frame, small with clean lines. Roofed in dark slate, its siding was of cedar shakes that had weathered a natural silver. There were blinds on the windows, square light fixtures flanking the door, and a wraparound porch with an Adirondack chair here and there.

A carport, absent a car, was tucked under the trees, a depleted wood bin against its side. Noah backed up the truck to unload the supply under his tarp, but before starting the task, gestured her toward the house.

The air here was dry, lighter, more . . . happy. It was a minute before Julia connected the last with balsams in the woods, whose sweet smell conjured holiday images. They crossed a small patch of packed dirt and pine needles. He had a key out by the time they reached the door.

And suddenly it struck her. "Is this yours?" she asked with a curious smile. It wasn't only the key. It was the feel of the place—appropriate for the setting, yet somehow different. Noah was that way—appropriate, yet different.

He opened the door and stood aside for her to enter. "I built it when I left New York. I figured a thirty-two-year-old guy with an ex-wife and a seven-year-old son couldn't move back in with his parents. I lived here until my mother died. Then my dad needed tending. I never formally moved back in with him. I just seemed to end up there more than here."

The house was as simple inside as Julia would imagine a man leaving the rat race would want. Living room, dining room, kitchen—there were no walls between them, just a comfortable collection of leather chairs, built-in appliances, and a round oak table with ladder-back chairs. A single large rug covered slatted wood floors; she guessed it to be Tibetan, knew it to be expensive. There were windows aplenty and a door leading to the back part of the wraparound porch. Above, on both side, were lofts. One had a pair of beds, the other a desk, replete with computer.

"There's more downstairs," he said.

"There's another floor?" she asked in surprise.

"It's built into the hill. You can't see it from the front." He pointed to a spot behind two of the leather chairs. "The stairs are back there. Take a look while I get my tools."

A burgundy runner cushioned the stairs. Holding a wide railing, she started down. Halfway there, the flight turned left, and there was suddenly more light than she would have expected. There was suddenly more *room* than she had expected. There was a bathroom here, and a walk-in closet. Primarily, though, this lower floor built into the hillside was a bedroom.

A large bed rested against a wall. Sitting on an even larger rug hooked in a myriad shades of blue, it had a simple white spread and, in lieu of a headboard, enough pillows to prop more than one person up for the view. And that view? No large-screen TV here, but a wall of French doors with a view of the world.

Immediately drawn there, she looked out on an expanse of sky and sea so seamlessly merged that, save the long lean shadow of the mainland far to the west, the horizon was lost. Like the rug underfoot, this view of the world held more shades of blue than she could name. Variations of blue spruce, blue sky, blue sea, blue land—one delineated the other. The only exception to blue was the spill of gold as sunset skimmed in over the waves from the west, and the weathered gray of the deck beyond the doors.

Her view had borders on three sides—trees left and right and, beneath, the spikes of spruce tips on the hillside—but the sky had no limit. There was possibility here.

She looked back at the bed, so neatly made, so clean. Quiet, confident, modest. And different. Yes, different. Like him.

Hearing footsteps above, she waited. When the sound stopped at a place far from the stairs, she went up herself. It was a minute before she spotted his bottom half protruding from under the sink.

She crouched down by his hips and peered into the dark cabinet. He had a wrench, but it wasn't quite attached to anything.

"How can you see?" she asked.

"I can't," he remarked wryly and lifted his head to meet her gaze. "There's a flashlight two cabinets down. Want to get it?"

She found it easily and trained it on the spot where he was working. "This is a fabulous place," she remarked. "How often do you stay here?"

"Not often enough," he said as he tightened the wrench around a section of pipe. "I drop by to use the computer."

"Will you stay here more now that your dad's gone?"

He grunted with the effort of pushing the wrench. "Not yet. I want Ian to know the other place. That's his heritage, y'know?"

"Will he be your sternman?"

"If he can hack it." He pushed himself out, holding a U-shaped piece of pipe, and spent a minute coating the threads with sealant. Then he was back inside, reconnecting the piece, adding putty to the outer edges of the fitting, before emerging for good.

Julia was on her haunches. "He could hack it more easily if I helped."

Noah sat up. Eye to eye, they were barely an arm's length apart. "He could. But he won't."

"Why not? I'm still available."

"You're still slim. And soft. Go lobstering, and you get hard. You don't want that."

She frowned. "Everyone seems to know what I want. Don't I have a say?"

He gave her a smug smile. "Not about this. It's my boat." He pushed himself up and put his tools away.

Julia wanted to be annoyed. It was the kind of statement Monte would make, laced with sexism and superiority. *Do this for me, like a good girl,* or the more outrageously chauvinistic, *Treat yourself to a new dress; I want you looking pretty for me.*

Noah's remark about her being slim and soft might have been chauvinistic, but he delivered it differently—as if it wasn't a put-down at all, but rather his protecting her from what was clearly hard physical work. And that was nice. She still wanted to go lobstering, but his protectiveness made the refusal more palatable.

Leaving the house, Julia perched on the running board of the truck. Lucas came out of the woods, approached only so near, and stopped. Wary, he stared at her. She held out a hand. He took one step, paused, took another step. Then he sat and looked at her, which left Julia with nothing to do but look back at him and think about hard physical work. She told herself that Noah was right, that it was his boat, and lobstering was rough. If she was looking for adventure, she could go whitewater rafting, parasailing, or bungee jumping. If she was looking to tempt fate, there were dangerous activities aplenty that wouldn't require anyone's permission.

But she wasn't looking for danger, or even for adventure for adventure's sake. She wanted to do something interesting. Looking back, she saw her life framed—like Noah's bedroom window, only with no opening at all. Her horizons were defined and finite.

In contrast to this island, where life followed weather and tides and the vista was open, that seemed stifling.

It struck her then that she had been singled out to make more of her life. It was an exciting thought; it was a *terrifying* thought. Where to head? What to do? Most people faced their life decisions on the cusp of adulthood, but she was well beyond that. Where to *begin?*

Noah emerged, went to the back of the truck, and tossed in his tools. Then he loaded his arms with wood, carried it to the bin, stacked it, and returned for more. As soon as he left with the second load, Julia went to the back of the truck and loaded up her own arms. This was a place to begin. It was simple, practical, helpful.

"What are you doing?" he asked when he straightened from the bin.

She didn't answer, just smiled and passed him by.

"You'll mess up your nice new T-shirt," he called.

"It'll wash," she called back. Her arms didn't hold half as much as his could, but if she made four trips, she would save him two, which she did.

Soon enough, they were back on the road. And for a little while, Julia was satisfied. She glanced at Noah. His face was darker than ever; the sun was far too low now to do anything more than gild the very tips of the spruces. He seemed preoccupied, focused almost absently on the narrow road as they descended Hawks Hill and headed toward Dobbs and her car. His headlights were on. Dusk was heavy and low.

"About Kim?" she asked softly. "Do you think I ought to do something?"

With a deep breath, he returned from wherever he'd been. "You? It's not just your worry. It's mine, too."

"We, then. Do we go to the police?"

He was slow in answering, clearly reluctant. "I hate to do that before Kim starts talking again. Think she will?"

"Eventually. At least, that's what my friend the psych professor says. She likens what Kim is experiencing to having surgery. Right now, the incision is so raw that the nerve endings aren't functioning, and everything's numb. In Kim's case, the numbness is emotional. It manifests itself in her inability to speak. When the nerve endings start to regenerate, the numbness wears off."

"How long does that take?"

"It depends on the case. So I guess you have to decide. You lost your dad. How fast do you need to learn the cause of the accident?"

"Very. But I don't want it to be Kim."

Neither did Julia. "If we say nothing, are we obstructing justice?"

"Not unless we know something for sure. Do you?"

"Know it for sure? No."

"Me neither." He shot her a glance. "Why don't you try talking with Kim again? I'll push John and see what his investigation's turning up. A pistol would be nice, especially if it's registered to a third party." Without humor, he added, "I could use a real villain."

Suddenly he sat straighter and slowed the truck, eyes sharpened on the road. Julia's followed. His headlights picked out several cars haphazardly gathered ahead. It was a minute in the stone blue of dusk before she recognized the spot as being the one where she had left her SUV. Moments later, she picked out Zoe's truck, along with the little Plymouth that Molly had taken to driving. The police cruiser was parked beside them; though the light bar on top was dark, the driver's door was wide open in a statement of urgency.

Noah pulled up close behind. Julia was out of the truck the instant it stopped. She had barely reached the ground when Molly started running toward her. She stopped just beyond reach, staring in horror.

"I found your car," she said in breathless accusation. "I sat here forever, waiting for you. I can't tell you what I thought."

Julia could understand Molly's fear, but only to a point. This was the island, after all, not the city. And she wasn't a helpless ninny. "What did you think?"

"That you'd been abducted. Or done something strange."

Julia was taken aback. "Strange, like what?"

"I don't know. Just something. You said you were bringing cookies to the Walsh kids. You were supposed to be back."

"You were supposed to be at work," Julia replied quietly. She wasn't arguing. She was simply stating fact.

"Rick needed my Social Security number, and I couldn't remember it, so I drove home for my papers, and you weren't there."

Zoe approached. "She was frightened. She called me, and then John."

"Why were you gone so *long*?" Molly asked without budging from that spot, just beyond reach.

"My fault," Noah offered, coming up beside Julia. "I passed her on the road and conned her into helping me run a few errands."

Julia felt a twinge of annoyance. She didn't need a cover. "He didn't have to con me. He asked, and I went. I had no reason not to."

Molly's mouth settled into a straight line. Seconds later, she turned on her heel and strode to the Plymouth.

Julia caught up with her there. They were far enough from the others to give them privacy; still, she kept her voice low. "Molly, what *is* it?"

"This doesn't look good. That's all."

"*What* doesn't look good?"

"You and him. Did you know him before?"

Julia was offended. "What are you implying?"

"Maybe there's *double* reason Dad's back in New York."

"Double reason?"

"Dad there. You here."

Julia wouldn't have picked this time or place, but the matter loomed. "Did you see something there last week?"

Molly drew herself straighter. "He's lonely. I think you should go back."

"Lonely?" Julia couldn't imagine it. "Did he say that?"

"You need to be there."

"Was someone with him?" It wouldn't be the first time, Julia knew, and felt a stab of anger toward her husband.

"You need to be there," Molly repeated and climbed into the car. "I have a job. I'm all set for the summer. Pretend I'm still in Paris."

Julia leaned down to window level. "You didn't answer me."

"I have to get to work," she said. She started the car, backed it around, and drove off.

"What's eating her?" Zoe asked, her tone kind.

Julia held up a staying hand and walked past, toward her own car, but before she could climb in, John Roman said, "Hold up. I have your things." At the back of the cruiser, he opened the trunk. Her leather purse was deformed, yet recognizable. She could only assume that the large plastic bag with it—the large green *trash* bag—contained the remnants of her other belongings that had been retrieved from the ocean floor.

Feeling mildly sick, she couldn't move, so he carried the bags to her. She managed to open the back hatch of the SUV so that he could put them inside, and thanked him for the effort. But these things were as unwelcome as Molly's accusations. Old horizons were crowding in on her, pushing her back into places she didn't want to be.

Given a shovel, she would have stopped on the way back to Zoe's and buried the bags under several feet of cleansing island soil. Lacking one, she settled for stashing them behind bales of fresh hay in a far corner of the barn. She was reemerging when Zoe pulled up, but she wasn't ready to talk yet. Sending Zoe back to her friend's house, she heated a can of soup for dinner. Putting her wedding band by the bathroom sink, she washed up, climbed into bed, and read the manual that came with her camera until she fell asleep. She didn't hear Zoe come in later. Nor did she hear Molly return from work, and she was out of the house, herself, the next morning before either of them got up.

Chapter 11

Julia drove with her window down and no destination in mind, at her own pace. She couldn't remember having done this before—just driving for the sake of driving. Leisure was one word to describe what she felt; defiance was another. Her life was a mess of tangled ends and open questions, yet she found herself smiling.

The air was damp but refreshing. She imagined it clearing her head of worries, though she didn't dwell on them any more than she dwelt on the concept of defiance. Island mornings were more about being than thinking.

She had her camera with her and stopped from time to time to take pictures of gulls on the rocks, a hermit crab in the froth of the surf, sandpipers on the beach. She followed the road all the way around the harbor to Foss Fish and Lobster, and, while the sky bled from lilac to pink, photographed the large box of a building against it.

The pictures were sweet but common. She could as easily have found the same ones on postcards at the island store, but that was fine. She was familiarizing herself with the camera, and the drive was therapeutic. By the time she returned to Zoe's, she wasn't quite as angry at Molly.

Since it was early still, she went straight to the barn. She was surprised to find her aunt already there. "I heard you leave," Zoe explained gently. She had a rabbit on the grooming table and was working a wire brush through its fur. "Are you all right?"

Sneakers whispering, Julia crossed the old wood floor and kissed the top of Zoe's sleep-mussed head. "I am. Thank you. How about you? My visit keeps growing more complicated for you, too."

"I'm not complaining."

"Were you up when Molly got back?"

"Um-hmm. She's still angry."

If anyone has a right to be angry, it's me, Julia thought. She was the one whose integrity had been wrongly questioned—and she might have said as much, if Zoe hadn't given her arm a gentle little shake.

"It's too nice a morning to deal with that yet. Want to see me pluck?"

Like Noah's offer to run errands, this one was perfectly timed. The rabbit at hand was Sugar, so named for the white in her largely cinnamon fur and her sweet personality. "I'll bet you didn't know she has multiple layers of fur," Zoe said.

"I didn't."

"They all do. At a given time, they can have one

THE SUMMER I DARED 231

coat that's three inches long, another beneath it half that length, and a new, very short one close to the skin. The longest coat is the one we pluck."

"I don't see layers," Julia remarked.

Zoe gently parted the coat. "Take a closer look." Beneath her knowing fingers, the different lengths of fur were clear as day.

"How do you pluck the longest coat without taking the shorter ones?"

"Easy. The longest fibers are released when you pluck, the shorter ones stay put. This is actually my argument in favor of plucking, rather than clipping or shearing. Plucking takes longer, nearly forty-five minutes per rabbit. I'd cut that time by half if I clipped, and by three-quarters if I sheared. The problem is, when you clip or shear, you do take multiple layers, and that's fine for the wool buyer but not for the rabbit. Angoras rely on their fur for warmth. Plucking removes only the top layer, leaving them plenty still. They may not need it now as much as they do in the winter, but their internal thermostats are calibrated for it. If you clip or shear and inadvertently take too much, you risk leaving the rabbit chilled."

Julia recalled Zoe's description of what happened when a hairless kit fell through the bottom of the cage to the unprotected tray beneath. "Chilled" was putting it kindly.

"Besides," Zoe said, "my rabbitry isn't that big. I can get everyone plucked." She saddened. "Todd was a help. I miss him." She resumed work with a metal comb, slowing at a tangle, separating it with care.

"His dysfunctionality was to my advantage. He had nowhere to go but here. I would have gone to his funeral, but the brother suggested I not. I'm part of a life the family can't understand."

"Or resents," Julia suggested, "if they blame the island for taking Todd away."

Zoe worked the comb through another matted patch. "Does Monte resent me?"

Julia gave her a curious smile. "Why would he resent you?"

"For taking you away from the city."

"You didn't take me away. I *went*."

Zoe's eyes were frank. "What's going on between you two?"

Nothing, Julia might have told anyone else. *Everything's fine. Why do you ask?*

But this was Zoe. Zoe loved her and wouldn't judge her harshly. And she had to be suspecting the truth, especially after Molly's behavior out on the road the night before.

Julia let out a breath. "I'd say that familiarity breeds contempt, only there isn't contempt. Monte and I are perfectly friendly when we're together. It's just that we rarely are. I was hoping it would change after Molly left. I was hoping there'd be a little passion, and I don't mean sex. I mean emotional involvement. I was hoping we'd be off doing things, just the two of us, like when we were first dating."

"Are you sitting home alone a lot?"

"No. I'm active—American Cancer Society, Friends of the Library, that kind of thing." This involvement gave her a sense of control. As she rose in the ranks of a charity's bureaucracy, there was even an element of power. "I exercise. I take courses. I'm in a book group. I have my own life, my own friends."

"The ones you email?"

"Yes. They're fabulous women. They were all associated with contacts of Monte's at one time or another, which is how I met them. Our friendships took off on their own. They're high-power women, but they love me because I'm not. They say I'm their touchstone."

"Does it bother you not being a high-power woman?"

Julia smiled. "Molly asks me that. She keeps telling me I'd have been a great school principal, or a great therapist, or a great florist. But I didn't want to be any of those things. Monte didn't force me to drop out of school."

"Excuse me," Zoe chided knowingly.

"Okay," Julia granted. "I got pregnant. But once Molly was born, I could have gone back to school if I'd wanted to. I didn't."

"In hindsight, are you sorry?"

"You mean, do I wish I had a career that would occupy me during those times when Monte is busy?" Bluntly, she said, "My not having a career isn't the problem."

Zoe had set aside the metal comb and was working with practiced fingers. "I remember when you met him. You were swept off your feet. Madly in love."

"Madly," Julia confirmed.

"Are you still?"

She sputtered out a sad laugh. "Madly? No."

"At all?"

"He's my husband," she said, which didn't answer the question, but she didn't know what other answer to give. She didn't hate Monte—should, perhaps, but she didn't. He had his strong points: he was a good provider, intelligent, charming when he wanted to be. She supposed she still loved those things about him.

Loved?

Well, she appreciated them, at least. Without them, she might have left years before.

"He's a good-looking man, and he knows it," Zoe said. "He loves the adulation of women."

"He does."

"Has he been faithful?"

Julia held Zoe's searching gaze, which was answer in and of itself.

"You seem calm," Zoe finally said, and Julia gave an uneasy laugh.

"Now maybe, but I wasn't always. I cried. I shook. I felt used. I felt *worthless*."

"Do you still?"

"Sometimes. How not to wonder whether if I'd been a little smarter, a little sexier, a little more of a dynamo, he'd have been satisfied at home?"

"Some men need conquest."

"So my therapist said. She let me vent, and she said all the right things, but in the end, there was only so much she could do. Couples therapy would have been the next step, but Monte refused."

"Too threatening?"

Julia rolled her eyes. "Way."

"Is he in love with someone?"

"I don't think so. He has short flings."

"Do you confront him?"

She made a soft sound of self-derision. Confrontation was something she had spent a lifetime avoiding. "He knows I've suspected it. There was the time when flowers mistakenly arrived at the house with a card from him addressed to another woman. He said she worked at the brokerage and was leaving, hence the flowers, but I'm not stupid. I checked the brokerage directory. She wasn't on it. Another time, I got a phone call from a woman. He had just ended it with her, and she was hurt enough to want to hurt him back. Calling the wife to tell all seemed like the best way."

"How did Monte explain that one?"

"He claimed she was a client who didn't like the performance of her portfolio, so she was looking to make trouble for him. Well, she was a client. That was true. I can't prove the rest."

"Why do you *stay*?" Zoe asked with feeling.

Julia shot that feeling right back. "Because there's been good *reason* to stay. There's Molly. There's financial security. There's a way of life. Monte has been my job for twenty years. He's what I *do*."

"But you came up here," Zoe reminded her quietly. "For two weeks, maybe more. That's a longer break from Monte than you've ever taken." More gently, she asked, "Is he with someone now?"

Julia touched the backs of her fingers to the soft spot between the rabbit's ears. "I don't know. I think so. He's out of the house a lot, and he doesn't have that many male friends. He may be working, but this time of year, New York is dead. So what's he doing?" Once started, the words continued to spill. "I'm afraid Molly saw something when she showed up unexpectedly last Monday night."

"Caught him with a woman?"

"Yes."

"Have you asked?"

"Indirectly. But how blunt can I be? Forget putting her in the position of telling on one parent to the other; if I ask bluntly, it suggests doubt on my part, and once doubt has been voiced, it never goes away. It creates insecurity. I never wanted that for Molly."

Zoe had taken up the metal comb again and was working it through the cinnamon fur. "Is that what you felt when I told you about George and me?"

"Insecurity? No. I'm not starry-eyed, like I was at Molly's age."

"A jaded lady at forty," Zoe teased.

Julia managed a small smile. "You know what I mean. I'm not saying that I wasn't shocked by what you said. I still am. Part of me—the not-so-nice part, I guess—may feel a little vindicated, like their marriage isn't as perfect as everyone thought, which means that I'm not such a failure by comparison." She paused. "I'm disappointed in my father."

"And in me?"

"No. I don't think you set out to seduce George.

It wouldn't have happened if Mom hadn't left him here alone."

"Isn't that what you've done with Monte?"

Julia was taken aback. "Maybe. Only he does his thing whether I'm there or not, and I needed a break."

"Break from the city? Break from Monte? Break from suspicion and insecurity?"

"All of the above."

"You're like Janet in a way, you know," Zoe said.

"I am not."

"Yes, you are. When something is troublesome, you opt out. Isn't that what Janet always did? When raising a family became a nightmare of custodial arrangements, she withdrew into her work and ceded the responsibility to you and George."

"What responsibility am I ceding?" Julia argued, annoyed by the suggestion. She had taken pains to cover every possible base before even suggesting she go away for two weeks. "I've set up Monte's world so that it's on autopilot. What responsibility am I ceding?"

"Responsibility for your marriage."

"Excuse me, Zoe. He's the cheater."

"You're allowing it."

"By leaving him alone in the house?" Julia asked. "Well, maybe that's what I want. Maybe I'm giving him just enough rope to hang himself. I'm not naive." Her voice began to rise. "Maybe I'm begging him to show his true stripes. Maybe I'm ready. Maybe the time is right. Maybe I didn't even know that when I planned this trip. Maybe the accident brought it all out." She took a quick breath and went on in the same high pitch. "I don't know. I don't *know*. But I do know that it's my life, and I'm not so obedient—or stupid—that I'm oblivious to his affairs, but I'll deal with them in a way that works for me. It might not work for you or for someone else," she tapped her chest, "but it's my life. *My* life."

Zoe smiled. "That, my dear, is the most force I've ever heard from you."

Julia exhaled. "You riled me."

"I'm glad. You're too nice sometimes."

"I meant what I said."

"I know."

"I will deal with it, but when I'm ready."

"I know."

Julia let out another breath, feeling uplifted, at least a little bit. She hitched her chin toward the rabbit. "Go on. I'm watching."

Starting at a spot at the rabbit's rump, Zoe formed her hand into a loose fist, took the longest fiber between her thumb and the curl of her forefinger, and gently pulled. The fiber came out easily. She repeated the procedure, working systematically along the rabbit's body, always pulling in the direction of the natural growth of the coat. As each piece was removed, she laid it in a tissue-lined box, adding a new tissue when one layer was filled. She demonstrated the way the nonplucking hand could ease trauma to the rabbit by holding its body not far from the area being plucked. She showed Julia how to separate out lower-grade mats from that considered prime pluck.

After a bit, she yielded the grooming table to Julia, and, as she took her turn, Julia was mellow. The ocean, ever in the background, sang a soothing rhythm, and the whispers inside the barn were few. It was a peaceful Friday morning. For a time, the worries of her life were far away.

You're like Janet in a way, you know. When something is troublesome, you opt out.

Julia thought about what Zoe said a lot in the ensuing hours. Molly slept on. It was only when noon neared that Julia realized she was doing precisely what Zoe had accused. Sitting back passively, waiting for Molly to wake up, was opting out. So she went to Molly's room, quietly opened the door—and found her daughter wide awake, propped up in bed, reading.

"Hey," Julia said with a smile. "And here I thought you were still asleep."

Molly didn't return the smile. Her eyes said, *So I'm awake. What do you want?*

Julia hadn't seen that look in years. "Hungry?"

"No." She returned to her book.

"Not even for fresh strawberries? I just picked a quart."

"No," she said without looking up.

"How's work going?"

"Fine."

"Will it be a good experience?"

"Yes."

"What're you reading?" Julia tried and—*again*—realized she was opting out, in this instance trying to cajole Molly into speaking her mind, rather than raising the issue herself.

"Stephen King," Molly said. "You wouldn't like it."

Julia left the door and went to the bed. "We need to talk."

Molly pushed the book down. "Not you and me. You and Dad. If you're cheating on each other, that's your choice. But don't let me go on thinking everything's fine. It's em*barr*assing to be told one thing and see another."

"I am not cheating on your father," Julia said. She didn't care that Molly was young and upset. She would not be wrongfully accused. "I have *never* cheated on your father. You've seen me talking with men before. I do it all the time when I'm out places. I've seen *you* talking with men. Does that mean you're sleeping with them?"

"I have male friends. You don't."

"I do. I just don't happen to go to lunch with them, because I don't have an excuse to do it that won't raise eyebrows—like *yours*," she couldn't help but add, "and I think that's too bad. Noah Prine is an interesting man. I could have a very interesting lunch with him."

"That's your choice," Molly said dismissively, but when she tried to raise her book again, Julia held it down.

"Talk to me, Molly. Tell me what happened when you got home last Monday night."

Molly stared across the room, her lower lip protruding the slightest bit. It was the same pout she'd worn occasionally as a child—nowhere near as cute now, nor taken as lightly. Petulance was one thing, unhappiness another.

Julia saw unhappiness, and suddenly the possibility of raising doubt seemed less risky than keeping silent. "I think someone was there. With him. Your father may not have explained it well—"

Molly's eyes stopped her cold. "She was in his *bed*. What other explanation could there *be*?"

There. Confirmed. Julia let out a dismayed breath and hung her head. Her heart was beating fast enough to acknowledge this as another life-changing moment. Turning marginally away from Molly, she sank down on the bed.

"Didn't you *know*?" Molly asked. "Didn't you have *any* idea that he'd be with someone else? What did you *think* would happen when you went away for two weeks?"

Julia was a minute in processing her daughter's words. Disheartened, she looked back. This young woman with the boy's haircut and the accusatory look felt like a stranger. "Are you blaming *me*? Like, if I'd been there, this wouldn't have happened? Do you think this is the first time?" she asked, gloves off now. The cat was out of the bag, Molly was an adult, and half-truths were dangerous things. "Well, it's not, Molly. It's happened before, and it may well happen again, and that's something I have to deal with. Me. Not you. Me."

Molly folded her arms over her chest. It might have been a belligerent pose had her eyes not filled with tears. "Are you divorcing him?"

"I don't know."

The book fell aside when Molly sat up quickly. "And you're going to find out *here*? I was right last night. You have to go back. Didn't you always tell me that I should go after what I wanted? Isn't the same true for you? You have to fight for him, Mom. Maybe that's not the way it's supposed to be, but if you want your marriage to last, you're going to have to let him know. Go back. If you catch the afternoon ferry, you could fly out of Portland and be there for dinner."

Julia could—and she might, another day. But not today. Quietly, she pushed herself up. She was halfway across the floor when Molly said, "Will you do it?"

From the door, Julia looked back, and the pleading on the girl's face nearly broke her heart. Julia understood. No child wanted her parents to divorce. Had Molly been younger, Julia would have done most anything to keep the marriage intact. She *had* done just that, all those years.

But Molly was grown and increasingly gone from home, and Julia had to think about herself. Unfortunately, she hadn't had much practice at it.

Stay and argue? Leave and wait?

Unsure, she let herself out of the room.

Close the door? Leave it open?

She started to close it, reconsidered, and left it ajar.

Molly slammed it shut when she was barely halfway down the hall.

*   *   *

Something about that slamming door turned a switch inside Julia—and the first thing she thought of was Molly's hair. She liked Molly's hair long, had thought it elegant and versatile. But it was Molly's hair, Molly's life, Molly's choice. Julia accepted—graciously, she felt—that Molly had decided to cut it. Molly was an adult. Julia had to respect that.

She wanted the same respect from Molly. She wanted respect and trust and even the smallest allowance for her own personal whims. Lord knew she had given that to Molly for years. That Molly couldn't give it back made her angry—and Julia didn't know how to deal with anger. It left her feeling frustrated and with a distinct lack of control.

Needing an escape, she got in the car and drove to the studio of Tony Hammel. Dominated by wide windows and large skylights, it was a rambling contemporary structure high on Dobbs Hill. Small cabins of a similarly contemporary style dotted the rim of the woods, housing for those of his students who had come to attend weeklong workshops. Had it not been for the crash of the *Amelia Celeste,* Julia would have been one of those students. Wandering through the studio now, catching bits of lectures given by Tony and others, studying the photographs on the walls and those on worktables, she was inspired.

Late that afternoon, determined to take advantage of the drama of oblique light and long shadows, she drove to the harbor with her camera. By the time she reached it, though, fog had rolled in, which meant that there would be no drama in the pattern of dock pilings, stone walls, or wood shingles. There was color in the newly painted buoys hanging on one arm of the dock, but no drama. There was continuity in the row of trucks waiting for owners to return from the sea, but no drama. These were the kinds of things Tony's students had photographed. Truth be told, Julia was more interested in watching the lobstermen return from a day's work.

So she wandered down the dock. She was wearing jeans, a T-shirt, and Zoe's Foss Fish and Lobster hat, and even with her blonde ponytail spilling from the hole in the back, she must have looked local enough to pass muster, because people glanced at her only in the most natural of ways. She didn't feel conspicuous, as she had the other day. The clothes, perhaps? Her own confidence? The presence of tourists who did look like tourists, making her one of the guys by comparison?

If she felt singled out, it was in her own mind and had more to do with having been given the gift of life than with her walk on the pier now.

A pair of lobstermen pulled into a slip. One was gray-haired under a ratty baseball hat, weathered and large in his oilskins; she guessed him to be in his late forties. The other was smaller and, even with no hair at all, clearly younger. Looking at two high foreheads, snub noses, and round chins, she pegged them to be father and son.

They secured the boat, produced scrub brushes and hoses, and began to clean. Within minutes, a lather was spreading, raising the same clean smell she remembered from Noah's boat. One man used the brush, the other the hose. They had the job down to a science.

Unable to resist, Julia went closer. "Do you pump fresh water out from shore to do this?"

The younger man looked up, but it was the older who spoke. "No sense doin' that, when salt water's just fine." Words and intonation—both were pure Maine. "There's a sea chest on the bottom of the boat. We got a belt-driven pump running off the engine. That brings it up."

"Do you have to use special soap?"

"Well, the wife calls it that when she tries to con me into doin' the dishes."

"This is dish soap?" Julia asked in surprise.

The older looked at the younger. "What's your mother use? Joy?"

"Dawn," said the son and told Julia in a milder accent, "It's one that'll lather in salt water."

"Ah," Julia said with a smile. "Thanks."

She would have loved to take pictures of them working, but she was grateful enough for their friendliness not to push her luck. With the camera hanging idly from her shoulder, she watched them work a little longer, then moved on.

Other boats returned, some to slips, some to moorings. Sitting on the edge of the dock with her legs hanging down, she watched several of the latter as the fishermen cleaned up, gathered their coolers and sweatshirts and the occasional lobster trap, tossed them into waiting dinghies, and motored to the pier. One such returnee, a young man working alone, pulled in not far from where she sat. Having seen enough of the others to know the drill, she scrambled to her feet, went to his boat, and took the line from him. She looped it once around the piling, and held it until he killed the outboard motor and jumped onto the dock. He unlooped the line and looped it again— securely, this time—so quickly that she had to laugh.

"How did you *do* that?" she asked, more an expression of admiration than a request for an answer. But the man untied the line and tied it more slowly, showing her the wrist motion as he went. She could see what he did. Didn't know if she could do it herself. But the method was there. "Thanks," she said sincerely.

He gave a small nod, slipped down into his boat, and began shifting his belongings to the dock.

"That camera work?" asked a voice.

Julia turned to see a man approaching. He wore glasses and a shirt splotched with green paint the color of his buoys. He was from one of the other boats she had watched. "It does."

He gestured that she should follow, and led her down another arm of the pier to where several men stood in a clump. When she arrived, they parted. Two lobster traps were on the dock, both badly damaged.

"We need pictures for evidence," said the man who had fetched her. His voice was quiet, but it held a certain strength.

"No seal made this kind of mess," said the father from before.

And his son. "It's man-made, made to look like seal."

Julia took one picture, then a second. She moved to a different angle for a third, moved in closer and took a fourth.

"See how the net inside's been torn?" asked the bespectacled man. "Can you get a picture of that?" While Julia did, he talked quietly, illustrating what he said with work-worn hands. "The net's called the head. See the funnel shape? Ideally, the lobster comes in through the wide part and gets the bait. When he can't go back, he goes through the next funnel into the other part of the trap, and he's stuck here. Problem is, with the net torn like that, he eats my bait, turns around, and walks out. These traps came up empty—no lobster, no bait. When do you think you can get us some pictures?"

"Tomorrow morning," Julia said, thinking to print them tonight. "Am I giving them to you?"

"No. Give them to Noah. They're just insurance, in case certain parties claim we're making this up, if you know what I mean."

Julia knew more than that. She knew, in that instant, why the men on the pier had been willing to talk with her. It had less to do with her clothing than it did with Noah Prine. Someone had seen them together the evening before—John Roman, certainly, perhaps others as well—and word had spread. She didn't know what they imagined. But they did assume she would be seeing him again, and soon.

With Molly's accusations still fresh, Julia almost denied it. Then she caught herself. She and Noah were friends in the most innocent of ways. She welcomed an excuse to see him.

Besides, she liked it when the lobstermen talked with her. It made her feel part of something. If her connection with Noah won her acceptance, it wasn't such a bad thing.

The *Leila Sue* was nowhere in sight when Julia left the harbor. She returned to the house and had dinner with Zoe, then printed out the pictures she'd taken. Having been up since dawn, she was asleep by nine.

Noah hauled traps late to compensate for lost days and, without a sternman, slower work. By the time he tied up at the slip and scrubbed down the boat, it was nearly ten. A few late diners were on the Grill deck, but they were finishing up. No matter that it was Friday night, with more tourists around than had been there the weekend before, most locals were home in bed. Saturday was a lobstering day. Hauling began with the sun, and the sun didn't sleep in. Acutely aware of that, Noah shouldered his things and started down the dock.

"About time," said John Roman, meeting him before he had gone far. "I won't ask why you're so late, but I gotta warn you. If you were out there shooting, you'd best bury the gun. They filed a complaint."

Noah paused. "Who filed a complaint?"

"The fruit guys. Someone's taking potshots at the hull of their boat, right at the waterline."

Noah smiled. "Did it sink?"

"Nah," said John with a slanted smile of his own. "They plugged up the holes and reported it to my buddy Charlie Andress over on West Rock. Charlie isn't stupid. He knows where Haber and Welk are dropping their lines, so he knows who's annoyed."

Noah started walking again. "What's he want you to do about it?"

John fell into step. "Warn you, I guess."

"Hey, it wasn't me."

"You were the one suggested it to the trap group."

Noah had nothing to hide. "I suggested it and would have done it in a minute, but the others voted it down. They chose knots, so I've been knotting. That's it. If there are holes in the hull, the bullet's from someone else's gun. Maybe it's the same gun that shot Artie."

"Uh, nope," John said, scratching the back of his head just below the line of his cap. "Don't think that's so. The Coast Guard called this afternoon. They found *that* gun in the wreck of *The Beast*."

Chapter 12

Having fallen asleep so early, Julia awakened again at dawn. Tiptoeing to the bathroom, she cleaned her face and teeth and brushed her hair, and put on her wedding band. Pulling on a sweatshirt and jeans, she slipped out of the house and headed for town.

She parked at the pier and turned off her headlights. Camera and tripod in hand, she wandered from spot to spot before choosing the landing at the top of the stairs to the Grill. She disabled the flash and adjusted the settings for dim light, as the manual had suggested she should. Extending the legs of the tripod, she screwed on the camera, opened the monitor, and took a look.

The harbor was quiet, the water as gentle as she had ever seen it. Lobster boats rocked at their moorings; those in slips seemed simply to rise and fall with each breath of the sea. Without the range of color that daylight would bring, the world was simplified. In this predawn dark, with the headlights of pickups raking the dock, the shadows of sleepy lobstermen carrying their gear, and lights going on in one wheelhouse after another, Julia found her drama.

She photographed from the distance, then zoomed in—zoomed back out when another piece of the harbor caught her eye. She captured men rowing to their boats, and those boats motoring out to sea.

As the minutes passed, the light bled from purple to blue to pink. The sky wasn't clear; clouds were strung out between bands of color. The play between the two was a subject in itself, evolving as she watched.

When she refocused on the dock, she saw Noah. He stood with his hands on his hips and was looking directly up at her. She straightened and smiled, feeling inordinately pleased when he left his gear there and headed her way. He wore jeans, a sweatshirt, and clogs. His hair was messed, as though he had just come from bed, which she realized he had. It was actually a lovely thought. He was an exceedingly virile man.

He trotted up the stairs and slowed at the last turn. Stopping with several steps left to go, he held the rail on each side. His face was relaxed, mouth gently curved. "Rick says you've been here awhile."

She was still smiling. Couldn't help it. She liked Noah Prine. His presence was a nice touch to the day. "Rick, huh? I wondered how you knew to look up. No one else has. It's like I'm hidden, which makes it even more fun taking pictures."

"Get anything good?"

"I don't know. I'm not taking the time to look."

"Isn't it early to be doing this kind of thing?"

"Not if you want to photograph the harbor coming to life."

"Are you always up at dawn?"

"In New York, never. Here, it could become a habit."

He paused and grew serious. "About the other night? I'm sorry if I caused a problem."

"The problem's not your doing."

"Did you work it out?"

She sighed. "If you're asking whether my daughter accepts that I'm a grown woman with a right to run *errands* with whomever I choose, I doubt it. In fairness, though, there are other issues involved." Not caring to go into the whole business with Monte, she reached into her camera bag and pulled out the photos she had printed. "These are for you."

"Thanks," he said with an appreciative smile. "I was told to expect them."

She smiled back, enjoying feeling useful. "The harbor grapevine?"

"Actually, the chief of police, who would love it if you could email these to him. Think you can?"

"Of course."

"That'd be great. It seems yesterday was a day of complaints," he tapped the photos against the rail, "like sabotaged traps. But John also got some news. They found a revolver in the wreck of *The Beast*. It was registered to Artie."

Julia's eyes widened in surprise. "To Artie? Was it the one that shot him?"

"They don't know for sure. They know that one cartridge is missing out of six, and that the caliber is consistent with the hole in Artie's shoulder. Problem is, if there was proof the gun was fired, the ocean washed it away. Short of finding a bullet lodged in debris from *The Beast*—something of a needle in a haystack—they can only speculate on whether he was shot by this gun. But there's another twist. Artie was under investigation by INS agents for smuggling illegal immigrants ashore."

"On *The Beast*?" Julia asked in disbelief. Forget stealth; a boat like that would announce itself everywhere it went.

But Noah said, "Artie has another boat. It's less pretentious, but it can handle itself a ways out from shore, where the transfer would be made. It has a cuddy cabin that could hold sixteen in a pinch. The INS isn't so much suspecting him of using that boat as of arranging for other boats to do the work."

"Illegal immigrants."

"Some used as mules."

Julia knew the term. "Carrying drugs?"

"Allegedly, enough to make it worth Artie's while. It'd go a long way toward explaining why he kept flying high after the market bombed."

"Could the shooting have been related to that?"

"They're assuming it. Problem is, they can't find a shooter. There's no other body with the wreck. There's no sign that anyone was with Artie at the house. A long-range rifle might do it, but not in that fog."

Julia was oddly relieved. In a voice barely above a

whisper, she said, "At least the gun wasn't Kim's. That would have pointed a finger at her." More hesitantly, she asked, "Is anyone suggesting she was involved?"

Noah, too, spoke quietly. "I didn't ask. Didn't want to put a bug in someone's ear. Far as I know, no one but us knows she wasn't on the *Amelia Celeste*."

"We don't *know*, really," Julia hedged, but Noah's eyes chided her, and she trusted those eyes. "Amazing, if she was on *The Beast*, that she survived the crash."

"Not so amazing," he remarked. "She could have been on the sun platform at the very back of the boat. Those platforms are flat. There's no railing around them. Sitting there, she'd have gone flying off at the first impact, even before the explosion."

"But how could she allow him to drive if he was shot?"

"He might have insisted."

"But surely when his heart gave out . . . ?"

"She wouldn't have known it unless she was watching him. What if she was facing the stern?"

"Would she have been able to drive *The Beast* herself?"

"Technically," Noah confirmed. "She grew up here. She knows boats. *The Beast* would have been bigger and louder, but the mechanics are the same."

"Do you think she was involved with the smuggling?"

He was slow in answering, clearly reluctant. "The guilt's so bad, she's not talking. Would a girl that young, with her whole life ahead of her, go totally mute because she survived an accident and others didn't? Maybe. But I keep thinking there has to be more to the story to explain the guilt she feels."

Julia thought what he said made total sense, which put her in a bind. Forget smuggling; she kept trying to muster hatred toward Kim for helping a married man cheat on his wife. Monte had had any number of Kims in his life. Julia and she should be worlds apart.

Still, she felt drawn to the girl. "Maybe it's time I visit the bluff again."

By the time she got there, it was late morning and the weather had turned. After those strips of color at dawn, the clouds had spread and thickened, bringing cool air and rain. Until Julia saw the small blue Honda by the ruins of the keeper's house, she wasn't even sure Kim would be there, and even then she had to search. She finally spotted the girl tucked in beside the porch of the house, where she was sheltered from vertical rain, though not the more slanted rain blown in on gusts of wind. She wore a yellow slicker, but the hood was down. Red hair, pale face, small hands—everything exposed was wet.

Tugging up the hood of her own slicker, Julia took an insulated bag from the seat of the car. The surf pounded and the wind had a bite, but the rain dampened both.

"Hi," she called, though she had no fear of startling Kim this time. The girl had been watching her from the moment she pulled in, and continued to watch as she approached. "I figured something warm was called for on a day like this." Several feet from Kim, she set down the bag, unzipped it, and pulled out a bag of cookies. "Fresh from my oven," she said, digging back into the pack and extracting, this time, two travel mugs filled with coffee. She offered one to Kim. "I figured if you were anything like my daughter, you'd take it with cream and sugar."

Kim said nothing. But she did take the mug. Opening the top, she took a drink. She held it in both hands, seeming to welcome its warmth.

Ignoring the rain, Julia sat down on the ground and opened the bag of cookies. "Still warm," she announced, cradling the bag in her palm and holding it out.

Kim took one, bit into it, and closed her eyes for an instant while she chewed. There was no mistaking pleasure on a face that was otherwise drawn. Julia wondered if she was eating anything at home. Huddled inside the slicker, she looked smaller than ever.

"Don't you want your hood up?" Julia asked and, of course, didn't get an answer. So she ate a cookie herself, between sips of her own coffee, and sat quietly for a time with her legs folded under her slicker. Kim finished one cookie and took a second, and still Julia didn't speak—and not by conscious design. Speaking seemed unnecessary. It was beautiful there on the bluff in the rain.

After a time, quite spontaneously, she said, "This is a special place. It's kind of like you're away from everything up here."

Kim nodded. When Julia passed her the bag of cookies, she took another.

"Have you been eating meals?" Julia asked.

Kim shrugged with her mouth.

"Not hungry?"

She shook her head.

"Keep thinking about the accident, huh?"

Kim took a drink of the coffee and tucked the mug in her lap.

For a time, Julia drank her own coffee and let the sound of the surf and the spatter of rain on the rocks fill the void. Then she said, "I don't know what it is about this island. I've felt something since the first time I was here. I was twelve then." When Kim seemed surprised, she said, "I was. Twelve. Zoe had just moved here, and my parents thought it'd be a good summer vacation place for my brothers and me. We used to come for a week or two at a time."

There had been rainy days then, too, and she hadn't minded at all. She remembered once sitting at the end of the town dock—a smaller dock, with fewer arms—and letting the rain soak her. She was wearing a bathing suit and must have been sixteen at the time, because she was a late bloomer yet remembered feeling sexy.

"Sixteen was a big summer for me," she reminisced. "That was when I became aware of men. Boys, actually, but they did look like men to me. Big Sawyer grows them rugged. I remember sitting in the rain in my wet bathing suit and wondering what the boys could see or if they even cared to look. I didn't have the nerve to look and see. I looked at them plenty at other times.

Even took pictures of them. Boy, did I love those tattoos. Do they still do that, the local boys—have that rope tattooed around their biceps?"

Kim nodded.

"That was a turn-on," Julia mused. "Where I grew up, only bad boys had tattoos. I thought they were the coolest thing." She lowered her voice—not that anyone was around to hear, but it just seemed like too personal a confession not to guard it somehow. "I kept the pictures all those years. The guys in them spawned many a fantasy."

She was embarrassed to think how recently she had indulged. Over the years, those fantasies had become a haven when things were rocky with Monte. In her dreams, Big Sawyer men embodied everything he didn't—honesty, loyalty, faithfulness. And muscles. *And* big-time sexuality. With Big Sawyer men, there would be no going through the motions. They would make love like they meant it. At least, she imagined they would.

She sighed, realized what she'd done, and looked quickly at Kim. The girl was watching her closely. She tried to recall if she had said the sex part aloud. That would have been embarrassing.

More neutrally, she said, "I actually brought the pictures with me. They were in my shoulder bag when the ferry went down. I got the bag back—they recovered it from the crash site—but I can't get myself to open it."

She had a thought. "Did you have anything with you that they might have recovered?"

Kim gave her head a quick shake.

"Just as well," Julia said. "Those things are from before. Everything after feels like a different life." She paused. "You don't feel that, do you." It wasn't exactly a question.

Kim's head shake was barely a spasm, but it told Julia what she wanted to know.

"If you could go anywhere," Julia tried, "anywhere in the world, where would you go?" She knew Kim wouldn't answer, but the question seemed important. "I think about that a lot."

Sipping her coffee, now only lukewarm, she looked out at the rain. Drips fell from the rim of her hood, but they weren't bothersome. Rather, they seemed part of this very separate piece of the world.

"It's so quiet here," she murmured, and it was. Waves hit the shore, wind hit the bluff, and rain hit the roof of the keeper's house, but in the midst of it all, there was a stillness. "This is a place removed. Can't think about the usual worries here. I understand why you come."

Actually, Julia realized, the sense of separateness applied to all of Big Sawyer. Perhaps that was what she felt when she had visited as a child. Worries had a hard time making the crossing from the mainland; in moments like this, they were spectral—not quite here, not quite gone, certainly nowhere near as ominous as they had been.

"I always imagined I could stay here forever," she said wistfully.

Kim shot her a horrified look.

"No?" Julia asked.

A short, sharp head shake said a definitive no.

"You'd leave?"

Kim nodded.

"Why?" she asked. Then, "Where would you go? What would you do? Who would you be?" She paused, then faced forward and gave a diffident snort. "I'm a fine one to be asking you that. Who would *I* be? I haven't a clue."

Julia wished she wanted to be a lawyer like her friend Jane. She wasn't too old to go to law school; she could see herself doing family law or even legal aid work, either of which would be time-consuming and rewarding enough to compensate for Monte's infidelity. Or she could become an accountant. She was good at math, and accountants were in demand. *Or* she could take a job in her friend's store; Charlotte was always begging her to.

If she did any of those things, she might craft a life that would allow her to leave her marriage intact. That would please Molly. It might even please Monte. It would surely please her parents.

But would it please *her*?

Shy of an answer, she spent Saturday afternoon alternating between the rabbits in the barn and her photo printer in the house, and spent Saturday evening with Zoe and her friends. These things kept her busy enough so that she didn't dwell on the fact that Molly was coming and going without a word. Sunday morning, when Ellen Hamilton called, desperate for help, Julia was more than happy to oblige.

Bearing a fresh batch of cookies, she drove to the weathered farmhouse on Dobbs Hill. Far from deserted this time, the front yard was filled with cars. A U-Haul was backed up to the door, and an army of friends were carting furniture and boxes from house to van.

This was moving day. The rain had moved farther offshore, and while the sky was filled with clouds, they were the palest of gray. Sun came and went. The air was warm. Julia wore shorts, a T-shirt, and Birks. She had a sweatshirt tied around her shoulders, and though she wasn't sure she would need it, it offered a kind of comfort. Leaving the car and approaching the porch, she felt a distinct knot in the pit of her stomach.

The girls were off in the side yard, playing with a woman Julia had met just the night before with Zoe. The woman waved; Julia waved back but continued on toward the house. She had barely reached it when Ellen rushed out. Sandy hair flying, she looked frantic.

"Thank you so much for coming," she said, grasping Julia's arm and pulling her toward the yard. "Deanna's been with the kids, but she has to leave, and the rest of us are trying to get things loaded so that I can make the noon ferry, and the girls just love you." Even as she spoke, Vanessa broke away and, little legs wheeling, ran toward them. Halfway there, she stumbled and fell, but Julia barely had time to start forward when the child was up and running again. Grasping Julia's leg, she tipped her head back and grinned.

Julia scooped her up. "How's my little sweetie?"

"Good," Vanessa said and curled an arm around her neck. "D'ya bring cookies?"

"I did," Julia said, adding more quietly to Ellen, "Go back to work. We'll be fine."

Ellen didn't need further encouragement. Deanna lingered to talk with Julia until she absolutely had to run, at which point Julia took the girls across the meadow, farther from the hubbub at the house. Sitting in the tall grass, she gave them cookies, told them stories, and played little games with them. She even asked questions about the move, which they answered in a way that suggested they had come to their own understanding of it and were okay.

That was before Ellen came looking for them, at which point Vanessa, who had been sitting snug against Julia's leg, wrapped that little arm again around her neck, so tightly now that Julia had no choice but to lift her. Annie stayed close, as well.

"We're ready to go," Ellen said, forcing an enticing smile for the girls. "The ferry's waiting for us." She held out a hand to Annie. "All set?"

Nodding docilely, the child took Ellen's hand. Following them, carrying Vanessa, Julia had a lump in her throat. She doubted the girls were old enough to realize that this part of their life was done. But they did sense something of the moment's import. She could tell by the way Annie held back a little when they approached the car with the U-Haul hooked behind it, and Vanessa's arm clutched her neck as though she would never let go.

The lump in Julia's throat grew larger as longtime

Walsh friends took turns saying good-bye to the girls. Some had tears in their eyes, others couldn't speak, simply gave kisses and hugs. They had known these girls since birth. Sending them off to a new life in Akron was like pouring salt on the wound of the loss of Evan, Jeannie, and Kristie.

Annie climbed into the backseat of Ellen's car, but when Julia tried to settle Vanessa there, she refused to go. Both hands held Julia's neck now. Small sounds of protest came from the child's throat.

Wanting to make the leave-taking as easy on the three of them as possible, Julia offered to drive Vanessa to the dock. The little girl played with the long end of the seat belt the whole way, weaving it here and there, twisting it and tying it in ways that took Julia long minutes to undo when they arrived, but the extra time allowed Ellen to drive the car with its trailer onto the waiting ferry, before returning for Vanessa.

Vanessa wasn't going. Winding both arms and both legs around Julia now, she started to cry. Ellen tried prying her limbs free. Julia did the same. The more they tried, the harder Vanessa held on and the louder she cried.

The waterfront was crowded with people. The deck of the Harbor Grill held Sunday brunchers; tourists who had come in on the ferry were just beginning to wander toward Main Street; lobstermen were spending their enforced Sunday off by doing work on their boats. Vanessa's cries were shrill enough to draw eyes right and left, but what was there to do? Julia crooned soft words of encouragement to the child until her own throat closed up, at which point she was relegated to stroking the little girl's warm hair as she struggled to pass her to Ellen. Vanessa's mouth was open in screams of protest; large tears streamed down her cheeks. She climbed Julia's body with startling strength. Julia's heart positively ached.

In the end, a small child was no match for two healthy adults. They managed to transfer her, twisting and fighting, to Ellen's arms, and Ellen managed to get her aboard the ferry with Annie moments before the ramp was drawn up, and still Vanessa held out her arms to Julia, screeching now, *"Nononooo!"*

It was when *Nononooo!* turned to *Mamamama!* with little hands opening and closing, trying to grasp what she desperately wanted but was surely losing, that Julia pressed a hand to her mouth and began to cry softly herself. Once started, the tears wouldn't stop—not when the ferry pulled away, nor when its engine drowned out the sound of the child's screams, reducing her to a mimed image of hysteria, nor even when Ellen carried her to the front of the vessel and out of Julia's sight.

Sobbing quietly, Julia watched until the ferry was out of the harbor, on open ocean and gone. She moved her hand from her mouth to her heart, hugged herself with the other arm, and still she felt bereft. She pressed her lips together in an attempt to regain control; when that didn't work, she simply took sunglasses from the top of her head and put them on. Crossing to a bench at the shore end of the dock, she sank down—and all the while, quietly, she wept.

"Mom?" Molly asked, coming down to the bench beside Julia.

Julia kept her eyes on the sea and her fingers hard against her lips.

"Did you know them?"

"Enough," Julia managed, but couldn't say more. She didn't know where the tears had come from and why they refused to stop. She wasn't Vanessa's mother. She had spent a total of three, maybe four hours with the child.

Vanessa's tears were more understandable. From the very first, the little girl had gravitated to Julia. Too young to understand what had happened to her own parents, she had sensed a maternal something and gone for it.

Julia's tears, though? She wasn't a novice at separation. With Molly her only child, she had felt it more keenly than most, but she had learned to accept what had to be. Molly had to go to kindergarten. She had to sleep over at the houses of friends, had to eventually spend the summer away at camp. These experiences were as crucial to her education as schoolwork, and there was that, too. Molly had to go off to college. Julia missed her terribly. But she knew that all these things were in Molly's best interest.

"What can I do?" Molly whispered now.

Nothing, Julia said with the shake of her head.

"I was just stopping by at the Grill, but I'm not working until tonight. Want me to drive you home?"

Julia shook her head. She couldn't leave the harbor yet.

Her daughter sat for a minute. Then, sounding embarrassed, she asked, "Are you going to just . . . *sit* here?"

That embarrassment hit Julia the wrong way. Wiping tears from her cheeks, she looked at Molly through her dark glasses and said brokenly, "Yes. I'm going to just sit here." The words were barely out when new tears began to fall.

Molly straightened, then slumped, then swiveled on her bottom to face forward, and it hit Julia that her daughter didn't know what to do. She had never seen Julia like this. She didn't know what Julia needed—remarkably, didn't think to put an arm around Julia's shoulder or even a hand on her hand as Julia had done so many times when the tables were turned. But that was it—the tables had always been turned. Julia was the giver of comfort, not the recipient. Molly had no idea how to handle this new turn of events—and that was one more reason for Julia to cry. If children learned from the example their parents set, either Molly was failing the test, or Julia had failed it on the teaching end.

"Well, then," Molly said unsurely, "if you want to stay here, I'll leave. I'll be hanging around the Grill. If you change your mind and want me to do something, come in and get me, okay?"

Julia nodded, but she didn't watch Molly walk away. Rather, she put her elbows on her thighs, pressed her quivering mouth to laced fingers, and closed her eyes. All she had to do was to picture Vanessa Walsh reaching out so futilely, and she began crying again. There was loss here, but it didn't stop with Vanessa. Julia cried for the failure of her marriage, for wasted years of heartache and hope. She cried for her life in New York, because, though it was all she really knew, she didn't want it anymore.

"Hey," came a low male voice. She didn't have to open her eyes to know whose hand was holding her knee. She covered it with one of her own. His warmth was a balm.

"That was a rough good-bye," he said.

She nodded and wiped at her cheeks. "It just hit me," she murmured nasally. "I don't know why."

"Sure you do," he said in that same low voice. "You're sensitive, and you're smart. You know what that little girl's lost."

She sniffled and rubbed her nose with the back of her hand.

"Need a tissue?" he asked and, as though summoning a waiter, raised his voice. "Tissue!" Seconds later, he gave her a fresh one.

She blotted her eyes and blew her nose—all one-handed, because somewhere along the way his hand on her knee had turned up and their fingers had linked, and she wasn't breaking that contact. She didn't care if people saw; she needed a friend, and he was there.

So was his dog, sitting quietly, facing Julia on her left as Noah was on her right. "Lucas is staring again," she whispered.

Noah whispered back, "He's never seen anyone as beautiful before."

"Beautiful? Omigod. I'm a mess."

"He doesn't see it that way."

Julia took some solace in that. Never one for public displays, she figured that anyone else passing by must think her a head case. But she wasn't ready to leave.

"It's more than just Vanessa," she said, her chin in her palm, her face inches from his. "It's every frightening little thing. We think a child is worse off because she doesn't understand the extent of what's happening, but an adult *does* understand, and *that* makes it worse. *Plus,* an adult has the responsibility of acting—planning—moving—doing." She met Noah's gaze. "I'd love to sit back and let someone else take responsibility for my life."

"Right now?" He smiled. "Okay. Are you hungry?"

"No," she said, then changed that to "Yes." Coming off a crying jag, she shouldn't have felt like eating, but there was a definite hole in her stomach. She assumed part of it, at least, was from hunger.

"Are you a vegetarian?" he asked.

"No."

"Then we're golden." He raised his voice again, this time along with a finger aimed at the food cart near the line of parked cars. "Four hot, Alfie—mustard and relish—and two cold."

Julia downed every last bit of two hot dogs with mustard and relish, and a tall glass of fresh-squeezed lemonade. She couldn't remember when she'd had a better lunch. She couldn't remember when she'd had a more companionable one, though neither she nor Noah said much. It was enough that he was with her there on the bench, watching the life of the harbor for an hour that Sunday.

Molly was livid. Julia could see it the instant she pulled up at Zoe's stone farmhouse and spotted her daughter on the front steps. She had barely climbed from the SUV when Molly rose, then stood stiffly still, grasping the railing behind her. Between the look on her face and the shortness of her hair—still startling to Julia—she was clearly a rebel with a cause.

Julia tried a smile as she approached the steps. "I thought you were hanging around the harbor until it was time for work."

"Well, that was the plan," Molly said with disdain, "then you kept sitting there with him and people were commenting, and I couldn't bear it a minute longer."

"People were commenting?" Julia asked. "Commenting about what?"

"About what is going on between you two," Molly said, giving each word due weight. "About the fact that Noah hasn't been interested in anyone for ages. About the fact that you're wearing a wedding band, and if he's interested in you, he's playing with fire. They were asking *me* if you and Dad were separated."

"Whoa. Noah and I were sitting on a bench," Julia argued quietly. "*Sitting* on a bench."

"He wasn't sitting. He was kneeling down in front of you, close as could be. You were holding hands. Your heads were together. Anyone watching would have reached the same conclusion."

"I was crying, Molly. I was upset. Didn't those people see what happened with Vanessa Walsh?"

"That was beside the point," Molly said.

Julia didn't think so at all. "It tore me apart to see her screeching that way—brought everything back, everything to do with the accident. I was upset, and I was crying. Noah held my hand—the way you might have," she said with a dare in her voice. She remembered the hurt she had felt that for all their closeness, Molly hadn't been able to reach out. "That's how people give comfort to those they know and like and care about."

"But you're married to someone else."

"Molly, *listen* to me," Julia said with more force now. Zoe had come to the screen door, but Julia kept her eyes on her daughter. "Noah Prine is a friend. I have no intention of poisoning that just because some people have small minds. I don't want you to be one of those people. Please, Molly. Support me here. Give me the benefit of the doubt."

To her credit, Molly looked torn. "It's just that you're acting so *strange*. You're staying here, even when you know that Dad's doing things he shouldn't in New York. You haven't even called him."

Julia might have said that she had, that they had talked while Molly was at work. The girl would never know if it was true or not.

But Julia wasn't a liar. "We've emailed. I've sent him pictures."

"He doesn't need pictures," Molly cried. "He needs *you*."

Solemn, Julia asked, "What about what I need? Isn't it important that I need this time away? I know it's upsetting to you, and it's upsetting to me, too. But I need this time, Molly. I *need* this *time*."

A car approached. Julia had no sooner heard its engine when Molly's eyes flew past her. A dusty red wagon came up the drive and pulled in beside Julia's car.

"That's our taxi," Zoe said, coming out onto the porch. "Who . . . ?" She stopped talking when the back door opened and a man climbed out. Not as tall as he had been in his heyday, nor as slim, he wore a tieless business shirt and pressed slacks. His thinning gray hair showed its share of scalp, his oval face its share of doubt.

"Omigod," Julia cried. "Dad!" She started forward, heart pounding as she searched the backseat for her mother. Janet wasn't there, but her disappointment was short-lived. The idea that her father had come through for her after all was enough to warm her heart.

Jogging to the car, she gave him a hug. "You should have told us you were coming," she scolded when she drew back. "I'd have picked you up."

"I didn't know it myself until I got here. It was a last-minute thing." He held up a hand, clearly agitated. "I've been patient. I sat back and followed her lead, but when she goes on and on about Zoe, and on and on about you—a man can only take so much. I kept telling her to listen to herself. Had she done that, she wouldn't have been pleased. But she doesn't listen. She simply says what she feels and assumes that it's the only correct way to view things, and, quite honestly, I've had it."

Julia felt something turn inside. "What do you mean?"

"Know when the last time was we took a vacation? If you do, refresh my memory, because the only times we go away are when she can tie it into work. It's not much of a vacation for me, when she's at meetings half the time. I think it's wonderful that she's so successful; she's done good things—I can't deny her that. Finally, though, I have to look at my own life. I need a break."

Julia could certainly identify with that. "A break from?"

"Work. Baltimore. And, yes, your mother. She hasn't been much fun to be with lately."

"Have you *left* her?" Molly asked, joining them, a horrified look on her face. When she angled that look at Julia, it held an accusatory edge.

"I'm here, and she's there," George said belligerently. "She needs time alone to think about the effect she has on people, and I need a vacation." He produced a thin smile. "I thought, what better place to be than with my daughter and granddaughter." To Julia, he said, "You always know the right things to say in situations like these."

Slowly and painfully, Julia absorbed the fact that

her father hadn't come to comfort her at all. Quite the opposite. He had come so that she could comfort *him*. And why not? She had certainly done it enough in the past. *Give her time, Dad, she'll calm down. She's so used to solving problems that when she can't, she gets frustrated and says things she doesn't mean. How about I take a train down and meet you for dinner, and Mom will be in a better mood by the time she gets home.*

Her mother never went to Julia with problems. Her father was something else. He wouldn't think of seeing a counselor, when Julia played the role so well.

Right now, though, she wasn't up for being a marriage counselor. She didn't want to deal with her parents' problems. She had far more pressing problems of her own.

Wary, she asked, "You're staying on Big Sawyer? For how long?"

He shrugged. "How long are *you* staying? I'll stay that long."

A day or two, she could have handled. Maybe even three. But an indefinite stay, with him tied to her own plans? The thought of it was enough to crowd her chest, making her want to gasp for air. What was unfolding here was *not* what she'd had in mind when she had planned her own trip. *None* of it was what she'd had in mind.

Fighting a rising panic, she was searching for words when Molly asked George, "Where will you stay? Mom and I are in Zoe's guest rooms." She paused, then offered a reluctant, "We could always double up."

"I'll stay in town," George said, with Molly quickly shaking her head.

"There are no places, unless you rent a house, and my boss was just saying everything decent is booked. Next weekend's the Fourth. From now to Labor Day, forget it."

George was undaunted. "Then Zoe'll make a call and find a friend with a spare bedroom. I'll get something."

Julia was still struggling with the larger picture— her father coming and going with his problems with her mother, Molly coming and going with her problems with Julia, and Julia feeling hemmed in by the detritus of her life—not to mention Zoe, who would have feelings about George being around, and whom would Zoe confide in? Julia, of course.

Suddenly, there was only one choice. "Stay here," Julia told her father. "Take my room. I'll find another place to stay."

Molly turned on her. "Where?"

Julia didn't care where. She only knew that she wanted out. "I could stay at the Walsh place," she said. "Ellen left several beds. I could also stay at Tony Hammel's photo camp. There are possibilities."

Zoe joined them, protesting, "But you were here first."

George added, "I never intended to displace you."

"Things have grown crowded here," Julia said. "I need time alone. I'll be back to help with the rabbits, Zoe. I want to do that. But this is my vacation. I need space."

"What about us?" Molly cried. "We came here to be with you."

Julia felt a moment's guilt—but only because that was what she had been conditioned to feel. Taking a breath, she let the moment pass and eyed her daughter levelly. "Would you have come here if the job in Paris had worked out? I doubt it, and I'd have been the first to tell you not to come." She turned to her father. "Would you have come here if you and Mom hadn't argued? Honestly?" Of course he wouldn't have come.

"But we were arguing about *you*," he reasoned.

Again, there was a moment's guilt, but this, too, passed. She wasn't a little girl, and she didn't need to be taught the meaning of responsibility; she was an adult who had more than paid her family dues.

Feeling remarkably resolute, even emboldened, she said, "If that's supposed to make me feel guilty, so that I'll turn around and do what will make all of you feel best, I'm sorry. It doesn't. And I won't. I've carried the weight of family responsibilities for more years than I care to count." She paused but didn't try to fight back the indignation that rose in her. "I deal with everyone else's problems. Who deals with mine?"

Chapter 13

Thirty minutes later, Julia was on her way, and at no point in those thirty minutes did she waver, though the pressure was fierce. Her father kept saying that he hadn't meant to cause a stir; Molly kept saying that Julia really could share her room; Zoe kept saying—albeit for Julia's ears alone—that she wanted Julia, not George, in her house.

All the hovering made Julia more determined than ever to find her own place. If having survived the accident meant that she had been chosen to restructure her life, she couldn't think of a better step than declaring her independence. She packed up her new clothes, plus a bagful of Zoe's things. She packed up her camera equipment and printer. She was actually driving away when she stopped, backed up to the barn, and ran in for the pocketbook that the divers had recovered. The leather had dried to a motley tan and was nowhere near as soft as it had been, but there were things inside that she wanted.

More to the point, there were things inside that she didn't want others to see. Tossing the bag into the SUV, she closed the hatch, slid in behind the wheel, and left the farmhouse behind.

And *still* she didn't waver. She actually felt free— and, yes, that brought twinges of guilt. She loved Zoe. She loved her father. Lord knew, she loved Molly. Loving herself—respecting her own needs— was something important and new.

Heading first for the harbor, she parked at the end of the pier, walked down the dock, saw that Noah wasn't on his boat, and returned to her car. A short while later, she drove up Main Street, turned left on Spruce, and cruised slowly past one fisherman's cottage after another until she spotted his blue truck. Pulling in behind it, she was barely out of the car when Lucas loped up and escorted her down the short walk. Passing bushes still redolent with lilacs, though the blooms were fading, she gave a hearty knock on the weathered frame.

Noah opened the door—and for the first time, remembering how Molly had gone on about heads together, hands held, and Noah not having been with anyone for a while, Julia did waver. He seemed taller than before, perhaps a fact of the darkness behind him. He wore jeans and a T-shirt with the sleeves torn off. She saw broad shoulders and firm biceps.

High on one of those biceps was a ropy tattoo. Glimpsing it, she felt a deep burning inside, something she hadn't felt in a while—not for Monte, nor for anyone else. She thought of herself as attractive, not sexy—probably because Monte thought of her as attractive, not sexy. If he found her sexy, the reasoning went, he wouldn't have strayed.

Noah smiled through the screen and glanced at Lucas. "What'd I say? He knows beauty. How're you doin'?"

"Not bad," she said. "Actually, not great. I have a *huge* favor to ask. I know this is a major imposition on my part. It's truly taking advantage of the fact that you and I just happened to be on the *Amelia Celeste* at the same time, and after the kindness you showed me earlier, I feel guilty asking for *anything*, but it's like, when the problem arose, I could only think of one answer. Of course, I couldn't tell Zoe and Molly and my dad what it was—"

"Your dad's here?"

She nodded. "Showed up a little while ago, right out of the blue, and suddenly there's all this family at Zoe's, and I really want none of it. I packed up my things and drove away—just like that. I know it's something I need to do, but I'm not used to acting on impulse, so now I'm in a bind, which is why I'm here on your doorstep. Please feel free to say no. This is the first place I've stopped, and if you're uncomfortable with this, I'm sure there are other options—"

Shhhh, said the finger he put against his lips.

She stopped talking.

"Are you looking for a place to stay?" he asked.

Apologetically, she nodded.

"Want my hill house?"

Besides, he liked her. She was different from the other women he knew. She had a mind of her own and could argue with him quite effectively, but she didn't pretend to have all the answers. *That* was refreshing, after Sandi.

She was also married, which made her safe. He didn't have to worry about impressing her, didn't have to worry about whether she liked the island, whether she would want to stay, whether she could possibly survive without culture and comfort. He didn't have to apologize for being early to bed and early to rise. He didn't have to dress up.

Since she was married, nothing could happen. Sure, people talked. But the ones he cared about knew how he felt about carrying on with married women. He didn't do it.

Lucas, of course, was totally smitten, but Lucas was a dog. What did he know?

Julia Bechtel was a friend. That made it okay for Noah to loan her the hill house and outfit it with food. He felt good doing it, actually felt *terrific* doing it. From the minute he opened the door and brought in the first of her things, the place felt warmer. The fact that she seemed to love the house made him feel even better.

She hadn't brought much with her. They emptied her car in no time, had the food put away, her clothes hung, her printer hooked up to his computer so that she could print and email pictures to her heart's delight. Overriding her protests, he even installed her photo-editing software, so that she could play and ex-

She took a quick breath. "Desperately."

"It's yours."

She exhaled in relief. "Are you sure?"

"Positive. I won't be going there, not with the boy coming tomorrow."

"I know it's where you keep your computer. Tell me when you want to use it, and I'll take off for however long. It's just such a perfect location, so quiet and out of the way. I need to think. I'll be able to do it there. I have a cell phone, so I won't rack up a bill on your line. And I'm neat. No mess. I'll take good care of the place."

"I'm not worried."

"Truly?" she asked.

He nodded and smiled. "There's no one I'd rather have in my bed."

Julia laughed in delight. Yes, she heard Molly warning her about the way it looked and what people were saying, but she figured Noah knew of the talk. If he wasn't bothered, she wasn't either.

"Thanks," she said, grinning still. She started to turn, paused, looked at Lucas and then at Noah again. "Um, maybe you can remind me how to get there?"

Noah did one better. He led the way in the truck. He stopped en route at the island store for food basics—which, against Julia's protests, he insisted on paying for but, as he saw it, she was doing him favor. At a time when he felt the loss of his father, th challenge of his son, and an acute need to do som thing to justify his having been spared death hims she was there. Helping her felt right.

periment. Then, since it was only four, he led her through the woods surrounding the house, over barely discernible trails and along crumbling stone walls, to spots that he knew—the ruins of an old cellar, an assembly of thick birches with peeling white bark, a boulder with a view. When they returned, it was nearly six, so he uncorked a Chardonnay and sliced French bread, while she washed red grapes and warmed a wedge of Brie. They took it all out to the bedroom deck, sat on lounge chairs, and enjoyed the serenity.

Noah didn't know whether it was the wine, the most pleasant social experience he'd had in years, or simply the fact that with Ian due in sixteen hours, he couldn't procrastinate any longer, but when he finally returned to his parents' house, he was motivated. No matter that dusk approached. For the first time since he had left for the mainland with his father that fateful Tuesday, he raised the shades, opened the windows, and aired out the house. He stripped both his bed and Hutch's, and washed the sheets. He made room in his closet for Ian's things, put his own things in Hutch's room, put Hutch's things in boxes so quickly that he couldn't dwell on the loss. Deeming half of the food in the refrigerator to be either moldy or spoiled, he tossed it out, wiped down the shelves in preparation for fresh food the next morning. He scrubbed the bathroom. He washed the towels, then his own clothes. He replaced a bulb that had blown out in one of the living room lamps. He cleaned ashes from the woodstove.

By the time he was done, it was nearly midnight,

and he was tired. But he had a sense of accomplishment. The house was clean and smelled fresh. It wouldn't embarrass him in front of Ian. Lying on newly washed sheets in his parents' bed—now his own—with the familiar tang of salt air filtering in through the screen and skimming his body, he felt more human than he had in days.

He thought of his parents then, and the years they had slept in this room, in this bed. They had been happy together. He remembered shared glances and brief touches, nothing obvious, but enough to suggest an intimate meeting of minds. He truly did find solace thinking of them together again.

On that reassuring note, he fell into a sound sleep. He didn't even wake at the usual predawn hour that lobstering demanded, but slept through until eight when, startled, he jumped out of bed into a rush of last-minute chores, raced to the store and back, filled the fridge and the cupboard, mowed the lawn, gave Lucas a bath.

With everything done, he thought of Julia at his hill house, totally accepting—even admiring—of him. Buoyed, he whistled for Lucas, climbed into the truck, and set off to meet Ian in Portland.

Julia slept late, in part because that was what vacations were for, but more likely because she had been so late going to bed the night before. One thing had followed the next—a short call to Zoe telling her where she was staying, a similar message left for Monte, a certain amount of unpacking, lots of trips up and down the stairs, poking around, familiarizing herself with what was where and how to use it all, and then going out on the deck to see the play of moon and stars between a shifting veil of clouds. By the time she had washed up, set her wedding band on the bathroom counter, and pulled back that simple white bedspread, she was flush with adrenaline as she relived the events of the day, swinging from disbelief to pride, to excitement, to fear.

Moreover, slipping between Noah's sheets, she was acutely aware of . . . slipping between Noah's sheets. That thought was a lovely distraction from the rest, though no more calming.

Eventually, it struck her as she lay in that bed that she had never, ever lived alone. She had gone straight from her family home to a dormitory with two roommates, and from there to life with Monte. Yes, he took business trips, but she didn't call being left behind living alone. This was living alone. For as long as she stayed, there would be no one else using the bed, no one else using the bathroom, no one else drinking coffee from the first pot of the day.

For now, that felt right. It felt like the kind of new experience she was meant to have after the accident. For the long run? She didn't know. And that raised the dilemma of what to do with her future, which was truly what kept her awake until three in the morning.

She fell asleep with no solution in sight, and bolted up once to the vision of a purple bow bursting out of fog. Short of breath and shaking, she was a minute realizing where she was and quite a few more before she calmed. But sleep did return.

When she awoke next, it was after nine and the bedroom was bright. Beyond the windows, a filmy haze made something mystical of the blues and greens that would have otherwise delineated sky, sea, and woods. Propped on all those pillows that she had admired the Thursday before, she let herself float in the haze awhile—so mesmerized that she didn't hear a car approach at the front of the house. Nor, apparently, did she hear the first sound of the doorbell. It was only when the ring came in a series of short, urgent trills that she realized someone had come.

Assuming it was Noah, she slipped on a robe and ran up the stairs. She was startled to open the door and find a visibly guarded Molly—which should have brought back the angst of the previous day, but didn't. Feeling instant pleasure, Julia broke into a smile.

"Molly!" she said, catching the girl's hand. "You have to see this." Drawing her into the house, she pulled her down the stairs and onto the deck. "Isn't this *the* best view?"

Molly looked at it awhile before turning to Julia. "It's really nice," she said quietly. "So's the house. Zoe said it's Noah's."

"Yes." Julia put both hands on Molly's shoulders. "Okay. You just showed up here unannounced. Was he here?"

"No."

"Do you see any evidence that he was here?"

"You're not wearing your wedding band."

"I never wear it at night. You know that. Try again. Any evidence he was here?"

"I haven't looked."

"Trust me," Julia said gently but firmly. "He wasn't. He doesn't live here, which is the only reason I can. It's the perfect place for me. Don't you think so?"

"I don't know what to think," Molly answered, losing all semblance of composure. She seemed completely rattled. "Everything's always been the same, and suddenly it isn't. You're here and Dad's there, and now Grampa's here and Gram is there. Of all the people in my life, I thought my family was the most together. What's wrong with Daddy? Doesn't he *know* you're the best woman he could ever have?"

Julia was touched. Inside her, a raw little spot scabbed over. Wrapping her arms around Molly, she held her—until Molly drew back, wanting an answer. "Doesn't he? What is he *looking* for?"

"Adulation? Adventure? Novelty? *Risk?* I don't know, Molly. All I know is that I'm really angry at him right now." It had been one thing when Julia was the only one hurt by his affairs. But Molly had been hurt now, too. That changed things.

"I called him this morning," Molly said. "It's the first time we've talked since that night, but I wanted him to know how upset you are. He says there's nothing going on with that woman."

Molly might believe that, but Julia couldn't.

"He says she was an old friend whose husband had locked her out of the house. She may be. I didn't see them *doing* anything. I told him you were staying alone here, so if he wanted to come, you'd have privacy."

"You didn't."

"I did, and he said he might."

Julia was appalled. "But I don't want him here. This is my time, my place, and it's my business. You had no right suggesting he come."

"He's my father—"

"You're grown, Molly. You may spend a few more vacations at home, but then you're out in your own place with your own friends. I'm the one who'll be with your father. I'm the one who has to decide what I want."

"He swore nothing happened," Molly insisted.

"This time?" Julia asked. "Or the one before that, or the one before that?"

"Can't you forgive him?"

"The issue isn't so much forgiveness as trust. But there's so much more going on here, Molly. This isn't only about my marriage. What I said last night, about filling everyone else's needs? I meant that. And I'm not blaming your father or your grandparents or you. I could have refused. But you all needed me, and I wanted to be needed. There's a pleasure in that, too."

"But not anymore. Is that what you're saying?"

"I'm saying that I've been defining myself in terms of other people—Monte's wife, Molly's mother, Janet's daughter. I don't have an identity of my own."

"Do you need one?"

"I think so."

"Suddenly? Now? Because of the accident?"

Julia settled against the rail, turning her back on the view. "Most of the people who died were younger than me. They had so much ahead of them. So here I am, spared. For what? Why? There has to be a purpose, something that goes beyond what I've done so far in my life. And it's not an activist thing—like I'm supposed to try to change the world. It has to do with me. With making me a whole person."

"I think you're a whole person," Molly said.

"Well, I don't. So maybe that's what's missing in my life. Maybe I don't *value* myself enough." The words were familiar. It took her a minute to realize that she had heard them in therapy years before. At the time, she hadn't paid them much heed. Change was painful. The devil she knew was better than the one she did not.

And now?

"Come back to Zoe's?" Molly asked pleadingly.

Julia looked around. "This is a good place for me right now. You can visit whenever you want."

"Can I stay here?"

Hel-lo, Julia nearly cried. After all her talk about needing space?

Slipping an elbow through her daughter's, she guided her up the stairs. "I want you at Zoe's."

"I want you there, too," Molly said, and launched in with, "What is going on between Grandpa and Gram? And what's with Grandpa and Zoe? They had zero to say to each other. I mean, really impolite. I wanted to make them blueberry-stuffed French toast, but Zoe insisted on cooking, and she wouldn't even sit and eat with us, just kept busy at the stove. Grandpa went back and forth between me and the *Wall Street Journal.* I think I'll call Gram."

"Margaret Marie, do not do that. Let your grandparents work out their own problems. Do you hear?"

* * *

It was good advice, if only Julia could have followed it. *Not your business,* Julia told herself. *Can't carry everyone else's baggage when you're trying to carry your own,* she argued.

But her mother was her mother, a woman whose husband of forty-odd years had not only walked out on her, but had taken refuge in the home of the *other* woman, the one with whom he'd once had an affair. Julia would have had to be made of stone not to feel for her.

Moreover, she was haunted by what Zoe had said about mother and daughter being alike. Julia didn't want to think of herself as opting out when the going got rough.

She called Janet at work. To her credit, Janet came on right away, but that was the extent of her concession.

"Yes, Julia," she said in a businesslike tone.

Julia felt the familiar stomach-jumping. "Are you okay?"

"I'm fine."

"You know Dad's here with me."

"Well, if that's where he's gone, that's where he's gone."

"Are you okay with that?"

"He's a big boy, Julia. He can go where he wants."

"That wasn't my question."

"No, but apparently what I'm *okay* with doesn't matter anymore. I was not okay with your going up there. You went anyway, and now your father has followed. If you really want to know, I think he's being as irresponsible with regard to me as you are being with regard to your husband. Neither of you has any business being there."

"To the contrary," Julia said, because they were avoiding the issue. "We're here because Zoe's here."

There was the briefest pause, then a dry, "So she is. I have a meeting now, Julia. Have a good day."

Ian's plane was late, which meant that Noah had an hour to sit at the airport with nothing to do but think of having his son for a whole three weeks and wonder what they would do, whether they would get along, what they would talk about, whether they could connect. Sandi was right: Noah had been an absentee father. He was going to have to deal with Ian's resentment, along with a mutual unfamiliarity. In ten years, they hadn't spent any significant amount of time together. For all practical purposes, they were strangers.

Noah wanted to change that. He had three weeks in which to do it—three weeks, and precious little understanding of how to go about it. Lobstering he could do. When it came to fathering, though, he was in a thick 'o fog without a horn. Times had changed since he was seventeen. His father's method of fathering wouldn't work with Ian. The problem was, Noah didn't know what method would.

Feeling decidedly adrift, he rose and stood at the window until the jet finally landed and taxied toward the terminal. He moved back then, hit by a wave of apprehension. He had failed as a husband, had failed as a father. No matter that he had greater reason to succeed with Ian now. Who was to say he wouldn't fail again?

Beyond the window, the plane loomed at the jet-port. By the time the jetway door opened, Noah's heart was beating faster. Forget how Ian would act; he wasn't even sure how Ian would *appear*. The last time they had been together was for an overnight in New York during the Easter weekend, little more than two months before. Ian had been presentable enough, wearing slacks, a shirt, and trendy shoes that would carry him through dinner at a decent restaurant, an evening of theater, and a stay at the Ritz on Central Park. Granted, his shirt had refused to stay tucked, the slacks were too long over the shoes, and his hair was *way* too long. He was good-looking enough to get away with it all, partic-ularly when he smiled, which he did for waiters, cab-bies, and hotel clerks, though never for Noah.

While in Manhattan, Noah had planned a visit to the Museum of Natural History, thinking to share his love of nature with his son. Ian had been bored.

The first few passengers emerged. Tall enough for a clear view, Noah kept his eyes on the door. More and more passengers came through, until he guessed that the majority of those who had been aboard had deplaned. The crowd thinned. Two more passengers came out, then a trio of teenaged girls. He began to worry, actually began to get *angry,* because if Ian had missed the flight and Sandi hadn't called—Noah could have made *far* bet-ter use of his morning, most notably hauling traps.

Then Ian appeared. He wore the latest in faded

jeans and a logo T-shirt, and his hair was shorter, had blond streaks, and stood straight up on top, but those good looks remained. He added a cocky saunter when the trio of girls slowed and called back to him before moving on. Friends from Baltimore? It didn't matter. Noah, who hadn't thought Ian was old enough to grin the way he grinned at those girls, actually felt a moment of sheer male pride. His son was a man, or at least was getting there fast.

When Ian spotted him, the grin died—and still Noah's pride remained. Ian was a young man with a savvy way about him. When Noah had been seventeen, he hadn't had that way about him. Kids nowadays grew up faster. Or maybe it was that kids on the mainland grew up faster.

"Hey," Noah called as he strode forward. He put out a hand to shake, but when Ian's met it, Noah impulsively drew him into a hug. It wasn't a smooth thing, and Ian's stiffness didn't help. He actually looked annoyed when Noah set him back.

But Noah wasn't sorry for the hug, not for a minute. He hadn't planned it, didn't even know he'd needed it. In lieu of words, though, it said something. Ian was his son, flesh of his flesh. That fact demanded acknowledgment. No, he wasn't apologizing for the hug.

"You look great, Ian," he said.

Ian shrugged.

"How was the flight?"

"Okay," Ian said in the deep voice that still surprised Noah.

"Did they feed you?"

"Peanuts," came that deep voice laced with disdain.

Noah had hoped they could have lunch in Rockland, but he figured Ian might need something sooner. "Did you check a bag?"

"No," the boy said with a slight, almost insolent rise at the end, and dipped an ear toward the duffle on his shoulder. "This is it. Like, your island isn't New York."

As put-downs went, it was a potent one. Noah had always been sensitive to the fact that he hadn't grown up with mainland sophistication. Sure, his time in New York was worth something, but there was still the matter of modest roots. Sandi had often used it to explain things she didn't like.

Noah knew he would be feeling defensive in a minute. Not wanting that, he tossed a thumb toward the exit. "Let's go."

Driving north on the Maine Turnpike, Noah did his best to engage Ian in conversation. "So, how's baseball?"

"Done," came the reply.

"For the summer?"

"Yes."

"Was it a good league?"

Ian shrugged.

"Is that a yes or a no?" Noah asked.

"A yes."

"Are you still playing shortstop?"

"Yes."

"But running cross-country in the fall. Do you like that?"

There was another shrug, then a grudging, "It keeps me in shape."

"How are the Orioles doing?"

"Lousy. Nothing's been the same since Cal Ripken retired."

"I thought there were some other good players."

"They sold them all off."

Noah sighed. "For what it's worth, the Red Sox are still breaking our hearts."

Tracking the coast, Noah left the turnpike at Brunswick and took Route 1 into Wiscasset, where they stopped for lunch at Red's Eats.

"Here?" Ian asked with a dubious glance at the small red building, its take-out window, plastic tables and chairs.

"See that line at the window? Red's has the best lobster rolls in the state."

"I don't eat lobster."

"Maybe that's because you haven't had a good lobster roll."

"I gag on lobster."

Noah sighed. "Do you eat fried clams?"

"Yes."

"Order fried clams," he said and got out of the truck.

Ian ordered fried clams and ate them all. When Noah told him to pass a napkin, he passed it. When Noah told him to use the rest room before they hit the road again, he used the rest room. When Noah told him to buckle his seat belt, he buckled his seat belt.

He could follow orders. That was something. Not fun or interesting or promising for an interactive relationship. But something.

Noah waited until they were back on Route 1, halfway between Wiscasset and Damariscotta, before trying again. "How's your mom?"

"Fine."

"Giving you a hard time?"

"No."

"She's proud of you, entering your senior year. How does that feel?"

"How does what feel?"

"Being a senior."

"It sucks," Ian said. "Everyone's on your back about college. I'm not going."

"Why not?"

"I don't know what I want to do. It'd be a total waste. Unless I could play ball, which I can't, because I'm not good enough."

"Who says?" Noah asked, glancing his way.

Ian returned a defiant look. "My coach."

"What does he know?"

"A lot."

"Open the glove box and pass me my sunglasses," Noah said. When Ian complied, he asked, "What colleges are you going to see?"

"I don't know. Mom planned the trip."

"Ian. This is your future. Find some places you like."

Ian didn't reply.

Noah let it go until, on the outskirts of Rockland,

they passed a cluster of girls. So he tried, "Did you know those girls who got off the plane in front of you?"

"No."

"They were pretty."

"They were townies."

Meaning, Noah knew, that they went to public school, rather than private school like Ian. "Nothing wrong with that. Your mother and I both went to public school. What're the girls at your school like?"

Ian snorted. "Cooler than those, that's for sure."

"Anyone special?"

"No."

"Not even the one you took to the junior prom?"

"She's a friend. And we went with other friends. It was no big deal."

Noah spotted an attractive girl as they approached the pier. "What do you think of that one?"

"She's okay," Ian said.

"If I were your age, I'd have called her a knockout."

Ian shot him a stare. "You're not my age."

"And grateful for it," Noah said, turning off the engine and returning the stare. "I don't recall having a chip on my shoulder, but I'm sure I pushed my parents plenty. If there's one thing they taught by example, it's patience. Ten minutes until we board the ferry," he added and faced forward.

Patience was one thing, Noah decided, and progress quite another. Standing at the rail as the ferry made the crossing, he wondered if the first would get him the last. He wanted a relationship with his son. Question-and-answer sessions did not make a relationship.

The good news was that, though the ferry offered places to hide, Ian didn't stray far. He stood at the rail six feet from Noah, watching the islands as they slowly took color and shape. Of the four in the ferry's path, Noah might have pointed out Little Sawyer from Big Sawyer from West Rock from Hull. He might have pointed out a passing lobster boat, the *My Andrea,* with Leslie Crane at her helm. He might have shown Ian the string of green-and-gold buoys Leslie was tending, how they were set north to south, how if you wanted to know where the catch would be good, you looked for those green-and-gold buoys, because Leslie was a highliner, consistently one of the most successful of the island's lobstermen. He might have shown Ian where the *Amelia Celeste* had gone down and taken the life of his grandfather with it.

But Noah didn't say a thing. He didn't trust that Ian wouldn't make a disparaging remark, one that might provoke anger in him. That was something he needed to avoid. Better, he decided, to let things unfold slowly.

But it wasn't to be. The ferry had no sooner docked at Big Sawyer and Noah driven the truck off when he was waved down by Mike Kling, whose shaved head gleamed in the sun.

"We got trouble, Noah," he said. "Those buoys you set last week up north of Main Mast rock? They're gray."

"Gray?"

"Painted. Once you spot the things, you can see blue and orange underneath, but the problem's spotting them. They blend right into the chop."

"Painted?" That was a new one. Lobstermen didn't carry paint in their boats. Novices might, if they were peeved that their pot warp was tied up in knots. "As in vandalized?"

"You got it."

"Just mine?"

"Looks it."

"Haber and Welk?"

"Most likely."

And so it went, Noah knew. You invade our turf, we knot your lines, you paint our buoys. Cutting warp was the next step. And he was game. Haber and Welk seemed to be picking on him. Why not pick back?

He ran a hand around the back of his neck. Something of a highliner himself, he had been expecting good things from the traps near Main Mast rock. They sat on rocky bottom, the bottom of choice for lobsters during the late-June molt, when, after walking out of their old shells, they were waiting for their new ones to harden and, in the meanwhile, were vulnerable to predators. Rocky bottom offered places to hide that sandy bottom did not.

He could still haul the traps; he had notations in his logbook of where each one was. But the buoys would have to be repainted. To do that, they had to be brought in, which meant hauling the traps and bringing those along, which meant either multiple trips or a mighty full boat, given the possible number of traps involved. It also meant the loss of a few days' fishing.

"Gotta be done," he said, as much to himself as to Mike. He put the truck in gear, thinking to continue on to the house to get Ian settled in, but then had another thought. Backing up, he pulled into a parking spot. It was early yet; he still had another few hours of daylight. Before he could decide what to do, he had to know the extent of the damage.

Chapter 14

After trying to talk with her mother, Julia took a long shower. She spread Lily of the Valley body lotion over every inch of her skin, slipped on her wedding band, and got dressed. Then she had an English muffin and tea. But it was only after a walk in the woods that she finally mellowed out. Back at the house, she brought a book to the bedroom deck and read until her stomach growled. She made a sandwich with the deli meat and rye bread Noah had bought, and returned to the deck. All the while, she refused to think about anything but the novelty of doing her own thing in her own time and being answerable to no one at all.

By midafternoon, sun no longer hit the bedroom deck, so she shifted to an Adirondack chair on the front porch and returned to her book. She was there when the second car of the day came out of the woods and parked. If she had been pleased when

Molly came, she was delighted now. This car was a small blue Honda with Kim at the wheel.

Closing her book, Julia came forward in the deep chair. When Kim didn't get out but simply sat watching her from the car, Julia rose. She went to the edge of the porch. When that didn't scare Kim off, she approached the car. Walking leisurely, she went to the driver's side. Kim bowed her head and looked at her lap, but the window was open, like an ear ready to listen.

"How'd you know I was here?" Julia asked and answered herself. "Ah, don't tell me. My father went to the island store for the *Wall Street Journal,* got into a conversation with Daryl, the owner, and let it slip that I was staying here. Daryl told June, who told Nancy, who told you."

The corner of Kim's mouth twitched. In the absence of words, that was progress. Even more so, the fact that she had come at all. From what Julia had heard, Kim had been nowhere in two weeks except her own house and the bluff. Noah's house certainly offered more privacy than either of those.

"Want to come in?" she asked. "I was about to put on fresh coffee, maybe even have a snack." She gestured the girl along. When Kim didn't move, she went into the house, leaving the door open, and set up the coffeemaker. By the time the first hisses and gurgles were coming from the machine, Kim stood at the edge of the room.

She was several inches shorter than Julia's five-seven, and built as nicely as her mother and grandmother—namely, fuller in the bust than anywhere else. Julia could see how men would be drawn. Her clothes were clean—a blouse, jeans, and a zippered sweater. Appearing freshly washed, her hair looked longer, thicker, and redder than ever.

Julia gestured her into a seat, but the girl didn't budge. So, opening the refrigerator, she took out what remained of the French bread and Brie from the evening before. In no time, she had the Brie on the bread, on a tray under the broiler. When the top began to bubble, she put half of the snack on each of two small white dishes. Again, she gestured for Kim to sit, and took a seat of her own this time.

Kim approached the table. She lowered herself to the chair's edge as though she had doubts and was poised to run.

Julia helped herself to a piece of toast, then got up and poured two cups of coffee. She set them on the table and sat down again. It was a full minute before Kim finally put out an unsteady hand and took a piece of toast.

"Well, that's a relief," Julia said. "I was worried I'd done this for nothing."

Brow furrowed, Kim kept her eyes on the food. With her pale skin and straight features complementing her hair, she was a striking young woman. Her eyes were chestnut, a warmer brown than those of her mother and grandmother. Her earlobes were pierced but earringless. Her mouth was wider than Julia had thought it to be, and looked all the larger in such a small face.

She ate in silence. When she had finished two slices of toast, she put her hand in her lap.

Quietly, Julia said, "If the grapevine told you I was here, it must be keeping you up to date on the investigation of the accident."

Kim swallowed. Julia took that for a yes.

"For what it's worth, no one has asked either Noah or me about you. Everyone seems to know, though, that you and Artie had a thing."

Kim studied her hands.

"If that's true," Julia went on more softly, "it's only a matter of time before someone will wonder which boat you were on."

Kim's eyes met hers in alarm.

"They'll wonder," Julia added, "but there's no way they'll ever know for sure. I can't swear that you weren't on the *Amelia Celeste,* and neither can Noah. Did anyone see you with Artie on the day of the accident?"

Kim didn't reply, simply stared at her with large chestnut eyes.

"Did you shoot him?"

No reply.

"Do you know who did?"

Still no reply.

Julia sat back. "I want to help you, though Lord knows why. Do you know how *wrong* it is to have an affair with a married man? Do you know how hurtful it is for the wife? And for the kids?"

Kim didn't move, didn't blink, didn't speak. Nor did her eyes leave Julia's.

"I ought to hate you, but I can't. There's a bond, Kim. We shared something that night. It doesn't matter where you were sitting or why you were there. You survived something horrific, just like I did. Don't you ask yourself why?"

Kim moved her head in a deliberate nod. At the same time, her hand went into the pocket of her sweater and pulled out something flat. She slid it across the table toward Julia. Her hand lingered in a last minute's unsureness before giving it a tiny shove and withdrawing.

It was a bankbook. Uneasy, Julia opened it. The account was in Kim's name, the first deposits dated eight years before. Those deposits were in the kinds of small amounts that represented a teenager's earnings from baby-sitting and such. Larger amounts, several thousand a pop, had been deposited more recently, most in the last eighteen months. The current balance was twenty-three thousand and change.

Julia tried to find meaning in the amount. "You've always worked and always saved."

Kim nodded slowly.

Baby-sitting was fine. Bartending was fine. The larger amounts, though, made Julia nervous. "Are these big ones from Artie?" she asked and, suddenly, even without a response from Kim, she wanted to push the bankbook away, forget she had seen it, pretend it didn't exist. It was incriminating. She needed to tell the girl that. "Did you know he was under suspicion for smuggling illegal aliens?"

Kim stared at her, eyes wide with a plea, and Julia

did try to slide the bankbook back then. Kim's hand
shot out and stopped the slide.

"If this is hush money," Julia began, "I don't want
any part of it." But something about the way Kim was
looking at her suggested that it wasn't hush money at
all. She wasn't giving the money to Julia. Rather,
"You want me to hold this for you?"

Kim gave a quick nod.

"So no one else sees?" Another nod. "But that
makes me an accessory to whatever you did for this
money."

Kim eyed her steadily, still with an element of
pleading, and it got to Julia. Adding everything Noah
had told her to everything Zoe had told her to everything her own gut instinct told her, she couldn't
think of Kim as evil.

"Did you love Artie?" she asked, because that made
the most sense. "Did he give you this money as a gift?"
Some men gave flowers, others jewelry. Julia couldn't
imagine Kim wanting either. Money, on the other
hand, Kim might want, indeed. "Were you saving up
for something? To buy your own boat? Or a house?"

Kim looked out the window, but not toward her
car and the road. Her eyes rose to the tops of the trees
and grew distant, then glassy with tears—and suddenly Julia recalled the horror on the girl's face the
last time they had talked, when Julia had dreamed
aloud of staying on Big Sawyer forever.

"This is your escape," she said, understanding.
"Do you know where you want to go? What you
want to do?"

Eyes still brimming, Kim rose from the chair and headed for the door.

Julia was up in an instant. "Don't leave, Kim. Tell me these things. If you can't say them, write them down. I can help."

But Kim didn't stop.

Long after the sound of the blue Honda's motor was lost in the woods, Julia sat at the table staring at the bankbook Kim had left. She probably should have refused to hold it, should have followed Kim right out to the car and tossed it inside. Yes, it was incriminating, though whether it was representative of the payoff a married man made to his mistress, or the payoff a felon made to his accomplice, Julia didn't know.

Not knowing, and feeling a loyalty to Kim that made picking up the phone to call the police seem wrong, she rose from the table, went down to the bedroom, and tucked the bankbook into the mottled leather bag that held her most personal things. On impulse, she took the bag out to the porch and removed those things. They were still vaguely damp from their time in the ocean. She guessed that if the zipper hadn't been closed, they would have been covered with seaweed.

Actually, if the zipper hadn't been closed, they would have dispersed. She was grateful they hadn't. Among the things that she laid out to dry were two envelopes. One held charge receipts and credit card bills that she had so carefully, guiltily gathered. The other held the photographs that were far older, but that were every bit as important to her.

Pulling the photos from their envelope, she was relieved to find that though their color was muted by moisture, the basic images were intact. Five in all, she spread them in a line. One was of the harbor, one of the pier. A third captured a stack of lobster traps, and a fourth the men building the pile. But the fifth was the one she wanted to see. Far from a close-up—she wouldn't have *dared* do that, at the age of fifteen—it showed six young men perched on and around the pier piling. They wore work boots and jeans, but were barechested. Each of the six had the tattoo around his biceps that marked him as part of the local lobster gang.

Lifting the picture, she held it in her palm and brought it closer, and there she saw him, or thought she did—Noah Prine at seventeen, far less mature in looks and build than he was now, but handsome nonetheless.

She was thinking of the fantasies that had been based on this particular picture over the years, when the phone rang. It was the land line. She debated letting it ring, until she realized that it might be Noah—and that she wanted to talk with him. Running inside, she picked up the phone by the bed.

The voice she heard was less deep than his, and more crisp. "Mrs. Bechtel, it's Alex Brier from the *Island Gazette*. Zoe said I'd find you there. I have a favor to ask. Those pictures you gave to the Chief? I want them for the paper. Think you could email them here?"

Julia was startled. She wondered if giving them to the newspaper was permissible. But no one had said she shouldn't. "Uh, sure," she managed. "When do you need them?"

"As soon as you can send them. Got a pen?"

Opening the drawer of the nightstand by the bed, she found pens, along with half-completed crossword puzzles with Noah's strong lettering in the squares. She jotted the editor's email address in the margin of one. As soon as she hung up, she took her camera from its case in the living room, went up to the loft, and sent the pictures along.

Then she called Noah on his cell phone. "Yeah," he answered, sounding irritated.

"It's Julia. I'm sorry, is this a bad time?" She knew he was with Ian and wouldn't have called if she hadn't felt an urgency.

His voice gentled. "No more so than another. We're on the *Leila Sue*." He told her about the vandalism to the buoys. "It looks like forty were painted. Someone was busy last night."

"The fruit guys?"

"Probably."

"Did anyone see them?"

"Nope. Hold on." He must have put the phone in his shirt pocket, because though his voice was more distant, the words were distinct. "Gaff it, Ian. Grab it with the hook. That's it. Bring it up now, right here over the winch. There. The hydraulic hauler'll do the rest." A motor started. He returned to Julia. "Can you hold another minute?"

"Sure."

To Ian, he said, "We're only in five fathoms, so it

won't take long. Keep a lookout. You'll see a bright thing coming at you fast before it breaks the surface. The hauler'll get it on the rail, but you need to get it in the boat. There. See it? Got it. Okay. Look for the next." He returned to Julia. "My boy didn't expect this when he woke up in D.C. this morning. It's something of a trial by fire."

"Things are okay with you and him, then?"

"Now."

"Ah." Clearly, he couldn't talk freely. "Forty buoys is how many traps?"

"I do pairs, so that's eighty, but I'm not hauling all of them." To Ian, he said, "Start a stack in the stern. There, on the trap skids." Back to Julia, he said, "I have extra buoys. Paint 'em, and they're good for exchange. Problem is, it has to be done soon. Traps without colors are fair game." He called, "Next string, Ian." Then, to Julia, "Everything okay there?"

"I just had a visit from Kim."

"Did you?".

"I need to ask your advice, but not on the phone. I know you'll be busy with Ian—"

"Come to the trap shed around nine tonight. You can help paint."

Julia smiled in relief. "I'd like that," she said and hung up feeling as though she might be able to pay for her keep after all.

Satisfied, she returned to the lounger, but she couldn't relax as before. Something had changed. The woods were as peaceful, the scent as sweet, the view as soothing, but her thoughts were on the real world now, on painted buoys and Noah, on Kim and her stash, on Molly and Zoe and George and Janet, all the loose threads in her life.

Call Monte, a little voice said, and she was instantly annoyed. She didn't want the reminder of who she'd been, not when she was feeling independent and strong. There was a shine in her world right now. Monte would tarnish it.

Zoe was another matter. Within minutes, Julia was inside again and calling her. "Hi," she said with bated breath, wondering if Zoe was furious at her.

But Zoe's voice held a smile. "Hi, yourself. I'm glad you called. I was worried."

"That makes two of us. Between the rabbits and Dad, I've abandoned you. How's it going?"

"Oh, it's fine. I put George to work with the rabbits. It keeps him busy and gets the work done. He's not a natural at it like you are—his heart isn't in it—but he does what I say."

"He does what Mom says, too—usually, at least. Is it awkward, having him there?"

"A little."

"I'm sorry."

"It's not your doing, Julia. It's mine and his, so we'll deal. At least I had Molly here for breakfast and lunch. She's at the Grill now. Tonight's lobster night. She's doing an appetizer of lobster crepes."

"Well, then, we have to go," Julia said. It was a perfect idea. "Let me treat you and Dad."

Zoe cleared her throat. "Uh, excuse me? Who wanted space?"

"Me. But I have it now. That means I can *choose* to be with people, and I choose to be with you and Dad."

"Your father and I are not a pair."

"I'm glad. I still want to take you to dinner."

"If you're feeling guilty—"

"Of course I'm feeling guilty," Julia said. "Feeling guilty is too much a part of me to be gone in a day. But I also want to do this. Please let me?"

Julia went to the Grill early, hoping to see Matthew Crane before the others arrived. Sure enough, he was in his usual corner, nursing his usual whiskey as he looked out over the harbor toward open ocean. He couldn't possibly see much; fog had rolled in. Still, he looked.

She slipped down on the bench, but he spoke before she could say a word. "Know why Monday night's lobster night?" he asked.

She shook her head.

"With no hauling on Sundays, the catch is bigger on Mondays, so the price is lower. It's all about money. It wasn't always that way. Lobster used to be so plentiful it was thought of as charity fare."

"Charity fare?"

"For widows and children and convicts and servants. Some of the servants got so tired of eating it, they had it written into their contracts that they couldn't be served it more than three times a week."

Julia smiled. "You're kidding me."

Matthew shook his head. He sipped his drink and sat it back on his thigh. "Native Americans used to pick lobster right out of the seaweed on the shore. They used them to fertilize their cornfields."

"Why are there so few now?"

"Fewer lobster? I don't know if there are fewer. Maine lobstermen hauled forty-six million pounds last year. The problem is demand. It used to be you had your lobster boiled live or steamed. Now you have it baked, stuffed, and grilled. You have lobster Savannah, lobster Newburg, and lobster thermidor. You have stew and chowder. You have lobster salad and lobster roll. You have lobster cakes, lobster pie, lobster puffs, lobster ravioli, even lobster ice cream. What's he got on the menu tonight—lobster crepes? Where will it end?" Matthew looked up as the waitress approached. "Me, I'm a boiled-live man."

"Here you go, Cap'n Crane," the girl said with a wink at Julia. "Our feistiest one-and-a-half pounder with drawn butter and a side of cornbread." She set the platter down on the bench in exchange for Matthew's whiskey glass.

"I thought you were a scrod man," Julia teased as soon as the girl left.

"Tuesday through Sunday it's scrod. Monday it's boiled live. My Amelia loved boiled live, too. 'Course, she could never quite get the hang of pulling the thing apart. She was too ladylike." He grasped the body in one hand and the tail in the other. With a sharp twist, the two came apart. "I used to do it for her. I never minded." Just as easily, he separated the knuckles from the body, then the claws from the knuckles.

Julia was amazed. "How do you do that without a cracker?"

Matthew guffawed. "It's not as easy as it used to be. The arthritis and all." He took the tail, bent it backward until it split, and neatly removed the piece of meat inside.

"Mrs. Bechtel?"

Julia looked up. A fair-haired man with serious eyes and an intense look hunkered down beside her. She didn't recognize him, but the voice was familiar.

"Alex Brier," he said. "Thanks for emailing the pictures. I'm using them in this week's paper, and my deadline was an hour ago. Want to take more?"

"Of the traps?"

"Of Noah's buoys and anything else that happens. More will. You can bet on that. I've been doing all the pictures myself, only my wife's expecting a baby in two months, and the doctor is making her stay in bed, so I'm running back and forth, trying to do the newspaper and take care of our two other kids. I could find you a ride out, if you're willing to do it."

"What fun," Julia said, grinning. "I'm willing."

"Great. Thanks. I'll pay you for this—"

"I don't need pay. There are no expenses on my end." Totally aside from that, she couldn't imagine being paid. She had no expertise to be paid for. She was simply a visitor to the island who happened to have had her camera with her in the right place at the right time.

Alex stood. "Thanks, then. I'll arrange a ride and give you a call."

"I'll take her," Matthew said. He held the last of the tail piece, dripping butter onto the plate. "My nephew's been offering me his Cobalt. Pretty fancy boat for a lobsterman, but not for a lady from New York."

For the first time, Alex smiled. "All my problems should be settled this easily. Thanks, guys," he said and left.

Julia wished her own problems were settled as easily. Those problems hit her within thirty minutes of sitting down with Zoe and George, which was as long as it took to order wine, devour Molly's crepes, and discuss Noah's sabotaged buoys, which were the talk of the place. By the time dinner salads arrived, George had grown quiet, and by the time lobster arrived—boiled live for Zoe, stew for Julia, and hash for George—he was looking despondent.

Naturally, Julia asked whether he had talked with Janet. When he said he had not, she suggested he call. When he argued that he wasn't ready to talk with her, he then turned the tables and asked if Julia had talked with Monte. She changed the subject.

Julia didn't regret having suggested dinner. She would do it again in a minute. George was her father, and he was distressed. Janet was her mother, and she was alone. Monte was her husband, and, as such, was still a part of her life. It all needed discussing.

But not now. Not yet.

After paying the bill, she was pleased to take her leave and head for Noah's trap shed. The same fog that had obstructed the sunset now produced a dusk that was thick and moist. She wore a sweater, and buttoned it up as she drove.

The shed was at the end of Spruce Street, where houses had given way to wild grasses and trees. She might have missed the small wood hut, had it not been for a glow in the window. She had barely parked when Lucas appeared from nowhere, ran back and forth in a moment's frenzy, then butted his muzzle against her hand. Delighted, Julia was patting his head when Noah appeared at the door, and suddenly it hit her—the way he was now with his hair messed and his sweatshirt and jeans spattered with paint, the way he had looked as a teenager with his buddies and all of them with that ropy tattoo, the way his voice had gentled earlier when she had called on the phone.

Her insides melted. The best she could do was manage a smile.

With a hand high on the door frame, he smiled back. "Hey. Mmm, you look nice. Just come from dinner?"

She nodded. Leaving a hand on Lucas's head, she raised her brows and looked around Noah into the shed. With the door open, the smell of fresh paint was quickly supplanting that of the salt mist.

He stepped aside to let her in. Lucas went first. "I sent Ian home. He was exhausted. I'd say 'poor kid,' if he hadn't been out until two this morning with friends."

The oil lamp threw enough light to show dozens of buoys newly painted a bright blue. "Oh my," Julia said, finding her voice. "Have you done all this tonight?"

"I had no choice. I don't want those traps lost. I'm about to start on the stripes."

"Give me a brush."

"Not dressed like you are."

Julia spotted a sweatshirt on a hook. "That'll do, won't it?" she asked as she unbuttoned her sweater. In no time, she replaced it with the sweatshirt. It was large, but large served the purpose. She homed in on an open can of orange paint. Several brushes lay nearby. She picked one up. "Show me how you want it done."

He showed her, and for a time they worked quietly, with Lucas sleeping nearby. They were done with nearly half before Noah said, "Tell me about Kim."

Sitting back on her heels, Julia told him about the visit. By the time she reached the part about the bankbook, he had stopped painting, too.

"Twenty-three thousand?"

"And change."

"Most over the last eighteen months?"

"That's right."

"So the question," Noah correctly concluded, "is what he was paying her for. She didn't indicate in any way?"

"Only that she was saving up so that she could leave here. She gave me the bankbook for safekeeping. I guess she's thinking that if she becomes part of an investigation, she doesn't want it drawing attention. But the bank has those same records. Investigators would come up with them in no time. If they start investigating her," Julia added, because that was the crux of her own dilemma. "What do I do, Noah? Is the bankbook an admission of guilt? I can't swear which boat she was on the night of the accident, but I now have that bankbook in my possession, which means I know something the police don't. Artie was paying her for something. The question is what."

"How did she seem?"

"Not evil or manipulative, that's for sure. Stricken," Julia decided. "That's the hardest part for me. I feel protective of her. She was there with us that night. Regardless of what she was or was not involved in, she's suffering."

Noah considered that thought. After a minute, he resumed painting, and Julia followed his lead. He was thinking, she knew. She could see the way his brow was creased and his mouth had tightened. He would talk when he had something to say.

Sure enough, when the last of the blue buoys wore orange stripes and had been carefully hung to dry, he put out the oil lamp and led her outside. There, leaning beside her against her car, he said, "Let me talk with John. He'll tell me what's going on. He trusts me. He won't think twice if I prod, what with my father having been killed."

She wanted to see his face to learn more than his voice conveyed, but with the fog obscuring moon and stars, the night was dark. Gently, she asked, "How are you doing with that?"

"Not bad. I've cleaned things up, and now Ian's here, so the house feels different."

"How was it with him today?"

"Awkward. He answers questions but doesn't initiate anything. The good news is he can follow orders. First thing tomorrow, we're heading out to replace buoys. He'll be fine with that."

"I may see you out there," Julia said on a lighter note. With her eyes adjusting to the dark, she saw Noah turn his head and look at her. "Alex Brier asked me to take pictures of your gray buoys. Matthew Crane is taking me out."

Noah tipped his head. His voice held a smile. "Matthew, huh? None of the working guys would do it?"

"Don't know. Didn't ask. Matthew offered. I said yes."

"You have him wrapped around your finger. Bet you do that to all the men."

"No. Not all."

"You've sure done it to my dog. Look at him sitting there, right by your leg."

Julia scratched Lucas's head. "Maybe he's just a lady's man, starved for female attention."

"Nah. There's plenty of females around. He's not interested in them. I told you. He knows beauty when he sees it."

Julia didn't reply. Noah had said those words more than once—three times, to be exact—but they were only words. She knew not to put much stock in them; Monte thought her beautiful, but it hadn't kept him interested for long.

Words were easily spoken. But there was something else here with Noah, something in the thick night air that sent a warmth through her veins. It could have been the way his body touched hers, arm to arm, hip to hip, or the way he looked at her, then away, then back, as though he couldn't control his eyes, any more than she could control the heat she felt inside.

"Oh, boy," he finally muttered.

She nodded. "Bad timing."

"My son, your husband."

"The accident."

"Gear war."

"Maybe that's all it is?" she asked. "A reaction?"

He shook his head and folded his arms on his chest. She did the same, and all the while good sense was telling her to get in her car and drive away. Had she been willing to listen, good sense would have had her on her way back to New York the next morning.

"So maybe," he said quietly, "this is what the accident was for."

"You and me?"

"Yes. What's your marriage like?"

"Don't ask that," she whispered.

"If it's good, I'll back off."

"Noah."

"Is it?"

She unfolded her arms and dropped her chin to her chest. In the next instant, though, she turned into him, and he was there. His arms went around her, drawing her close. Cheek settling on his chest, she closed her eyes and breathed in far more than the paint on his shirt. He was beneath it—Noah Prine—heart pounding loudly, limbs trembling slightly, body smelling of man and exuding a penetrating heat. If she wanted to be wanted, the proof was here. He made no attempt to hide it—all the less so when, shifting, he pressed her against the car.

She sighed at the sheer pleasure of it.

"You can say *that* again," he muttered hoarsely.

She repeated the sigh.

He chuckled. His breath was warm by her ear. "Can I kiss you?"

She shook her head, but her arms were around him now, too.

"Not even if I keep my mouth closed and my tongue inside?" he asked.

She laughed. "What fun would that be?"

"None. I'm good with my tongue."

"I'm sure you are," she managed, though her knees had gone soft. Without his body propping hers up, she might have slipped to the ground and melted away.

Taking her face in his hands, he turned it up. His eyes were serious. "I messed up my marriage because my priorities were wrong, and they've probably been wrong in the ten years since, because the only thing that's mattered to me is work. Mattered? That's a rel-

ative word. All I've done is go through the motions—
wake up in the morning, work all day, come home
exhausted and go to bed. Since the accident, I've been
thinking about missed opportunities. I blew it with
my parents and now they're gone. But Ian isn't. So
I'm working on that. And now there's you. Tell me
what you want, Julia."

Unable to do that, with so much else in her life
up in the air, Julia pressed a hand to his mouth. His
lips were firm and lean. Her fingers lingered there a
minute, then withdrew. Slipping out from under
him, she rounded the car and slid behind the wheel.
After nearly closing the door on Lucas, she eased his
head out of the way and started the car.

Noah stood several feet away. She backed around
and drove off, alternately watching the road and her
rearview mirror. All too soon, the mirror was dark, but
his image remained in her mind, a glow that reminded
her what it was like to be wanted. Coming off a long
emotional night filled with insecurity and hurt, she
was elated. She could love him for that alone.

On impulse, driven by a combination of strength
and guilt, she walked into the hill house and phoned
Monte. It wasn't the first time she had tried him; they
were playing phone tag, leaving messages for each
other every few days. She heard her own voice ask
the caller to leave a message. This time, though, she
hung up before the beep.

She might have reached him on his cell phone.
Where would he be at ten o'clock at night? She
wasn't sure she wanted to know.

That wasn't true. She did want to know. She *badly* wanted to know.

But would he tell the truth? She doubted it. Monte had an answer for everything. She was so convinced of *that,* that even if he did tell the truth, she probably wouldn't believe it.

What's your marriage like? Noah had asked.

Sad, she thought. Very sad.

Chapter 15

Noah was up before dawn, shaking Ian awake, then monitoring the NOAA weather broadcast while he fried a package of bacon and half a dozen eggs, toasted six slices of bread, and poured large glasses of juice.

Entering the kitchen when everything was on the table, Ian looked at the food and shook his head. "I hope none of that's for me. I can't eat this early."

"You're going to be working this early. You'll need energy."

"Just coffee," Ian said, and helped himself to a mugful.

Noah didn't argue. It wasn't worth the breath. If Ian was hungry, he would eat lunch. If he was very hungry, he would know to have breakfast tomorrow. Here was one of the things he and Sandi had disagreed upon. Noah had never insisted that Ian eat, not when Ian was four, not when he was twelve. Nor had he insisted that the boy wear a winter jacket when the weather cooled. These were things a child could learn for himself. Not so homework or manners, which were musts, and alcohol and drugs, which were must-nots.

Noah chose his fights—another legacy of his parents, he realized now.

So he ate his own full breakfast while Ian drank his coffee. The boy sat at the table looking at anything but Noah, while Noah made four tuna sandwiches and packed them in a cooler along with canned soda and chips. He put his logbook beside the cooler. He cleaned up the kitchen.

Pulling on a sweatshirt, he suggested Ian do the same. Ian said he'd be fine without. So Noah said, "Take the cooler." Logbook in hand, he opened the front door. There was fresh air here, all the more so, figuratively speaking, when Lucas bounded out of the deep purple dawn. Lucas was enthusiasm. He was energy and loyalty. He was unconditional love, and Noah was hungry for that.

Taking the dog's head in both hands, he scrubbed his neck. "Hey, guy, how're you doing?" Lucas's tail wagged wildly. "Have a good night? The bed was lonely without you. Where you been?" Lucas's tongue lolled in delight.

"The dog hates me," Ian said.

Noah opened the truck door. Lucas scrambled into the extended cab. "Why do you say that?"

"He won't come near me."

Noah might have said that dogs, like young children, were drawn to warmth and to genuine affec-

tion, neither of which Ian had shown. More diplo-
matically, he said, "He doesn't know you, so he's cautious. That's typical of this breed of dog."

Ian didn't say anything more, not when they
stopped at the trap shed to load the truck up with
buoys, nor when they backed onto the pier and trans-
ferred the buoys to the boat. To his credit, the boy was
no weakling. Noah saw firm biceps under the sleeves
of his T-shirt. He also saw goose bumps, lots of them.

There were sweatshirts on the boat, hanging in
plain sight. He figured Ian would take one if he was
cold. Same with a hat. Noah wore his Patriots cap. He
half hoped Ian would ask about it, which would open
up talk about both sports and Hutch, either subject
being something they shared. But Hutch might never
have existed, for the interest Ian had shown. There
hadn't been a word since he arrived—no offer of con-
dolence, no question about the accident investigation
or whether he was sleeping in Hutch's bed.

Once the truck was unloaded, Noah parked it
back at the pier. He stopped briefly at Rick's for his
thermos and found two there, along with a bag with a
penciled note on the front: *Something special for the boy,
in case he suffers withdrawal at ten.*

Smiling, he tucked the thermoses under his arm,
took the bag, and returned to the boat. He pulled on
oilskin overalls and rubber boots, and was relieved
when Ian followed suit. Hauling those few traps yesterday, they had only worn boots, but Ian would have
had to be dim-witted not to realize that a full day's
work would be wetter.

Mickey Kling called over a weather update from the deck of the *Mickey 'n Mike*. Leslie Crane gave Noah a thumbs-up as *My Andrea* motored out of the harbor.

Whistling for Lucas, Noah directed Ian to untie the lines while he got the engine humming. He had to jiggle the wires connecting the VHF before the local channel sputtered out a sound, but that was nothing new. Backing out of the slip, he actually felt pretty good. Yes, Ian was a pill; yes, the gear war was escalating; yes, he was worried about Kimmie Colella and about his hankering for Julia Bechtel. But he was going out lobstering with his son, and that was special.

Fog remained, though it wasn't nearly as thick as it had been the night before. With sunrise somewhere beyond it and the cottony world inside a pale gray, the *Leila Sue* motored to Foss's for bait, then held to headway speed through the harbor. Once past the markers, Noah edged up the throttle. In no time, with his radar screen providing what the fog took away, they were headed for Main Mast rock at eighteen knots.

Julia was less than an hour behind. In stark contrast to Ian Prine, she wore jeans, a T-shirt, a light sweater, a sweatshirt, and a jacket, plus wool socks and sneakers, plus a hat. She packed her camera, along with warm corn muffins fresh from the oven, a pair of thick turkey sandwiches, and a thermos of hot tea. At the last minute, she even added an extra pair of socks to serve as gloves.

By the time she reached the dock, Matthew was

idling beside it in an elegant boat. He wore his usual khakis, but now with a navy blue jacket and a captain's hat. He looked pleased with himself.

"She's a twenty-nine-footer with six hundred horses, GPS, real leather wheel, wood dash, heating, AC, you name it. I wasn't sure how a gem like this'd run," he said as he helped her aboard, "but she's easy. They have to make 'em easy. Folks who can afford craft like this don't know much about the sea. Me, I cut my teeth running lobster boats. I may not be up on the latest with trim tabs and thrusters and all on this thing, but I brought her over here just fine. It's the knowledge of wind and waves that counts. Store your stuff in the cuddy while I tie us off."

But Julia didn't want to be chauffered. At times she felt she had spent the better part of the last twenty years in the backseat of a cab. Here, she wanted to *do*.

So she said, "I have a better idea," and dropped her things out of the way. "I'll tie off. You drive."

Noah knew the waters around Big Sawyer like the back of his hand. Barely checking the radar, he navigated the boat through the deeper channel before heading for the shoals. With Lucas close by his leg, he stood at the wheel, absently monitoring the VHF and the intermittent chatter of his friends, as he drank coffee from the cap of his thermos. Ian was behind him, attaching fresh-painted buoys to the warp of the traps stacked in the stern.

"We'll set those first," he said when the boy was done. "See how low the stern rides under their weight?

Not good if the chop rises. Once they're gone, we'll have room to work."

Ian stood beside him, peering into the fog. "How do you know where they go?"

"They go where I want them to go."

"Where do you *want* them to go?" the boy asked, his tone snooty and vaguely mocking.

"I want them to go where the lobsters are," Noah shot back. Snootiness rubbed him the wrong way. It smacked of superiority, which roused the old inferiority complex in Noah. Sandi said it was in his mind, but he knew he wasn't alone in his reaction. Condescension from mainlanders, and the defensiveness it spawned, was something islanders fought all their lives.

Defensiveness wasn't the best approach now, though. More constructively, he said, "This time of year, I want my traps in the shallows. Lobsters are molting right about now. Once they shed those old shells, they hide in the rocks until the new ones harden and give them protection from predators. We pulled these traps yesterday from five fathoms. We'll set them in three fathoms today. Even without the buoy problem, I'd have moved them soon anyway. You can't leave traps in the same place all summer, not if you want a decent catch. You have to follow the lobsters." He brought the engine down to a putter and pointed at one of his screens. "Eighteen, twenty feet. Let's go."

Taking traps from the stern, he showed Ian how to balance a pair on the starboard rail, slide the first overboard, then the second, then the buoy. Doubling back, they laid a second string and a third. Farther north, they laid another two strings, then another two farther north again. When the stern was free of traps and the boat rode higher, Noah headed for others of the gray buoys he had seen the day before.

Today, though, there was lobstering to do. Approaching a gray buoy, he threw the boat out of gear, gaffed the buoy, and pulled it aboard. While Ian exchanged the bad buoy for a newly painted one, Noah threw the line over the hydraulic winch, started the hauler, and pulled each of the two traps aboard as they shot up from the depths. Water came up with each, splashed across the deck and out the scuppers. It was North Atlantic cold even at the turn of July.

"You're my sternman," he told Ian. "Your job is to empty the trap, measure what's inside, band keepers, and rebait." He handed him a pair of thick cotton gloves. "Wear these. And don't get your fingers in the way of a claw. They don't call those things cutters and crushers for nothing."

Ian was staring at the first trap. "What's that?" he asked uneasily.

"Dogfish," Noah said. Wearing gloves of his own, he lifted the fish from the trap. "Dogfish is a small shark. This one's just a baby, but the teeth are sharp and there's poison back here near the dorsal fins." He pitched the dogfish back into the sea, and did the same with a hermit crab and several pieces of seaweed. Three lobsters were left in the trap. He dumped them onto the banding table, where they waved their claws and slapped their tails. "These two are shorts," he said, tossing the two smallest back into the ocean. "Here's a maybe." He took up a small measuring tool. "The carapace is the body as measured from the eye socket to where the tail starts. We can't keep anything smaller than three and a quarter inches or larger than five—the small ones so they can grow and hopefully breed, the large ones because if they've survived this long, they're among the fittest, and we always want the fittest to breed. See? This one's nearly three and a half. It's a keeper. Likely a one-pounder. That's a chick."

Taking the banding tool, he showed Ian how to fit a small, wide elastic band onto the end and stretch it enough to fit it over the claw. "Come on, bud," he murmured when the lobster refused to close its claw. He finally blew on the claw, and the lobster complied.

"Cool," Ian remarked in his first show of animation.

Thinking of Hutch and the myriad things he had taught Noah in his noncommunicative way, Noah tossed the lobster into a tank. "Now for the bait. See the bag inside the trap? Reach in and take it out."

Ian got the bag out. It contained nothing but fish bones and small bits of flesh. "This is gross."

Noah ignored the remark. "Bait like this has become part of the ecological system. The smallest of the lobsters walk in and out of the traps feeding on it." He pointed to a small rectangular opening at the bottom of one side of the trap. "This escape is for them. As they molt and grow, they become food for other marine species."

Ian continued to stare at the bait bag, now with his upper lip curled. "What're we supposed to do with this?"

Noah reached in, scooped out what remained of the bait, and tossed it overboard. The pieces had no sooner hit the waves when a seagull swooped down, caught one up, and carried it off. A second seagull followed suit.

"Now, restuff the bag," he instructed. When Ian had done it—albeit with a pinched look that decried the smell—he showed him how to retie the bag in the trap. Setting that trap aside, he turned to the second one. It contained more seaweed, a starfish, and a lobster with one claw. The seaweed and the starfish went overboard; the lobster remained. Noah didn't have to measure it to know it was a keeper, but he had Ian do it anyway. "A one-clawed lobster is called a cull. It won't command as large a price, but it's worth something."

"How'd it lose the claw?"

"A fight, maybe. Lobsters can spontaneously drop a claw if it's that or death. Once in a while they grab on to the wire of the trap when you're trying to pull them out, and lose a claw that way. If they were still in the ocean, they'd grow another. It won't be as big, but it'll work."

He let Ian struggle with the bander, which was what he remembered his father doing when he was young and had been learning. He had been seven at the time and lacked the strength in his hand to properly do the job, but he could stuff bait bags. He was paid a nickel a bag.

Ian eventually had the lobster banded and the trap baited, at which point Noah put the boat in gear and the traps went back over the transom, one by one. As soon as a newly painted buoy was bobbing in the waves, they moved on. They had hauled twenty pairs of traps and were about to gaff the last of the vandalized buoys when the sound of a motor came out of the mist.

Noah straightened. He knew the local fleet well enough to tell the *Mickey 'n Mike* from *My Andrea* or *Long Haul* or the *Nora Fritz* sight unseen. This was none of those. It was too smooth, too oiled, too content. He was feeling a sense of anticipation even before the Cobalt materialized, and smiled helplessly when he saw the cockpit. Julia stood there with Matthew Crane. She broke into a grin and waved.

He raised an answering hand.

Matthew throttled down and sidled up as close as was wise in the ocean swells.

"How's it going?" she called.

"Getting there," he called back. "How about you?"

"I've gotten *terrific* stuff. Now I want you."

He grinned. "Want me how?"

"Doing your thing. You know, lobstering."

"You mean, I should pretend you're not there. Act like I'm just doing a day's work."

"Exactly," she insisted and looked past him. "Is that Ian? Hi, Ian!"

Noah glanced back. His son had taken advantage of the small break to open Rick Greene's bag and was devouring a chocolate croissant. With the bits of seaweed on his oilskins, the windblown mess of his spiky hair, and his upper-body musculature, he could have been taken for a lobsterman. Noah felt a glimmer of pride.

The boy raised his chin in greeting as he chewed the last of the croissant. Tossing the bag aside, he went to the rail as Noah caught up the last buoy and put the line over the winch. As the line coiled into a pile on the deck, they watched for the first trap. Ian grabbed it, then the second one. While he removed the spoiled buoy and worked at attaching a fresh blue-and-orange one, Noah sorted through the contents of the traps. He tossed back a small cod, several sea urchins, and one undersize lobster, leaving three legal ones on the table. He banded these while Ian rebaited the traps, and all the while he did his best to forget Julia was there.

Outwardly, he succeeded. Her camera might capture the lobsterman at work, but it wouldn't record the fact that his heart was beating faster than normal and his hand was less than steady.

Ian noticed. Julia had no sooner given him a thumbs-up and the Cobalt disappeared into the mist when he said, "What was *that* about?"

"What?" Noah asked, buoy in hand as he waited for the line to play out with the second of the traps sinking fast.

"That woman."

Noah dropped the buoy into the water. "Her name is Julia. She also survived the crash. She's from New York."

"Figures, with a boat like that."

Unable to ignore Ian's arrogance this time, Noah throttled up the *Leila Sue*. "That boat belongs to a local fisherman. You may find this hard to believe, Ian, but many local lobstermen do quite well."

Ian seemed unimpressed. His mind was elsewhere. "Was that her husband?"

"No. He's in New York," Noah said in an end-of-discussion tone. "Here's the next buoy. Gaff it, will you? We have a hell of a lot of work to do before lunch."

Noah drove his son hard, steaming from one string of traps to the next, hauling, emptying, rebaiting, resetting, and starting all over again minutes later. He demanded a level of stamina from Ian that he doubted any baseball coach had ever demanded, and felt little sympathy when the boy began to flag.

But fatigue caused accidents, and had Noah not looked back at the right moment, seen what was about to happen, and lunged to push Ian out of the way, the boy might have gone right over the side.

"What the *hell*?" Ian cried. He was sprawled on the deck, while Noah dropped the second trap into the water.

"Didn't you see the coil of pot warp?" Noah called back. Heart pounding, he dropped the buoy in after the trap and turned, feeling suddenly drained. "There's *always* a coil of rope under the hauler. Put your foot there like you did, and when the line plays out fast, you either lose the foot or go right over the side and down with the trap. I had a childhood friend who died that way."

Ian sat up, a sullen expression on his face.

Noah returned to the wheel and killed the engine. "I need lunch," he muttered and pulled out the cooler. He turned over two pails and sat on one. Tossing Ian a sandwich, he unwrapped one himself and ate, but it was a while before his pulse returned to normal and a while after that before he tasted the food he was wolfing down.

"I would never have forgiven myself if anything had happened to you," he finally said.

"What about *me*?" Ian cried in a higher voice. "Think I want my life to end up *here*?"

Noah considered that. More to the point, he considered how to answer. Ian's dig could only hurt if it was valid—if there were truly reason for Noah to feel inferior about Big Sawyer. Suddenly, though, he didn't believe there was, and he was upset enough to say it. "If your life has to end, you could do a whole lot worse than here. People think here. They care here. They feel here. Your grandparents died here, and your father probably will, too. You have roots here, Ian. You may not want to admit that, but that's because you're ignorant." He had meant to say shortsighted, but the other word had popped out, and Ian was quick to react.

"Ignorant of what? *This*?" the boy asked, shooting a disparaging glance at the marine debris strewn on the deck. "Am I supposed to care about this? This is what you wanted, not me. You hide here."

"Hide?"

"You ran here after the divorce and you haven't left."

"Left to live elsewhere? Why would I? I like it here."

"But you used to *do* something. This can't compare to that."

Noah bristled. "You don't think so? You *are* ignorant, making a statement like that. I didn't have to come back here after the divorce. I could have gone anywhere I wanted. I was good at what I did. Do you know that? You didn't have a clue at seven, but at seventeen, you should. I was earning big bucks, and it had nothing to do with luck. Luck only takes you so far. What was carrying me was smarts."

"But you gave it all up," Ian charged, smug in the indictment.

"No," Noah said slowly. "I didn't. I still do consulting."

Ian was skeptical. "What do you know about what's happening in the world?"

"Probably more'n you do."

"How?"

"Phone, fax, email. We're not backwards."

Ian snorted. "You're not connected. I looked."

"You didn't look in the right place," Noah said, though he had no intention of elaborating. Ian wanted to email his friends—Sandi had warned that he would. Noah had no qualms about letting the boy rough it a while. "You know nothing about my life, Ian. You might, if you asked a question or two, but you never seem to want to do that."

"You're the one who won't talk," the boy muttered.

"I'll talk," Noah countered, putting his elbows on his knees. "Go ahead. Ask."

"Do you get HBO?"

"Only when the cloud cover is light enough so the satellite can connect."

"What about Thai food?"

"At the Grill. Rick serves lobster pad Thai, gingered scallops, and curried mussels."

"Till what time?"

"Nine."

"What do people do after that?"

"Go to bed, because they'll be up before dawn the next day, like we were today, so they can do most of their fishing before the seas rise. People do an honest day's work here, and it isn't just physical. There's a lot of know-how that goes into successful lobstering. This may not be your choice of work, but there are generations of families who've been lobstering, passing the knowledge on from grandfather to father to son, to daughters now, too. These people could have gone elsewhere and been successful, but they chose to stay. Just like I chose to return." He straightened. "So don't ever think I'm hiding here. I choose this life." He was deliberate in his use of the present tense. "*Choose* this life."

A thrumming came from the fog. He turned his head, easily identifying the approaching engine as that of the *Trapper John*. Devouring the remaining half of his sandwich in a single bite, he went to the rail. The other lobster boat emerged from the fog and came alongside. Noah had just caught her rail, so that the two boats rose and fell in tandem, when the *Willa B.* joined them.

"That your boy?" asked John Mather.

Noah made the introductions. He was grateful when Ian came to the rail to shake hands with John and acknowledge Hayes Miller aboard the third boat.

Hayes called to Noah, "Saw your new buoys."

Noah nodded. "The bad ones are gone."

"Tell us what to do," John said.

"I'm gunnin' for bear," Hayes called.

But Noah knew what he wanted. "They singled me out, so I'm singling them out. The way I see it, a few cut lines won't hurt."

Grinning, Hayes pumped a fist in the air.

John was more quiet but no less approving. "Want help, I'll do it."

"No," said Noah. "Me and my boy can handle it. Thanks, though."

Noah finished hauling the traps he'd set out to haul, and the catch was good, particularly since damage control had taken much of their time. His tanks held three-hundred-some pounds of lobster, averaging out to more than a pound per trap. Yes, the catch was good.

Even better, he and Ian hadn't argued since lunch. Granted, they hadn't said much at all. But they had fallen into a rhythm of hauling that lobsterman and sternman didn't always find. Noah might have told Ian that, if he hadn't feared a snide remark in return. He didn't want to have to deal with more anger. The waves had risen, and there was still work to do.

With the fog finally starting to thin, he directed the *Leila Sue* to a heavy concentration of purple-and-lime buoys, then pulled Ian to the wheel. "See these buoys? Go to one and let her idle," he threw the gear into neutral to demonstrate, then into forward again, "go to the next and let her idle," then neutral again. "I'll be quick."

"I've never driven a boat," Ian said.

"No better place to learn. The only danger here is that you'll mangle pot warp. Be my guest. Any line you cut with the prop is one less I do by hand. Here you go," he said, indicating the first buoy. Taking a sharp knife from the cuddy, he leaned over the rail and freed the buoy from its warp with a decisive upward cut. The *Leila Sue* was idle longer than she needed to be, bucking in the waves, and when she finally moved forward, she wasn't as sure as she would have been with Noah's hand on the throttle. The next time was better, though, and the third time even better.

"You learn fast," Noah called as his knife neatly severed another buoy from its warp.

Ian had his legs planted wide for balance. "Isn't this illegal?" he asked as he headed for the next buoy.

"Not by local law."

"But you're destroying someone's property."

"That someone is trespassing. Technically, since he's on my turf, it's my property."

"Who says it's your turf?"

"Same people who make local law. People who've fished here for generations. People like your grandfather."

Ian might have asked about Hutch then. Instead,

coming up on the next buoy, he asked, "What if they bring charges?"

"They won't."

"Why not?"

"Because there's ten guys who'll testify that they painted my buoys, and zero guys who'll say I was cutting these lines."

"What happens to the traps attached to these?"

Noah held the rail with one hand while, fighting the waves, he leaned down with his knife. The boat rose and fell, rose and fell before he was able to make his slash and cut the line. "They're lost to Haber and Welk, unless they want to send a diver down, but without buoys, they won't have a clue where the traps are."

"What if lobsters are in them—big ones, that can't get out the escape hatch?"

"These traps have a panel held on by hog rings. Hog rings are biodegradable clips. In time, they fall apart, the panel opens, and the lobsters get out."

"Alive?" Ian asked, moving the *Leila Sue* forward.

Noah waited for the next buoy. "If not, they're food for other fish. The system works."

They didn't cut free all of the purple-and-green buoys. The point was for Haber and Welk to find a few tied to traps and know that the rest had been deliberately destroyed. Not that Noah wasn't enjoying himself. He slashed lines for himself and his father, for Greg Hornsby and Dar Hutter and Grady Bartz. He slashed a few for the Walshes. And for Zoe's assistant, Todd Slokum. Haber and Welk might not have had anything to do with their deaths, but they were bad guys all the same.

Noah might have done a few more, if the *Leila Sue* hadn't been suddenly rolling in six-foot swells. With Ian starting to look a little unsteady, he retook the helm and put in for the harbor; there was work to do there as well. First stop was Foss Fish, where they unloaded the day's catch. Then it was over to the fuel wharf for diesel, then back to the slip to clean up the boat.

At four in the afternoon, he dropped a clearly exhausted Ian back at the house. Then he went back into town to see the police chief.

Julia had come ashore far earlier. She and Matthew had actually eaten their sandwiches while tied up at the dock, soon after which she was back on Hawks Hill, sitting at Noah's computer and playing with the pictures she had shot. She cropped some and lightened others, sharpened a few and rendered others in unusual color tones.

In time, she sent those of Noah and Ian replacing vandalized buoys on to Alex Brier. She sent a few of the others to Monte, because she wanted him to know she was using—and loving—the camera. She even made prints of her favorites, playing with this program as well.

Then she drove to Zoe's, fully expecting to find her in the barn, but when she walked in, she found only her father. He was cleaning out trays under cages, refilling hay racks, apparently content to putter around. But why shouldn't he be? With the misters

THE SUMMER I DARED　　　　341

giving aromatic puffs every few minutes, the rabbits scrabbling and shifting, and fog muting the rest of the world, the barn was as peaceful as ever.

On closer look, she realized he wasn't entirely content, but rather wore the same furrowed look he'd had at dinner the evening before.

Letting him be, Julia checked out the babies in the nest boxes. As always, though, she gravitated toward Gretchen. She didn't even have to sit down now; she could easily hold the rabbit in the crook of her elbow, stroking her while swaying gently from side to side.

"So," she said after a bit, "are you enjoying yourself?"

"Very much," her father declared with a bit too much zeal. "It's nice not to be programmed for a change."

"Are you talking about your work, or Mom?"

"Both."

"So. Tell me about your day. What'd you do?"

He gave a lopsided shrug. "Oh, walked around."

"Where?"

"In town. On the dock. Wherever. I talked with people. You know."

What Julia knew was that he sounded less than enthused. "Have you called her?" she asked.

"Not yet."

She waited for him to say more, but he simply removed a depleted water bottle from the wall of a cage and replaced it with a full one. So she asked, "Do you plan to?"

"Eventually," he said with renewed bravado. "I can't stay here forever. I have a business to run. She isn't the only important person in our house. Fortunately, the second quarter is over and estimateds are paid, so this is my quiet season."

"Mom loves you, you know."

"So you've said."

"Come on, Dad," Julia coaxed as she had so many other times. "She has to be autocratic at work; that's how she succeeds. She just has trouble turning it off." She watched him replace another water bottle. "You don't really plan to divorce her, do you? That'd be a mistake. She's a good person."

"Is she?" her father asked. "After what she's done to you?"

Julia bit her tongue. No, her mother hadn't been there for her after the accident. Nor, though, had her father, so it was the pot calling the kettle black. Besides, Janet's greatest sin in Julia's opinion was what she had done to Zoe. Wasn't George the source of *that* problem?

"Tell me something, Dad. You could have gone to visit Uncle Martin in Hilton Head or Charlie Payne on Mackinac Island. Why'd you come here?"

"Because you were here. You needed me."

"What about Zoe? It's clearly more hurtful to Mom, your coming here rather than going to one of those other places."

Her father stared at her long enough to see that she knew what had happened between Zoe and him. To his credit, he didn't deny it. Further to his credit, he finally sounded less spiteful and more adult. "We're talking a one-time thing an awful lot of years ago, Julia. It's time your mother got over it. We've avoided the issue for too long. Maybe facing it will help." Reaching for two more freshly filled water bottles, he walked off to the cages at the end of the row.

Facing it by walking away? Facing it by refusing to call?

Oh, yes, Julia was guilty of those things herself. What to do? Agonizing over that thought, she continued to stroke Gretchen before returning her to her cage, at which point Ned began rubbing her leg. Squatting, she scratched his ears until he'd had enough and wandered off. Julia headed to the house. "Zoe?" she called out.

"In my bedroom!"

Passing the rooms Molly and her father were using, Julia went on to Zoe's. It had been added several years before, and was larger and brighter than the others, for good reason. Zoe did much of her spinning here. There was a bed, a nightstand, a dresser, an armoire, and an easy chair with a hassock, but the skylights in the cathedral ceiling channeled light onto a beautiful walnut spinning wheel. Zoe sat there, her bare feet rhythmically working a pair of treadles while her hands were neatly lined up, one in front of the other, guiding newly plucked angora to the wheel.

Julia watched for a while from the door. The motion of the wheel was steady and smooth, the rapid little tick-tick-tick of the turning bobbin hypnotic. Even the treadles seemed to whisper with each depression. The peacefulness here was much like that in the barn. Zoe's world was a resonant one, indeed.

Quietly, Julia approached the wheel. "Whose fur are you spinning?"

"My lilac. See the color?" She stopped the wheel and pointed with her thumb. "It's a subtle lilac, really a mauve. The color is deeper at the end of the fur. When I spin it, it comes out striped." Julia had just enough time to look close and see the stripe before Zoe got the wheel spinning again. "When someone knits this, it'll work up as a heather."

"This is for knitting then, not weaving?"

"Oh, it could be used for weaving, but not rug making. It's one-ply and way too fine. I'm doing this on special order for a woman who owns a yarn store in Boston. She stocks some of the most beautiful and unusual yarns. If she likes this, she'll order more. It would be a good market for me."

Her hands were deft, holding the fur between forefingers and thumbs, moving in a little, out a little, while the wheel whirred, the treadles whispered, and the bobbin made that soft tick-tick-tick as it turned.

Julia took a deep breath and smiled. "I could watch this forever. It's as calming as working with the rabbits. Dad is keeping busy out there, by the way. How's it going with you and him?"

Zoe continued to spin. "The awkwardness is starting to fade."

"Are you still drawn to him?"

"No. He has aged, and so have I. There have been other men in my life. You know that. Each one lasted longer and meant more to me than George did. I'm not belittling your father. He's a wonderful man. But

I've grown into someone different from the woman I was back then." She paused. "Haven't you?"

Julia had. Definitely. "But you loved him once. Are you saying love doesn't last?"

"I'm saying that, in my case, what I thought was love wasn't. Your case is different," Zoe went on, correctly tracking Julia's thoughts. "What's happening with Monte and you may be a factor of growth. Sometimes you grow in the same direction as the person you're with, sometimes you don't. It happens over a period of time, not overnight."

"I've felt different about so many things since the accident."

"My guess is you felt different before the accident but refused to see it."

The bobbin continued its tick-tick-tick, the treadles their soft little puffs.

"I saw it," Julia said at last. She simply hadn't been ready to act.

"So, what if you were to tell this to Monte?"

Julia had asked herself that dozens of times. "He would go on and on about how understandable this is after a traumatic experience, but that it'll pass, because I do have a good life and, yes, he and I may have some differences, but every couple does. He'll say how can I possibly think there are other women. He'll say I'm the first and the last. And he'll convince me, Zoe. He's the ultimate salesman. He has an answer for everything."

Zoe stopped pedaling. The wheel slowed, the tick of the bobbin came to a stop. "Counseling?"

"Been there. It might have helped if Monte had come, but he didn't think he needed counseling. As far as he was concerned, it was all about my insecurity."

"What if you were to say you want a divorce?"

Julia had considered this, too. "He'd say I had no grounds."

"Adultery isn't grounds?"

"He'd say it never happened and that I just jumped to conclusions. He'd say I was upset. He'd say that I don't have a clue what divorce means. He'd say that if I ever knew how badly I could end up, I wouldn't even *mention* the word."

"Is that a threat?"

"Vaguely."

"It certainly isn't the voice of a loving husband."

That was the hardest part for Julia. Nothing Monte did showed real love. He never went out of his way for her, never made a sacrifice for her sake. Everything was programmed: *She is your wife, therefore you buy lingerie for her birthday, flowers for our anniversary, jewelry for Christmas.*

A loving husband? "No," she said with an inner loneliness that physically hurt. "Just a stubborn one."

"But why?" Zoe cried. "What's in it for him? If he has affairs, if he doesn't feel love, why does he want the marriage to last?"

Julia laughed bitterly. "He knows he has a good thing in me. Lots has happened in the world since we got married. Another woman would be younger and more demanding. She wouldn't put up with his playing around. Nor would she be alone in the kitchen at ten-thirty at night cleaning up after a dinner for six, while Monte sits with his feet up on the hassock and watches the late news."

"Oh, Julia."

She smiled. "Not a nice situation."

"And Noah? You like him, don't you."

She nodded.

Zoe's eyes held compassion. "Danger, Julia. Danger."

Chapter 16

The police station on Big Sawyer was little more than a storefront office. It sat on Main Street, beside the post office and across from Brady's Tackle & Gear. There was no jail cell, as such; a lockable back room served for those who needed sobering up or cooling off for a night.

When Noah walked in, John Roman had his ankles crossed atop a weathered wood desk and his eyes on the computer screen. Dropping his feet, he sat forward. "Just the man I wanted to see. Had some fun today, did you?"

"You bet," Noah said without remorse. Contrary to what Ian might think, he didn't believe in the willful destruction of property, except when it came to violators of local law. Those violators stole the livelihood of far more needy fishermen than Noah.

"Take a look at this," John said, pointing at the computer screen.

Putting thoughts of Kim on hold, Noah rounded the desk. He didn't recognize the face on the screen—hadn't been at the Grill at the right time—but the text beside the picture was clear. "Kevin Welk," he read and perused a short but impressive criminal record. He had no sooner finished when John brought up another page, this one devoted to Curt Haber. Between the two, they had convictions spanning the last dozen or so years for bank theft, breaking and entering, and assault.

"Their names kept cropping up," John explained, "so I decided to check them out. Not your usual lobstermen."

No. They weren't even the usual poachers. The usual poacher was either a newbie who didn't know any better, or a fisherman from another island who simply wanted to muscle his way into more fertile grounds. "Do they have licenses to lobster here?"

"Sure do. I checked that out first. Everything with the state was filed in good order. This other . . ." John raised his brows, scratched the back of his neck, shook his head. "So, I'm asking myself what they're doing here, and my mind keeps going places it probably shouldn't be going."

Noah knew those places. He often returned there himself. "What's the latest theory on Artie's death?"

"For lack of anything better, they're saying he shot himself. The INS has gone back to the smuggling part. They're focusing on a guy in Florida who's supposed to be the mastermind. Someone, or a group of someones, has been shuttling illegals from large boats outside the two-hundred-mile limit to private docks on the mainland. They don't see Artie as doing the actual transfer, just arranging for it."

No mention of Kim. Relieved, Noah said, "Haber and Welk are from Florida."

"Yup. So I ask myself why they're here and whether there's a reason behind their making public nuisances of themselves. Hell, the guys are loud. Makes you wonder if lobstering's just a cover."

Noah agreed. Most poachers were subtle. Most responded to the first warning. It was almost as if Haber and Welk were going out of their way to let everyone know that they wanted to haul traps. Only wanted to haul traps. Only wanted to catch lobster.

"Still," he pointed out, "there's no way they could have shot Artie in that fog."

"Unless one of them was on the boat with him."

"If so, he would have died, too," Noah tried off-handedly.

"Not necessarily," said the chief of police, watching him closely now. "Who's to say someone couldn't have been thrown off *The Beast* like you were thrown off the *Amelia Celeste*? Who's to say it wasn't Haber or Welk, or maybe even a third person?"

John knew, Noah realized—and if he didn't *know,* then he suspected—and that, without knowledge of the bankbook.

"So here's the story," John went on. His voice was quieter, holding an element of resignation. "They know Artie was connected to Kim. They just don't know how. Could be it was sexual, could be it was something else. There's only one person who knows, and that's Kim. Now, don't look at me like that, Noah. The Colellas are cousins on my wife's side, so I'm protective of her, too. Even if sex was all it was, she might know something that can help us. She was around Artie. She was at his house, and she was on his boat. I keep telling her there's nothing to worry about because I'll protect her, but she still won't say a word."

"Maybe she can't," Noah said, because it occurred to him that if Kim had been more than a mistress, and something had gone awry, leading to Artie's death, she might be in danger herself.

"I've been out at the house every day for a week now," John went right on. "Most days she isn't there. When she is, she just sits on that sofa and looks at her hands. How long'll that go on, before someone higher 'n me decides it's time she tells them what she knows, and brings her in?"

Noah caved in about the computer, but only because he wanted Ian to have something to do while he and Julia talked to Kim—or so he told himself. Deep down, he probably wanted to impress Ian. The hill house wasn't the typical Big Sawyer home, any more than the electronics inside were the toys of a hick.

So he called it quits on the water Wednesday at three, which was just as well, with the dense fog and rough seas. He got them both home to shower, and was at the hill house by four. Expecting them, Julia had left the front door ajar, and Lucas raced right on through. By the time they joined him, she was bent over rubbing his ears, laughing between wet doggie kisses. Laughter lingered on her face when she straightened, beautiful in plain old jeans and a blouse, with her blonde hair brushing her shoulders and her features alive. She had just taken scones from the oven; some were moist with chocolate chunks, others crunchy with Heath Bar bits, still others dotted with wild blueberries. She had clearly gone food shopping on her own. He wanted to think she had done it for him. If not that, he wanted to think she had done it for Ian.

He was actually more touched by thought of the second option. She understood what he was trying to do with the boy and seemed to want to do her part to help. Given the appetite that Ian had developed in the last day, she couldn't have picked a better way.

"Scones usually go with tea this hour of the day," she told Ian affably, "but I figured you wouldn't be the tea type. So I bought Coke and a Frappuccino."

Ian's hand hovered over a Heath Bar scone. "Cool enough to eat?" he asked.

"Should be," Julia said, handing him a napkin and offering one to Noah, who reached for a chocolate scone.

Seeing unsureness in her seconds before he took a bite, Noah's heart melted right along with the chocolate—but the scone was delicious. He indicated as much with a low moan of pleasure. After a heartfelt "Thank you," he led Ian to the loft.

At the top of the stairs, Ian's eyes lit. "Oh, wow. This is really yours?"

"Yes. Julia's just staying here until a room opens at

her aunt's." He turned on the computer, but that was all he had to do. By the time the programs were loaded and the desktop displayed, Ian was on his way to the Internet.

Noah became irrelevant then. For a minute or two he watched, fascinated by the ease with which his son worked the web. He wasn't even sure Ian heard him when he said, "I'll be back," and headed downstairs.

He helped himself to another scone on his way out the door with Julia, but when he told Lucas to stay with Ian, the dog wasn't having any part of it. Pushing his way into the backseat of the truck, he sat behind Julia and looked defiantly at Noah.

So Noah caved in on this, too, and the dog came along. "Bluff or beach?" he asked Julia.

"Bluff," Julia said. "I just talked with Nancy."

Sure enough, the small blue Honda was there by the stone keeper's house. Both were shrouded in the mist. Even harder to see was Kim, sitting on the rocks beyond it, looking warily back at the truck.

Pulling on a sweatshirt, Julia climbed out. When her hair began to blow, she held it back. "Hi," she called over the pounding of the surf as she started over the rocks carrying a small bag of scones.

Noah got out and held the door open for Lucas, but between the hammering surf and the wind, Lucas looked dubious. Nervous eyes trailed Julia, but the rest of his body wasn't moving. He finally curled up and put his chin on his paws.

Noah closed the door and started toward the

rocks. This was the first time he had seen Kim since the accident. She was bundled in a jacket, red hair tucked away; her face was thinner than he recalled. He guessed she had lost weight that she couldn't afford to lose, and understood why Julia had wanted to bring food.

That said, she didn't look sick. Pale, perhaps, and frightened. But sick enough to be unable to speak?

Kim raised anxious eyes to Julia. They moved to Noah, then returned.

"You know him, he's a friend," Julia said with gentle insistence. Settling herself close to Kim, she opened the bag and handed her a scone. Kim took it and began to eat, but she remained guarded, her body not quite relaxed, her eyes never far from Noah.

He sat on a nearby rock and looked out into the fog, while he tried to decide how to begin. He didn't envy John Roman his job. Pressuring people—interrogating them—wasn't a fun thing to do. Or maybe it was just that Noah was a lousy communicator. Sandi was probably right in that. If he couldn't communicate with his own son, what was he supposed to say in a sensitive situation like this?

He waited until most of Kim's scone was gone. As carefully as he could then, he explained why he had come. "The Chief is doing everything he can to keep investigators away. He doesn't want them bothering you. He wants to give you time to heal. The problem is that the investigation is going nowhere. John is afraid that he won't be able to keep them away much longer." He sat forward. "Because you and Artie were involved, they figure you know something. They don't care if you were having an affair with Artie. They want to know other things you might have seen, like who called Artie, who visited him, what names he used to mention."

Kim swallowed hard, but said nothing.

Noah looked out at the gray again. This kind of fog was more typical of August than July. Global warming? If it wasn't that, it had to be something else. They were predicting a week of storms. Going lobstering, he could live with fog. He could even live with a moderate chop. Increase the chop and add rain, and he had to sit home, and that was frustrating.

So was this. He wanted to help Kim—*really* wanted to help her. It was suddenly very important, part of the responsibility he felt in the aftermath of the accident. Ian was important. And now Kim.

"Why can't you speak?" he blurted out with less finesse than he might have, but he didn't know how else to get through. "Is it a physical thing? Emotional? Because here's the problem. Silence can sometimes be taken as a sign of guilt. If they ask you questions and you refuse to answer, they're going to think you're guilty. They don't know you like we do. They won't give you the benefit of the doubt. Talk to us, Kim. Tell us what you know."

Julia touched his arm.

"I can only hold John off so long," he told her more quietly. "He can only hold the *others* off so long."

Leaving her hand on his arm, Julia asked Kim, "Could you write the answers to questions we asked?"

Kim closed her eyes. Turning away, she put her head on her knees.

"Okay," Noah tried. "Here's another thought. They know that Artie was involved in bad stuff, and they know he was doing it with bad people. Those people are dangerous. You may think you're safe as long as you don't talk. But if those bad people get nervous enough, they may want insurance that your silence will last. John can protect you, but only if he knows what you know."

The hand on his arm tightened, but he didn't need the warning. He knew the danger of pushing Kim too far. Julia wasn't the only one who could imagine the girl throwing herself over the cliff. What Julia didn't know, though, was that he had a weapon to fight that.

Crossing to where Kim sat, he hunkered down in front of her. Very quietly, he said, "I know who he is, Kim."

Her eyes grew wider.

"There are times when you thought it was me," he went on, "but I was never with your mother. Talk to us—give us information—help us, and I'll help you." Nancy might not want the man identified, but Kim was over twenty-one, and perhaps this was part of Noah's responsibility. "He never knew, you know. He was here and then gone."

Kim was hanging on his every word. She pressed her lips together, then opened her mouth, and for a minute he thought she was going to speak, but the only sound that came out was a short bit of breath, immediately lost in the headland wind.

Having offered the carrot, Noah said, "Artie was working with a man from Florida. Do you know who he is?"

Kim gave a frightened head shake.

"Did he ever mention the names Curt Haber and Kevin Welk?"

Another frightened head shake.

"Did he tell you anything about his work?"

A third frightened head shake.

"Were you having an affair with Artie?"

This head shake was firmer.

"Were you on *The Beast* with Artie that day?"

This time there was no head shake at all. Kim straightened and was looking at him as if to say, *I'm not stupid. You're trying to trip me up.*

"I'm not the enemy, Kim. I don't even know who the enemy is. That's why I need your help. But okay. Here's another thought. Have you been on the water since the accident?"

Distrustful still, Kim simply stared.

"I didn't think so," he concluded, deciding that this was a brainstorm. "Me, I've been everywhere else but where the accident happened. Same with Julia. So let's put that demon behind us. We'll go out together, the three of us. Plus my son, whom you've never met. He's seventeen and wants to pretend nothing ever happened. He could use the reminder." And Kim could use the jolt, Noah figured. Even if it didn't help, nothing was lost. "I'll be at the dock tomorrow at four o'clock. We won't be out more'n an hour. You know where the slip is. Four o'clock."

*   *   *

Driving back to Hawks Hill, Julia kept glancing at Noah—kept remembering their time at the trap shed and feeling the warmth, kept telling herself that she had no business flirting with him, kept marveling that it felt so *good*.

But he was looking distracted, clearly concerned about Kim, so she refocused. "Do you think she'll be there tomorrow?"

He drew in a long breath and pulled himself back from wherever he'd been. "I don't know. It just seems like the right thing to do. Maybe it's a selfish thing. Gives me an excuse to take Ian there." He shot a questioning look at Julia, eyes haunted in a way she hadn't seen since the days immediately following the accident.

"It's a great idea," she said. "It certainly can't hurt."

"Assuming she shows up. The fact is, she needs a shrink."

"She won't see one. I've asked her. I've asked Nancy to ask her. She's clearly afraid to talk."

"Or guilty. Very guilty."

"Of what?" Julia asked, desperate to know. "Do you really think she was involved in smuggling illegal aliens?" She couldn't imagine that Kim would knowingly do that. The girl seemed too innocent—too sensitive—to be involved.

"My problem," Noah replied, "is that she's been silent now for more than two weeks. If it's from shock, that should be easing. Same with grief at losing Artie. So maybe she's silent out of guilt. But guilt at having slept with a married man? I don't buy that. She's seen it too often. She certainly wouldn't be scolded for it by Nancy or June. But she is scared of something." He shot her another glance. "Do you agree?"

"I do. Do you really know who her father is?"

He nodded. "My first college summer, three of my buddies came back here with me to work. He was the wildest of them. He waited tables that summer and went back to school with grand plans to do Wall Street after graduation, but he played too much, and his grades showed it. He settled for the family business, which folded a few years later. He hasn't made any money, so it's not like he could have helped Nancy or Kim. He's a nice enough guy—clueless professionally, clueless socially, but nice enough."

"Is he married?"

"Yes, with two kids, maybe three."

"Would he want to know about Kim?" she asked. She guessed that the only thing worse than not knowing the identity of your father was knowing that he didn't want to have anything to do with you.

"I could convince him," Noah replied.

Julia didn't ask how. She didn't want to know. Her concern in this situation was Kim. She was thinking that she ought to take Molly along for the boat ride on the chance that someone Kim's own age might make a connection, when Noah pulled off the road into his drive. Several minutes later, when the truck made the last turn and the house appeared, it was as though thinking of Molly had conjured her up. There was the little Plymouth of Zoe's that she was using, parked by the front door.

Julia shot Noah a quizzical look and climbed from the truck the instant it came to a stop. The activity inside the house was centered around the kitchen. Molly was there, as was Ian, along with food on the counter, pots on the stove, dishes on the table. Half a dozen things seemed to be in the works. Something smelled divine.

Seeing her, Molly said an indignant, "I came over here thinking you'd be alone and hungry, in which case I'd cook you dinner, since I have the night off. Instead, I found Ian. We're making bouillabaisse and, quite honestly, there isn't enough for four."

Noah passed Julia and went to the stove. He peered into the largest pot. "That smells incredible. What's in it?"

Ian answered. "Scallops, mussels, clams, monk-fish, and lobster."

"I thought you didn't like lobster."

"Cooked this way, it's palatable."

"Palatable?" Molly echoed, pulling her chin back as if from a blow. But she was strong on the rebound. "It's more than that. If you don't *love* this, there's something wrong with your taste buds. Could be im-maturity," she added with a smirk. "Hand me the cayenne, would you?"

Ian handed her the cayenne. Seeing them side by side, Julia couldn't help but think that they were two handsome children. Molly was adorably chic with her short blonde hair—yes, she had to admit that her daughter's short hair was chic—her etched features and slender curves, and Ian was appropriately taller, more muscular, and apparently willing to help.

Noah was still at the stove, albeit now out of the line of immediate work. "There's lobster meat in the freezer," he offered. "If we defrost it, there might be enough in there for four."

"*Frozen* lobster?" Molly asked. "In this bouillabaisse? I don't think so."

"What if I drive down to the store for extra ingredients?" he tried, but she summarily vetoed that idea.

"The island store doesn't have the freshest. Rick has the freshest."

"Then I'll drive down to the Grill."

"Rick's off for the night."

Noah pulled his cell phone from his pocket. "How about I call Rick. He'll tell whoever is *on* to give me what we need. Would that work?"

Julia tried not to grin. It looked like he had her.

But Molly wasn't so easily bested. Quick-tongued— she was, indeed, her father's daughter—she began ticking off a list. "You'll also need another baguette, a leek, and a fennel bulb. And pick up a starter—let's say two orders of escargot and two of the hearts of palm salad. And a blueberry tart for dessert. Buy the large size. Ian's starved." She grinned at Noah.

"Thank you," Julia said several hours later. She and Molly sat on the leather sofa in the living room, alone now, both slouched low with their heads on the back of the seat. Sealed in by fog and drizzle, the house was more homey than ever, made even more so by the lingering scent of the stew's garlicky tomato base. "Dinner was fabulous."

Molly smiled. "It was good."

Julia reached sideways and caught her hand. "Thanks for being civil."

"Civil?"

"Warm. It wasn't that hard, was it?"

Molly grunted. "No. They're okay people. They did the cleanup."

"What did you think of Ian?"

"He's too young for me."

"Not that way. As a person."

"Ask me again in five years. Right now, he's still into adolescent angst."

"Spoken by a veteran twenty-year-old."

"You know what I mean. He's angry."

"So are you lately."

"I have cause. My life is in chaos. I don't know what's happening. There have been so many changes since high school, and now this—you. You just seem so different, so independent."

Julia tried to make light of it. "Isn't that a good thing?"

"Yes for you, no for me. You were always predictable. Now it's like I don't know what you're going to do next."

In fact, Julia didn't either. Spontaneity was a luxury she hadn't tasted much of in the past. "Some things never change. I'll always love you. I'll always be there for you." When Molly slid toward her, she opened an arm. "We do things I never did with my own mother."

Molly looked up from the crook of her shoulder. "You had the time. She didn't. She worked."

"Many working mothers have the kinds of relationships with their children that I have with you. It has to do with attitude."

"Quality time."

"Uh-huh."

"So, how does it feel being independent?"

"Novel."

Molly grew more cautious. "You've had time to think. Do you know where you're going?"

Who am I? Julia still wasn't sure. There were no manuals for reinventing a life. It was all trial and error, feeling her way along, one day at a time. "I'm still working on it."

"But you're not going back to New York," the girl said, laying down the gauntlet, and the old Julia would have hemmed and hawed and said what would be of comfort to Molly. The new Julia needed to be more honest.

"A year ago, I would have said yes, because that's what everyone there seems to want. But it's not a simple decision. There's nothing win-win about divorce." She felt a tremor in Molly and held her tighter. "I've been blessed with a healthy daughter who is on her way to a fabulous career. You'll be taking your own roads, Molly, and I wouldn't dream of holding you back. You'll be finding things that make you happy. I want to do the same. I'm only forty. With a little luck, I may have another forty years to live."

"Dad loves independent women."

He certainly did, Julia realized with a stab of bitterness. Unfortunately, he didn't consider *her* to be one. Independence wasn't part of his definition of her. She wasn't sure he could change that definition, any more than he could control his need for other women—and for the first time she wondered if she cared. She was angry at Monte. Time and again, he had betrayed her. He might say that she had abandoned him this summer, but the truth was that he was content to have her gone.

Another truth? She was content to *be* gone. It was nice not feeling the pressure of seeing to his every need—nice not having to suffer the backhanded little jabs he was so adept at slinging. If it wasn't, *Your man didn't give you the best piece of swordfish today,* it was, *Don't you need to comb your hair?* or, *You're not wearing that suit tonight, are you?* or even, *Once in a while, it'd be nice if you got on top.*

Julia was delighted to be free of that. She didn't know whether saving the marriage for the sake of saving the marriage would work anymore.

"If you didn't go back to New York," Molly asked, "would you stay here?"

"Does it matter?"

"Yes. I feel like you're getting involved in a world I don't know, like I'm going to lose you."

Julia smiled. "That's just how I felt when you started college. I was convinced that what we'd had between us was over and done, that my little girl was off on her own and that things would never be the same—and I was right. They won't ever be the same. But different isn't bad. Actually, different is good. It can even be better. I like the relationship we have. It's very adult."

"You seem peaceful about this."

Julia did feel peaceful, surprisingly so, given that her stomach still churned when she thought about Monte. He was unfinished business, a huge question mark. Saying the word "divorce" aloud was one thing, facing the reality of it was far more terrifying. Her future was a mystery. That, alone, was cause for fear.

Peaceful? Committed was probably a better word.

"This feels like the right thing," she said, "like I'm heading in the right direction. Actually, it feels good to head in *any* direction. I've been static too long." But not since the accident. Like Kim, she felt a jolt, reliving that night. Her past had exploded right along with the *Amelia Celeste* and *The Beast*. The result felt like liberation. "As for my getting involved in a world you don't know, that doesn't have to be. There's actually someone I'd like you to meet. What time do you start work tomorrow?"

"Two," Molly said.

"Oh, dear. That's too early. We're taking Kim out on the *Leila Sue*. She hasn't been on the water since the accident. We're hoping it'll give her a little push, maybe some closure. You and she are close in age, and you're so good with people. You could be a real help."

"What time are you going?" Molly asked.

"Four."

Seeming pleased, the girl smiled. "I'll be there."

"But work—"

"Rick is as worried about Kim as everyone else. He'll give me a few hours off."

* * *

Naturally, Julia brought food. It wasn't that this was a party, though it was in fact a rite of sorts, but bringing food was simply what she *did*. She doubted that part of her would ever change—and in this case it wasn't bad at all. For one thing, Noah and Ian were starved. They had just finished washing down the boat after a day of work, and though they had put on dry clothes, they were flagging. Their eyes lit up at the sight of Julia's insulated bag. Warm drumsticks, wedges of thick grilled cheese, and hot cider hit the spot on another foggy day, when the dampness defied the arrival of July and gave the salt air a chill. Her choice of offerings was validated when Rick Greene, who lived with Maine weather all the time, sent Molly along with bacon-wrapped scallops and grilled portobellos, all hot. They opened the bags on the console and helped themselves while Julia filled cups from the thermos. And that was another thing. Noah was pretty adorable when he was famished and trying to be civilized about it, while his son, the supposedly civilized one, scarfed food down.

Noah was pretty adorable anyway, Julia thought— and she wasn't, no, she wasn't flirting with him. But being near him gave her a buzz. Who wouldn't want that?

Four o'clock came and went. Noah and Ian had eaten the bulk of the food but were deliberately leaving some for Kim. By 4:05 Noah was glancing at his watch. Pulling his Patriots cap low on his brow, he exchanged a worried look with Julia. By four-ten he was scanning the shore through the fog, and Julia was fearing that their efforts were in vain.

At four-fifteen, a blue car appeared. When it parked a distance from the pier, Julia had her doubts, but the woman who climbed out did look to be Kim. She wore the same hooded jacket she had worn on the bluff and presented the same diminutive figure. Head lowered, she hurried down the dock toward the *Leila Sue*. As she neared, Julia saw that under the hood she wore a black watchman's cap, under which she had piled every last strand of her hair. With that hair hidden and no other distinguishing feature in sight, she could pass for any one of the local women.

She didn't want to be seen. Julia could only begin to imagine the courage it had taken for her to come. Courage, desire to heal, need to revisit the site of the crash, perhaps simply the wish to cooperate with Noah, who had information she wanted—whatever, she was there. She kept her head down as she climbed aboard. It was only when she was hidden half inside the wheel-house that she raised her eyes to acknowledge the others, but those eyes were worried. She looked from face to face when she was introduced to Molly and Ian. She shook her head when they offered her food, at which point Noah said, "Are you sure?" When she nodded, he and Ian finished off what was left.

Noah backed the *Leila Sue* from her slip and picked his way out of the harbor. There were more boats now than had been here two weeks before. Pleasure craft had joined the usual gang of lobster boats at moorings. The summer folk had arrived.

The *Leila Sue* passed a particularly handsome boat. Her canvas was up; inside its cover, lamps lit a group of forlorn boaters.

"They can't be happy with this weather," Julia remarked. "Will it clear for the weekend?"

"Doesn't look it," said Noah. "Lobster boat races are a fixture on the Fourth of July weekend, but word is they may be canceled. The forecast isn't good. They're predicting wind and rain late Sunday and Monday. Hear that, Ian?"

Ian was with Molly—and Molly with Kim, to Julia's gratitude—all three crowded as deep into the wheelhouse as they could be without disappearing into the cuddy. Jackets were zipped, hoods tied, and hands pulled up into the shelter of sleeves. Julia was hooded herself, rain slicker over sweatshirt, over more layers both above and below.

"I could use a day off," Ian said.

"Sorry," Noah said, sounding not sorry at all. "If the forecast holds, we're working Sunday, too. The law won't allow us to lobster, but it gives us leave to move traps if a storm is brewing." To Julia, he said, "Traps in the shallows will be knocked around by high wind and storm surge. We'll haul them up and set them deeper. It's either that or risk losing half the stock."

Julia was peering out the front window. "How can you *see* to do anything?"

Noah tapped the screens before him. "Besides, I know these waters." He gave the radio an extra jiggle. It came right on. There was static and strands of conversation, but they filtered out into the wind.

"Do you know where the accident was?"

"Longitude and latitude, yes."

She didn't say anything more, nor did she move from his side. In weather eerily reminiscent of the day of the accident, he represented safety.

The *Leila Sue* picked up speed. Assuming that Kim was thinking back to that day too, Julia caught the girl's eye. "Okay?" she mouthed.

Kim had removed the watchman's cap, so wisps of red hair blew around the edge of her hood, but she didn't appear happy—actually looked as though she might scream, which would probably have been the best thing in the world for her.

In the end, she didn't scream, just gave a nod.

As the boat pitched ahead through the seas, there was no talk, just the thrum of the engine, the sputter of the radio, the rush of the wind, and the slap of the hull. It wasn't a long ride. The *Amelia Celeste* had been nearly home when *The Beast* hit. Keeping a close watch on the instrument panel, Noah plowed on. Finally, he said, "This is it," and killed the engine.

The boat rose and fell, and the wind whistled over the wheelhouse, but all else was still. Noah went to the gunnel and stood somberly. Moments later, Ian joined him there. He didn't touch Noah. A solid arm's length separated them. Julia was nonetheless grateful for the gesture.

Wanting to give them time alone, she went to the stern. It was here, on the *Amelia Celeste,* that so many people had died. The *Leila Sue* was a different boat—smaller than the *Amelia Celeste* and outfitted for lobstering, not ferrying—but Julia was instantly transported back to that night. She didn't recall the details of the boarding. She had been rushed; they were still a blur. But she felt the presence of the eight people who had been lost—felt it so clearly that she shuddered and wrapped her arms around herself. Moments later, Molly was there. Seeming to know what to do this time, she gave Julia a hug.

"Do you feel it?" the girl whispered.

"I do," Julia whispered back.

"Did those people know what hit them?"

"They knew *The Beast* was coming."

"Did he do it *intentionally*?" Molly cried with more feeling now.

Julia was about to say she didn't know, when something cold touched her hand. With her hood up, she couldn't see on her left. Now she turned and saw Kim.

The girl's eyes were filled with sorrow. They went from Julia to Molly and back. In a deliberate motion, she shook her head.

"Not intentionally?" Julia asked.

Kim repeated the head shake and touched her own shoulder.

"Because he was shot," Julia interpreted. "But why was he still driving the boat?"

Kim shook her head in bewilderment.

"You don't know?"

Another head shake, more vehement this time, with a hint of panic.

"But you were there," Julia whispered.

Panic gave way to something so far beyond regret as to be painful, and the answer was suddenly clear. Julia would have asked more, if it hadn't seemed irrelevant to the moment. Explanations could come later. Right now in Kimmie's eyes were agony and need—agony over what had occurred, need to be accepted despite it.

Julia pulled her close on the right while Molly stayed locked to her on the left, the three of them steadying one another against the roll of the boat as they looked out over the stern. They were buffeted by the wind, but appropriately so—reality pushing, pushing, pushing against what the human soul could bear.

Larger than the women and more used to the roll of the boat, Noah stood firm at the starboard gunnel staring out at the sea. He barely noticed the wind or the spume that rose up when the bow of the boat dug into a wave. Taking deep breaths, he felt the life of his father consolidate and rise from the depths. Scenes scrolled up over the whitecaps—Hutch working dawn to dusk without complaint; Hutch saving to buy his wife a new and finer wedding band for their fiftieth wedding anniversary, though she was terminally ill; Hutch standing at the side of the truck that September morning when Noah left for college, watching him go, just watching, not moving an inch until the ferry was out of sight.

With these memories came the connection Noah sought. He and his father had shared more than an occupation and a house. They may never have said it aloud, but there had been feeling between them. That feeling now crowded Noah's throat.

And he had thought Kim needed this? *He* needed it. He hadn't been to this spot—to this *very* spot—since the accident. Since then he had lived through the funeral and the cleaning-out. He had returned to work, hauling traps through the day and using Haber and Welk as an outlet for his anger, filling in the quiet times by thoughts of survival, opportunity, and mission. But he was the one who needed closure. Here now, at the place where his father had breathed his last, he felt that.

Eyes filling with tears, he took the best of Hutch, tucked it inside, and prayed he could be as good a man. It struck him that if he had been spared death for nothing else, it was to gain this understanding of what, at the core, his father had been.

He felt someone beside him and looked over quickly. Ian was close now, awkward and unsure. "I didn't know him," the boy said.

Noah nodded. He faced the sea, faced the fact that it was his fault. He should have had Ian here every summer. He always told himself that the boy was busy with other things, that Sandi wouldn't want him on Big Sawyer so long, that Noah and Hutch had serious lobstering to do summers and couldn't be slowed down by a child. But they were all excuses for Noah's own insecurity. He could try to blame it on his marriage, but that didn't get him anywhere. It was time he took responsibility for his behavior. That was another reason why he had survived the accident.

He had three weeks. He was determined to make the most of them, starting with dinner tonight at the

Grill. He wanted to introduce his son to his friends. They might not have the advanced degrees that Sandi's friends had, but they were good people. He wanted Ian to hear their stories about Hutch.

Grateful to have direction, he glanced back at the stern. Julia's eyes met his. Worried still, they said that Kim hadn't talked.

He refused to be discouraged. If this hadn't worked, something else would. Returning to the wheel, he started the engine. As soon as the women were in the shelter of the wheelhouse again, he turned the *Leila Sue* and headed for shore. Riding with the tide, they made better time. But the fog remained thick. He had to slow to a crawl inside the harbor markers to avoid hitting other boats, and was relieved when he pulled into the slip.

Kim was off the boat the instant the lines were tied. Head bowed again, she hurried down the dock to the shore. Each step took her farther into the fog. She was nearly at the gauzy bit of blue that was her car when Molly cried, "Oh, look—she dropped her hat." Snatching the black watchman's cap from the deck, she scrambled out of the boat and ran after the girl.

At the same time, Kim must have realized she had left it, because she had barely closed herself in the Honda and started the motor when she climbed out again. Leaving the car running, she ran back toward the pier. She had just met Molly when an explosion rocked the Honda, and it burst into flames.

Chapter 17

Within seconds of the explosion, Julia was out of the boat and racing down the dock. She was vaguely aware of Noah and Ian passing her, but her focus was on Molly, who had sunk down to the wharf with Kim, the two of them a conjoined shape in the mist. She ran with her heart in her mouth, frightened enough not to see the pier, where people stood unharmed but in shock, far closer to the blazing car than were Molly and Kim. It was only when she reached the girls and pushed her way through the cluster that now included Noah, Ian, and half a dozen others that she found Molly unhurt, holding Kim, who was sobbing uncontrollably.

Molly raised terrified eyes to Julia's.

Even as more people came on the run, some heading for hoses to put out the fire, Julia dropped down and held them both, quaking bodies and tremulous limbs, hoods fallen back, faces pale and wet with tears.

"Oh God . . . oh God . . . oh God." The voice was fractured, words a sobbing whisper, but they definitely came from Kim.

Molly said shakily, "Someone bombed the car."

"He wants me dead," Kim cried between sobs. Her voice was reedy and high, but there was no mistaking the words.

"Who?" Noah asked gently.

"He tried once," she wailed brokenly, "but I grabbed the gun. It wasn't supposed to go off—but he just kept holding on—and then it *did*."

Artie. The pieces fell into place. As stunned as Julia was by the bombing, as shaken by what might have happened to her own daughter, as muddled by memories of another explosion and death, she was still able to think. Those thoughts painted a new picture of what had happened that day on *The Beast.*

Noah's eyes met hers. They reflected the same picture.

"Let's get her out of here," he said softly, because more and more people were crowding around, and a public confession wouldn't do. As he said it, John Roman was breaking out of the fog at the far end of the parking lot and running their way. Off to the other side, hoses had doused the worst of the flames, leaving Kim's car strewn in pieces around a smoldering core.

"My office," John said.

Noah shook his head. "My house. It's less threatening. Besides," he added in a warning to John, "I want to hear what she has to say before I turn her over to you." He helped Kim up. With Ian dashing ahead and a number of the townsfolk coming along, he held her against his side and walked her down the dock to his truck.

Julia helped Molly up and then held her, just held her there on the dock for the longest time. People hovered, offering comforting words, a quick touch, the gentle squeeze of an arm—all gestures that helped. They showed caring and support in a place that, three weeks earlier, had never heard of Julia Bechtel or her daughter. Still, the panic that had been so instinctive in the seconds after the blast now returned in lurid detail. Had Molly been faster or Kim slower, the two would have been at the car when the blast occurred. They would have died. Thinking of the possibility, Julia had trouble breathing.

But she wanted to be with Noah and Kim. When she had recovered a measure of composure, she wrapped an arm around Molly's waist and started walking. There was no talk about Molly returning to work at the Grill. Rick Greene was one of those on the dock and accompanied the two women to Julia's car. He even offered to drive, but Julia smiled, shook her head, and thanked him. She needed to feel in control of something. By the time she arrived at Noah's, she was sure enough of Molly's safety to focus on Kim.

They were gathered in the living room, where upholstered furniture, aged wood side tables, and amber lamps offered comfort, while the corner woodstove gave dryness and warmth. The room was an escape from the fog and fear beyond.

Kim had sunk deep into a corner of the sofa. Her mother and grandmother arrived shortly after Julia, but they stood apart, seeming wary of what Kim might say.

Noah sat on the coffee table near Kim, elbows on his knees, a compassionate look in his eyes. "What happened today—that's why you need to tell us about Artie. We can't protect you unless we know what kind of danger you're in."

Kim was looking at him, clearly clinging to the assurance in his voice. She held a glass of water braced in her lap, but it was none too steady even then.

"Were you on *The Beast* that day?" Noah asked.

She nodded.

"Had you been at the house first with Artie?"

She nodded again, and with that second silent gesture, Julia feared the muteness had returned. But then Kim took a drink of water, cleared her throat, and said in a rusty voice, "I went to talk with him. I needed him to explain what he was doing."

"What he was doing with you, you mean?"

She shook her head. "We never did that."

"Never had an affair?"

"No. It was just supposed to look that way." Her eyes fell. It was another minute before she cleared her throat again and raised her head. "It was supposed to cover up the other."

"The other?"

"The money." She shot John a wary look.

"Ignore him," Noah said. "What you say here is not any kind of formal confession. It's just friends wanting to know what happened that day. He hasn't read you your rights. Nothing you say now can be held against you, and if he dares quote anything from this discussion, we'll all deny it was said."

That would be perjury if they were under oath at the time, but Julia knew she would commit it in an instant if someone tried to railroad Kim. She felt passionately about this. It was good to be passionate about something that mattered. Her life had lacked passion. She had never had to fight over Molly, which was probably a good thing. Then again, perhaps if she'd had to—if she had been forced to show passion—she would have grown up long before now.

Noah shared the passion. His was quiet and controlled, but there was no doubting that he meant every word he directed at John.

Kim seemed to calm. She swallowed. "I was making cash deposits for him in Portland. He was paying me to do it." She faltered and took a drink. "He said he was sheltering it from taxes. I knew it was wrong for him to do that, but he was offering me good money to make runs to the bank, and I"—her voice cracked—"I really wanted that money."

"For what?" John asked.

Does it matter? Julia cried silently. She knew what the money was for; Kim had told her, in no uncertain terms. But how could the girl tell these people who loved Big Sawyer that she did not? She couldn't afford to offend them. In the legal sense, they held her future in their hands. She was in a precarious position.

But Julia didn't know the Kim who had tended bar prior to the accident, a woman who could hold her own against the roughest of auto mechanics, shipyard workers, and lobstermen. She had more moxie than Julia imagined.

Her chin grew firm. With only the slightest glance at Nancy and June, she said, "To leave here. To go somewhere else." Raspy though it was, her voice strengthened. "I didn't know what he was doing— didn't have a *clue* that the money was from smuggling illegals into the country until I overheard a conversation. I was at his house and the phone rang. I didn't want to answer it because it might have been his wife, and she *really* would have gotten the wrong idea. But the phone kept ringing, and once before he yelled at me for not answering it when he was expecting a call, so I picked up. We both did at the same time. He said hello first, and he didn't realize I was on the line, and then it was like if I hung up he would know I was. there and think I was snooping. It seemed better to be invisible. So I held the phone and listened, and even then it took me a while to figure out what was going on. I went home, and I went over and over what I had heard. That was when it hit me that he was using me for something way past evading taxes. So I went to his house to ask him about it."

"What did he say?"

"That I was wrong. That I had misheard and misunderstood, and why didn't we go out for a ride on the boat, because he really needed some air. So we did, and before I knew it, he pulled out a gun." Her voice was shaky now, her eyes wide. "He aimed it at me. He didn't say anything, but I knew he meant to kill me, and I didn't want to die. So I jumped at him." She jerked back. "The gun went off, and he was, like, totally unable to believe he was shot. He kept touching his shoulder and looking at the blood on his hand, and touching his shoulder and looking at the blood again. By the time he went looking for the gun, I already had it. I went way back to the sun deck, as far away from him as I could get, and I held that gun and would have killed him if he'd come at me again."

"Good girl," said Nancy.

Kim turned on her, eyes brimming with anguished tears. "I shot him, Ma. I shot him, and I got the gun, and then I was so upset about the whole thing that I looked away at the end, and because I did, we hit the *Amelia Celeste* and nine people died! I'm not good. I don't think I'll *ever* be good!"

Julia pressed a hand to her mouth, because Kim wasn't just saying the words. She meant them. That was what two and a half weeks of silence had been about. Just because she was speaking now didn't mean the guilt was gone. Things like that lingered— Julia knew. She hadn't planned to get pregnant, had been raised thinking that good girls were responsible for preventing the unexpected. When Monte was eager to get married, the pregnancy seemed like nothing more than an advance on a good thing. At some point, though—possibly around the time of his first affair—she began to wonder if he had felt trapped.

He hadn't actually said those words, but she felt them. An argument could be made that his affairs were a way of punishing her, and that she put up with them to ease her own guilt.

Noah's voice soothed. His words might as easily have fit her as Kim. "What happened wasn't your fault. There were two of you involved."

"But I shot him."

"With *his* gun, which he had taken along on *his* boat, for the purpose of killing you. You acted in self-defense, Kim."

"Were you aware that he was impaired?" John asked.

Kim looked back in surprise. "No. I thought the gunshot was nothing from the way he insisted on driving. If I had known his heart was going to stop, I'd have *done* something."

"Didn't you hear the calls from the *Amelia Celeste*?"

"I couldn't hear *anything*," she cried hoarsely. "I was sitting on top of the engines, and I was so upset that I couldn't think straight. The first I knew anything was wrong was when we hit the other boat, and the next thing, I was in the water. I honestly thought he had deliberately run us into the rocks, like he was trying to kill me that way. He *will* kill me. Look at what happened today."

"That wasn't Artie," Noah said. "Artie's dead."

Kim looked at him. Her eyes went to John, then to her mother, then to Julia. They stayed there for a minute.

Tapping into the trust that Julia believed they shared, she said, "He is dead, Kim. Someone else set that bomb."

"Who?" Kim asked in bewilderment.

John said, "I was hoping you could tell us. Do you know who was on the other end of that phone call?"

Kim took a drink of water and carefully returned the glass to her lap. "Dave. No last name."

John nodded. "That's one of the men they're watching. Anyone else?"

"They talked about 'the drivers.' No names, just 'the drivers.'"

"Those'd be the men who captain the boats bringing the cargo ashore."

"Cargo?" Kim cried. "They're *people*."

John told Noah, "The INS figures they're using old trawlers. No one looks twice when a boat like that passes by in the dark. They suspect Artie's job was arranging it. He and *The Beast* were so loud that it was a cover. He didn't ever try to be subtle. No one around here suspected him of being anything but obnoxious."

Noah asked, "Has the smuggling stopped now that Artie is gone?"

"No. Another transfer is in the works."

"If the authorities know all this," Julia asked in frustration, "why don't they make arrests?"

"Unless they catch them in the act, they won't have a case. But catching them in the act is hard. There's an awful lot of ocean and an awful lot of shoreline."

"What about Kim?" Julia asked John. "If she didn't know about the crime, is she in any way responsible?"

"Not if she helps us out."

"But if she helps you out, she'll be in worse danger than she already is."

"We're protecting her now."

Julia wanted to be alone with Noah. After yet one more incident showing the fragility of life, she wanted to talk about losing a parent, losing a spouse, losing one's own self-esteem. She wanted Noah to hold her the way he had outside the trap shed. She had never felt so alive.

Noah felt the same, if the way he looked at her meant anything. But Ian was there, as was Molly, and somehow the four of them ended up at the Grill. Thursday was hash night. At an inside table out of the rain, Noah ordered roast beef hash, Ian corned beef hash, Molly scallop hash, and Julia lobster hash. They didn't talk much among themselves, because there was always someone new drawing up a chair and wanting to discuss the explosion and Kim. If it wasn't one of Noah's fellow lobstermen, it was the manager of the island auto shop, the owner of the marina, or Alden Foss of Foss Fish and Lobster. Several of Zoe's friends stopped by, now Julia's friends, too. Zoe, herself, was there for a while.

Alex Brier came by wondering if Julia had any pictures of the burned-out car. While he was there, he pulled out the newly printed *Island Gazette* and pointed to three of her pictures. All were on the front page, with *Photo by Julia Bechtel* beneath each. She smiled and felt vaguely embarrassed—they were only snapshots. But Molly leaned over to look and said they were fabulous, and Ian leaned over to look and agreed, and Noah, who regularly read the weekly, broke away from Joe Brady, reached for the paper, and said that they were the best pictures the *Gazette* had printed in ages and that he hoped Alex was paying her what she was worth.

Matthew Crane approached, took a seat near Julia, and listened to the talk. He looked better than he had—less tired, more involved. Julia was pleased. He wasn't elderly. There was plenty of life in him yet.

And still Julia wanted to be with Noah, wanted to talk about what had happened that day. If she had felt an urgency after the accident to be heading somewhere, she felt it even more acutely now. At one point, seeing Monte in one of Molly's expressions, she thought to call him to talk it through, but immediately vetoed the idea. Monte wouldn't understand. He didn't have the patience to listen to Julia's problems. He was a glib answer man.

She didn't want Monte. She wanted Noah.

He looked at her often, and she had to settle for that. Though they sat with coffee long after the meal was done, a group remained there—as well as a sense of safety and comfort in the company of friends. In time, the friends wandered off, but even then Julia had no time with Noah. She was Molly's mother, and Molly wanted her back at Zoe's for a little while, at least.

So Julia went. She found her father bored with the book he was reading, and she talked with him. Mostly she sat on the bed with Molly, who wanted to talk about what Kim would do with her life, what Molly should do with her life, and what Julia would have done if Molly had died in the explosion.

"Don't even *think* those words," Julia scolded.

But Molly was determined. "If I died, would you leave Dad?"

"That's an awful question."

"Mom. Answer me."

It was something Julia didn't want to discuss with Molly, but they had reached a better place in the last two days, a grown-up place, and while Julia could never forget that Molly was her child, there was something to be said for honesty between adults. Molly could handle it. She, too, had grown since she had come here.

So Julia said, "There was a time when you were younger when I would have done most anything to hold my marriage together. I don't feel that way any longer. You're grown. You're strong. I have a feeling that whatever I decide to do, you'll understand. You may not be happy, but you'll understand. So your being here or not is no longer the issue."

"What is?"

That was the question of the night. Julia thought about it driving back to Hawks Hill, thought about it as she put her wedding band on the counter and showered, brushed her hair, and climbed into bed. She thought about it as she lay in the dark.

The issue was not Monte. She had spent twenty years trying to please him—trying and failing and trying again. As she lay there, miles away from him physically and emotionally, what he wanted no longer mattered. What mattered now, at last, was what *she* wanted.

Who am I? Who do I want to be?

At that moment, only one answer came. She might attribute it to the fact that she was in Noah's bed, but that hadn't been a factor when she had first seen him washing his boat. She had been physically drawn to him then—and again at the trap shed—and again when she had seen Ian and him out on the ocean. She had been drawn to him all evening—and yes, that might have been because of the danger they had faced that afternoon. Danger stirred the senses. It also fed into thoughts of mortality, which fed into thoughts of limited time, which fed into thoughts of splurging.

Wanting Noah didn't feel like a splurge. It felt like a necessity. And it had little to do with talking. She needed to be held. She needed to know that if she died, she would be missed. She needed to be *loved*.

The telephone rang. It was the land line, on the nightstand not far from her head. Her insides quickened.

"Hello?"

"I just turned onto the road to the house," he said in a voice that was husky and low. "Tell me to stop."

She couldn't do that. Yes, she was Monte's wife. But she was also Julia. Julia was a woman whose obedience was stifling, whose loyalty had been ignored along with her needs. Julia was a woman who wanted. Yes, she did.

Her heart was beating loudly, but not so loudly that she couldn't tell when Noah disconnected the call. Out of bed in a flash, she ran up the stairs. She opened the door just as headlights appeared and lit the gossamer nightgown she wore, so innocently purchased in Camden. Barefoot, she stood on the threshold until the truck came to a stop. The headlights went off, but their glow hung in the fog, and Julia didn't hesitate. She had spent a lifetime waiting for others to act. *Who did she want to be?* She wanted to be a doer.

She reached the truck just as Noah climbed out, and in a heartbeat her arms were around his neck as fast as his circled her back. The sheer relief of it made her cry out. Her mouth was still open when it found his, and he didn't hesitate here, either. The way he devoured her lips said he was as hungry as she.

Cushioned by mist, they made love against the side of the truck, and it was like nothing Julia had ever known. This was pure adult lust, dire adult need. She didn't think about Monte; he had no place in a world that smelled of balsam, spruce, and salt air. Like the explosion of the *Amelia Celeste,* the darkness offered a passage from one life to the next. In that darkness, her world was alive with sensation. She was so consumed by it that no single detail registered—not Noah's hardness and heat, not the breathy sounds between kisses, not the rasp of a zipper—only the larger realm of desire. Braced against the truck with her legs around his hips, she barely felt his entry when her insides burst into spasms. Stoked further by his own climax, the spasms went on and on.

Even when they faded to a pleasurable pulse, she refused to let go, and he seemed fine with that. With remarkable grace, keeping her legs around him and her head tucked into his neck, he got them into the house and down the stairs, but she would have expected no less of a man who so easily hauled traps from the sea. Laying her on the bed, he put the lamp on low and, in the warmth of a golden glow, drew the gown over her head—and Julia thought she would die. His eyes were as hot on her as his hands and mouth had been. When she worked at his clothes and got them off, the reward was heavenly. His body was long and hard, spattered with hair, warm with sweat, and trembling with arousal.

It began all over again, only this time was different. This time she could see him, and the pleasure was even more intense. She could see his mouth on her breast, could see her own hands on his belly, could see the joining of their bodies. He said sweet things that set her on fire, and they found a rhythm. Moving with it, they shifted and sped, and her eyes were open, mating with his until the very end, when the surge of sensation was simply too much.

Lying with him in the aftermath, her cheek against the damp hair on his chest, she did think of Monte, because what she was sharing here was like nothing—*nothing*—between Monte and her. Monte didn't say sweet things. He issued orders, like *Move your hips*, or *Open your mouth*, and there was always the self-involved *Yes, yes, yes*. He never said her name. She often suspected that he was imagining she was someone else. They always made love in the dark.

Who am I?

Monte would have said, *My wife*.

Who am I?

I am Julia. She couldn't possibly forget, because Noah said her name over and over. He was making love to Julia. His eyes were on her the entire time.

Who am I?

I am a woman. She couldn't forget that either, because he used his hands and his mouth to recognize everything about her body that was different from his—from her breasts to her belly to the warmth between her legs. Blossoming as a woman, she grew bolder. She answered his daring with a daring of her own. There was no judgment or shame, only the joy of being alive.

Who am I?

I am appealing. Monte had let her forget this, perhaps as a justification for his affairs, but Noah didn't let it go for a minute. Everything about him spoke of how appealing he found her, from the trembling of his limbs to the hammer of his heart to the sweat on his body and the heaviness of his sex. And then there were those husky groans. After the fourth or fifth, he simply laughed.

"What?" she asked, looking up at him.

"I don't believe it, you're so incredibly sexy."

So was he, she decided, and told him so—and they did talk about other things, though the physical had them enthralled. It was a celebration of life, filled with passion and heat, and they pushed it as far as it would go. Things that had given Julia pause with Monte were deeply satisfying with Noah. He didn't have to urge her to open her legs or use her mouth; she did it naturally, did it because she wanted to, did it because she needed to be closer, always closer to him. By the time dawn approached, she knew more about this man and his needs—knew more about herself and her own needs—than she had learned in twenty years of marriage to Monte.

"I have to go," he whispered. They were spooned together. Now he turned her in his arms. "Ian will be waking."

She nodded. Ian would be waking. The world would be waking. *She* would be waking.

He kissed her once, then again. With a groan that this time very clearly said, *I don't want to leave,* he tore himself away. He sat on the side of the bed to pull on his pants. Rising behind him, she snaked an arm over his shoulder and across his chest. The other hand fingered the ropy tattoo. It undulated over muscle as he dressed.

"It's a hemp chain. Know why?" he asked quietly.

"No. Why?"

"Because we are."

"Are what?"

"Chained. Chained here. Not physically. But

emotionally. We're lobstermen, born and bred. We might leave, but it's never for long."

It was a warning. He didn't look at her as he said it, but silently finished dressing in the predawn light.

She watched without rising. Reality loomed, which wasn't to say that guilt held her down. She didn't regret what she and Noah had done. Like so much of what had happened to her this summer, it was empowering. The fact that it had happened, though, made her a different person. That was the reality she had to face now.

He started for the door, stopped, and returned. Catching her up, he held her tightly for a long minute before very gently setting her back on her knees on the bed. He stroked her cheek. The look in his eyes could only be called yearning, and it took her breath away.

"I love you," he whispered.

He took more than her breath with the words—took her whole heart; and it wasn't fair—she wasn't free, the timing was wrong. She would have told him that if her eyes hadn't filled with tears and her throat closed up. He took it in and gave her a fierce kiss, then broke away and went up the stairs.

She came off the bed and, pulling the sheet free, wrapped it around her as she ran after him. She reached the front door, but he was already starting the truck, and it was surely for the best. All she could do was watch him through tears, fog, and rain.

She stayed until neither sight nor sound of the truck remained, then slowly closed the door. Back in bed, she wrapped her arms around his pillow and held the scent of him a bit longer, but she didn't sleep. Everything about her body screamed of Noah, but her mind was off on its own trip, headed in the direction she knew she needed to go.

Rising, she showered, dressed in her nicest clothes, put on makeup. Putting on her wedding band was harder today, but she did it. She was still Monte's wife.

She made the bed, neatened up, and packed her things. From the leather pocketbook that had been rescued from the bottom of the sea, she took her key ring and the two envelopes—one with photos she had taken so many years before, the other with the papers she had more recently, painstakingly gathered—and put them in her new bag. She sat in the kitchen with a cup of coffee until the hour was decent, then cleaned up, locked the door, and drove to Zoe's.

The rabbits were starting to stir. After pausing to scratch Ned's ear, she walked down the row of cages. The misters puffed, but other than the occasional wren song in the meadow or the more distant cry of a gull, all was still. She went first to Gretchen, but found herself more interested today in the babies. One by one, she held them, amazed at how they had evolved from leggy little things into warm handfuls of fur, eyes, and ears. Life passed. Things grew. Within weeks, these babies would be taken from their mother and placed in homes far away.

"The only reason anyone on Big Sawyer gets dressed like you are at this time of day is to go off-island," Zoe said from the door, then came forward.

She wore a robe and clogs, and her hair was mussed. She must have heard the car and come straight from bed. "Headed back?"

Julia nodded. "I have to talk with Monte. It won't wait any longer." Gently, she slid the baby she held back into the nest box. Then she took Zoe's hand. "I don't want to see the others. Will you tell them I've gone?"

"Molly will ask. How much should I say?"

"Just that . . . I have to talk with Monte."

Zoe's eyes held understanding. Lightly, she touched Julia's cheek. Then she hugged her and let her go.

Chapter 18

Julia took the first ferry of the day. Teary-eyed still, she parked the car and stood at the deck looking back at the island until it was lost in the fog. Hood up against the spray, she barely felt the chop. It was rougher than at any other time she had made the crossing, but she wasn't afraid. She and the sea had reached an accommodation after the sinking of the *Amelia Celeste.* It wouldn't take her now.

Once in the car again, she headed out of Rockland, hit the turnpike, and drove south. Flying would have been faster, but she needed the familiarity of the car—Julia's car, with Julia's purse on the seat, Julia's map in the glove box, Julia's belongings in the back. She also needed the time. The fog lifted as she drove, and her plans congealed. By the time she reached Portland, she was able to think of Noah without welling up, in part because the traffic demanded her attention. Once past Portland, the traffic eased again, but it had been enough of a reminder of what lay ahead that the break was made. From then on, she refused to look back.

She made several phone calls as she passed through New Hampshire, stopped midday in Massachusetts for something to eat, then drove on through Connecticut and into New York, and all the while traffic flowed smoothly. Neither accidents nor construction slowed her down. Likewise, she was steady at the wheel. She took both as good omens.

Noah's mood was as lousy as the weather. He had known he was playing with fire; Julia's wedding band stared him in the face when he was with her, and she hadn't talked of getting a divorce. Now she was gone, left on the morning ferry, information radioed by Leslie Crane. Noah felt he'd been stripped bare and flogged.

Gone for good? He didn't know. And he did care—which made the not knowing hard.

Rain had begun midday and now fell steadily into four-foot waves that had the *Leila Sue* pitching and rolling. Add to that the forecast, which wasn't good, and the paucity of lobsters in the traps he had hauled, and he had little to smile about. Things got even worse when he neared the traps he had set at the upper ledges north of Big Sawyer and saw a field filled with grape-lime-grape buoys.

"God *damn* it," he muttered, holding the wheel steady against the yaw of the boat. "They just don't *learn*."

Ian came to stand beside him. "Are those the ones you cut?"

"No. The ones I cut will have been swept off there into the rocks. These are new ones."

"What're you going to do?"

Noah's first thought was to check with his buddies. Then his second thought came, and he was feeling just raw enough to go with it. Throttling up, he pushed the *Leila Sue* ahead until he reached the first of Haber and Welk's buoys.

"We're haulin'," he said through gritted teeth and threw the throttle into neutral. "Gaff the buoy." As soon as Ian had done it, Noah hooked the line over the winch and started the hydraulic hauler. The first trap came up from the bottom with two good-sized bugs inside.

"We're taking their catch?" Ian asked, sounding doubtful.

"Nope," said Noah. He opened the trap, but instead of dumping its contents on the deck of the boat, he dumped it right back into the sea. He did the same with the second trap, then slid both traps over the transom. When the buoy was in the water again, he moved on to the next.

He might be lousy at reading women, but he was good at this.

By late afternoon, Julia entered Manhattan. A teariness returned then, though it was as much from apprehension as anything else. Leaving the car in a garage, she walked in the late-day sun, up along the park to the Metropolitan Museum, over to Madison Avenue, and down to Charlotte's boutique. She spotted her friend inside—but walked on past. She couldn't talk yet.

The workday was ending, and sidewalk traffic increased. That brought a greater sense of anonymity, which made it easier for Julia. In a crowd, she didn't feel quite so conspicuous. She stopped for coffee, though she hardly needed the caffeine. She thumbed through the latest copy of *Real Simple,* sipping her coffee, checking her watch. When the time was right, she headed for the address she had jotted down during the drive south, and the next hour passed in a blur. When she hit the streets again, her stomach was in knots, but she was certainly more well informed.

Still she had time on her hands, so she stopped for dinner at a small restaurant far enough from her usual haunts that she wouldn't bump into people she knew. Even then, she picked an out-of-the-way table and kept her head down, eyes on her magazine.

A man approached at one point. Nattily suited, he was close to her age, tall, and trim. "Excuse me," he said, looking bemused, "aren't you Susan Paine?"

She smiled. "No. Sorry." She returned to her magazine.

"Do you know who she is?" he asked.

She looked up again. "I'm sorry, I don't."

"That makes two of us," he said, sounding less bemused now than smug, and it hit her that he was making a pass.

She raised a warning hand, shook her head, and

returned to the magazine, flattered but so disinterested that she actually felt sorry for the man.

He left. She had a refill of coffee. When she reached the point of having read the magazine twice through—the second time with her mind elsewhere—she gestured for the bill and left. And still she had time to spare. So she walked around as the evening lengthened, always with others on the sidewalk, cars nearby, horns honking, and she refused to think of the quiet on Big Sawyer.

She sat in front of the Plaza for a while, watching the comings and goings. She walked down to Rockefeller Center and did the same. These were things she had done during the first days of her life in New York, before the pattern of day-to-day living had inured her to the wonders of the city. She saw them now again, appreciating them as she hadn't in so long a time.

Every few minutes she glanced at her watch. As the time drew near, she grew more committed. That terrified her.

Ten-thirty came and went, then eleven, and she grew edgy. At eleven-thirty, taking deep breaths and praying for calm, she headed uptown again. Shortly before midnight, she reached the address she had called home for fourteen of the last twenty years. The doorman stood watch out front, but she didn't want to be seen. So, using her key, she slipped into the building through the service entrance and took the elevator to the top floor. She went down the hall and paused at the door, one hand pressed to her thudding heart, the other clutching her key, and all the while she told herself that her stealth would prove stupid if he wasn't even home.

But she remained steadfast. Quietly, she fitted her key into the lock, opened the door, and slipped inside. There was Monte's briefcase at the foot of the credenza where he dropped it when he walked in each night. A light came from the bedroom hall, and soft music from the bedroom itself. For a split second she had qualms.

Who am I? I'm an ungrateful, disloyal, conniving thief, she thought.

No. *No.* This is my home. I have a *right* to be here.

She walked down the Persian runner toward the bedroom, familiar enough with the wood floor under the rug to avoid creaky spots. Her heart was nowhere near as silent. It was beating loudly by the time she reached the bedroom door and looked inside.

Monte was asleep in a tangle of sheets, his arms around a dark-haired woman. Both were clearly naked under what little covered their loins.

Julia had known. Seeing it, though—actually seeing her husband in bed with another woman, the familiarity of him and all that other bare flesh—was like taking a blow to the belly. The reality of it hit her so hard that, for a minute, she feared she might throw up. She swallowed once, then again, and breathed in through her nose. On the tail of sickness, though, came anger, and anger made her bold.

The music played softly. Monte snored faintly.

There were no clothes strewn about, as there would have been had this been a first passionate encounter. His things lay neatly on the loveseat, hers over the dressing table chair. Everything about the scene suggested that they had done this before.

Julia passed the dressing table on her way to the bed. On impulse, she took a high-heeled pump from the floor and slipped it into her bag—and, instantly, she hated herself for it, but she didn't put the shoe back. It would be insurance, should Monte later try to deny what she had seen by arguing either that she had been delusional or—as he had said about Molly—"on" something.

Resenting him for making her think and feel and act this way, she went right up to the bed. Anger gave her distance; oddly disengaged, she stared at the twining of bodies. She hadn't slept so close to Monte in . . . in . . . she didn't remember when the last time was. He hadn't asked; she hadn't offered. Perhaps this was a need of his that hadn't been met.

His low snoring faltered. His lids flickered, then rose. He focused on her without seeing at first, and she knew that myopic look. He had removed his contacts.

But he did figure it out. Eyes going wide, he bolted up, and it was almost comical, the passage of his thoughts, the way he realized she was there, then realized his mistress was there as well. He pulled at the sheet, as if to cover her up and pretend she wasn't there, but that left him more exposed and, in his nakedness, truly condemned. In tugging the sheet back to himself, he woke up the woman, who took one look at Julia and burrowed under the sheet.

Pulling now at the blanket to cover himself while he climbed out of bed, he took the offensive. "You've been away for two and a half weeks with barely a call. You gave me no sign you wanted to return. What are you *doing* here, Julia?"

Julia had imagined this conversation many times, the last hundred or so during the drive down from Maine. She was angry but in control. "This is my home," she said.

"How did you get here? Why didn't you call? If I'd known—"

"If you'd known, you wouldn't have had her here? That's why I didn't call." Feeling a wave of disgust, she looked at the figure under the sheet. "This is a sleazy scene. I'll wait for you in the living room." She turned and walked out.

He was a minute in following, apparently believing he would have an edge if he was at least marginally dressed, because when he appeared he wore pants. He also wore dark, horn-rimmed glasses, which gave him gravity. "I never knew you to be a conniver, but this is underhanded," he charged. "Were you deliberately trying to trip me up?"

"Monte," Julia cried, "you were in bed with her. *Naked.*"

He held up a hand. "It's not what it seems."

"Oh, please," she said with some force. "Don't take me for a fool. I caught you. Molly caught you."

His eyes narrowed. "What did Molly say?"

"That you were with an old friend who was going through a rough time, and while she may believe that, I certainly don't. I want a divorce."

In a heartbeat's silence, the soft music played on. "A divorce," he finally said, sounding stunned. "Where did this come from?"

"Years of affairs. Years of put-downs. I'm done, Monte."

He pushed a hand through his hair and looked around, seeming confused. "Why didn't John call to say you were on your way up?" John was the doorman.

"I came in the back way."

"With what? I sent you car keys, not a house key."

"Yes. I noticed that. But they recovered my purse from the ocean floor. My house keys were inside."

"So you plotted to show up here unannounced and catch me by surprise?"

She was angry enough to smile. "I sure did. Caught you with your pants down, literally and figuratively." The smile faded. She curbed the anger in an effort to sound cool and sure. She wanted Monte to know that she meant every word. "I've talked with an attorney."

"An attorney."

"About a divorce."

"You aren't serious about this, Julia."

"I am. Totally."

"On what grounds?"

"I have a choice. I can use irreconcilable differences. Or I can bring an alienation of affection suit against your paramour."

"You'd never prove that."

"I would. I have copies of credit card bills from the last few years." She didn't mention the shoe in her bag.

He went red in the face. "You had no business going through my files."

"Our files, Monte. My name's also on the credit card you used. I have a right to those records."

He stared at her for a minute. "Julia, this is not *you*." When she simply stared back, he shot a look around the room. "If you think you're going to take all of this, think again. You deserted me—just packed up and moved to Maine. This is abandonment."

"Not according to my lawyer."

"Who is this lawyer?"

"Mark Tompkins."

"Ahhh," he said snidely, "the champion of every disgruntled wife in New York. Is he talking you into this? That's his job, you know."

"My mind was made up before I ever called his office," Julia said, holding her ground. She was actually getting into the swing of it, answering him point by point.

"Is it Zoe?" he asked now. "Has she brainwashed you? She hates men."

"A, she doesn't hate men. B, I haven't spent enough time with her to be brainwashed. C, she doesn't know I'm doing this."

He looked confused. "But—I don't *want* a divorce."

Monte didn't want a divorce, Julia reflected and thought, What about me? Who am I? I'm a woman who is tired of being walked on. I'm a woman who has more to give than lip service to a marriage that ceased working years ago. Sensibly, she said, "Of course you don't want a divorce. It's very nice to have someone seeing to all your needs, so that you can spend time on the sly with women like the one in there. I know you don't want a divorce. But I do."

He stiffened. "I'll fight you."

"I have credit card bills *and* phone bills." And that shoe. Caught in the act.

He drew himself up straighter. "You went through phone bills, too?"

"Yes. I knew you'd try to talk your way out of it if I didn't have proof."

"What about Molly? Have you thought about how this would affect her?"

"Have I *thought* about it?" Julia burst out, losing a bit of composure then. "I might have done this *years* ago if it hadn't been for Molly. She's a grown woman now. She knows what she saw that night, but you're her father, so she'll believe your tale. If you're really concerned about Molly, you'll keep this as civil as possible."

He put his hands on his hips, raked his teeth over his lip, frowned. Quietly, seeming for the first time to actually care, he said, "What happened up there? Did you meet someone?"

"Yes. Me."

He looked peeved. "I'm serious."

So was she. She wasn't telling him about Noah, because although Noah was pretty momentous, he wasn't the most important part of what had happened to her. "I found out that what I think and feel matters. It's something I've overlooked all these years."

He lowered his voice to a whisper and hitched his chin toward the bedroom. "Give me five minutes, and she's history. She doesn't mean anything to me."

"Well, then, I'm sorry for you. Maybe you'll find someone who does."

He looked at her, but it was a different look from what she had seen. He looked at her as though he saw a new person. More curious than accusatory, trying to figure things out, he said, "Is this why you went up there in the first place? You must have collected those bills before you left."

"I didn't know I'd use them."

"It was the accident, then?"

"I think yes," she said, reflecting his own quiet. In the same tone, she revised that. "I *know* yes. Accidents like that turn your world upside down."

"Maybe all you need is therapy."

She smiled, but not in anger. She was feeling relief. Of all the times over the years when she had imagined this confrontation, she had felt dread. But the worst was over now. She felt mellow, even sad. "Therapy won't fix what's wrong. You have needs, Monte, but I have them, too. Do you know what a woman feels when her husband has affairs? She feels hurt. She feels angry. She feels ugly. She feels used."

"What if I promised—" He stopped short when she held up a hand. She shook her head and let her eyes say what she didn't want to say aloud. His promises weren't worth a thing. Trust was gone.

"I've felt unloved for too long," she finally offered.

"I do love you."

"In your way. But it isn't enough."

"You *said* that to him?" her friend Donna asked a short time later.

"I did," she confirmed, sinking lower on the sofa, legs sprawled in an unladylike way that she didn't have the strength to change. Walking the five blocks to Donna's small place through streets that were emptier now, she had been hit by the shakes. She was grateful to arrive, grateful that Donna had waited up, grateful for warm arms, a generous heart, and a place to sleep. She was terrified by what she had done. She was also suddenly, overwhelmingly exhausted.

Donna wore a robe, hair rollers, and a face shiny from soap. The successful real estate lawyer? Hard to believe. Just then, she was simply a friend whom Julia was blessed to have.

"Thank you for Mark," Julia said. "He might not have taken me on if you hadn't made a call."

"Lawyers listen to lawyers. He'll do right by you."

"What is right? I'm not sure that I want a whole lot of what Monte has."

"No," Donna said, regarding her thoughtfully, "you never did."

Julia yawned. She listened to the city night. She turned her head on the sofa. "So, did you all know?"

"About the affairs? We suspected."

"Did you think I was a fool not to see?"

"Julia," Donna chided, "no one of us has *ever* taken you for a fool. Women are pragmatists. We do what we have to at a given time. When times change, we have a window in which to act. Not all of us are brave enough to do it. You are. When the others hear, they'll admire you as much as I do."

Julia loved Donna. She loved Charlotte and Jane. What she most loved about them—impressive women, all three—was that they loved her, too.

She reached for her friend's hand. "And if I leave New York?"

"Leave New York?" Donna cried lightly. "*Leave* New York? No one leaves New York. Not for good. You may live somewhere else, but you'll be back. And do you think we won't want to visit you wherever you are? Think again, sweetie."

Under a blanket on the sofa, Julia slept soundly until Donna woke her at the agreed-upon time. She showered and dressed, then picked up her wedding band and turned it in her hand. Stones circled the front half; the back was pure platinum. The stones were shiny, the platinum scuffed—polished outside, bruised inside.

It was time. Tucking the ring in her purse, she joined Donna for a bagel and coffee, but she didn't linger. She had driving to do.

Saturday morning traffic was light. The trip to Baltimore would take three and a half hours. It was a buffer; she needed the time to sort through her thoughts. The significance of what she had done was all the more stark in the light of day. A major life change, legal action ahead, emotional ups and downs—she didn't take it lightly. Each time she turned the steering wheel and saw her naked finger, she felt a jolt.

Hearing Noah's voice would have calmed her, but she refused to call. She wasn't divorcing Monte for Noah. She was doing it for herself.

After cutting over from the East Side, she drove down Ninth Avenue thinking about the life she had known in New York. Once out of the Lincoln Tunnel, though, she focused on Janet. That meant gearing up to buck a pattern of behavior that had been forty years in the making.

Who am I? she asked over and over again in what amounted to a three-hour pep talk. *I am a strong woman. I am capable. I am sensible and thoughtful and thorough. I am an independent woman who has her own convictions and is willing to act on them.*

Phrases became part of a mantra, because Julia knew that first appearances mattered. Janet had to take one look at Julia and see the change.

She took a steadying breath when she entered Baltimore and repeated the mantra as she negotiated the familiar route. *I am a survivor,* she added. *I have a responsibility to speak up for what I think is right. I won't be minimized any more.*

Her parents' tree-lined street, with its large brick homes and lush green lawns, was as elegant as ever. She pulled into the paved driveway and parked behind the garage that held his-and-her sedans. The humidity hit her the instant she stepped from the car, more a flash from the past than anything oppressive, but it unbalanced her. Going up the bluestone walk, she wondered if her hair was too long, her capris too wrinkled, her wedged sandals too low and islandy. These qualms were another flash from the past. Her mother was an opinionated woman who didn't shy from saying what she thought.

I have a responsibility to myself, Julia insisted. Shoulders back, she rang the bell. She did have a key, a relic of childhood, not to mention of later years when she had raced back from New York to cover for Janet. It was another on the key chain that had been rescued from the sea. Instinct told her, though, that this wasn't the time to open the door herself and walk in.

The sidelight curtain shifted. Her mother's startled eyes appeared. The door opened quickly—and, just as quickly, Julia forgot about being aggressive. This was a Janet she hadn't seen before, slim as ever though less tall, wearier, and older, far older. She wore faded knee-length shorts, an untucked blouse, and no makeup, and her normally striking silver hair wasn't combed—not at all the appearance of a woman who did "important work." Julia couldn't remember the last time she had seen her mother looking disheveled. She couldn't remember when she had seen her mother looking anything but perfectly put-together. Unsettled—because this was her *mother*—Julia lost all taste for a fight.

Janet's eyes flew to the car, then back. "Is your father all right?" she asked in alarm.

"He's fine."

"Molly, then?"

"She's fine."

"You?"

Julia managed a smile. "I'm fine, too. Can I come in, Mom?"

Seeming startled by the question, Janet stepped aside. "I was on the patio. I didn't expect anyone. I was just sitting there with the paper. It's been a week from hell. This is the first time I've been able to catch my breath." She closed the door on the heat and started down the cool hall, then turned and eyed Julia with unease. "Did he tell you to come?"

There was no mistaking whom she meant. "No. He doesn't know I'm here."

She turned and continued on, only to stop several paces later. Her eyes were somber this time. "If you've come to argue his case, please don't. He needs to do that himself." She went on through the kitchen and out a pair of French doors to the patio. Crossing the flagstones to the sun, she lowered herself into a lounge chair with more care than she would have taken if she had been twenty years younger. The paper was on a table by the lounger. Pages pristine, it looked unopened.

Julia's heart broke. Her mother was clearly unhappy.

Pulling up a chair, she said, "I'm not arguing his case, Mom. I just want you to know that there is nothing going on between Zoe and him. There was that one time however many years ago, but nothing since and nothing now. He went up there because I was there, and because he was angry at you and knew that going there would be the most hurtful thing."

"That was childish of him."

"Yes."

Janet closed her eyes. Julia was fearing that was the end of it, when her mother said, "How do you know nothing's happening?"

"I've seen them together. There's no chemistry."

"Would you be able to tell if there were?"

"I think I would."

"You didn't notice anything last time."

"I was fifteen then."

Janet said nothing. Lacing her fingers together over her waist, she lay in the sun for a time. Her nails were polished—she had a manicure every Thursday at noon—but everything else about her hands looked tired and tense.

"There's nothing," Julia insisted. "Trust me. Twenty-five years have passed. They're both different people from who they were then. Dad is bored. She's put him to work in the barn, but she doesn't want to be anywhere near him, so he's there alone, and he has only so much patience for that. He hangs out at the Grill, waiting for Molly to come out of the kitchen and say hello. He hangs out at the dock and talks with anyone who's there."

"He's living in the house with her," Janet argued, but wearily.

"That's my fault. Neither of them wanted it, but there was one other place to sleep, and I took it."

Janet sighed. She turned her face to the sun.

"Are you wearing sunscreen?" Julia asked.

"No."

"Aren't you supposed to?" Several suspicious spots had been treated in recent years.

Janet slit open an eye and said without humor, "I'm living dangerously." She closed the eye. "If you're staying somewhere else, how do you know he isn't sneaking down the hall to see her at night?"

"Zoe told me."

"And you believe her?"

"Why would she lie? If she was at all interested, she would be gloating. But she isn't. She has never forgiven herself for what happened. There's no way, no *way* she would ever let it happen again."

Janet said nothing for a while. Then, "If he's bored, why's he staying there?"

"Because you haven't called!"

Her mother raised her head and met her gaze. "He hasn't called me, either. What if I fell down the stairs and lay at the bottom needing help? What if I died in my sleep? Doesn't he care?"

"I was in an accident that could have taken my life, but you didn't call," Julia cried. "Didn't *you* care?"

"I knew you were well. You called and told us so."

"I also told you I was upset!"

"Yes. Can we get to this later?" It was typical Janet, scheduling things in. "Right now, we're discussing your father."

Julia sighed in exasperation. "Of course, he cares."

"I told your brothers I sent him up there to be with you. I didn't know what else to say. Does he plan to come back?"

"Yes."

"When?"

"After the holiday weekend."

"Tuesday? Wednesday?"

"I don't know, Mom. Why don't you call him and ask?"

Janet shot her a caustic look and returned her head to the chair.

Julia let it go. She needed a breather. She consciously relaxed her hands, then lifted her hair off the back of her neck. She had forgotten the heat and humidity of Baltimore summers. Island air could be warm, but there was always a breeze. Here, nothing moved. If the past was any indication, half of the neighborhood was at the shore for the Fourth of July weekend, if only to escape the heat. Not that Julia minded either the heat or the neighbors' absence. Both were childhood memories. Revisited now, as she stood on the brink of a major change in her life, they brought a surprising comfort.

"The yard is beautiful," she said. "Do you still have the same gardener?"

"Yes. *He's* very loyal."

Julia sighed. "So is Dad."

"Well, it would be nice to think so, but once a man cheats on his wife, it is hard. You have no idea what it's like to live with that fear all these years."

Julia held her breath. It was time. If Janet was going to fight her on this, she wanted it over and done.

Carefully, she said, "I know what it's like, Mom. I've lived with it myself."

Janet opened one eye, saw that Julia was serious, and opened the other—and for the first time since seeing her mother looking so vulnerable at the door, Julia let loose with the defiance she had drummed up during her drive from New York.

Chapter 19

I've just come from New York," Julia said in a rush of courage. "I'm divorcing Monte."

Janet raised her head off the lounge. "Divorcing?"

"It isn't working. It hasn't for a while. Monte's had a string of affairs. I walked in last night and caught him in bed with the latest."

She was so braced for an I-told-you-so about having left Monte alone and run off to Maine that when Janet said a simple, "Oh Julia," she was already on to the next point.

"Molly saw the same thing when she flew back from Paris and showed up unannounced." She realized that Janet was looking stunned—actually sympathetic—but still she hurried on. Janet was a big one for "studies." She liked statistics telling about the people her charity served and the success of the service. Julia needed to bolster her case. "All the signs pointed to it. He was relieved when I said I wasn't coming home after the accident, and relieved when Molly decided to stay on Big Sawyer. I think back on how he urged her to spend the summer in Paris instead of New York. He knew I planned to be in Maine for two weeks. He had been counting on that time to play on his own."

"A *string* of affairs?" Janet asked archly. "Going back how long?"

Julia was quickly defensive. Old habits died hard. "Well, I don't *know,* Mom. I didn't come home from my honeymoon expecting it. Maybe it started way back then. I didn't monitor his comings and goings. I'm not that kind of wife."

"I know."

"I had suspicions, but only because he seemed disinterested in some regards—"

"Sex."

"—and I really didn't want to believe it. What woman does? I've only documented the past three years—and yes, I put up with it," she hurried to say before Janet-the-activist could scold, "for all the usual reasons. But it's gotten harder to look the other way."

"And then there's the fear," Janet said quietly.

"Oh, yes," Julia agreed indignantly, and was about to tell Janet that she knew very *well* what the fear was about, when she realized that Janet was commiserating with her. Commiserating. The archness had been directed at Monte, not at Julia. "You've felt that fear?" she asked more meekly.

"I have."

Gratified, Julia relaxed some. As she did, though,

the pain emerged. "It was sharpest the first time I realized what was going on. I was convinced he had fallen in love with someone else and would divorce me. I learned to live with the fear, but there was always a new doubt. Did I look young enough? Did I dress stylishly enough? Was I deferential enough and agreeable enough and interesting enough? Was I accommodating enough? Did I do enough for him, so that he would *need* me?"

Janet slid her feet to the ground and sat up. "You were far better at all those things than I was."

"I doubt that," Julia said. "I pale next to you. But Dad's different from Monte. He's proud of your career, and anyway, he's a background kind of guy. Monte's not. He wants to be up there on a pedestal. He likes being seen and admired. He likes being coveted. So I worked harder to be deferential and agreeable and interesting. I knew that if I became a negative asset, he would sell me off."

"Buy you off," Janet corrected.

"That's an awful pressure to live with. After the accident, it just seemed self-defeating."

"What will you do? Where will you live?"

Julia hadn't thought that far. All she knew was that having slept with Noah, she had to end her marriage. "For now, I'll stay on Big Sawyer."

"You need a lawyer."

"I have one. I met with him yesterday, before I saw Monte."

"How did Monte take it?"

"He tried arguing, but I caught him red-handed. I

honestly think this is the first time I've ever won an argument with him. Toward the end, he was almost looking sad."

"Almost?"

"I'd say 'truly,' if I didn't know what a good actor he is. That's the saddest thing of all."

"The lack of trust."

"Yes."

Janet sat back in the lounger again, eyes focused on the pair of tall oaks at the end of the yard. After a bit, without looking at Julia, she said, "You think you're above it. I run an organization that deals with people who are down-and-out, dysfunctional, impoverished on so many levels, and it's been easy to feel superior, because I'm none of those things." She aimed stricken eyes at Julia. "The hubris does you in. Suddenly you see that you're not above anyone or anything, because right in your own home, things aren't so good."

"But they are," Julia countered. This was part of the awakening she'd had after the sinking of the *Amelia Celeste*. "We're alive. We're healthy. What a gift that is."

Pensive, Janet looked at her dogwoods. Closer to the patio than the oaks, they had lost their blossoms but were lush in size and rich in color. An old wrought-iron bench sat under one. Julia had spent many summer days on that bench, many quiet moments. With so much changing in her life, being here with her mother was a cushion.

After a time, Janet faced her. "You've had reason to think about death."

Julia had. Mere mention of it brought back all the hurt she had felt. In the comfort of the setting, she found the strength to say, "I needed you, Mom. You didn't have to visit. A call would have been enough."

"I know."

"You have an aversion to Big Sawyer, but this was me, not Zoe. I'm your daughter."

"I know. I'm sorry."

Julia heard the apology. Being Julia, though, she couldn't make her mother grovel. So she went on, reasoning, "It's been a growing experience for me. I managed on my own. I'm better off for that. Actually, Mom"—there was more to say, but she needed a time-out—"I'm hungry. Are you interested in lunch?"

Janet looked nervous. "I don't have much; it's just your father and me, and now with him gone . . ."

What she didn't say was that George did the shopping, and that with his being gone nearly a week, the refrigerator was bare. "I'll run to the market," Julia offered. "Want anything special?"

Janet insisted on coming, and it was a first. Julia couldn't remember a time when she and her mother had walked these aisles together. From the way Janet studied the array of food, she wondered when her mother had last been here, period. Cleaned up and dressed now in a skirt and blouse, she looked more her usual composed self.

Julia chose to take credit for that—and found that it felt good. She was, after all, a nurturer. Yes, the nurturing had been one-sided and she had neglected herself in the process. That had to change. But if she took pleasure in caring for others, she didn't see why she had to stop.

Understanding that, she relaxed with Janet, who pushed the carriage and pointed at things she wanted to buy, things that went well beyond lunch. But then, lunch wasn't the point.

"Do they have a market up there?" Janet asked after they had picked up lettuce and fruit in the fresh-produce aisle.

"Not a supermarket, per se," Julia replied, "just the island store, but it's upscale."

"Zoe was never a picky eater. Raisins, Julia. Over there. Is she still slim?"

"Very," Julia said, putting the raisins in the cart as Janet rounded the corner into the next aisle.

"Too thin?"

"No. She's just right."

"Um, that cereal, I think. Your father never buys that one. But I like it."

Julia took the cereal off the shelf, put it in the cart, and they went on.

"She probably hasn't turned gray, either," Janet remarked, but questioningly.

"She has. But she colors it. She looks good. She likes her life."

"Zoe and the rabbits."

Snide? Julia didn't know. Giving Janet the benefit of the doubt, she said, "The rabbits are a means to an end. They connect her with people. Some of those people buy the babies, some buy the wool."

"We need bottled water," Janet said. She took the

bottles as Julia handed them to her, and neatly lined them up in the cart. "Does she smell of rabbit?"

"No, she does not. Angoras don't smell."

Janet pointed at coffee, then, in the next aisle, applesauce. They turned onto the pasta aisle. Janet picked up a box of tortellini and read the directions on the side. "Have you ever made this?"

"Not that brand."

Janet replaced the box and pushed the cart on. When they started down the detergent aisle, she said, "What about men?"

"What about them?"

"Fabric softener sheets, please. Yes, those. Isn't she interested?"

"She has many male friends."

Softener sheets went beside applesauce, and the cart moved on. "That's not what I meant."

"She's been with men. Two were long-term."

"What happened?"

"She decided she liked her independence too much to give it up. She has a nice life, Mom."

Janet studied the shelves of dishwasher detergent. "But she has no family."

"Her friends are her family."

They rounded the end of the aisle and came face-to-face with condiments. "I need mustard. And cucumber chips. Choose whatever brand you like. Did she never want children?"

Julia chose her favorites and set the jars in the cart. "She kept waiting for a husband. She's pretty conventional that way. By the time she realized there wouldn't be one, when she might have considered a sperm donor, she was already perimenopausal. It hit early."

"With me, too. Maybe you, in a few years."

Julia thought of what she and Noah had done, all unprotected, because they were, after all, forty, with children who were grown, or nearly so. Women with twenty-year-old children didn't get pregnant. At least, she hoped they didn't. This wasn't the time for it at all.

"Why does that embarrass you?" Janet asked curiously.

Julia's eyes flew to hers. "It doesn't."

"You're blushing."

"Oh. No. Here's the bread. What kind would you like?"

"I like rye. Your father does not."

"I do." Julia reached for rye.

They hit the deli department next, took a number, and waited their turn. They stood close and spoke low, similar in height and looks, if years apart.

"I didn't expect Zoe to stay on that island," Janet said. "She used to be adventurous."

"She used to be twenty."

"She was reckless then. What's her house like?"

"It's nothing like yours."

"Obviously. What kind of sandwiches do we want to make? I like their seafood salad."

Julia's first instinct was to go along with that. Old habits died hard. But no seafood salad here could compare with that at the Harbor Grill, and the new

Julia had a voice. "Turkey breast for me. Let's buy some of each," which was what they did.

At the dairy case, Janet reached for a quart of milk. "So, what's it like?"

"Zoe's house?" Julia described the farmhouse as they returned to the front of the store. "Is there anything else you need?"

"Yes. Paper towels. I want the eight-pack. Your father buys one roll at a time. Can you imagine? Not only does it cost more, but he has to think about it every week, rather than once in two months. He shops like a man."

"If you went with him, you could teach him."

"But then I'd have to go myself, and I'm too busy."

Julia thought about that during the drive home. Out on the patio again, now with sandwiches and drinks, she was comfortable enough to be bold. "Dad feels some of that, you know."

"Some of what?"

"Your being too busy. It's the bottom line of why he went to Maine."

"He was angry that I didn't call you," Janet argued.

Julia disagreed. "He was angry that you said you were too busy to do it, because it tapped into his anger about *that*. He wants more of your time, Mom. He's getting old enough to relax some about work. He wants you to do the same."

"Retirement. It's a frightening word. I'm not ready."

"No one's asking you to retire. Can't you just cut back some?"

To her credit, Janet didn't summarily dismiss the idea. "I can, but I'm not sure I want to. Cutting back—going into even semiretirement—it's a whole new stage. Some of my friends are having a hard time." She shot Julia an awkward look. "You know, being with their husbands all the time."

"Do you love Dad?"

"Of course."

"Then, what's the problem?"

"We've been used to something else. I'm not sure how it would work. He might hate having *me* around all the time."

"He wouldn't. He worships you. He would feel *honored* if you chose to spend more time with him."

Janet was clearly unsure of that, because she got blustery. "Well, he needs to tell me that."

"Maybe he's afraid. You're an intimidating woman."

"He's my *husband,* for goodness sakes. He can say what he likes to me."

"Not always."

The words lingered. Julia could feel them in Janet's silence and wondered if she had gone too far. Janet hadn't asked for her opinion. Janet had opinions aplenty of her own. Traditionally, Julia did what Janet asked, not the other way around.

But the status quo didn't work for Julia anymore. She wanted a better relationship with her mother. As she saw it, this was one way to make the most of surviving the *Amelia Celeste.*

They didn't talk much for a while, and Julia was fearing the worst. As soon as they finished their sandwiches, though, Janet suggested—as amiably as you please—that they go shopping. She claimed that she wanted to pick up a few things she needed. In truth, she seemed more intent on buying for Julia. When she took yet one more pair of slacks from the rack and said, "Try these on. They would look good on you," Julia called her on it.

"I thought we were shopping for you."

"I have plenty. You're the one whose clothes went down with the ship."

"It was a boat, not a ship, and the clothes I lost were for a two-week vacation."

"The rest are back in New York with your husband, from whom you are now separated. Are you aware of that?"

Julia felt a tiny jolt. Being separated from Monte was still totally new. "It's okay," she said. "Those clothes aren't appropriate for Maine."

"Well, these are," Janet remarked. The pants she pulled out were casual, and the tops sporty. She even led Julia to the workout section and insisted she buy warm-up suits for hanging around the house, and again she insisted on paying.

"I can afford these, Mom. Monte won't leave me penniless."

"I'm not thinking of Monte," Janet said. "I'm thinking of me. Indulge me, please."

Noah and Ian were late returning to the dock, not because they chose to work longer, but because the sea was that rough. Even with spindles sticking up, finding buoys was a challenge. Same with pulling traps onto the boat. The surf swelled and sucked with enough force to make even emptying the lobster tanks at Foss's harder than usual. Back in the *Leila Sue*'s slip, the shouting from boat to boat was on that theme.

"You goin' out tomorrow, Hayes?" yelled Mickey Kling as he hosed off the *Mickey 'n Mike*.

From the deck of the *Willa B.*, Hayes Miller yelled back, "Gonna have to, if the forecast holds, or I'll lose a bundle. You?"

"We'll move a few in the morning, but if it gets much worse than this, I'm turning around. Hey, Noah! I hear you dumped some rotten fruit!"

Noah raised a hand in acknowledgment and went back to scrubbing his deck. After emptying out Haber and Welk's traps, he had moved a few of his own to deeper water, but there were many more in the path of the storm.

Ian wanted his Sunday off. His body was still adjusting to the daily rigor of hauling. Noah might take pity on him and leave him home, but he was surely going out himself. He was a lobsterman. Women might come and go, but there were always buoys, traps, and bugs. Totally aside from the practical need to get his traps away from the rocks, the work was a diversion. Add the risk of angry seas, and it was even better.

Julia and Janet hung out back at the house doing not much of anything at all, and it was time well spent. For Julia, the patio was an oasis. Even without talk, she felt closer to Janet. Then came dinner. Dressing up some, they went to a restaurant on North Charles. There, surrounded by teak, marble, and brass, they shared a bottle of wine and an order of Chateaubriand, and it was so startlingly companionable that Julia dared sit back and ask, "What do you think of me?"

Janet gave her a quizzical look. "What kind of question is that?"

"I've always felt overshadowed. Irrelevant, often. Do you see me that way?"

"Good Lord, no. You're my daughter."

"Do you like me?"

"You're my daughter," Janet repeated, as though that answered the question. But Julia was mellow enough to continue on.

"Are you proud of me?"

"Other than the state of your fingernails?"

Which were clean but bare. "I'm serious."

"Yes, I'm proud of you."

"Why?"

"*Julia.*" Janet seemed almost embarrassed.

"I really want to know," Julia insisted and realized she sounded like Molly, which wasn't a bad thing at all. Molly was forthright when it came to her own needs and wants. Julia had to be more like that. "Remember what I said to you on the phone from Maine? I haven't done anything like what you have in life. Are you disappointed? Did you have higher hopes for me? Would you find value in me as a friend?"

Janet seemed startled. "How could I be disappointed, when you do all the things I can't?"

"You could if you wanted to."

"No. I don't have the patience you do. I don't have the temperament you have. I'm not the agreeable person you are."

"Maybe being agreeable isn't always good."

"Turn that around, please. What if everyone in the world were—for want of a better word—as *difficult* as I am? How would anything get done? You're the grease, Julia. You make things happen. What I do is only a small part of the job."

"What you do is *important*," Julia said. For all her resentment of the word, it had to be used.

Janet sighed. "Not as important as I'd like to think."

You're the grease, Julia. You make things happen.

Julia slept on those thoughts. When she woke up in the middle of the night realizing that her marriage was done, the words gave her a sense of hope. If she could make things happen, she could take care of herself. That was what she needed to do.

Noah slept fitfully. He kept his cell phone close, thinking he could snatch it right up if she called, which she didn't, but he was in and out of bed anyway, monitoring the weather band. Though the fog remained thick, the wind eased and the rain held off. Reports had the storm approaching over water from the southeast, which meant it could be volatile, but not until noon. He figured he could accomplish a lot before then, and return to port with time to spare.

At four in the morning, he began fixing breakfast. He had his cell phone beside him here, too, on the chance she woke up from wherever she was, remembered what they had been doing at this time two nights before, and decided to call. She didn't. Which was just as well. Because bacon had just begun sizzling when Ian appeared. The boy's feet were bare, but he wore a sweatshirt and jeans, and appeared to have every intention of coming along.

"You could've slept," Noah said

Ian leaned against the doorjamb. "You can't go out alone."

"I've gone out alone many a time."

"None of the others will be working alone today. It isn't safe."

"The storm'll hold off. I'll be back by noon."

"I'm coming."

He sounded determined, and, argument aside, Noah was pleased. It was a bright spot in what promised to be a dismal day. Still, he felt obligated to ask, "Are you sure you want to?"

"I don't think you should go alone, and there's no one else you can take."

"You're it by default?"

"Looks that way," the boy said, folding his arms on his chest. In that instant, everything about him—looks, build, stubbornness—spoke of the grandfather he had barely known.

Yes, a bright spot. Feeling strengthened, Noah added

extra bacon and eggs to the pan. "Make some sandwiches, okay? You're hungry by ten."

Thirty minutes later, they set off. Riding that
surge of strength, defiant almost, Noah left the cell
phone on the kitchen counter. If she hadn't called
during the quiet times, she wouldn't now, and he was
tired of waiting. He had more important things to do.
He tried to close Lucas in the house, but the dog
squirmed out of his hands and ran toward the truck.
Noah wondered if Lucas was feeling as brash as he
was. Lucas had loved Julia, too.

The fog was even thicker at the harbor. Rick met
them with muffins at the side door of the Grill.
"Rain's coming, Noah. Are you sure you're game for
the ark?"

Noah snickered, handed Ian a thermos and took
his own. "If I'm not back by noon, send the troops."

Once aboard the *Leila Sue,* he got the engine
going and turned on the electronics. He figured he
would need all the navigational help he could get,
starting with leaving the harbor. Dawn was barely rising, the black of night had just begun its first fade
into gray. With Ian and Lucas a muted shadow in the
stern, he carefully piloted the boat around moorings.
More lobster boats were tied up than gone. Either the
fleet was staying ashore, or he had simply beat them
to it. The VHF was correspondingly quiet.

Clearing the harbor marker, he opened up the
throttle and, using the loran, headed full tilt for the
farthest of his traps. They lay forty minutes out, in an
area of rocks and ledges that might have been an is-

land in the days of Atlantis but, in modernity, had never quite made it to island status. This was prime molt territory. The shallows here had been fertile lobstering ground for the past several weeks.

The waves were light. He stopped once along the way to move a trio of strings, simply because they were close. Then he continued on. The world was a soupy, monochromatic gray, the fog thick enough to wet his windows. He kept his wipers on. Following his instruments, he reached the first of these most distant bright blue-orange-orange buoys, and threw the throttle into neutral. Ian gaffed the buoy and pulled it aboard; Noah hitched the warp over the hauler and turned it on. In no time the first trap was up, then the second. They each took one, tossing back seaweed, a cod, two shorts, and a handful of starfish into the sea, and dumping a total of three keepers in the tank. When the traps were stacked in the stern, ready for deeper water, Noah headed for the next buoy. The traps they pulled here held no keepers. Once the rest was tossed back, they joined the pile.

Bound for the third buoy, Noah returned to the wheel just as the idle stumbled. He raised the throttle and got a sputter, a surge, a misfire. He shifted back, then forward again. Another sputter came, then the rattle of an almost-catch, then nothing. Other than the sound of waves slapping the hull and wipers on the windshield, all was still.

"Swell," he muttered under his breath.

Ian came up beside him. "You can't be out of gas. We filled up two days ago."

"It's not gas," Noah said, heading for the stern.

Ian followed. "A dead battery?"

"No. The wipers are working." He began moving traps. "Give me a hand." When the traps had been shifted out of the way, he opened the engine compartment. He checked the fuel tank, fingered the lines, searched for anything else that might be amiss, and saw nothing. Then, on the impulse of a split-second premonition, he scrambled around traps, hung over the stern to see the exhaust, and swore softly.

"What?" Ian asked, leaning over beside him.

"Steam," Noah said in dismay.

"What does that mean?"

"Water in the tank. We're not going anywhere."

"How'd water get in the tank?"

"The same way my buoys were painted gray."

"Haber and Welk?"

"Them, or someone else."

"Maybe the gas you bought was bad."

That was Noah's first thought, too, but it couldn't be. "I'd have known it long before now."

"But—why are they picking on *you*?"

"Consolidating their efforts? Who knows?"

Still, Ian fought it. "If there's water in the tank, how'd we get *this* far?"

"Water's heavier than gas. It sinks to the bottom of the tank, which is where the fuel line pulls from. At the end of a day, there's always gas left in the fuel lines, the filter, and the carburetor bowl. That's what got us here." Unfortunately, they weren't going anywhere else without help. Scrambling to his feet, he went to the VHF, but when he tried to get it going, nothing happened. He fiddled with the connectors. That usually did the trick. This time the wires came free in his hand. They had been cut and tucked back in, which he would have seen if he had been more diligent back at the dock.

He swore again.

"No radio?" Ian asked.

"No."

"Cell phone?"

"Back at the house."

"How do we get the water out of the tank?"

"We pump out the whole thing," which he knew they couldn't do here and which would be a waste of effort even if they could, since they had nothing to put back in its place.

"So how do we get help?"

Noah ducked into the cabin and emerged with a flare kit. On the deck again, he opened it, loaded the flare into a gun, aimed the gun in the general direction of Big Sawyer, and fired. He and Ian stood looking up.

"I don't see anything," Ian said.

"It's up in the fog."

"If we can't see it, how can anyone else?"

"They may not," Noah said, "but this is the best we can do. We have six flares. We'll shoot them up every few minutes. Either someone will see it, or catch us on radar. Or noon will come and go, and they'll send someone out."

"How will they know where we are?"

"They'll know." His friends knew where he fished. They would find him, but only if the *Leila Sue* stayed put. Anchoring would work for now. A thirty-five-pound plow was more than enough anchor for a thirty-four-foot boat. If the seas rose and the wind picked up, that would change things. Being anchored this close to the rocks could become dangerous then. Traps had the buffer of water. The potential damage to a boat against rocks was that much worse. And to the people aboard?

He couldn't go there yet.

"The radar's still working," Ian pointed out hopefully.

"The instruments work off the battery," Noah said and promptly turned them all off, though not before getting a fix on the *Leila Sue*'s bearings and entering it in his log. "The battery gets its charge from the engine."

"How long will the charge last on its own?"

"An hour, give or take. The radar drains more, the horn less. We'll sound the horn. If anyone's near, they'll come."

"What if they don't?" Ian asked.

"Then they'll come looking for us once we're missed."

"What if the weather gets bad, and they can't?"

"We'll ride out the storm. Then they'll come looking."

"Can we ride it out in one piece?"

Noah knew Ian was frightened. He was none too

happy, himself. He couldn't have known his fuel would be fouled, but he should have made sure the radio worked. No good fisherman left port without a radio. And without a cell phone? No modern fisherman did that.

Stupid, Noah decided in disgust. And with his son aboard? *Stupid and irresponsible.*

He had been on the *Leila Sue* in a storm. She could hold her own in waves up to eight or nine feet. Much higher, and there'd be trouble. Last time, at least, he'd had power and had been able to steer into the waves. He had no power now, no way to control his position. Pitching and rolling were one thing, yawing something else. If the *Leila Sue* yawed so much that she ended up broadside to the waves, she could roll right over under a high one. Once underwater, she might not recover.

"Tell you what," he told Ian as he tried to control his own fear. "Let's take a lesson from Lucas here. See how calm he is?" Lucas was sitting in a corner of the wheelhouse, watching Noah with his tongue hanging out, a smile on his face, and adoration in his eyes.

"He doesn't know any better," Ian said.

"Well, neither do we. The sea's not bad right now. It may not get bad at all. Let's give it an hour before we panic."

It didn't take an hour for the weather to worsen. After shooting one more seemingly futile flare and twenty minutes of bobbing at a tight anchor, the *Leila Sue* began to roll in a rising surf. A third flare and another twenty minutes later, the pull on the boat grew fierce, and still Noah resisted. He liked knowing where he was. The thought of being blown loose around the North Atlantic didn't appeal to him at all.

When yet another twenty minutes had passed, though, he had no choice. The waves were too large and the wind too strong for the boat to be yanked around on a cord. Fearing structural damage that could actually sink the *Leila Sue,* he raised the anchor, and for the next few minutes, grasping the gunnel for balance against the roll and pitch of the boat, he held his breath. With the fog unremittingly thick, he couldn't see if they were about to hit rock or not. When enough time had passed, he gave the depth finder a quick look. Only when he saw that they were in deeper water did he relax.

It was a mixed blessing, of course. Rocks could destroy the *Leila Sue.* But rocks were something to cling to if the *Leila Sue* sank.

Negotiating the roll of the deck, Noah went forward and pulled life jackets from a bin in the bow. He tossed one to Ian, who quickly put it on and asked, "What about Lucas?"

"He's a good swimmer."

"So am I," Ian said just as the boat crested a wave and pitched down. He nearly lost his footing and had to grab at the edge of the wheelhouse.

Lucas stayed in his corner, alternately putting his head down to try to sleep and raising it to send Noah questioning looks.

Seeming to speak for the dog, Ian said, "It can't get much worse than this, can it?"

"Sure."

"Much worse?"

Noah gave a half shrug as he fastened his life jacket. He loaded the flare gun again.

"Do you think it *will*?" the boy asked, sounding either impatient or imperious.

Neither sat well with Noah, who was wallowing in "shouldas"—shoulda checked the VHF, shoulda taken the cell phone, shoulda stayed in port, to hell with a few traps.

"Do I look like a weatherman?" he shot back and fired the flare gun, but even as he did, he wondered if it was futile. They were ten miles out. In this kind of fog, the glow cast by the flare wouldn't carry more than a mile or two, or last more than a minute. Even if someone was in the area, he'd be working hard to control his boat, not looking up into the sky for a flare.

Ian was staring at him hard, jaw tight and square. "Can't you talk to me? I haven't done this before. You have. Tell me what we're going into. I don't even care if you don't know, but it would be nice to hear that. I can't read your mind. When you don't say anything, I think the worst. Like, you hate my clothes, hate my school, hate the way I talk and the way I look."

Noah was startled. "What are you talking about?"

"You don't *talk*. I don't *know* what you're *thinking*. You don't give compliments. I don't remember your ever saying I did something right. Do you even *like* me?"

Noah was bewildered. As precarious as his footing was on a rolling deck, this was worse. "You do lots of things right."

"Like what? Name one thing."

"This isn't the time, Ian."

"See? I called it wrong. Why isn't it the time? What else are we supposed to be doing?"

"Checking the bilge, for one thing. The pump's not going to work on its own. Water starts collecting there, and we'll sink. While I do that, you keep dry," Noah said. Grabbing the oilskin at Ian's elbow, he pulled him inside the wheelhouse. "And hold on to something. The swells are getting higher. I don't want you going over the side."

"What about Lucas?"

"Inside the cuddy," Noah instructed and grabbed Lucas's collar. The dog didn't want to go, and Noah was torn. If Lucas was in the cuddy and the boat went down, he was doomed. If he stayed where he was, though, with the boat pitching forward and back, he would slide out of his corner and be swept off. The dog might be a good swimmer, but he wasn't any match for a mountain of water driven by an angry wind.

One hour passed, then a second. A light rain was falling, and the waves didn't let up. Broad daylight was a dense, steely gray, broken by absolutely nothing at all. The *Leila Sue* continued to seesaw, but what water she took on ran out the scuppers, and the bilge remained dry. Noah checked the radar from time to time, looking for other boats in the area, but the few blips he saw were easily a handful of miles away. He used the fifth flare, then the sixth. They started sounding the horn, but it seemed lost in the echo of water on water as the waves crashed in on themselves.

Soon, the rain began in earnest. They wore full oilskin jackets, now with hoods raised, and even under the wheelhouse roof their faces were wet. Ian's was pale. Seeming frightened enough to have moved past his snit, he asked, "Do you think we've hit the worst of it yet?"

"Can't tell," Noah replied, but he was still annoyed. Ian's accusations hit home—and were all the worse because he thought he had made inroads with the boy. And then there was guilt. He had dragged Ian to Maine. His own carelessness had put them in a mess. And now he was back to the same old silence.

He owed the boy more than that. He owed *himself* more than that. Hell, he owed the people who had died on the *Amelia Celeste* more than that. If he had been spared death for the purpose of making more of his life, he was botching it good.

So, holding the wheelhouse roof for balance against the pitch and roll of the boat, he spoke loud enough to be heard over the commotion of the storm. "Let me explain something, Ian. I grew up working with my father on a boat just like this. He didn't chatter, so I didn't chatter. We'd hear friends on the radio, and sometimes we talked to them, but we were busy hauling, and we liked hearing the sounds of the work. We were caught in lots of storms. Weather forecasting wasn't as good then. Storms could come on you out of the blue. We didn't talk about it, because we knew what we faced, and what we faced was not knowing. The sea has a mind of its own. I don't care what pictures satellites beam down, it can be different under those clouds. My guess is we're in for another eight hours of this. Could be more, could be less."

"What do we do until then?"

"If we start taking on water, we bail. If we broach, we pray."

"Broach?"

"Turn sideways. That's risky."

"Do you think help'll come?"

"Hard to say. It'll be at least another hour before anyone starts thinking we might be in trouble. If conditions are bad enough, my friends won't dare it. Same with a helicopter. It wouldn't get close in this fog. A Coast Guard cutter might. That's our best chance."

"Best chance of survival?"

"Best chance of rescue within the next few hours. We'll live, Ian," Noah vowed. "I didn't survive the loss of my father three weeks ago just to go down with him now."

Chapter 20

Julia slept late in her childhood bedroom. The decor had changed; Janet had turned it into a sitting room. She had tried to get Julia to sleep in her brothers' room, now the guest bedroom, but Julia chose the pullout sofa here.

This room held memories. The furniture might be different, but the sun streaming in through the blinds was the same, as were house sounds, like the washing machine running in the laundry room and the whoosh of cool air through the vents. With the rest of her life in flux, she needed the familiarity of these things. In a sense, she had come full circle and was about to set out on her own once again.

She wondered if it was sunny in Maine, wondered if Noah had to move his traps after all. She wondered if he was thinking of her, wondered if he was wondering why she had left and when she would be back. She was starting to wonder that herself.

When she went downstairs, she found Janet on the patio, looking far better than she had the day before. This time, the paper had been read. She smiled and nodded toward the mug Julia held.

"You helped yourself. Good. I still make it awfully strong."

Julia sipped the brew. Yes, it was strong—stronger than her usual—but it was good. "Why does coffee always taste better when someone else makes it?"

"It does, doesn't it," Janet mused, then asked, "Can I get you some breakfast?"

"Not yet," Julia said, though she was tempted. Like drinking coffee made by someone else, breakfast made by someone else was a treat, all the more so with her mother doing the making. At that moment, Janet did seem like a mother, which was what Julia needed far more than food. Satisfied with her coffee for now, she slipped into a seat.

"Would you like the paper?" Janet asked, solicitous.

"No. I'll just sit."

"So, what should we do today?"

Julia heard enthusiasm, the eagerness of a woman who seemed delighted to have a companion, which raised the issue of George. They would have to discuss him. But later. Julia didn't want to argue with her mother, not when they were on such comfortable footing. Part of the fence had been mended; she wanted to bask in the pleasure of that before she tackled the rest.

"I could just sit awhile," she said.

"Not bake cookies? Or cut flowers? Or paint

something?" Janet countered. "You were always doing something homey, making me feel totally inadequate."

"No. *Did* I?"

"You did."

"I'm sorry."

"Why?" Janet asked with a curious half smile. "I *was* inadequate—here, at least. Remember when you painted the mudroom? We each got to pick a wall color. You got the ceiling."

Julia hadn't dreamed that Janet felt inadequate about anything, and it wasn't that she liked the idea of it, so much as Janet's ability to say it. Their relationship was taking a more honest direction, which was behind much of what Julia had said the evening before. That realized, she let it go and thought of the mudroom.

"I picked blue," she recalled. It was a clear, fair-weather blue, the likes of which they hadn't seen in Big Sawyer in days. Something told her that they weren't seeing it now either. Feeling oddly uneasy, she pushed it out of her mind. "I'll just sit. It's truly lovely here. Not everyone has what we do, y'know?"

Noah wasn't happy. Rain pelted the *Leila Sue,* blowing horizontally at times, and the occasional wave rose up and broke on her deck. It drained easily enough. But they had already lost several traps, and the storm continued to worsen. He rationed use of the battery, only briefly turning on the depth finder to verify that he wasn't about to run into rocks, or the radar to look for other boats. He kept Ian at the horn. The fog remained opaque.

With a wind out of the southeast, the waves were carrying them in a northwesterly direction, and the *Leila Sue* kept turning. That was the most frightening part. Without the ability to steer, he couldn't control their position. At least they hadn't been broadsided yet.

At the rate they were being swept along, he guessed they would pass north of Hull in five or six hours. Hull was the northernmost of Big Sawyer's three closest neighbors, and the waters above her were littered with rocks. That didn't bode well for the *Leila Sue*. Nor did the fact that he saw no boats near them now. Small-craft warnings might be ignored by lobstermen bent on moving traps, but gale warnings were not. Noah estimated that the wind was blowing close to thirty-five knots, definitely gale force. Even the last foolhardy stragglers must have turned around and gone in.

"What time is it?" Ian called.

They were standing side by side, trying to brace themselves against the instrument panel, facing the stern, on the premise that it was less disconcerting to look at the boat than at the nothingness of fog. Even with this shelter, the noise of the rain, the wind, and the waves would have drowned out a quiet remark. Lucas had begun to howl in the cabin, but this, too, was muted.

"Almost twelve," Noah called back. "They'll be missing us soon." He wished he could see something. Between the rise and fall of the boat and the hemming-in of the fog, he felt vaguely queasy, though that was more from their predicament than from seasickness. Mercifully, Ian looked pale but not green. "Are you feeling okay?"

The boy nodded.

"Not what you expected when you agreed to come up, huh?" Noah asked, trying to lighten the mood. The words were barely out when curiosity got the better of him. "Tell me what you thought you'd do."

"Catch lobsters."

Noah nodded, then said, "You do that well." He had certainly thought it often enough, but, no, he hadn't said it aloud before.

Ian shot him a surprised look. In the next breath, though, he repositioned his hands and bent his knees to take the pitch of the boat. He came out of the motion looking more nervous than before. "Can this boat sink?"

"Any boat can sink."

"What'll we do if it does?"

"There's an inflatable life raft."

Ian gave him an incredulous look: *Like, we'd survive in an inflatable life raft and not in the boat?*

Noah was grateful he hadn't asked the question aloud, because he didn't know the answer. The ensuing silence was filled with water, wind, and fear.

Julia ate on the patio, more of a brunch than a breakfast, given the lateness of the morning. Then she fell asleep. Right there in her mother's lounger. Fell asleep. Again.

She awoke to find that the sun had shifted past

the midday point. She had barely taken that in when Janet said, "You were exhausted. Confronting Monte must have drained you."

It wasn't only that, Julia knew. She had barely slept the night before leaving Big Sawyer. Thinking of that night now, she felt a tingling inside, and suddenly she wanted to talk with Noah. She wanted to know he was safe, wanted him to know she was thinking of him.

"I'll be right back," she told Janet and went into the kitchen, where she had left her cell phone. She dialed his numbers, first cell, then home, and got no answer at either. She was thinking that that was odd, and that she hoped the weather had improved—when her cell phone rang right in her hand.

"Mom, it's me," said Molly. "Where are you?"

"Gram's."

"In Baltimore? Oh, God."

"What's wrong?"

"It is storming so bad here, and Noah and Ian aren't back. No one's seen or heard from them since they left at dawn."

Julia's stomach dipped. She had sensed something amiss even before trying to call—had felt that odd uneasiness. Heart thudding, she asked, "Has anyone gone out to look?"

"They can't. I mean, it's *really* bad, and it's not supposed to clear until tonight. The Coast Guard's going to try it. John Mather will go with them. He knows where Noah sets his traps, but there's a lot of traps and a lot of ocean."

A lot of traps and a lot of ocean. Once upon a time, Julia might have pictured the scene in a horizontal way. Now she pictured it vertically, as well. The ocean depths were real to her. Likewise, death at sea.

Feeling a terrible dread, she was holding the phone to her heart when her mother walked in. One look at Julia, and the older woman paled. Her first thought, again, clearly was of George.

So Julia said quickly, "That was Molly. Dad's fine, but the weather's bad up there. Two really good friends are lost on the water."

"Lost, as in *dead*?" Janet asked.

Julia's eyes teared up. "Lost, as in no one knows where they are. The Coast Guard's going out. I have to leave, Mom. Those friends? They're Noah and his son. Noah is special. I need to be there."

Janet opened her mouth, seemingly to interrogate. *Special? How? Who is he? What does he mean to you?* Then she closed her mouth for an instant, shifted gears, and said sensibly, "Do you want to fly and leave the car here?"

It made sense, of course—until Julia called the airline and realized that with bad weather in Maine causing air traffic delays, flying might actually take longer. She couldn't see herself sitting, stuck, in an airport. Better to take her chances on the road.

"It's a long drive," her mother warned when Julia made her decision.

"Ten hours. Molly will call with updates. I can do it, Mom. There was a reason why I got so much sleep here."

She left to go upstairs and pack her things. When she returned, her mother was waiting in the hall with her own small bag and her mind made up. She was coming along.

The waves were fierce, looming six, then eight, then ten feet above the *Leila Sue*. She was carried along at their mercy, twisting and turning at times, at others rising on their crest, then plunging headlong into a trough with force enough to break her back if she hit bottom. Noah figured they were in deep enough waters to preclude that. But the water shallowed out in the trough when it was pulled up into a crest. And then there was the danger of twisting and turning. Each time the *Leila Sue* turned broadside, waves broke on her deck with greater force. The good news was that they didn't roll over. The bad news was that between the volume and the force of the waves, the bilge began taking on water.

With the bilge pump lacking power, Noah pumped by hand. He didn't care if the engine got wet; with a fouled tank, the engine wouldn't be taking them anywhere, anyway. No, his concern was the weight of water collecting in the bilge. Enough, and the *Leila Sue* would sink.

They took turns at it, with the person who was not pumping holding a tether tied to the waist of the other. The hits were drenching; the rest of the traps had been swept from the deck long before. Noah didn't want Ian or him washing overboard, too.

His muscles began to scream. He was working ten

minutes to every five that Ian did, but he figured the boy was hurting, too. Taking a break, he sent him into the cabin to console a howling Lucas. Ian emerged with the tether tied to the dog's collar.

"I can't leave him in there," he said. "It's worse than here."

Noah was frankly pleased that one decision, at least, had been made for him. Actually, another one had. The battery, drained by the horn and those brief instrument runs, had just died.

"That's fine," he told Ian. "Just hold him good."

The boat was running before the seas now, being swept up to the crest of a gathering wave, then plunged into the trough, all the while buffeted by wind-driven rain. Noah had never been in anything as bad before. But then, he had never been sabotaged before.

Furious at Haber and Welk or whomever, feeling betrayed by Julia and cursed by the gods, he returned to pumping the bilge with a vengeance. Lacking a villain to yell at, he settled for yelling at Ian.

"I don't disapprove of you," he shouted over the roar of the sea. "I don't know why you say that."

"You don't say positive stuff," Ian shouted back.

"Do I say negative stuff?"

"You don't come to Washington. You don't phone me much or see me much. You don't want me living with you, you just leave me with Mom."

"You have more opportunity living there. Your Mom agrees."

"Then summers," Ian shouted. "You never ask for those."

"You're always booked up with things that sound better," Noah shouted back.

Neither waves nor rain diluted the disbelieving look Ian shot him. "Better than my being with my dad?"

"Better than lobstering. Better than hanging out here."

"I thought you liked it here. You chose to come back."

"Only after I experienced other things," Noah called, working the pump. "I had choices. I want you to have choices, too. That's what going to college gives you."

Molly called once when Julia was driving through Delaware and again when they were crossing New Jersey. Both calls were as discouraging as the gathering clouds. A third call came shortly before five, after Julia had skirted New York City and entered southern Connecticut. Her heart ached.

Ending the call, she relayed the news to Janet. "There's no sign of them. A Coast Guard cutter is out searching, but they haven't a clue. They're thinking something may have happened to them early in the day, because very few of Noah's traps were moved."

"Maybe they're riding out the storm somewhere else?"

"If Noah did that, he'd have called to let someone know."

"What about emergency signals?"

"He carries flares. The cutter hasn't seen anything. But the fog is thick, thick, thick."

"Can't radar cut through fog?"

It certainly could. But if the boat had hit a ledge and broken up, there wouldn't be a blip for radar to catch. Likewise if the boat had *blown* up.

Julia fought tears. She would never have entertained the thought of an explosion if Kim's car hadn't been blown up. Like death by drowning, this, too, was real. If a bomb was planted in Noah's boat, set on a timer to hit when he was far enough from shore so that others wouldn't see . . .

"Julia?" Her mother's voice brought her back with a start. "Where were you?"

"Somewhere I don't want to be," Julia said and drove on under threatening skies.

Ian's peanut butter sandwiches had been long since devoured. Huddled in the wheelhouse with the boy and the dog, exhausted and worried, with nightfall less than two hours away, Noah gave Ian one of the PowerBars he kept stashed in the cuddy, precisely for emergencies like this—which was truly pathetic. He kept PowerBars, but not a radio beacon, dye markers, or a backup ship-to-shore. He kept flares, as the Coast Guard required for a boat his size. But the flares were used up. So here were a whole other bunch of "shouldas"—all worthless. He could beat up on himself forever, but what good would it do?

He reasoned that Julia hadn't betrayed him. Truly, he had no cause to think that. She had left to take care of unfinished business. She would be back.

And the storm would let up. Once that happened, they could drift on the *Leila Sue* until they were found. All they had to do was to hold out until then.

"We need pails," he told Ian and pushed himself up. Snatching two from a stack inside the cabin, he passed one to Ian, then, holding on to the side of the boat, worked his way back to the bilge hatch and began bailing.

Ian joined him, with Lucas still tethered to his waist. They were both soaking wet—Lucas looking sickly thin with his fur plastered down—but there was no fighting that. Nothing was dry. Absolutely nothing. Noah could feel the wet through his oilskins, through his boots, through his jeans and shirt, through his *skin*. If he wanted to be morbid, he could say he was halfway to becoming a sea creature.

"I'm not going to college," Ian declared loudly as he scooped up a pailful of water and heaved it over the side.

"That'd be dumb."

"There you go. Calling me dumb."

"I said not going to *college* would be dumb," Noah shouted. He had a feeling using pails was going to be as ineffective as the pump, but he had to do something. Better to stand here, feet anchored in the bilge while he weathered the tilt and tip of the boat, than slide around the wheelhouse floor. "If you want me to talk, you have to take the good with the bad."

Ian didn't respond.

"Wise move," Noah called.

The boat angled sharply to port, and another huge wave broke on the deck. Lucas was washed to a corner of the stern before the tether attached to Ian played out. Staying low to the deck, Ian scrambled over and carried him back.

"Why no college?" Noah called when he returned.

Ian retrieved his pail. "I need time off. Lots of kids are doing that now."

"What would you do?"

"I don't know," he said and dug the pail into the water, "but what's the point of college if I don't know what I want to do with my *life*?" He hurled the contents of the pail into the sea.

Noah did the same once, twice, five times, ten times, while the boat yawed and pulled. Rain was indistinguishable from ocean spray, and with the bilge filling faster than they could bail, it suddenly seemed important to Noah that he keep talking. "That's what liberal arts programs are for."

"I hate the colleges I've seen. The classes are big, the dorm rooms suck, and the weekends are an orgy. You want me to do that?"

"Try small colleges," Noah said, throwing another pailful over the side.

"Small means selective. My SAT scores stink."

"Ah." The bottom line. Noah straightened. "You're afraid you won't get into the schools you apply to."

Ian, too, stopped bailing. "Do you know how embarrassing that would be for Mom?" he shouted.

"Like, here she is, a big person at my school, and even with the pull of the college counselor, who is her friend, her own son can't get into a college?"

"No one's asking you to go to an Ivy League college," Noah argued as the boat headed up another wave. With water in the bilge, they were riding deeper now.

Ian braced himself for the descent. "You went to one."

"You're not me."

"Not as smart."

The *Leila Sue* crested the wave and soared down. "*Just* as smart," Noah shouted, bracing himself as Ian was doing. "Maybe smarter, only growing up in a different time and place."

They hit the trough. The bow went way under, water poured up against the wheelhouse windows, then rose to the roof and threatened to continue on over into the body of the boat—it seemed forever that the *Leila Sue* hung there, forever that Noah waited in horror, until the whole thing reversed itself and the bow was buoyant again.

Then he heard a strangled cry. He looked back at the stern in time to see Ian off the boat on the tail of a wave—boy and dog both—and Noah whirled, lunged for the end of the tether, and grabbed it tight. Losing his footing, he slid through several inches of water all the way into the stern before his boots caught, but he came up pulling the rope, pulling as hard as he could. Ian was ten feet behind the *Leila Sue* and being dragged right along into the next wave.

He would be immersed. Human lungs were no match for the power of the storm. Even if Noah could go back for the life ring—which he couldn't— Ian could be pushed underwater and held long enough to nullify the effect of the life jacket.

Keeping his eyes on the boy, he pulled at the rope; the water fought him, or maybe it was the weight of boy and dog, but he kept at it. He pulled harder, pulled faster, saw Ian moving closer, but at the same time felt the upward surge of the boat. He didn't shout to Ian, just pulled that rope, then, when the boy was close enough, reached down, grabbed his wrist, and hauled him up and aboard, all six feet, 170 pounds of him, as though he were a child. Lucas was next. Noah got him aboard seconds before a huge wall of water hit the deck.

Just south of Boston, the rain began. Julia put on the wipers and tightened her hands on the wheel, but she didn't slow down. Mind, heart, soul—all were on Big Sawyer with the rest of the people who were gathered at the Grill, anxiously awaiting word on the *Leila Sue*—and when mind, heart, and soul weren't at the Grill, they were out in the storm. Julia felt the water again as she had the night of the accident. She relived the pull of the waves, the submersion, the terror. She was over her head in memories: split-second flashes of faces and cries, the pointed purple bow of *The Beast*.

"He must be something," her mother remarked gravely.

Returning to reality with a start, Julia shot her a blank look.

"Noah Prine," Janet said. "We've been out of Balti-more all this time, and you haven't once asked how I feel about going up there. It's not going to be easy, Julia. Seeing your father is only the first challenge. The bigger one is seeing my sister. It's been twenty-five years. I'm sitting here remembering everything, everything before and everything after. You haven't asked about that."

No. Julia hadn't. Nor did she plan to. This was one of the things she had learned in the past three weeks. There were times when her own needs came first. "I'm sorry, Mom. I'm on overload here. I can't deal with that right now."

"That's why I say he must be something." Janet paused. "Yes?"

Julia checked her rearview mirror. Putting on her left blinker, she moved into the passing lane. "Yes."

"Is he the reason you're divorcing Monte?"

"No. I'm divorcing Monte because our marriage has no meaning anymore. I'm divorcing him because he's a hopeless cheater. I deserve better."

"Where does Noah come in?"

Julia passed one car, then a second, cleared it comfortably, and blinkered right. "He is . . . just . . . a breath of fresh air."

"That could mean anything," said Janet. "What about him is so fresh?"

"The way he looks at me," Julia offered without having to think. "The way he talks. The way he smiles. It's all genuine." She did think then. "His *silence* is fresh. We don't have to be talking. There's stuff up there that takes the place of words. Everything is sensual."

"As in pleasing the senses," her mother correctly put in. "Is that what Zoe loves about the island?"

"I don't know. We haven't talked about it, but I'd guess it is. Life there is rich." She shot her mother a curious look. "I don't know if that makes sense to you."

Janet didn't confirm or deny. Instead, she said, "You were enthralled with the place right from the first. That's one of the reasons I sent you and your brothers back. They had other things to do, but you had less, and you always looked forward to going. Could you live there?"

"I think so." Actually, she knew so, all the more the nearer they came. She was returning to a place she wanted to be. As frightened as she was for Noah, as much as he filled her mind, there was room for that knowledge.

"What if Noah's not there?"

"Dead, you mean?"

"Would you want to stay there then?"

She hadn't gone that far. She did know that her feelings for Big Sawyer were wrapped in and around her feelings for Noah. Big Sawyer without him?

She teared up. "He'll be fine," she insisted and took one hand from the wheel only long enough to brush a tear from her cheek. "He won't die. He'll be fine."

Darkness snaked into the fog. There hadn't been a monster wave since the last once, and though the boat continued to buck and turn and rise and duck, Noah was too exhausted, too numb with relief to do anything but sit in the wheelhouse with Ian. Their backs were against the console, their sides were touching. Ian had lost his boots to the sea, but he was alive. Same with Lucas, who lay sprawled, trembling, across their legs. Each had a hand on the dog. He was the connector, the one they touched in lieu of touching each other.

In a situation that was grossly surreal, Noah picked up where he had left off. Quietly now, lacking the strength for more, he said, "The thing about Ivy League schools? It's okay." He breathed, shooting for greater calm. "Barely a third of my high school class went to college, and none of those applied to the ones I did. That gave me an edge in the admissions process." He drew in another breath, though the air was saturated with water and salt. "I know that competition is bad in your class. But opting out is worse."

Ian was totally drained. His voice was weak. "What am I supposed to do?"

Noah felt an inkling of strength. "Apply to different schools from those your friends choose. Pick ones you like. Don't be pressured by anyone else, not by me or your mother or the college counselor, and certainly not by your friends. Here's a chance to do what you want, for a change. Go for it."

"If we live."

"We'll live," Noah said, feeling even more strength. "We've come this far, haven't we? If you didn't die back there in the water, you won't die now."

Nor would Noah, he realized. He had been spared dying on the *Amelia Celeste* so that he could mend his relationship with his son, and he was on his way to doing that. There were things they could do together, things that went beyond lobstering. And then there was Julia. For a little while, sitting there beside Ian, with the weight of Lucas holding them down against the rock and reel of the boat, he let himself think about her. It started with images of the night they'd shared and went on to more innocent ones. Work, play, travel, family, sex—he could share it all with her, could do it in a heartbeat. He had let his marriage die of attrition. Julia was his second chance. Wasn't this another reason why he hadn't died with Hutch?

Go for it, he had told Ian. The same applied to him. Realizing that, he felt conviction, and feeling conviction, he was suddenly calm.

Then he realized that the calm wasn't only internal. The *Leila Sue* continued to roll in the waves, but the waves were no longer as angry, nor the rain as fierce. Sure enough, as night fell, the storm waned.

Chapter 21

Thirty minutes shy of Rockland, Julia got word from Molly that the weather had begun to improve. By the time she parked at the pier, the rain had stopped. Even in the dark, the fog had lifted enough for her to see Matthew Crane and his nephew's Cobalt, in full canvas, waiting to take Janet and her to Big Sawyer.

Matthew helped Janet board, then Julia, who gave him a hug. Drawing back, she asked, "Any word?"

"Not yet."

"Can you see enough to get us back?"

"I got me here, didn't I?" Matthew said lightly. "There's no one else better in these waters than me. Know how many times I've made this crossing? There's reason they sent me to get you. Besides, the others are heading out to search for Noah."

Julia didn't ask him to speculate on what had happened to the *Leila Sue,* but just let him pilot the Cobalt.

Inside the boat's canvas, the three of them were pro-
tected from the lingering mist and sea spray that rose.
The waves were hearty, but the Cobalt cut neatly
through, and the fog continued to lift. Increasingly,
Julia could see the running lights of other boats, lobster
boats that would never be leaving port this late at night
if one of their own weren't in trouble.

In less than fifteen minutes, Matthew steered into
the harbor, and the chop was considerable even here.
Julia could only begin to imagine what it had been
like at the height of the storm. It was hard to imagine
what docking would be like in less-skilled hands than
Matthew's. True to his word, he did know wind and
waves, and negotiated the boat neatly alongside the
wharf. Of all the people gathered there in jeans, slick-
ers, and hats, front and center were Molly and
George.

Julia glanced at her mother. She had seen them,
too. She looked unsure of herself, which was so uncharacteristic that Julia moved close and said, "He's
waiting for you. He loves you."

Janet didn't answer. Eyes brimming, she simply
swallowed.

The lines were tied. So many hands were there
helping them from the rocking boat onto the dock
that Julia didn't know whose was whose, but she did
know Molly's arms when they wrapped around her
and held her with a desperate need. Molly would
have to know about Monte and her, but not now, not
when so much else was at stake.

Julia looked around. George was hugging Janet,

and the hug was mutual. Janet's arms held George as tightly as his held her.

"Where's Zoe?" Julia whispered to her daughter.

Molly whispered back, "Just ashore, at the end of the dock. She doesn't know what to do. I've never seen her like this."

Shifting a bit, Julia spotted her through a hole in the crowd. She stood alone, arms folded across her middle, but in a gesture of self-protection, not obstinacy. Molly was right; Zoe didn't know what to do. Julia wanted to go to her, but she wasn't the person Zoe needed.

Suddenly, there seemed a lull in the voices of those on the dock and the sounds of the sea. It was in Julia's mind, of course, because there was Janet, separating herself from George and the rest, and walking down the dock.

Zoe dropped her arms as her older sister approached.

Julia would never know what words were said. It was not her business to know. She saw Janet stop several feet away, saw her stand there for a minute, then move closer, raise a hand and touch Zoe's cheek.

Julia looked away, then. It was a beginning, and it was between Janet and Zoe. More crucial now, Julia needed to know about Noah.

They drifted, exhausted as much by the aftermath of terror as by the physical exertion of keeping the *Leila Sue* afloat. In short bursts of strength, they bailed enough water from the bilge to avoid sinking. For the most part, though, they sat in the wheel-house, rode the gentled ocean swells, kept their eyes out through the thinning fog for the lights that would mean their rescue.

For all the times Noah had wondered what to say to his son, there was no wondering now. They didn't have to talk to know what they had shared. Noah would never have invited an adventure like this, and they had yet to be rescued. But he knew that what they had been through would be with them always. It was a bond. He didn't need words to say that. He could feel the knowledge in Ian, who was working with him now, not against him—feeling with him now, not against him—thinking with him now, not against him. As initiations went into the brotherhood of lobstermen, Ian had suffered trial by fire. He'd made Noah proud.

At ten o'clock, after seventeen hours on the water, the first lights emerged from the lifting fog and headed their way. With the sighting, they let out whoops of relief and stood at the gunnel, energized despite their exhaustion, shouting and laughing. In his exuberance, Ian threw his arms around Noah, and the rescue was complete.

Revisiting that morning two days and a lifetime before, Julia couldn't keep tears at bay. Then, the emotion had been sadness at leaving Noah and fear of facing Monte. Now she also felt fear—fear that Noah had rethought his feelings for her. Her fear, though, was paired with happiness. Regardless of what happened between Noah and her, she was thrilled he was safe.

Leading a parade of lobster boats, the Coast Guard cutter entered the harbor shortly before eleven. The night waters were lit by running lights, searchlights, and torches blazing on the dock. Noah and Ian were off the cutter the instant it docked—and Lucas! Julia hadn't known Lucas was aboard the *Leila Sue.* The dog looked damp but glad to be on his home turf, to judge from the exuberant way he raced down the dock. Noah and Ian had none of that freedom. Friends converged on them in a circle of backslapping and hugs.

Julia stood at the shore end of the dock. On this eve of the Fourth of July, there was much to celebrate, all the more so after the tragedy of three weeks before. This time, the story was life all the way.

Noah wasn't a hero. Each time Ian repeated the story to those gathered around them of how his father had fought the waves to pull on that rope and save him from drowning, Noah felt more awkward. He had done the only thing he could.

Suddenly, incredibly, he felt itchy again. He wanted to go after Julia, but he couldn't do that now. He could go after Haber and Welk, though. That was a start.

Breaking out of the circle, he was immediately intercepted by John Roman, who fell into step and asked, "You're sure it was water polluted the tank?"

"I'm sure," Noah said. "I know the signs."

"And the radio wires were cut."

"Clean through."

"Haber and Welk?"

"Got another suspect?"

"Not me," John replied. "You call it, friend. We'll pay them a visit whenever you want."

"I want now," Noah said.

"It's pretty late."

"Too late for you?" Noah challenged.

"Hell, no. Not for Charlie Andress, either. We live for things that break the routine. I'm thinking of you. You've been up since, what, four? Five?"

"I'm not ready to sleep, but they should be. This time of night we'll have the best chance of finding them home. Your boat has radar. The ocean's into the calm after the storm. Give me ten to change clothes, and we'll take a ride to West Rock."

"I'm game," John said.

It was a plan. Noah felt good.

In the next instant, he stopped walking. As if to compensate, his heart began to race. Julia stood not ten feet away, breathlessly beautiful with her hair shining in the night. She wore white pants, a lime green blazer, and stacked sandals, and looked more cosmopolitan than he had seen her look since that first night aboard the *Amelia Celeste*. She had a hand pressed to her mouth and tears of regret in her eyes, and she didn't move toward him.

I've lost her, he thought. She's come back to say good-bye.

Then he noticed the strangeness of the hand that was pressed to her mouth, and suddenly realized the tears he saw weren't of regret at all, but unsureness—and things clicked. A handful of steps took him to where she stood, and all the while she looked at him with a kind of fearful yearning.

He touched her hand—touched the spot that looked so odd without its wedding band. Linking his fingers through hers, he brought her hand to his heart so that she could feel its thud, and she smiled through her tears.

What that smile did to him! For a minute he couldn't breathe—thought it was his runaway heart and that he might suffocate, then realized it was emotion gathering in his chest.

"Dad?" Ian came up behind him. "John's waiting."

Noah cleared his throat. He took a breath to steady himself. "We're going to West Rock," he told Julia softly. "Bearding the lion in his den."

"I'm coming," she said. She was holding his eyes like she would never let them go, holding his hand the same way.

"No, ma'am. And neither is he," he said, tossing his head at Ian.

"They nearly got me killed," Ian argued. "I have a right to go."

"These are criminals, Ian," Noah said, though the message was meant for Julia, as well. "I'll be with John and Charlie. They have guns."

"But—"

"I messed up bad with the boat. No radio, no cell

phone—it was stupid of me, and it nearly got you killed. Don't put me in that position again. Tell you what. We need dry clothes. Then you stay at the house with Julia. That way, I'll see both of you when I get back."

In the end, Ian came. For a boy who had been sullen and silent less than a week before, he wouldn't stop talking now, and he was eloquent. *It's my fight, too,* he said. Then, *Four against two is better than three against two.* And the clincher, *If it had been your dad and you when you were seventeen, would you have gone?* And, of course, once Noah said Ian could come, Julia looked ready to rebel. *I've spent my life sitting on the sidelines,* those beautiful hazel eyes said in protest. It took a quiet moment with her, and the sharing of bits of his heart and his hopes, before she acquiesced.

John's boat made the crossing to West Rock in seven minutes. Charlie Andress met them at the dock and drove them to where Haber and Welk were staying. It was a typical fisherman's cottage, more a bungalow than a house, and as run-down as any on the road. Not so the black Porsche sitting in front. Charlie's headlights picked it right out.

"Whoa," said Ian. "Cool car."

"A little out of character for a lobsterman," John remarked.

Charlie said, "The car's registered in Florida. We figure they could suffer the shack, but couldn't resist having the car."

"Now there's a pattern," Noah observed, leaning in from the backseat, where he and Ian sat. "They go to some effort to pass as regular lobstermen—get a lobstering license, paint their buoys, put tags on their traps. Then they ignore local law and start a gear war, like they couldn't resist that either."

"They're thugs," Charlie said, parking in front of the house.

"No lights on," observed John. "They must be sleeping."

"Good," Noah declared and opened his door. As far as he was concerned, the more disruptive their visit, the better.

Charlie took the lead, since this was his jurisdiction. He knocked on the door while the others waited—knocked loudly, with confidence and intent. Totally aside from the remark about thugs, that knock said he had no love for Haber and Welk either. He wanted to wake them up.

A light came on. The door opened. One man stood there and was joined seconds later by another, but neither had been asleep. Both were wide awake and fully dressed. Of average height and build, they were bearded, as many lobstermen were. One had a shaved head, the other did not. Both wore rain jackets.

"You know me," Charlie said in a lazy way. "This here's John Roman from over Big Sawyer. We need to talk with you."

Even with the only light coming from behind the two in the doorway, their tension was obvious. "Bad time, man," said the hairless one—Welk, Noah decided, recalling the picture on John's computer. "It's kinda late."

"Doesn't look to me like you were in bed," Charlie remarked.

"We just got back."

"Oh? Where you been?"

Noah wanted to hear the answer, too. West Rock was half the size of Big Sawyer. The only eatery was a diner, and it closed at eight—and even if that wasn't so, he didn't think they had eaten out. Faint cooking smells wafted through the open door—garlic, onion, fried ground beef—smells now several hours old. Thugs? They were goddamned felons. No, they hadn't been out for dinner. Where then? Rain jackets notwithstanding, given the storm had so recently ended, he didn't think the boys had been out for a cruise.

Welk gave a halfhearted shrug. "Here and there."

Charlie grunted. "Not in that car. I touched the engine cover as I went past just now. It's cold."

Welk darted a glance at Haber, who said, "We were out walking. Is there any law against that?"

"No. If you ask me, though, you look a little too dry to be just coming in. There's still a wind blowin' up rain from the storm. No, I'd say you're on your way out. Where you headed?"

"To bed, as soon as you leave."

"Well, now, that may be a while," Charlie said in an easygoing way. "Like I said, we need to talk. How 'bout inviting us in?"

"How 'bout getting a search warrant?" Welk snapped back.

Haber made a small *stay calm* gesture with his hand.

Still leisurely, because that was clearly annoying the two, Charlie said, "I'm not searching anything. Just wanting to talk. We can either do it here or back in the office."

"In the morning," Welk said anxiously. "Okay, man?"

"Actually," Charlie mused, "it's not okay. I got folks here who have a gripe, and they've come all the way over to see you. My friend Mr. Roman and his friend Mr. Prine think you sabotaged Mr. Prine's boat. He's prepared to bring charges. I want to hear your side."

Welk checked his watch and, with a calm that said he wasn't calm at all, lowered the wrist.

Haber said, "Our side is he shot at our hull."

Noah was about to deny it when Charlie advised, "I wouldn't make that charge, if I was you. I looked into it when you first filed the complaint. I got witnesses saw you do that yourself."

"They lie."

Charlie shrugged. "You wouldn't be the first. Others have done even worse to justify a gear war." He looked to be enjoying himself, which gave Noah an idea of how much of an annoyance Haber and Welk had been on West Rock, too. In the same exasperatingly slow way, the police chief went on. "I'm just telling you what my witnesses say. They say you go out in the boat at night, and I'm asking myself why you do that. Are you pulling traps in the pitch black? Or spray-painting buoys? Or sliding up to the dock at Big Sawyer and fouling the fuel tank of its most respected citizen?"

"They also cut the radio wires," Ian charged, making his presence known, which was precisely why Noah hadn't wanted him along. Knowing of his existence gave Haber and Welk another weapon to use against Noah.

Noah drew their attention to him with an anger that was just rearin' to go. "Fouled the tank and robbed me of my radio right when a storm's about to hit—which resulted in our being out on the ocean in a disabled craft through the whole of that storm. Bottom line? That's attempted murder."

"Why're you looking at us?" Haber asked. "We're just lobstering for the summer. So you guys don't like outsiders. That's your problem, not ours."

"Wrong," Noah said. "You trespassed on *my* property when you disabled my boat. Willful destruction of property is a state crime."

Haber produced a snide smile. "What about the traps we lost when someone cut our lines?"

Noah was about to call him on the painted buoys, when Charlie stopped him with a hand. Calmly, he told Haber and Welk, "Pot warp is cut all the time. You won't find any witnesses to that."

Haber still wore his smile. It seemed plastered on his face, despite the fact that he was putting a hand in his pocket, taking it out, shifting his weight from one hip to the other. "I want a lawyer."

Charlie smiled right back at him. "Maybe in the morning."

"Okay," Welk said quickly. "Morning's fine. Come on, Curt." He seemed eager to close the door.

"You sure you guys aren't heading out?" Charlie asked curiously.

"At twelve-twenty?" Haber countered. "It's late, man. If you're gonna charge us, do it. If not, get the hell off my doorstep."

"I might remind you," Charlie mused conversationally, "that this isn't really your doorstep. This house belongs to an old friend of mine who hasn't lived here in six years because his wife isn't well, and she wants to be close to her family in Indiana. So he rents it out. Too bad, but it's vacant most of the time. Not many people come to West Rock. So it was a boon when you two showed an interest in renting, and you didn't even dicker with the amount of the rent. Pretty steep, if you ask me, but my friend can use the money. I don't think he'll be happy to hear that you've broken the local laws."

Haber shot an urgent look at Welk, and Welk looked so like a man trying to ignore a snake crawling down the back of his shirt—both of them seeming on the edge of panic—that Noah had a thought. He was about to nudge John, when John said, "Okay, Charlie, I think we've imposed on these gentlemen enough. Let's let them get their sleep. We'll all be fresher in the morning."

The two men at the door visibly relaxed.

"I was just getting started," Charlie protested.

But John gestured him back to the car. As soon as they were all four inside, John said, "Go round the corner, Charlie, just like you're meaning to leave, then park and put out the lights. I want to see what they do." Pulling a small notebook from his pocket, he flipped through it in the cast-off light of the dashboard.

"Are you thinking what I am?" Noah asked.

"That there's reason one checked his watch and the other knew the exact time? I'll bet I am." He found the page he wanted. Flipping open his cell phone, he punched in a number.

Charlie pulled around the corner, out of sight of the house, parked, and killed his lights.

"What?" Ian asked Noah.

Noah remembered the meeting of the trap group on the day of Hutch's funeral, when Mike Kling had suggested that they would be killing two birds with one stone if they could prove that the fruit guys, already in trouble for intruding on Big Sawyer turf, had also shot Artie. That wasn't the case; Kim had shot Artie. But there might be another stone . . .

"What if Haber and Welk are heading off to do business?"

"In the middle of the night?" Ian asked skeptically.

"That's when smuggling is done," Noah replied. He could hear John on his phone in the front, using words consistent with INS talk.

"But if they were involved in smuggling," Ian persisted, "why would they do all the rest?"

Noah snorted. "Stupidity?"

"Seriously. Wouldn't they want to be *invisible* here?"

"They may have thought being lobstermen would

do that. Artie let people think he and Kimmie were having an affair as a cover. Haber and Welk might have used lobstering as theirs. They got their license, rented a place, did the things they thought they had to do. They didn't check out local law, because it's not written down. So they unwittingly set traps in our space. When we called them on it by knotting their lines, they lashed back. Didn't have the good sense just to move their traps. Had to try to best us."

"Why?"

"Because they're no good. Violence is all they know."

"There's the Porsche," Charlie said as a black car sped past.

John ended his call. "Follow it, Charlie. We're witnesses on this end. The INS has already boarded the big boat. They have the crew in custody. Now they want the driver of the smaller boat—or drivers, as the case is here."

Ian leaned forward. "They're smuggling illegals in a *lobster boat*?"

Noah confirmed the possibility. "Their boat's a forty-five-footer. They could easily pack thirty or forty people in on one night. If they make a trip on each of three nights, all told they land over a hundred people and God knows how many kilos of smack."

"Smack," Ian echoed. "Wow."

Noah asked John, "Do we think they were the ones who bombed Kimmie's car?"

"They know how," John remarked. "They haven't spent the last ten years in a church choir. My guess is we'll find evidence of explosives when Charlie goes back to that house with a warrant. Right, Charlie?"

Once they saw Haber and Welk park at the pier, board their boat and head to sea without running lights, and once that information had been duly reported to John's INS contact, there was no point in hanging around West Rock. John guided his own boat in the other direction, and just in time. Exhaustion had suddenly hit Ian, who dozed off even during the brief ride to Big Sawyer, and Noah wasn't in much better shape. They had been up for nearly twenty-two hours, much of that under severe stress.

He still had one thing to do, though. When he arrived back at his parents' house, he found that one thing to do sound asleep on the sofa. Her body was covered by the mint green and lilac afghan his mother had crocheted years before; her feet were covered by Lucas, who was now dry and fluffy and sound asleep as well.

"She's been cooking," Ian whispered, sniffing the air. No garlic smell here. This smell was of warm chocolate, shortbread, coffee cake—made from flour, sugar, butter, chocolate bars, maybe cinnamon or vanilla extract, or aged remnants of them, which was likely all she had found in the house.

"Go take a look," Noah whispered.

Momentarily revived, Ian left for the kitchen.

Noah hunkered down beside the sofa and just looked at Julia. He guessed he could do that for hours any day, but all the more so now, sluggish as he was with exhaustion. He could watch her sleep. He could look at every one of her features, could trace every curve, but it wouldn't be the physical that held him here. The beauty he saw went beyond that. She was peaceful. She was together, and reasonable, and compassionate. She was a giver, which was both a gift and a challenge. She was generous to a fault.

And she was smiling.

He smiled back. "Hi," he whispered, not knowing what else to say.

She mouthed the word in reply. A hand came from under the afghan and touched the stubble of his beard, then his mouth. She left her thumb on his lower lip. "Did you get them?"

He nodded. "We got 'em good."

"No one hurt?"

"No one hurt."

She let out a pleased sigh. "I'm sorry I fell asleep."

"Don't be. You were exhausted. Driving all day, cooking all night." He sobered enough to say, "You didn't have to do that."

"I know. But I wanted to. I like cooking."

Ian appeared. His mouth was full, and his hands held more. He worked at chewing and swallowing, then said to Noah, "Wait'll you see what's in the kitchen." To Julia, he said, "It's all *so* good."

"All?" Noah asked. "You didn't eat it *all,* did you?"

"Nuh-uh. This is for you." He passed a napkin filled with brownies, cookies, and chunks of some kind of cake. As soon as the hand-off was done, he went down the hall to his room.

Noah sat back on his heels. Suddenly ravenous,

he put a cookie in his mouth whole and grinned while he chewed. When he was done, he ate a brownie, then the cake. In no time the napkin was empty. He wiped his mouth, crumbled the napkin, and bobbed a little on his heels. When that felt good, he bobbed a little more. "I could be spoiled," he finally said.

"Everyone needs spoiling from time to time."

"Even you?"

She nodded. "My mother made me coffee this morning. Sounds like nothing, but it was a treat. I felt pampered."

Noah's smiled faded. "He never made you feel that way?"

"No."

He took her hand. "I would."

"I know."

"But you want to take it slow."

"I have to. I'm at the bare beginnings of a legal process, and there's a home to dismantle. I want to make things as easy as possible for Molly."

"But you came back here." He clung to that thought.

She squeezed his hand tight. "How could I not?"

"Could you live here?"

"I don't see why not."

"I'll tell you why not. Summer's fun, but winters are bad." Sandi had come back with him for Christmas one year, and had refused to do it ever again. "The island is bleak and cold and isolating then."

Julia smiled. "If you're trying to scare me off, it

won't work. I can think of lots of things I can do when summer's done."

"Like what?"

"Go lobstering."

"I don't do that in winter."

"What do you do?"

"Go skiing."

"Not here," she said sweetly.

"No. In Vail, Aspen, wherever."

"I can do that."

"You can. But not lobstering." He stood firm on that. "What else?"

"I can take pictures of you lobstering."

"If you think that'll get you in the door for the real thing, think again."

Her smile grew smug. "We'll see. I can also work with Zoe's rabbits. That's so calming. And I'd like to learn how to weave. I used to knit and crochet, but I've never weaved. Zoe's friends have looms. They'd teach me."

"They would," he said, loving the image of Julia creating. She had an artistic eye. Her photographs told him that. "What else?"

"Whatever comes up," she said, growing serious. "I don't want to be programmed. I understand that the past had to be. I went to school, I got married, I raised a child, I kept Monte's house."

"You were his doormat."

"At times. But it's like the accident held up a hand and signaled a time-out. Now I need to breathe. I need to regroup. I need to leave myself open to things that have meaning for me. *Personal* meaning. Does that sound totally selfish?"

He was as serious as she now, because it was his future, too. "Not selfish. What you want is important. You need to be happy, Julia. You need to be satisfied and fulfilled. I would never want to stand in your way."

She was suddenly incredulous. "Stand in my way? But you're *part* of what I want."

"I am?"

"Oh, yes. I *choose* to be here. Like you did." Using forefinger and thumb, she squeezed his chin. "The other night, while I was waiting to speak to Monte, I had a cup of tea. Know what the tag said?"

He shook his head.

"It said, 'Real intelligence is like a river; the deeper it is, the less noise it makes.' You don't make noise, but you're deep. I've had the other." Slowly, meaningfully, she shook her head.

Noah's heart swelled. She hadn't said those three words, but did he really need to hear them? What she had said was what he needed to hear.

"If it weren't for the boy," he said, "I'd climb up there with you."

She actually blushed. After what they had shared the Thursday night before, that blush came as a surprise. But it was honest and sweet, one more thing for him to love.

Epilogue

Julia gave herself a year. She figured she wouldn't need half of that time to realize that she loved Noah, but she was gun-shy. She had loved Monte, too. Older and wiser now, she understood that defining herself in terms of one man or another wasn't enough. Nor was defining herself in terms of her parents or her daughter. She needed an identity of her own and the confidence that would bring. Giving herself a year to develop those seemed like a plan.

July was a month to coast. Everything was new, from the freedom of being with Noah, to the pleasure of watching him with Ian, watching her mother with her father, and watching Janet with Zoe. Even the sun felt new. It returned following the storm and stayed, bringing days that were warm, occasionally hot, but relieved by breezy nights.

Julia and her camera became inseparable; it was

her entrée to parts of Big Sawyer that she mightn't
have otherwise dared explore. She meandered around
the marina where boats were being repaired, around
Foss Fish and Lobster while the day's catch was tallied, around the dock when lobstermen were doing
the myriad little chores of their trade.

Noah still refused to let her haul traps, but once the
Leila Sue's fuel tank was drained and refilled, the radio
rewired, and he was satisfied that he had taken every possible backup safety measure, Julia was welcomed aboard.
She spent many days photographing Ian and him at
work. Other days, she spent time with Molly, who was
truly unbalanced now that the divorce was real, and who
needed coddling. And then there was Kim. With all of
Artie's cohorts in custody, she was no longer in physical
danger, but she was determined to reshape her life in the
aftermath of what had happened. She wanted to go to
New York, and Julia knew New York. Together, they
hatched a plan that began with Julia's friend Charlotte
hiring Kim to work in her boutique, and went on to include helping her find a small, rent-controlled apartment, sign up for courses at City College, and take the
first steps toward contacting her dad.

August was a month of legal doings, most notably
a formal separation agreement and exploratory settlement talks. Monte's lawyer fought to maximize his
client's holdings, and Julia understood that. It was
part of the game. But she was prepared to play hard-
ball. When Monte dared suggest that she had imagined his alleged affairs, she produced the shoe she

had taken from the condo that night, at which point his infidelity became a given. He did argue about almost everything else, though, starting with the contents of the condo and ending with investments he had made over the years, and that kept the phone lines humming between Big Sawyer and New York.

Julia wanted few of the material goods she had accumulated in the course of her marriage, nor did she want a large alimony check each month. She wanted a settlement that would give her a nest egg, assets enough to enable her to live with total independence. Part of that meant having money to spend on Molly, though she didn't fear for the girl's bank account. For all his other faults, Monte was desperate to have his daughter in his life. Once the legal proceedings began and he accepted that his marriage was ending, he bent over backward to reach out to Molly.

Noah did reach Ian. The boy agreed to look at colleges before the start of school, but only if Noah came along. He apparently had it fixed in his mind that his father was more attuned to his personal feelings than his mother. Whether it was true or not, Noah was pleased to be involved.

September was the prime lobstering month, the time when lobsters were fully grown in their shells, which meant that each lobster caught weighed more than it had back at the time of the molt. With Ian in school again, Noah considered hiring another sternman. In the end, he chose to work alone, though he was rarely truly alone. Julia went along often, both to keep him company and to take pictures. The local paper was regularly printing her photos now, often on the front page, so she had excuse enough. While she was there, she pitched in to help with whatever Noah allowed. The more she handled well, the more he let her do the next time. He absolutely refused to call her his sternman, but she didn't need the title. Nor did she need an income, and they did fight over that. Staying at the hill house, she paid no rent, and her daily maintenance needs were few. Yes, Monte was stalling about producing financial records. But the separation agreement covered her needs.

Noah paid her anyway. He tallied her hours and deposited money each week in the local account she had opened.

October produced a phone call to Julia from a man who had seen her pictures in the paper, and who was writing a book on lobstering and wanted to illustrate it with more of the same.

"A book? I can't do a *book*," she told Noah with a nervous laugh.

"Why not?" he asked. "Photographs are the same whether they're printed in the newspaper or in a book."

"But he has a publisher," she argued. "He has an advance. This is more serious than working for the *Island Gazette*."

"That's why you should do it," Noah maintained. "Your pictures deserve more than local exposure, and they're good, Julia. This man wouldn't be asking you to do this if he didn't like your work. Besides, you've already taken most of the ones he needs. A few more, and you'll fulfill whatever agreement you sign with him. What's the downside here?"

After several days of grappling with her own insecurities, Julia agreed. Within two weeks, her name was on the book contract as the "photographs by" person. She used the initial money she received to buy a computer, software, and a printer sophisticated enough to produce ever better prints.

Molly came up to visit during her fall break. She loved seeing Julia, Noah, and Zoe, but was nearly as excited to see her friends from the Grill. While there, she convinced Rick Greene to offer yogurt pancakes topped with kiwi at his Sunday brunch.

Monte continued to waffle. He claimed that some of his major investments had soured. Julia's lawyer put a forensic accountant on the case.

Come November, the weather turned raw. The shortness of the days had already taken a toll on lobstering, and by the end of the month, Noah pulled his traps for the season. Haul traps, load up the boat, return to shore, unload traps, truck them to the trap shed for cleaning and storage—it was no easy task. Lacking the brawn needed for most of it, Julia kept the home fires burning, and Noah was right: she had photographs for the book done in no time, which gave her a sense of pride and accomplishment, not to mention more free time.

The home fires, by the way, were largely at Noah's house in town. Though she worked at the hill house, she had tired of sleeping alone—or perhaps not tired of it so much as found she wanted to sleep with Noah more.

Falling into a comfortable routine, she rose each morning at dawn for breakfast with him. After he left, she read the newspaper online, answered emails, then headed out to help Zoe with the rabbits, to work on a loom with a friend, or simply to visit. Island people were interesting people, she found. They read. The shorter the days and the colder the air, the *more* they read. Fiction, nonfiction, sci-fi, mystery, biography—their tastes were as eclectic as the furniture in their homes. Give them a wood fire, a glass of mulled cider, and an easy chair, and they talked about those books for hours.

Well, not only about those books. Gather a group of—especially—women, and the talk strayed to other topics. Julia might have kept at it forever, if she hadn't wanted to be back at the house before Noah. He never asked for it, but the pleasure on his face when he opened the door and felt the warmth, smelled the food, and caught sight of her there was reason enough to return.

December was for family. With the traps cleaned, examined for broken parts, and stacked in tall piles behind the shed, all needed pieces duly ordered, and the *Leila Sue* out of the water, Noah went to Washington. He visited the school where Ian studied and Sandi worked. He sat in the bleachers cheering the varsity basketball team, of which Ian was a member. He helped Ian with college applications.

Julia spent this time in New York. The accountant had uncovered the heftiest of Monte's hidden investments, which was reason enough for Monte to give up the fight. Julia chose to believe, though, that he was either feeling goodwill at the holiday season, or just growing up. Add to that the fact that she was more rooted elsewhere now, and seeing him wasn't as painful as it had been at the start.

The condo went on the market. Molly's things would be moved to Monte's new place, but Julia's would not. She sorted through them all, deciding what to save and what to toss. It would have been a tedious task, had it not been for the wealth of distractions at hand. She saw friends. She saw Kim. She visited her old haunts and did her holiday shopping. And the treat at the very end? Ten days skiing in the Canadian Rockies with Noah, Ian, and Molly.

In January, Janet turned sixty-five, so George threw her a party. It wasn't a surprise—Janet would have never stood for that. She had loosened up since her time on Big Sawyer, but she still felt *very* strongly that there had to be *plenty* of hors d'oeuvres, because you didn't call a party for seven o'clock with plans for dinner at nine and *not* feed people during the interim. And the food had to be *good,* she insisted, which was why the catering had to be done either by Fred of Elegance at Home, or by Susan of Mason-Dixon Eats. She let George pick which one.

She also requested that Zoe come.

Zoe was apprehensive. This was a family shindig, and she hadn't been part of family for years. She feared she would be on display and would come up short.

"How could Zoe possibly come up short?" Noah asked in disbelief. "She shines wherever she goes."

Julia cleared her throat. "Excuse me? Who was it who agonized over what clothes to wear visiting his son's school? Who wanted to look totally urbane?"

"I didn't want to embarrass him."

"You could never do that. I told you so at the time, and I say it now. Ian was so proud to have you there. I think he was actually disappointed that you looked so urbane. He would have preferred you wore an old T-shirt, so that his friends could see the tattoo."

Noah winced. "His mother hasn't forgiven me for that."

"For your tattoo or Ian's?"

"Either one. But Ian earned it. After what he went through that day in the storm, how could I say no?"

Julia wrapped an arm around his waist and smiled up into smiling eyes. "Oh, and you did fight, all the way to the tattoo parlor."

"Same one I used," Noah said with pride.

February was bleak. A cold wind blew off the ocean, rushed up the hillsides, and whistled through the trees. Noah had warned Julia. But she didn't complain—because February, it turned out, was for *them*. There were no kids, no parents, no aunts. A few friends stopped by, but they were incidental. Julia and Noah moved up to the hill house and burrowed in. They had books and food and a fire in the hearth. What could be better?

Well, that was for the first two weeks of the month. They spent the last two on a sailboat in the Caribbean.

Julia returned to two pieces of news. First, Charlotte was so pleased with Kim that she was taking the girl with her to Europe on a buying trip. And second, Monte had agreed to the last of the divorce terms, so the papers were being filed.

March brought work thoughts. For Noah, that meant attacking the traps that were piled behind the shed, repairing broken ones, fixing latches, replacing hog rings, painting buoys. It meant looking over the *Leila Sue* and deciding what she needed to get her in tip-top shape. It meant doing the paperwork for his license.

For Julia, it meant helping organize the local spinners and weavers for a show of their products in Boston. It meant taking pictures of their goods and producing a publicity flyer. It meant making travel arrangements for twenty-some artisans.

Midmonth, Janet and Molly made a surprise appearance. Janet complained some about the chill of the wind, but was otherwise in good form.

Then came April, and Julia found herself wondering where winter had gone. The days were noticeably longer again, and the sun warmer. With the *Leila Sue* tuned up, cleaned and polished, and back in the water, Noah loaded on his newly tagged traps and freshly painted buoys, and set the first strings of the year.

Julia went along for the ride, taking pictures to her heart's content, giving Noah a hand with an ease that came from being totally familiar now with the job.

Alex Brier marked the start of the lobstering season by printing four of her pictures on the front page of the *Gazette*.

In May, Julia's photographs made their formal debut when the lobstering book was published. Since the book held local interest, it was reviewed prominently by the Portland press, one member of whom happened to be putting together a book on the culture of Maine. Would Julia work with him to illustrate it? he called to ask. This time, the subject matter went beyond lobstering. If Julia agreed, she would be traveling around the state.

"Is that a problem?" Noah asked gently, when she expressed her qualms.

"I do lobstering," she reasoned because this other project was large and intimidating. "I don't do potato farming, or innkeeping, or blueberry growing."

"You do spinning, and weaving, and rabbitries. You do skiing in the Canadian Rockies and sailing in the Caribbean. You just bought a second camera—"

"A small one for my pocket."

"It packs four megapixels, and the test shots you made with it were fabulous. You also bought a Telephoto lens for the bigger camera. Seems to me you're perfectly set up to do the job."

"You think so?" she asked, still dubious.

He smiled his answer, then added, "Unless you don't want it."

"I *want* it," Julia said with more than a glimmer of excitement. She loved taking pictures. But she wasn't a professional photographer. She was a daughter and a mother. She was a significant other, sometimes a sternman to Noah. She was the first one to pitch in when a friend was sick, and she made a mean batch of cookies.

But she was also a survivor. She never quite forgot that. There were no longer middle-of-the-night jolts from the burst of a purple boat in her dreams, but she rarely awoke in the morning without thinking, *Here's a new day.* Life was fragile. Happiness and fulfillment, even success, weren't things to postpone.

Allowing that glimmer of excitement to grow, she took Noah's hand and said, "Yes, I could do this."

In June, with the first anniversary of the accident approaching, Noah turned the tables and took her hand. She kept saying that he had saved her life, but the opposite was true. For knowing Julia, he was more open and relaxed. He communicated better than he had. His relationship with Ian continued to solidify, and he was in love.

He waited until her divorce was final, but not a day longer. A whole year had shown him how perfectly Julia fit into his world. But he knew of the fragility of life, too.

So, the very first morning she was formally free, he forwent lobstering in favor of sleeping in with her at the hill house. Then he brought her breakfast on the bedroom deck, and, with sea, sky, and trees looking on, he put three stones in her hand. They were diamonds, set vertically in platinum, and they hung from a chain that was as elegant and as delicate as she was.

"The two small ones at the top are from earrings my father bought my mother. She didn't live long enough to enjoy them, so I want you to do that in her stead. The big one, here, is from me. If you'd like all three put into a wedding band, I'd love that. But a simple gold band would work, too. Whatever you want. It has to be different this time. For both of us. Y'know?"

She did.

Barbara Delinsky recently took time from working on her next book to talk with us. Here are excerpts from that conversation.

Q: What was the inspiration for *The Summer I Dared*?
A: Several events were haunting me in the spring of 2003. One was September 11, a second the D.C. sniper attacks, a third the tragic night club fire in Rhode Island. In each of these three instances, the victims were random people who were in the wrong place at the wrong time. But I kept thinking about the other victims, those who were just that little bit removed from the people who died and were living the rest of their lives knowing that they came this close, *this* close to the end. I wondered what effect this would have on a person's life. So I created Julia Bechtel, Noah Prine, and Kim Collela, all different from each other except for having survived a tragic accident.

Q: Julia Bechtel is closest to you in lifestyle. Do you identify with her?
A: Yes. My version of the tragic accident was being diagnosed with breast cancer. Nine years later, I am healthy and strong. But facing mortality, I began looking at life differently. Julia and I are alike in that we are inveterate peacemakers who thrive on obedience. After being diagnosed with breast cancer, I began speaking up more, began expressing my own opinion more, began trying new things that I had avoided because they didn't necessarily fit into my family's life. Like Julia, I asked myself, "If not now, when?"

Q: Have you ever been on a lobster boat?
A: No. Can you believe it? I wrote this whole book and then actually put my research material together for a little nonfiction book called *Does a Lobsterman Wear Pants?*, and during all that time I never saw a lobsterman in the flesh. Oops. Bad choice of words. But you get my drift. The fact is that I've written about many places—or in this instance, occupations—I've never visited. I was able to get more than enough information from books, the Web, and a few sources who were, uh, intimate with lobstermen. These lobstering wives gave me incredible information.

Q: How did you learn about Angora rabbits?
A: Aha. That I *did* do in the flesh. I discovered a farm where Angora rabbits are raised, only ten minutes from my home. The owner of the farm turned out to be a long-time fan of mine. She invited me over, showed me everything I needed to know about raising Angoras and plucking and spinning their fur. Debbie went so far as to sponsor a signing at her farm for *The Summer I Dared* and for *Uplift,* my book on breast cancer. She has been extremely generous in giving the proceeds to my charitable foundation.

Q: *The Summer I Dared* is set on the Maine coast. Don't you have ties to the region?
A: Actually, my ties are to Portland, where my mother grew up, and I spent seven of my happiest childhood summers in the lakes region of Maine. But I have visited the Maine coast many times. I adore Camden. Of

course, I knew it as the setting of the movie made from the book, *Peyton Place,* by Grace Metalious.

Q: Grace Metalious. Haven't I heard that name recently?

A: Very possibly. The year 2006 marks the 50th anniversary of the original publication of *Peyton Place,* so there has been renewed interest in Grace and her book. Word has it that Sandra Bullock is producing and starring in a biopic based on a biography of Grace written by Emily Toth.

Q: And how do you know this?

A: I know it because I have lived and breathed Grace Metalious and *Peyton Place* for the last year. They were the inspiration for my newest novel, *Looking for Peyton Place.*

Q: *Peyton Place*? Wow. That got my attention. Where did this idea come from?

A: In recent years, I've enjoyed books that take a non-fiction element and weave it into a novel, books like *I Was Amelia Earhart* and *Girl With a Pearl Earring*. When I was looking for the challenge that would become my next book, that concept stood right there in front of me.

Q: When did you first read *Peyton Place*?

A: Read? Well, I'm not sure I'd call it "read," in the most serious sense. I was a teenager, huddled with friends over our mothers' copies, flipping through to find the racy parts. I read it seriously as an adult when I was writing an early book, *The Passions of Chelsea Kane,* and I was duly impressed. I loved the richness of the

New England setting, the quirkiness of the myriad characters, and the ring of truth.

Q: Is your novel based on the Grace Metalious book?
A: No. Though the town I've created in *Looking for Peyton Place* believes that it was the model for the original *Peyton Place,* my own book is more about Grace.

Q: I don't know much about Grace.
A: That isn't surprising. She died at the age of thirty-nine, barely eight years after *Peyton Place* was published. The television series—which, by the way, was the first prime-time soap opera and, in that, the first of a genre still going strong today—debuted after she died. In all the hoopla, her name was largely forgotten. She died so young that there was precious little information on her. But I did locate a biography of her—two, actually—and found the information I needed.

Q: Do you compare yourself to Grace?
A: Compare? Lord, no. She was a free-thinker who was way ahead of her time where the plight of women—indeed, women's rights—was concerned. And she was an extraordinarily talented writer. I'm simply someone who is deeply impressed by her work.

Q: What is your favorite part of the book?
A: That's a toughie. I'd have to say it comes at the climax of Selena's trial. She wins. But she loses. In that irony, she embodies the dilemma of women in the 1950s.

Q: Do we need to read the original *Peyton Place* in order to enjoy *Looking for Peyton Place*?

A: Absolutely not. I tell the reader what he/she needs to know as my story progresses. That isn't to say that the reader who has indeed read *Peyton Place* won't see certain connections. For one thing, there is Road's End Inn. For another, there is the scene between Nicole and Aidan that so closely mirrors the much-touted scene in the original *Peyton Place* between Rodney Harrington and Betty Anderson.

Q: So can we expect a contest to see who can find the most Peyton Place-isms?

A: Now there's an idea. If I decide to do it, I'll let you know.

Q: What about your readers? Will you let them know?

A: Definitely. I'll post it on my website. The address is www.barbaradelinsky.com. Any reader who wants to comment on this or any other topic can write me through the post office there. As always, non-emailers can write to me c/o PO Box 812894, Wellesley, MA 02482-0026.